Praise for Little River

'*Little River* is a fascinating work by Dr Velma McClymont which looks at the unmistakable link between Scotland and Jamaica. We are always taught about the bond between England and Jamaica, but the Scottish connection is present among the surnames of Jamaicans today and *Little River* reveals this. The storytelling aspect of the book is riveting; from the childhood journey of Duncan Hutchinson in the Highlands of Scotland to his sailing to Jamaica as an adult to start a new life as a member of the plantocracy, who made their fortunes from the sugar plantations on the island. *Little River* gives readers a great insight into the story of *sugar and slaves* and really explores issues of race, class, gender, religion, colourism and rebellion, all of which speak of a time when Jamaica's colonial history was being sewn. Dr McClymont's hero is the revered Jamaican writer Claude McKay and his influence on her writing can be seen in *Little River*.'

– George Ruddock, The Weekly Gleaner UK

'This first volume of Velma McClymont's exquisite historical novel is set across the backdrop of upheavals in the West Indies between 1765 and 1812, stopping five years after the abolition of the Transatlantic slave trade in 1807. Her fiery dialogue brings an array of characters to life with stylish abandon, providing a penetrating insight into a patriarchal colonial world in which Scotsmen went to Jamaica to make a fortune. As a scholar of early modern Scottish philosophy, I learnt a great deal from McClymont's historical contextualism and anticipate the next instalment with fervour.'

– Professor Constantine Sandis, University of Hertfordshire

'*Little River* by Velma McClymont is a splendidly fascinating journey through a period in Jamaica's past that many wilfully forget. This work of fiction proves the power in truth.'

– Professor Linn Washington Jr, Temple University, USA

'A gripping and enthralling novel reflecting the inequalities of human beings, mirroring colonial injustices, the strength and resilience of a people denied of privileges and equal opportunities. *Little River* is an essential read for those interested in Jamaica's past and should prick the conscience of the descendants of the enslavers in Britain. The novel brings to the fore the atrocities committed, such as the sexual abuse of innocent girls and the brutalisation of Africans on sugar plantations – a past that should weigh heavily on the conscience of those who have benefitted from the wealth of this inhumane system. I commend Dr McClymont for writing and publishing this important novel that should set aflame the reparations conversation as it exposes the evils of the plantation system.'

– Rev'd Delroy Sittol JP, Jamaica Baptist Union

'*Little River* is an engrossing novel in which the plantocracy and the canefields come alive. Dr McClymont brings to the fore the appalling experiences of enslaved Africans in Jamaica and the tortuous life they experienced and the brutality they endured. The author demonstrates the physical, social, psychological and the sexual traumas that the enslaved Africans had to bear, and how they triumphed through their resistance and resilience to colonisation and white racist oppression. In spite of the trauma, their mental strength has left successes for future generations of Africans worldwide to emulate. The novel is a captivating read, full of historical information, and the author must be applauded for successfully taking on this enterprise.'

– Professor Tony Leiba, London South Bank University

Little River

**Other Books and Stories by the Author
(aka Kate Elizabeth Ernest)**

Hope Leaves Jamaica (1993)
Festus and Felix (1994)
Birds in the Wilderness (1995)
Tricky-Tricky Twins (1997)

Short Stories:
"Jumping the Broom" (1994)
"Disobedient Children" (1995)

Little River

Velma McClymont

WOMANZVUE LTD
61 BRIDGE STREET • KINGTON • HEREFORDSHIRE • HD5 3DJ

A WOMANZVUE BOOK

This hardback edition first published in Great Britain in 2022
by WomanzVue Ltd
61 Bridge Street, Kington, Herefordshire HD5 3DJ
Copyright © Velma McClymont, 2022
Velma McClymont has asserted her right under the Copyright,
Designs and Patents Acts, 1988,
to be identified as the Author of this work.

A catalogue record for this book is available from the British Library.

ISBN: HB: 978-1-7397247-2-6

Cover design and layout by Paul Medcalf, Avocet Typeset,
Bideford, Devon EX39 2BP
Printed and bound in Great Britain by CPI Group (UK) Ltd,
Croydon CR0 4YY

To find out more about the author and her books visit
www.womanzvue.com

This book is dedicated to the memory of my beloved grandmother, Mrs Carmel Smith-Morris (1909–2008),
my father, Stephen Benjamin Morris (1930–1995),
my father-in-law, David McClymont (1928–2010),
my great-grandmother, Mrs Katherine Harrison-Smith (1880s–1967),
and my favourite writer, Claude McKay (1889–1948).

'A people without knowledge of their past history,
origin and culture is like a tree without roots.'
Marcus Garvey

'I have forgotten much but still remember
the poinsettia's red, blood-red in warm December.'
Claude McKay

'There is no greater agony than bearing
an untold story inside you.'
Maya Angelou

Contents

Family Tree   xv

Foreword   xvii

Introduction   xxi

VOLUME 1: The Patriarchs   1

1: Calabash Estate   3

2: The African Empress   62

3: Canongate   119

4: Casualties of Empire   187

5: Lafayette   253

6: Riverhead   317

Acknowledgements   389

Family Tree

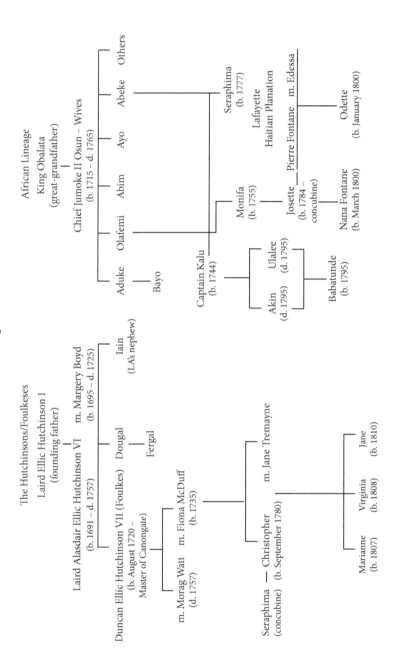

African Lineage
King Obalata
(great-grandfather)

Chief Jumoke II Osun – Wives
(b. 1715 – d. 1765)

Aduke   Olafemi   Abim   Ayo   Abeke   Others

Bayo

Captain Kalu
(b. 1744)

Monifa
(b. 1755)

Seraphima
(b. 1777)

Lafayette
Haitian Planation

Josette
(b. 1784 –
concubine)

Pierre Fontane   m. Edessa

Nana Fontane
(b. March 1800)

Odette
(b. January 1800)

Akin
(d. 1795)

Ulalee
(d. 1795)

Babatunde
(b. 1795)

The Hutchinsons/Foulkeses

Laird Ellic Hutchinson I
(founding father)

m. Margery Boyd
(b. 1695 – d. 1725)

Laird Alasdair Ellic Hutchinson VI
(b. 1691 – d. 1757)

Dougal   Iain
(LA's nephew)

Fergal

Duncan Ellic Hutchinson VII (Foulkes)
(b. August 1720 –
Master of Canongate)

m. Morag Watt   m. Fiona McDuff
(d. 1757)   (b. 1735)

m. Jane Tremayne

Seraphima — Christopher
(concubine)   (b. September 1780)

Marianne
(b. 1807)

Virginia
(b. 1808)

Jane
(b. 1810)

Foreword

Little River is a timely historical novel based on the enslavement of Africans in Jamaica. There were about 800,000 enslaved Africans in the British West Indies in 1800, a period covered in the novel. At the time, Jamaica's portion of this number was around 300,000 Africans. Dr Velma McClymont, the author of this timely book, is a distinguished scholar-activist and writer who was born in Jamaica in the late 1950s. Her novel reminds me of the haunting title of Robert Wedderburn's book, *The Horrors of Slavery.* Wedderburn was born in Jamaica and was rejected by his white slave-owning Scottish father, James Wedderburn.

In this evocative novel, Duncan Hutchinson (Foulkes), from the Scottish Highlands, sails to Jamaica in 1765 to make a fortune. He soon acquires a sugar plantation, marries a white Scotswoman and establishes himself. In keeping with the theme of 'miscegenation' and the fear of otherness, the narrative explores notions of white legitimacy through the mixed-raced children in *Little River.* Many of the children on plantations in Jamaica were of mixed-race, being the offspring of white men and their Black concubines. The horrors of the acquisition of Africans and the 'Middle Passage' experience are also vividly captured in the novel.

Although Henry Dundas is hailed by some of the sugar barons, such as Duncan Foulkes, for delaying the abolition of the slave trade, Dundas himself gave similar descriptions, rather like Dr McClymont, of the destruction of African families by white raiders in West Africa. During this period, thirty percent of the plantations in Jamaica were owned by Scots, leaving many Jamaicans today with Scottish genes and surnames. This theme is woven into the fabric of *Little River,* which is also a study in colour consciousness, as explored through the mixed-race characters fathered by the Scotsman named Ezekiel Darnley.

Concurrent with Duncan's role as a sugar planter is the threat of the Maroons and the politics of the powerful Scottish politician Henry

Dundas who, at the time, was suppressing a rebellion in Grenada: the Fedon Revolt 1795. Dundas selected the Scottish governor of Jamaica, who managed the last Maroon War, and supported Dundas's attack on St Domingue, where about 40,000 British troops died. In this revolt, the former enslaved African Toussaint L'Ouverture was successful. In *Little River*, Duncan writes 'epistles' to his brother Dougal, in Scotland, telling him about the rebellion in neighbouring St Domingue, the fear of slave revolts in Jamaica where some of the French planters from Haiti had escaped to (eg., Pierre Fontane and his wife Edessa) and anxiety over abolitionists such as William Wilberforce and Granville Sharp.

Influenced by the term *transculturation* and food culture, the novel highlights conspicuous consumption in plantation society. This includes luxury items such as wines, cigars and even reproduction paintings of classical/European landscapes and antiquity, hanging in the drawing rooms and dining rooms in plantation houses, to symbolise the transportation of British culture abroad. Likewise, the author also describes the regular celebrations and parties on sugar plantations where the starving enslaved Africans are flogged in the fields and threatened with death.

One theme that stands out in the novel is the use of clocks, chiming or ticking, to mark the passage of time. As the years pass, Duncan laments to his adult son, Christopher, who has fathered girl-children only, that he longs for a legitimate white grandson before he dies. Towards the end of this engaging novel, a clock sounds ominously in the plantation house while outside a barefoot white boy is caught up in the drama unfolding on the lawn at Canongate plantation. Duncan's son, though married to a white woman, is in an abusive relationship with the house slave named Seraphima, who is forced to abort her unborn children fathered by Christopher. The theme of concubinage is a common feature of the relationship between white men and enslaved women in slave society. Ironically, in his pursuit of class-based 'whiteness,' it did not occur to Duncan that the enslaved Africans on his plantation had come from African families torn apart by the institution of slavery, as Dr McClymont describes so movingly in this important book.

Little River also reflects Robert Burn's 'Man's inhumanity to man,' which says that, despite the horrors of slavery, and consequences such as racism, we are 'One Humanity.' Chattel slavery has consequences – it was not just 'the past' – the legacy continues today. Comparing slaveries, in contemporary times, to negate the horrors of chattel slavery is a 'false equivalent.' Importantly, to readers interested in historical fiction, this book is relevant both socially and educationally.

Professor Sir Geoff Palmer OBE,
Chancellor of Heriot-Watt University,
Edinburgh.

Introduction

Velma McClymont's *Little River* is a work of historical fiction that sets out to offer a reparative history of life on a Scottish-owned Jamaican sugar plantation in the period leading up to the Slave Trade Abolition Act of 1807. It brings to light and reconnects the often-ignored links between Scotland and the transoceanic trafficking and enslavement of African peoples in the West Indies and Abya Yala (or the so-called Americas) more broadly, while rooting itself academically in some of the most interesting and current research on slavery.

Today, many nations, cities, institutions, companies and estates are acknowledging and responding to calls from reparations activists and organizations at grassroots and state levels to recognize and address their historical connections to African enslavement. These calls are giving rise to an ever-increasing body of research that is seeking to unearth the specific details of those connections. This research also requires working with affected communities to understand how the past continues to shape our present-day world and its socio-political relations, while identifying reparatory strategies for a better future. The first step is to understand the depth and the breadth of our collective entanglements with slavery; a call to which *Little River* responds.

Until recently, Scotland's role in slavery had been swept under the carpet. This situation is neatly captured in the evocative title of Stephen Mullen's book, *It Wisnae Us – The Truth about Slavery and Glasgow,* which outlines the links between Scotland and the transoceanic trafficking and enslavement of African peoples. *It Wisnae* Us refers to the popular belief in Scotland's 'noble and heroic' past, lionised through figures such as William Wallace, and its political/economic subservience to England. As Mullen notes, these national mythologies have enabled Scots to view themselves predominantly, as the 'victims of oppression,' rather than as 'collaborators in the enslavement of nations.'

Such mythologies have thus hidden the less palatable truth that 'Scots played a major role in the British Empire.' Indeed, as the UCL Legacies of British Slave-ownership project has revealed, Scotland had the highest rates of ownership of enslaved Africans in proportion to the population, with the Scottish enslavers being particularly dominant in the Virginia tobacco and the Jamaican sugar plantation economies. Hence, by 1800, Scots owned 30% of estates in Jamaica; an island that imprisoned 40% of West Indian enslaved Africans. This in turn led to major economic growth in cities like Glasgow and Edinburgh, the remains of which can be seen in its material and architectural culture today.

Little River confronts this history head on by focusing on the rapid development of Scottish-led slavery in Jamaica and the rise of the sugar barons. As a polyphonic text, it is told from the perspective of multiple narrators, including enslavers from Britain/other European nations, West African traditional leaders and communities, enslaved Africans in both the canefields and in the plantation house, the Maroons and the free men and women 'of colour.' While the novel is a fictional account, it anchors itself in the key historical events that gave rise to Scotland's imperialist ambitions. In fact, the Acts of Union between England and Scotland in 1706 and 1707, for example, removed the former political and legal barriers that had prevented Scotland from participating legally in the trafficking and enslavement of Africans, and opened up a wealth of other colonial opportunities.

The novel cites the Battle of Culloden in 1746, which put an end to the Jacobite Risings and acted as an important push factor for the defeated Jacobites to emigrate to the British West Indies to 'find their fortunes.' The enslaver Duncan Foulkes is a case in point; he is a Jacobite who heads to Jamaica after Culloden brings his family into financial ruin. The same is also true of the Highland Clearances, which saw thousands of tenants from the Highlands and Islands being evicted from their homes (to make room for sheep farming and other forms of land enclosure that were more lucrative to Scottish landlords) between 1750 and 1860. In the novel, Duncan's second wife, Fiona, is a working-class woman and crofter's daughter who lost her home.

Perversely, the evictions of women like Fiona are directly linked to the profits of African enslavement. According to Alison Campsie, the newly enriched tobacco lords and sugar barons bought up 'more than one million acres of land relinquished during the clearances.' The profits of slavery, as MacKinnon and Mackillop have discovered, led to the purchase of at least 63 estates, which equates to a staggering 33.5% of all the land in the western Highlands and Islands.

By weaving these historical facts into *Little River*, McClymont brings to life some of the latest research findings into little-known aspects of Scottish history and African enslavement. Simultaneously, this raises questions about issues of reparatory justice over land.

The novel can also be seen as reparative in the sense that it draws our attention to the voices, thoughts and perspectives of those who were enslaved. There are the polyphonous voices of African captives imprisoned and violated in the hold of the *African Empress* (the slave ship), then tortured and violently abused in the canefields and in the many plantation houses. It is through their multiple acts of resistance and struggles against oppression that we hear their denunciation of the inhumanity of slavery.

In this sense, McClymont unearths the subaltern voice that has been subsumed in Euro-centric, and particularly white women's, writings about slavery, such as the eighteenth-and nineteenth century writers Janet Schaw, Emma Carmichael, Lady Nugent (wife of the Governor of Jamaica 1801 to 1806) and Anna Maria Falconbridge. For this reason, the figure of the enslaved woman Seraphima is key. For as readers, we participate in Seraphima's struggle as she is forced into concubinage with Duncan's son, Christopher. We witness the difficulties that she faces in negotiating/resisting the oppressive world of the plantation house, while still retaining her identity and integrity.

Likewise, the figure of the West African woman Monifa stands out in the text. She is captured and trafficked to Jamaica at ten years old, before being sold and taken to nearby Haiti. She keeps meticulous records of her family line, a promise to her dying mother, in a bid to preserve the links to her African heritage and familial roots for future generations. She also seeks to preserve and pass on her intimate knowledge of plants and their reparative properties that goes together with the practice of African spirituality (in this case *Kumina*) and its reparatory potential.

This preservation of African culture complements the theme of *Sankofa* that underpins the novel. *Sankofa* is an Adinkra symbol often represented by a bird with its head turned backwards to fetch an egg. It symbolises the need to go back and get that which has been forgotten: African ancestral heritage. One of the key settings in the text is the Motherland of pre-colonial West Africa (Chief Jumoke's compound), which is remembered by characters such as Monifa and her brother Kalu and their desire to return to their ancestral and spiritual roots.

I am reminded here of Ta-Nehusi Coates's brilliant exhortation that what is needed, where slavery and reparations are concerned, is not 'a handout, a payoff, hush money, or a reluctant bribe, but rather a national reckoning that would lead to spiritual renewal.' Acts and actions, such as Monifa's, stand in direct resistance to, and defiance of, the rapacious system of slavery, while offering a spiritual path out of the traumatic sexual, physical and psychological abuses inflicted upon the enslaved Africans.

In working against the tendency to downplay or deny Scotland's role in a crime against humanity, and in bringing history to life through creative writing, *Little River* contributes to Coates's call for 'the full acceptance of our collective biography and its consequences...an airing of family secrets, a settling with old ghosts...' To summarize then, this novel is a work of historical reparative fiction, that grows out of McClymont's scholar activism, and sets the scene explaining why the descendants of enslaved Africans are today calling for reparations for past injustices.

Dr Nicola Frith,
Senior Lecturer in French and Francophone Studies,
University of Edinburgh.

Volume 1:
The Patriarchs

1
Calabash Estate

Three boys could be seen through a stained-glass window bearing religious iconography, playing in the wood panelled hallway at Inverkin House in the Highlands of Scotland. Born on 19 August 1720, the eldest boy, eleven-year-old Duncan Hutchinson, exhaled. His pale face contorted beneath the blindfold as he listened to the creaking floorboards. Judging from the sounds made by the ageing wood, he believed that his brother, Dougal, and his cousin, Iain, were leading him towards the great hall where logs from the family's vast estate in Inverness burned in the massive fireplace. Reluctant to go any further, he halted with his arms outstretched until a small push caused him to stumble forward.

'Ouch!' Duncan's eyes shot open under the loose-fitting blindfold. He had hit his left foot on an object. 'Where are you?' Rain battered the roof, sheeting down the windows.

'Uh-oh.' Dougal looked around, signalling Iain to follow. 'Shh!'

The boys were united in a collective gasp when a window flew open in the draughty hallway. Outside, raindrops made patterns on the stained-glass windows, one of which depicted a man holding a sword (St Michael), angels and a king on a throne, flanked by twelve men. Visitors to Inverkin House had often remarked that this window reminded them of the Ascension.

'I've had enough of this childish game.' Duncan halted when a gust of wind came into the hallway. He was by nature astute and, though blindfolded, was aware of a pair of violet eyes observing him from the landing above. Even in child's play, he could not fully relax. Conscious of the paintings on the tall walls, he pictured the look of disapproval on his governess' face.

'Er.' Giggling nervously, Iain kept pace with Dougal, who changed direction rapidly.

'It!' Duncan grabbed a handful of material, clinging to the back of Dougal's shirt. 'Got you.' He felt satisfied that he had won but Dougal wanted to continue. 'If you're not following the rules of the game, how will Iain ever learn to play fair?'

'You cheated.' Five-year-old Iain adored Dougal, not because his uncle had told him that it was his duty to love his family but because his cousin was considerate. Dougal was Iain's rescuer, often putting a comforting arm around his cousin. Whenever the older boy climbed onto a wooden bench beneath one of the large stained-glass windows, he would beckon his cousin to hide in another box nearby that doubled as a window seat. Iain, eager to please, now climbed into the box. Once inside, he closed the lid and waited. He had no idea why Duncan disliked him, but he obeyed his older cousin out of deference.

'Ouch!' Duncan bumped into another object. *I'll gie ye a skelpit lug!* He snarled, 'I'll give you a slap on the ear!' He undid the blindfold and discovered that Dougal had placed a coat stand in his way, causing his anger to boil over. 'Daft thing.' He tossed the tartan blindfold aside and made his way towards the stairs to lodge a complaint with his governess, Miss Euphemia Booth. 'I'm going to tell her. She'll punish you.'

'It's just a bit of fun.' With a fleeting smile, Dougal jumped off the bench and lifted the lid of a wooden box, peering in. 'Come on out.' He hated it when Iain became emotional, coaxing him to climb out of the box. 'Come on, *Jack-in-the-box*.' He offered him a reassuring hand. 'It's not comfortable in there, is it? It's dark.'

'That's because there's no light in there, silly,' Duncan tatted, rolled his sea-green eyes upwards and walked with an exaggerated limp, doing his best impression of the injured party. 'I stubbed my toe on that blasted wooden stool. That wasn't hide-and-seek. I'd rather play chess than blind man's bluff. You ought to learn to play fair, cheat.'

'It's blind man's buff.' Dougal smiled at Iain, whose big dark puppy eyes looked up at him adoringly from within the box. 'He's annoyed with us because he lost.'

Duncan observed his brother's dark hair and deep-set brown eyes. 'Game over. Father's taking us to Edinburgh tomorrow and I've got to finish my homework today. I can't wait to see the Canongate leading to Holyrood, and Market Cross.' He issued a threat, 'If Iain annoys me today, I'm going to put him in the Tolbooth prison.'

'Not if I'm there.' Dougal walked over to the open window, grumbling that he was too small to close it. 'We're the only family he's got.' He sniffed. 'The rain is coming in through that window. If I were as tall as you, I'd climb onto a box and shut it. Go on then.'

'Oh, all right.' Duncan closed the stained-glass window whose images reminded him of the eleven disciples, and the twelfth was often said to be Our Lady. 'You're not going to Edinburgh with us.' He watched Iain climbing out of the box. 'You're a pest.'

Iain looked defensive. 'You're mean.' He was beginning to make sense of the world around him and did not like it when Duncan picked on him. 'He scares me, Dougal.'

A reflective child, Dougal wore a kindly expression. 'Poor thing.' One night, the then feverish Dougal was awakened by shadowy figures in the nursery. 'Don't be scared.' A messenger had arrived at Inverkin House with a grizzly baby. Pinned to the child's swaddling cloth was a note from a clergyman in Edinburgh. This *Good Samaritan* had been searching for the child's next of kin: Laird Alasdair Ellic Hutchinson VI (the patriarch of Inverkin House). He later told Duncan, for Dougal was too young to understand, that the baby was his nephew and the boys' cousin.

Fighting back tears, Iain said, 'I want to see Edinburgh Castle.'

'Don't cry.' Dougal did not care to visit Edinburgh where a jeering crowd would gather to leer at citizens in the stocks and pillories. When he was a year-old, his mother had died of smallpox. 'See what you've done, Duncan.' Since the funeral, he was loved by everyone, especially the servants and the tenant farmers. Duncan was tolerated. 'Come, Iain, let's go and find Jamie and Andy. They'll play hide-and-seek with us.'

Iain shuffled his feet. 'I like Jamie and Andy: they're kind.'

'Snivelling brat.' Duncan had reached the foot of the stairs. 'His father was a lackey. Rumour has it he seduced Aunt Livy by encouraging her to take the *handfasting vow* with him. He belongs with the servants below stairs, Dougal. Go away, Iain. There's a good dog.'

As for Laird Alasdair Ellic Hutchinson VI, the two older boys' father, he had objected to the ancient *handfasting vow* whereby the lovers' hands were bound together with a cord, symbolizing that they would marry. He had cautioned Livy, his late father's mistress' child, against the betrothal. But she, a romantic young woman who was reared in Oban, had insisted that the *handfasting vow* was valid. Defiant, she had exchanged rings with her lover who had promised to marry her as soon as he left service at the Palace of Holyrood. Three months later, she found her stomach swelling and was dismissed from Holyrood. Her lover had sailed to Holland with his new Dutch employer and threw the ring into a canal in the city.

'Go stand on that box, brat.' Duncan, loitering at the foot of the stars, felt that Iain's mother had done a bad thing. His own mother, Margery Boyd, a virtuous yellow-haired woman with rosy cheeks, came from a wealthy clan and had made a good marriage with the Laird of Inverkin House. 'Why are you shivering like a nervous puppy? Go and pee before you wet yourself. If you do, I'll lock you in that cupboard under the stairs. I will.'

'Booth locked me in there once; it's pitch black.' The image of a dark void disturbed Dougal's mind and a lock clicked inside his head. 'Get off the box, Iain.' The child climbed down readily and held out his hand. Dougal took it and walked across the hallway towards a set of doors leading to the servants' quarters. 'Let's go find Andy and Jamie.'

'You're always running about with them like mice trying to put a bell around a cat.' Half-way up the stairs, Duncan looked down with smug self-satisfaction. 'They only want to play with your hobby horse.' At eleven years old, he was more secure than Dougal, who was sensitive to what others were feeling, to the extent that he often changed his opinions to make the servants' children feel better about their status. 'Don't come crying to me when they break your toys.' His face hardened. 'You're not coming to Edinburgh with us, Iain.'

'Don't worry.' Dougal squeezed Iain's hand gently and proceeded towards the servants' quarters. 'He's all talk.' Descending the stairs, he felt wretched because he did not know if the boys really wanted to play with him or just his hobby horse, which he had deliberately left behind. 'Andy, Jamie, coming out to play?' He could not see them but he heard two boys with weak pale blue eyes laughing with their own father, the bearded gamekeeper, whose wife was the cook at Inverkin House. 'Oh bother.'

* * *

Alone, Duncan's gaze moved from the silk hangings in the wood panelled hallway below to the paintings on the high wall leading up to the first-floor landing. From this position, he studied his forebears whose images stretched back to the reign of Mary Queen of Scots. Those were turbulent years, when two of his male ancestors were found hanged and strangled near the Palace of Holyrood. It was believed that the two Protestants had been slain, for they were disciples of the long-bearded firebrand preacher named John Knox. Inspired by Knox's rhetoric, one Sunday evening in 1562, the Hutchinson brothers had been swaggering through the streets of Edinburgh when, confounded, they saw a handful of Roman Catholics publicly mouthing choice words: *God save our Queen.*

According to the patriarch, Laird Alasdair Ellic Hutchinson VI (the family's memory keeper), this defiance inflamed his anti-Catholic relatives who called the Monarch a papist for daring to attend Mass in a Protestant country with a reformed church: *The Kirk.* Conversation had turned to ridding Scotland of all Catholics. The brothers had urged the spectators to participate in a game of *priest-baiting*, stoning Catholic priests in the streets in an irreverent and political act. They then proceeded to Lawnmarket where a jeering crowd had gathered and had threatened to rid Scotland of *the harlot of Rome.* A day later, they were dead. It was said that they were murdered by Borderers and Highlanders who backed the queen.

'What have I told you?' A woman's voice was audible. 'It is a sin to worship images.' Miss Euphemia Booth appeared on the landing with her austere black dress trailing behind her. 'You are no match for the Patriarch, Laird Ellic Hutchinson I, and his sons. They say he was too obese to mount a horse.' She studied a portrait of two debonair young men in burgundy velvet capes, white lace collared ruffs and black Cavalier hats. 'Don't you know when you say horrid things you upset timid boys like Iain? Admittedly, his mother was a worthless *chit,* but that's no reason to be unkind to him, not in front of Dougal.' She began to murmur that she had frostbites on her hands and feet because, reluctantly, she had fished his velvet-lined gloves out of the icy river that morning. 'As time goes by, there'll be less need for relying on old masters to reaffirm your identity, Laird of Inverkin House.'

'Hurrah.' Duncan fixed his eyes on the *priest-baiters*. 'Look at those tartan shawls, draped carelessly across their shoulders, and the odd-shaped heads on those skinny necks.' His bottom lip hung loosely. 'If they had lived, they would have inherited this house and their sons after them. Father should have his portrait painted before he gets old and lardy like Laird Ellic. When I grow up, I am going to have my portrait painted: The Much-Honoured Duncan Ellic Hutchinson VII, Laird of Inverkin House. Booth, can I call myself Lord?'

Miss Booth slapped him down. 'A laird is not of noble birth, albeit his wife is styled Lady; hence your late mother was Lady Margery...' She loathed the image of the founding father, Laird Ellic Hutchinson I. The big, blonde, bearded Highlander in the MacDonald tartan kilt was grossly overweight by the time his portrait was painted. 'Your lessons can't wait. If you slacken today, you won't see the ships sailing to the New World tomorrow. Your father is accompanying two kinsmen to the Port of Leith. You ought to invite Iain along.'

'Whatever for?' The suggestion threw Duncan. '*He's a bastard*, you said as much.'

'Language, Master Hutchinson.' Miss Booth shot him a stern look and peered over the banister, down into the hallway, to ensure that no one had overheard them. The morning had begun with a jaunt down to the river that ran through the estate. The Much-Honoured Alasdair Ellic Hutchinson VI, Laird of Inverkin House, known as Squire Hutchinson, had insisted she take the boys for their morning exercise. All was going well until Duncan threw his velvet-lined gloves into the icy water and ordered Iain to fetch them. Miss Booth had given a wry smile and had pulled the child back, for she had anticipated Duncan's action. She was constantly in a state of hyper-vigilance. 'Mind your language.'

'*You taught me language; and my profit on't is I know how to curse. The red plague rid you for learning me your language!*' Duncan stood at the top of the stairs, parroting Shakespeare's Caliban. When she first became his governess, she would cup his face with both hands and gaze into his eyes, kissing him on his pink lips. She guarded his mind too and dreaded the day when this seventh-generation Hutchinson would leave Inverkin House. It was a place of quiet reflection, stunning views and images of power-hungry patriarchs inviting you to walk into their world. 'I don't like it when I punish Iain.'

'Tisk.' Miss Booth's views were shaped by the religious and political events that had engulfed Scotland since the sixteenth century, a time of suspicions and intrigue. The daughter of a deceased merchant from Glasgow, she had erased anything that linked her with her faith. She feared religious persecution as much as she dreaded excommunication. A flying object hit the window outside. 'That boy is a parasite.'

'Unlike Iain, I am not a bastard,' Duncan fired back. 'Or a parasite.'

'Think before you speak.' For a moment, Miss Booth was stung by his words. She did not understand how Iain's late mother, Miss Olivia Hutchinson, could have had a child out of wedlock. Soon after Miss Booth had taken up the role of governess, Livy ran away and found a job as a chambermaid at the Palace of Holyrood where she was privy to royal secrets and scandals. At the time of her disappearance, Miss Booth was secretly elated because Livy had been instrumental in providing a backbone for the family when Lady Margery Boyd-Hutchinson first passed away. Miss Booth had felt threatened by Livy, whom the servants got on well with. She had told Duncan that he had nothing in common with a base-born boy like Iain, whose mother had given away her virtue.

Duncan grew bolder. 'Words have consequences, Booth.'

'Come along, Master Hutchinson.' Miss Booth hastily entered the schoolroom. 'I am looking forward to seeing dear old Edinburgh. You know how much I like going to Kirk-o'-Field to see the place where Lord Darnley was murdered by the queen...'

'I dislike that place.' Duncan had been hoping that they would not visit dismal Kirk-o'-Field. 'Father believes there was a conspiracy against Mary Queen of Scots,' he said, blocking the schoolroom door. 'Allegedly, the queen was a naive woman whose enemies blamed her for the murder of her second husband. She was beset by problems and foolish to marry the Earl of Bothwell so soon after the king's death.' The boy relished Scottish history. 'Those were exciting times.' He loved to stand outside the Palace of Holyrood and imagine himself at court during the reign of Mary Queen of Scots. 'I think Elizabeth I planted English spies in Scotland to cause maximum disruption to Mary's rule. Between Queen Elizabeth I, Catherine de Medici of France (who hated Mary when she was Queen of France briefly), the fanatic John Knox and the ambitious Protestant nobles, all seeking favours, the Catholic queen stood no chance. May I speak my mind?'

'Stop thinking.' Miss Booth felt more irritated than usual. 'You are becoming your father's mouthpiece.' She pulled back her chair and sat stony-faced. 'Does he really think the queen was innocent of all the terrible things that happened? Think on, dolt.'

'I am not an idiot.' Duncan pulled back his chair and sat down. 'First you tell me not to think, then you tell me to think.' He picked up his falconer's whistle off the desk and blew it until she told him to put it aside and take up his quill pen. 'You know, Father has promised to get me some new hawking gloves and a bell for my hawk.' He dipped the pen into the inkwell, wishing she would stop butting into his life. 'I can't wait.'

'I hear your hawk killed a falcon.' Miss Booth stood and walked towards his desk. 'Your father expects you to excel in all you do. Pray tell, what lessons can you learn from watching a hawk tear a falcon apart? Hawking is barbaric.' Little did she know the servants, deferential to her face, called her Attila behind her back. 'Hawking is a sport for kings, noble men and aristocratic boys. Och! I daresay your father is meeting your physical needs.' She had taken a hiatus from intimidating Iain. 'Hawking is a manly sport, Master Hutchinson; you are a boy. To be called Lord of Inverkin is ridiculous. Hubris.'

Duncan flushed when she held his face with both hands and gazed into his eyes. He loved hunting with his father but she had made him feel wretched for enjoying the thrill of the kill, seeing his hawk swooping and ripping its victims apart. He knew that she was trying to sway him, compelling him to abandon his favourite sport and relinquish the time he spent hunting with his father and the gamekeeper, Bill. He knew she would go to her room soon and fall on her knees by her bedside, praying and reciting *The Sorrowful Mysteries of the Holy Rosary.* When he was much younger, he liked to look into her mesmerizing violet eyes. He no longer enjoyed her gazing into his eyes and stroking his face with her soft white hands. She continued to cup his face with both hands.

'Stop it.' Squirming in his seat, Duncan put down the pen and picked up his whistle. 'We are not in puppy-land.' His sandy hair fell forward, obscuring his face. 'Go get yourself a Maltese puppy.' He blew the whistle close to her ear until she released his face from her grip. 'Father is thinking of sending me to boarding-school, away from you.'

'What, leave the schoolroom?' Miss Booth gently stroked his face with mock concern. His father's plan had been brought to her attention a month ago. 'Actually, I do want you to kill a hawk for me.' He had the longest eyelashes she had ever seen on a boy and whenever he blew his whistle, his lips were soft and sensuous. She remembered holding his delicate frame in her arms when she first became his governess. 'Your father took Iain hunting last week. It would give me pleasure to curb his enthusiasm for the sport.'

'I shall do no such thing.' Outside, grey rain was sheeting down. 'No.' Duncan felt as if he were balancing on a plank. She had started a hateful campaign against his aunt Olivia and expected him to follow her lead. 'I've changed my mind about Iain.'

'I never change my view about a person.' Miss Booth confiscated the whistle and stared into his sea-green eyes. 'That was bad of you, flinging your velvet-lined gloves into the water and ordering Iain to fetch them. Given your new admiration for the waif, I must assume you are taking a different trajectory along the way. In my experience, people who change sides are always untrustworthy. They are liable to say one thing in private and do something different in public. Is that the kind of man you are going to be, Master Hutchinson? As part of your lesson, I would like you to translate my thoughts into Latin.'

'*Sic transit gloria mundi.*' Bored, Duncan picked up the quill pen and swallowed saliva. '*Thus passes the glory of the world.* Or, hero today, outcast tomorrow.'

'I want you to lock Iain in the cellar with the dead hawk.' Miss Booth felt certain that he was unaffected by the deaths of flying creatures. 'Then I would like an essay on the Acts of Union between England and

Scotland in 1706 and 1707.' Her lips puckered, saying, 'If that's too complicated, I shall fetch you a bucket with which to draw *the waters of truth*.'

'*Bleurgh*!' This remark was met with derision and a long sigh. 'You are making me uncomfortable.' Hunching over the desk, Duncan looked down at a sheet of blank paper and began to write in his neat handwriting. On hunting trips, his father had taught him not to fear animals. It was women, *weaker vessels*, who feared insects and wild animals.

'You will do as I suggested.' In truth, Miss Booth's vitality was gone. 'Write.' She stared at Duncan, who shifted awkwardly on the chair and dipped his pen into the inkwell. 'Never outshine those above you. You will lock Iain in the cupboard because I say so.'

'I'll do no such thing.' Unconsciously, Duncan bit his bottom lip in defiance. 'He's a little boy.' A door slammed below stairs and he shot to his feet, relieved that his father was home. 'See what you made me do. If you bully me again, I'll tell Father you're trying to convert me, papist. I'll tell him you said his favourite stained-glass window represents Catholicism: The Ascension. He hates religious zealots – *wolves in sheep's clothing*. By the way, Father despises your *moral hypocrisy*. There, I've said it.'

'Really, really!' Miss Booth, staring at the dark ink seeping between the gaps in the floorboards, repeated, 'Really!' She placed the whistle on his desk. 'Is it your ambition to be as opinionated as your father?' She could not believe that he had knocked over the inkwell. For a time, she watched the ink slowly spreading, as if it were blue blood and, in desperation, searched the room until she found a rug to cover the area. 'I can see the man you are going to become: strong, determined and ruthless.' With tears hovering, she stood by his desk and thought that if there was a sliver of a chance to change his father's mind about sending Iain away to school, she would try. 'I'd like an Aristotle quote.'

Thoughtful, Duncan mused: '*To avoid criticism say nothing, do nothing, be nothing*.'

'Aha! The Greek philosopher.' Miss Booth stared at her inky hands, recalling a half-remembered dream. In it, a man-child led her into a cave where sharks with terrifying teeth swam in an inky-blue lake. It was as if a door had opened inside her head and the memories were pouring out. She thought, *Oh, how could you be such a fool, Euphemia Booth?*

* * *

Dawn was breaking when they set out for Edinburgh. The boys, out-fitted in green velvet jackets, wore matching MacDonald kilts and sporrans. Iain must have fallen asleep because when he sat up and opened his eyes, half-listening, Duncan and Dougal were squabbling. Squire Alasdair Hutchinson, forty years old, wore a hand-pleated kilt and matching shawl. The tall, green-eyed patriarch broke his gaze from the trees and galloped ahead of the horse-drawn carriage. Two Highlanders rode on either side of him. Due to the high increase in rent, these men were about to take a one-way trip to North America.

Around 9.30am, they caught up with the Duke of Argyll's crested carriage. Squire Hutchinson had cast a withering look at the soldiers, muttering that every man had a duty to protect his *kith and kin*. Unarmed, he was conscious that it had been six years since the Disarming Act of 1725 was passed, prohibiting Highlanders from carrying arms in public. Cantering, his grey steed and his carriage dared not overtake the bewigged duke's horses until the aristocrat had given him the go ahead. Duke and Laird then passed each other with a cursory nod.

The Acts of Union of 1706 and 1707 had joined England and Scotland into a single kingdom, the United Kingdom, and brought about major changes in Scotland, particularly after the Jacobite Rising in 1715. These events resulted in the Government at Westminster garrisoning the Highlands by building army barracks and military roads. Under the Fortified Estates Act of 1707, Highlanders who participated in the uprising in 1715 had their lands and estates forfeited. Already, the Highlands were becoming a hub for British soldiers, known as Redcoats, who were still hunting Jacobite supporters in the Highlands.

'I'm scared, Dougal.' Iain felt a bolt of anxiety when a tree fell across the road in the distance.

'Ouch!' Miss Booth cried out when the two-horse carriage lurched forward. 'Mercy.' She put her head in her hands, for she had banged it on the carriage window. The boys beamed and it struck her that they wished her dead. 'Banish those bad thoughts, Messrs. Hutchinsons.' She perked up immediately, thinking that all the logs on Squire Hutchinson's land could never equal those on the Duke of Argyll's estate. Although she was aware of danger, she was more disturbed by the thought that Squire Hutchinson wanted to remove the boys from her influence and place them into masculine hands. She had left Inverkin House in a calm rage and now she thought to herself, *You are surplus to requirement, Euphemia.*

'Don't be scared, Iain.' Duncan had been pondering, for he was due to attend an interview at the Royal High School in Edinburgh. 'Father will know what to do.' He tried to reassure Dougal and Iain, who were both scheduled to attend interviews at James Mundell's School.

Ever since her redundancy notice had been served, the black-haired Miss Booth had feared teaching slow-witted children and showing interfering mamas her non-existent lesson plans. 'Pouf!' She blew air like a goldfish in a glass bowl and gazed at Duncan with the creeping realisation that she no longer had any influence over him. 'I hope they catch those brutes,' she said gloomily, observing the crest on the side of the Duke of Argyll's carriage that had come to a standstill. 'Oh Lord.' Two Redcoats dismounted and removed the log from the road. 'What is the world coming to when Scotsmen cannot bear arms in their own country?' Immediately after the crested carriage departed, she vented, 'Why should the Duke of Argyll be the only noble in the land to have his own private army?'

'Because he has the English King's ear and sits in the House of Lords at Westminster,' answered Duncan.

'I don't like it when you think, Master Hutchinson.' Miss Booth closed the carriage window and imagined fat old men snoozing in comfortable leather chairs in the House of Lords. 'Whatever is the matter, Iain? You are as white as snow.' The red-coated soldiers surrounded the carriage and the boy needed to pee. 'Why are they searching your kinsmen?' She stood up, got out of the carriage and, holding the door open, she said impatiently, 'Come along, boy. Those are Highlanders – harmless.' Not satisfied with being dismissed from her job, she grew even more tetchy when Iain told her that he could not urinate. 'The horses will run you down if you take all day. Why do you always want to empty your bladder when we are on the road, child? You are a *piddler*, always picking at your food.' A beetle fell from one of the branches above her head onto her left hand. 'If you keep this up,' she said, flicking it away, 'I shall cut off your tiny tiddler.'

'Leave him be.' Duncan alighted from the carriage and placed his hand on the child's left shoulder. 'Don't take all day, Iain.' With Miss Booth in a flap, his eyes gleamed at the thought of seeing Holyrood with its tapestries, continental carpets on the floor and gilt framed mirrors in every room. Being the eldest boy, he felt that he had a responsibility to protect Iain. 'Why are the Redcoats accosting Father's kinsmen, Booth?'

'I'll hold you responsible if he wets himself, Booth.' Hesitant, Dougal looked out the window before stepping down from the carriage. 'If you'd only taken him outside when he asked earlier, we wouldn't be standing here now.' His eyes settled on the anxious child, whose bottom lip was trembling. 'Don't just stand there, Booth. Do your duty.'

Duncan was surprised to see Miss Booth drop to her knees beside the child. 'On the count of three, Iain,' he said coaxingly. 'When I was little, I wanted to pee whenever I was afraid but, somehow, I couldn't do it.' An hour ago, his only worry was his new, pinching leather shoes. A dark shape dashed across the road. 'Did you see that?'

'*Sabre rattling*, gentlemen?' Miss Booth's authority had been greatly diminished, but she tried to put a bold face on it. 'I have a wee boy trying to relieve himself.' She watched the Redcoats approaching, knowing that they were hard and unflinching. 'Good Lord, gentlemen! You think I'm a *priest-harbourer*.' They proceeded to examine the carriage in silence, poking and prodding beneath the seats. 'There are no fugitives in there. You've got them on the run.'

Dougal called out, 'They've got him!' A dark, huddled shape had been cornered against the nearest stonewall. Shots were heard, followed by a commotion in the brambles nearby. 'Father, what's going on?' The naive portion of the boy's brain desperately wanted to believe that the Redcoats were merely harmless toy soldiers. 'What is happening, Duncan?'

'How should I know?' Duncan raised his shoulders, disguising his own fear when a shapeless mass collapsed into a heap beside the stonewall. 'I'm not a child, Booth.' He was aware of his governess standing behind him, protecting his back. 'Is he dead, Father?'

'Yes,' Squire Hutchinson replied. 'We are on a military road, which is hazardous at the best of times.' He rode over to the carriage, brought his grey steed to a halt and scanned the area in the brambles with hawk-like eyes. 'Get back into the carriage. I'll join you in a minute.'

Duncan, standing in the centre of the road, surveyed the landscape. 'Um!' The colour drained from the sandy-haired boy's face when he heard howling in the brambles and saw two bleeding men being dragged from the bushes. Struggling violently, they broke free and ran along the road, searching frantically for cover. 'A hanging!' Ropes were tied around the two Jacobite sympathizers' necks before the soldiers carried them off. 'They're not the Duke's men, are they?' Nothing he learned in the school-room prepared him for what he saw. 'A real hanging!' The corpses would soon be swinging and sun-dried. 'Hurry, Booth. Father is waiting.'

Miss Booth climbed into the carriage and sat with her embroidery on her lap, plotting her future. She had an older sister in Leith whom she planned to visit as soon as they reached Edinburgh. Short of stature, the sister had married a baker from Berwick-Upon-Tweed. Their younger brother, balding and bulky, had been apprenticed at a goldsmith's shop in Elphinstone Court in Edinburgh. She would walk around the city with them to discuss her future; she needed her family. The longer she sat in the carriage, the more despondent and alienated she felt, for she had had a frank discussion with Squire Hutchinson last night. He had explained that the boys required instruction from male tutors, silencing female protest by informing her that women could not teach boys how to become men.

'Why don't you say what you are thinking?' Miss Booth threw Duncan a side-eye. 'It can't do any good keeping it to yourself.' Her protégé had refused to lock Iain in the cellar and had undermined her by refusing to study under her tutelage. 'If I've ever needed a boost, it is now.' She deeply regretted doting on Duncan as a way of protecting her job and was dismayed by her maternal feelings for him. She worried that he would be bullied at boarding school by the more rumbustious boys, or by a stern-voiced headmaster taking morning assembly. 'I am grateful for the time I had with you boys. I shan't forget it.'

From the beginning, Squire Hutchinson had had reservations about employing Miss Booth but had needed a governess urgently. Riding along a military road on high alert, he had avoided her since terminating her contract. She had looked defensive when he brought up her less than glowing references. Anxious that the boys should experience no further discomfort, he barely noticed the wild scenery and the high hills as they made their way to a relative's house in Crieff, in the town of Perthshire, where they would rest over-night. This thriving cattle market town was where the Hutchinsons had bought and sold their cattle for generations, some of which ended up at Smithfield market in London.

* * *

The next day, they set off for Stirling Castle, stopping mid-morning for a comfort break at a roadside inn. Once inside, Squire Hutchinson had his ear to the ground. The half-whispered conversations flitted between talk of the Redcoats garrisoning the Highlands, undercover government spies seeking Jacobite sympathisers, and stories about young men being pressed-ganged. There was also talk of the importance of the Port of Leith to the West India merchants, of another Jacobite Rising and of the new wave of emigration from the Highlands to North America.

With her nose in the air at dawn, Miss Booth had been relieved to leave Crieff. She abhorred the stench of cattle dung and stale urine. Twenty-four hours had passed since she had experienced her first bout of anxiety. The second came upon their arrival in Edinburgh where a dishevelled woman yelled outside the carriage and was immediately ostracized. Elegant young men swaggered about or sat proudly on their prancing horses, barely stopping to enquire about the commotion. The pressing crowd had gone wild.

'I am so glad you boys will be attending school here in Edinburgh.' Miss Booth shook her head unconvincingly, peering out the window to see what was going on. 'Pickpockets!' The talk was that a street urchin had filched a gentleman's pocket watch and had been trampled by no less than six horses while making a dash for it in the High Street. 'It sounds as though the *Furies* have been let loose on the streets of Edinburgh.'

There was a sense of unease in the carriage. Any feeling of optimism Duncan had about attending boarding school, or feelings of excitement at seeing the Palace of Holyrood with its towers and crenelated battlements, had evaporated. The palace looked down on the city with its neat High Street, stone houses boasting wooden galleries and stone channels to take away the city's rainwater. Built on a hill to keep outsiders and marauding armies out, Edinburgh Castle seemed to be watching them enter the city.

'Aren't you glad you came, Iain?' Dougal admired a group of kilted warriors and Highlanders in tartan ensembles. 'What an adventure.' He suppressed the memory of two corpses dangling from an oak tree. 'I want to see the stallholders, too. I'm so hungry,' he added uneasily, staring out the window to where a clergyman was in the act of retrieving the dead body of a nine-year-old pickpocket. 'Forget about Duncan's threats, Iain. He can't send you to the Tolbooth prison. If he's mean to you today, I'm going to tell Father.'

'I have high hopes for you and Duncan.' Miss Booth's violet eyes scanned his face and, with a worried expression etched across her face, she turned briefly to look at the chaotic scene outside. 'I taught you boys to keep your thoughts to yourselves, especially if they happen to be bad thoughts about other people.' The carriage jolted and came to a standstill when the unforgiving crowd surged forward. She gazed out the window.

'Make way, make way!' The clergyman was carrying the dead boy whose distraught mother was being harassed by the baying mob; they seemed to be swallowing her up. *Alms for the poor,*' called the clergyman.

'Do-gooder.' Miss Booth looked away. Despite the indignities and humiliation heaped upon the destitute mother for training her son to become a pickpocket, she did not plead for mercy. It was unthinkable that anyone could be unmoved by such a scene. Grimacing, Miss Booth tutted, 'I remember another such incident when the crowd rushed the little thief. His mother was smothered with eggs and rotten tomatoes.'

'Out of the way, guttersnipes,' barked a *Good Samaritan* with a dark birthmark on his bald head. *'He that is without sin among you, let him first cast a stone at her.'*

'Father.' Transfixed and bewildered, Dougal's jaw dropped when the unkempt Scotsman whipped out a knife. 'Father,' he leaned out the carriage window, 'what's happening?'

'He's got a pistol.' Iain was visibly moved. He clung to Dougal's arm and looked up into his reassuring brown eyes. 'I don't like it here.' He gazed out the window. 'I've never seen so many people. I don't want to go to school in Edinburgh. I don't! I hate it here.'

'I fear it is time to take the crutches away from him.' While Dougal comforted Iain, Miss Booth appeared startled by the child's outburst and said unguardedly, 'He will take a few steps at a time before galloping away from Inverkin House like a horse bolting the stables; his sort always does.' The child was five feet away from her in the carriage, yet she could not find it within herself to offer him any reassurance. *Inverkin House is one of the most elegant homes in the Highlands – all those antiques*, she thought, imagining a Moroccan-leather claret jug that dated back to the fourteenth century. 'I can't blame you for wanting to return to the bosom of the schoolroom, child.'

Duncan's eyes scanned the crowd. 'You are really mean, Booth.'

'I apologise, Master Hutchinson.' The corpse was deposited at the carriage door for a speedy dispatch away from the crowd. 'Thieving boys must learn to keep their grubby hands to themselves.' Miss Booth had a knack of planting unpleasant images in people's minds and did not feel the need to play the do-gooder. 'We don't want to traumatize Master Hutchinson, Jr, by hosting the dead body of a pickpocket in the carriage. He has awful nightmares and the corpse of a child, a beggar no less, will only compound matters.'

'You have no feelings.' Duncan's eyes went to the weeping mother, elbowing her way through the crowd to keep up with the clergyman who was taking her son's body to the Kirk of St Giles. This was the church where John Knox had railed against 'petticoat government' and had denounced the young French-reared Mary Queen of Scots.

'She's weeping.' Dougal listened to the haunting cry of the deceased pickpocket's mother, which sounded like a wailing banshee. 'I pity her, tearing her clothes into rags.' He loosened his grip on Iain's trembling hand and wiped the boy's eyes. In front of his father, the uncaring Miss Booth had nothing but praise for Iain; behind the squire's back she was cold and calculating. 'We ought to go to St Giles and give that poor woman some money, Duncan.' He leaned out the carriage window. 'Father, I'm scared. Come into the carriage, please.'

Scanning the crowd, Squire Hutchinson was alerted by a movement beside the carriage. Instinctively, he kicked at the door, sending a thief flying. The mob soared forward when a third pickpocket lunged for the carriage door but was stopped by a heavy foot. At this, Dougal and Iain huddled together, wishing that Squire Hutchinson would dismount and join them. They did not speak but kept their eyes on the door. Duncan, leaping to his feet, placed himself between the door and the boys. His fears came to the fore when a lanky thief snatched a gentleman's wallet and was pinned against the rocking carriage until the mob seized him and frogmarched him away.

'Father, we ought to do something to help that woman,' cried Dougal.

'You are never happy unless you are worried about a waif or a stray,' replied Squire Hutchinson, trying to calm his jittery horse while the crowd continued to press against the carriage. 'Keep the doors closed, Booth.' With the mob growing bigger, he sensed that the boys were in danger and moved closer to the window. 'Keep your head inside, Duncan.'

'I think it's appalling the treatment she's been given.' Duncan patted his sporran, glancing up at Edinburgh Castle in the distance. 'That woman needs our help, Booth.'

'We cannot help every wayfarer who falls on the road. Mark my words, it will be your undoing.' Miss Booth was clean out of sympathy. 'She's a professional beggar.' The incident so aroused her anger that she could not help adding, 'That woman turned her son into a thief and now she is trying to save her own good-for-nothing hide. She reminds me of *a harpy*. Filthy monster, bad mother, perfectly loathsome.'

Duncan waved away the remark. 'You haven't got any children, Booth; you don't know what it's like to be a mother.' An hour had passed since they'd entered Edinburgh and the trip had become a disaster. 'I want to give that poor woman my pocket money.'

'I wouldn't give her the sweat off my brow,' Miss Booth said. 'It is a virtue to stand up for what we believe, though we must not reward bad behaviour. We must not succumb to weakness. Take my advice: kindness is a vice, not a virtue.' Since her redundancy notice had become known to the servants below stairs, she had given up on biting back her words. 'I do not agree with your desire to feed the world. It is good to demonstrate charity, occasionally, but you will grow up to become a pauper if you think it is a good thing to take off your kilt and gift it to vagrants who refuse to work for a living.'

'This crowd is swelling.' Squire Hutchinson dismounted and handed the horse's reins to one of his kinsmen nearby, who tethered them to his own horse and rode alongside the carriage with his other kinsman on the opposite side. When he told Miss Booth that he was terminating her contract, she'd pleaded with him to at least let her tutor Iain. Her persistence disgusted him and now he entered the safety of the carriage, thinking, *There is nothing distinguished about this nettlesome woman, except for her unusual violet eyes.*

'This mob is disorderly.' Miss Booth had lain awake for most of the night, agonising over losing her job. She was going to miss Inverkin House in autumn, particularly her morning walks with the boys. The leaves turned to gold, bronze and copper before the breeze swept them along the ground. Lowering her eyes to the embroidery on her lap, she knew it was futile to butter up Duncan. The minutes passed and she got back to work on her embroidery with frustration woven into every stitch. 'A penny for your thoughts?'

'*Change is essential*, your words.' There was a calculated aloofness about Duncan, who voiced his thoughts, repeating: '*To avoid criticism say nothing, do nothing, be nothing.*'

'Oh look, the great unwashed, shedding their dirty skin.' The carriage proceeded towards the Royal Mile while the childless governess fretted that even the deceased thief's mother had had a child. Hanging over the incident was the shadow of Iain's late mother, Miss Olivia Hutchinson. The arrival of the orphan had changed everything at Inverkin House. Miss Booth, realising she no longer had the youthful appearance to bluff her way into another widower's home as a tutor, abandoned the embroidery. 'You are delightfully down to earth, Master Hutchinson. If you really want to help the poor, you've got to challenge the *status quo*, which has turned some Highlanders into landless paupers…'

'That is revolutionary talk, and these are perilous times for Jacobite sympathisers.' Making a point, Squire Hutchinson silenced the governess with a stern look. 'Think before you speak, Booth.' She had come to Inverkin House with the air of a noble woman who had fallen on hard times. 'There are three impressionable young minds present.'

* * *

When Duncan was at boarding school in Edinburgh, he often played truant from school on a Friday afternoon and would go down to the Port of Leith to watch the ships sailing to the British colonies. He vowed that, like Christopher Columbus, he would explore the world one day. However, the Battle of Culloden of 16 April 1746 and the Highland Clearances had changed his destiny. His father, who saw action during the ill-fated Jacobite Rising of 1745, lost the family estate and Duncan's dream of circumnavigating the globe went up in flames. After decades in a dead-end job as a bookkeeper, he decided to leave Scotland.

Twenty years after the Jacobite Uprising, on a dreary September morning in 1765, Duncan stood on the deck of the *Ballantrae*, which was known as a *Jamaica packet*, having had dinner with Dougal last night. Earlier on, a strong breeze had caused the ship to change course, heading away from the Port of Leith, bustling with its merchant ships, towards the north of Scotland. The ship had passed three notable landmarks: Shetland, the Fair Isle and the Orkney Islands, the latter having once been used as a look-out post for the Viking warlords. Ever vigilant, Duncan now paced the deck; meantime, a handful of crofters wept as they approached land.

'Watch out!' Without warning, a dinghy drifted into the path of the *Jamaica packet*. Duncan mused, thinking about what lay ahead of them and looking over the side of the ship into the grey water. He had boarded enough ships in Leith not to be fazed by human error. 'That rower is heading for the stern.' He squinted and tried to make out the shape of the man in the boat. 'He'll be torn to pieces.' The ship's horn punctuated the air, urging the careless crofter to steady his boat. 'Out of the way, *ya dafty*.'

* * *

Three weeks later, the *Ballantrae* was struck by a rogue wave, followed by three towering waves smashing down on her. Duncan heard his own voice, trying to mobilise and organise the female passengers. Sea and rainwater deluged the deck when a gash of lightning struck the mast pole, causing the ship's bough to lift out of the water. There was an odd roaring sound and the passengers clung to the ropes when a fourth wave crashed into the ship, which was poised on the brink of what resembled a whirlpool. Before the storm, Duncan had hoped it would be plain sailing all the way. Now the crew struggled with the masts, desperately trying to steady the sails and control the riggings.

'Grab hold!' Duncan shouted when a sailor, clinging to the topsail and trying to reef the bowsprit, fell into the hold. Taken by surprise, he could still hear the boy's blood-curdling scream above a group of women wailing when a fifth wave hit the ship. 'Hold fast, ladies.' He pitied the Glaswegian boy, Tom, who had run away from home to find work and had been press-ganged. The sight of sailors lashing wooden planks together with ropes catapulted Duncan back into the past: at ten years old, his cousin Iain ran away to sea and was never seen again. The redundant Miss Booth had sent a letter to Iain's school master to recount his life story. It came to light that hardly a day had gone by without him being bullied. Iain was forgotten when the ship's cat was washed overboard. 'So much for nine lives.' In his mind, Duncan rebuked the winds and the waves. He ignored the screaming women and reasoned that the swelling water would at least rid the ship of rats in the hold. The well-dressed Scot remembered his clothes in his cabin; they would get a soaking. 'Better the rat-catcher than a human.' He looked steadily at a hysterical woman on deck.

'Lochaber nae maer,' said Captain Buchan, a big Scotsman with a loud voice and a penchant for whisky. 'Heaven preserve my bonny Scotch laddie.' Bearded and standing with his feet wide apart, he spoke in Gaelic, tossing backwards and forwards on the deck. After three decades at sea, first transporting enslaved Africans to the British West Indies, the old sea dog had conquered many a storm. 'All passengers below deck.'

'We're all going to die!' wailed a proxy bride in her mid-thirties, longing to return to Scotland. 'Sweet Mary, Mother of Jesus, don't let us drown at sea. Save our souls!'

'Hold fast, Pip.' Buchan turned to a puny sailor with a scar from his left eye down to his cheek and handed the helm to the great-grandson of a pirate who had frequented Port Royal. 'You okay down there, Tom?' He was concerned for the injured sailor-boy. 'Steady yer course, Pip.' He made his way into the hold where he scooped the vomiting Tom into his arms and smiled at him indulgently. 'Be still.' His face was strained, but his soothing voice had a soporific effect on the ten-year-old while the waves continued to beat into the ship. 'God is in control.'

'Blind faith.' Battling against the elements, Duncan clung to the ropes with water running down his face. A wooden barrel with pickled herrings, and another with salted beef, rolled about on the water-logged deck. 'It seems we're heading back to the Highlands, gentlemen.'

'*O ye of little faith,*' said a cynical chancer named Evan Brown. 'I am looking forward to seeing Port Royal, haunt of the buccaneers, and to becoming a sugar baron.' Unperturbed by the fierce winds and the killer waves, he clung to the ropes, whistling, '*Oh! Ye'll take the high road and I'll take the low road. And I'll be in Scotland afore ye…*'

'Steady yourself, ma'am.' Duncan held his nerve, swallowing air, when the proxy bride tripped and fell into his arms. He was on the way back to the rank-smelling cabin that he shared with six bilious-looking Scots. 'Sometimes a man must catch the nearest wave.'

* * *

Back in the stuffy cabin, united by the desire to gain a West India fortune, Duncan's companions described an idyllic life of wealth and status. As the dreams became more outlandish, the banter turned to the proxy bride's rounded bosoms. She had earlier flashed Duncan a come-hither smile, but he did not yield; he had no desire to fritter away his future on loose living. Much of the money he carried was to buy a sugar plantation; hence he focused his mind on the myth of the Minotaur and Minos, King of Crete, who offended Poseidon by refusing to sacrifice a bull that had emerged from the sea. With plenty of whisky to go around the cabin, Duncan climbed into his hammock and proceeded to tell the story of Minos's wife, Pasiphae. She had fallen in love with the bull and their union produced a child who was half-beast and half-man. However, the offspring of Pasiphae and the Minotaur, whose appetite could only be sated by virgin maids and Athenian youths, held no interest for money-hungry men who spoke enviously of William Drax, the Younger, who had founded a large plantation in St Ann, Jamaica: Drax Hall.

'If this storm continues, we will end up in *New Atlantis*.' Duncan lay in his hammock clutching Sir Francis Bacon's utopian novel. 'I am an optimist,' he said absently, listening to the crew battling in the hold where seawater had seeped up through the planks.

* * *

The next morning, with his tartan shawl draped across his shoulders like Rob Roy, Duncan stood on the *Ballantrae's* deck. Curious, he leaned over the side, listening to the unmistakable sound of a dolphin. The ship ploughed through the trackless ocean while the dolphin somersaulted, hitting the water fast, amusing the passengers until they spotted a *Jamaica packet*, escorted by a frigate, bound for Liverpool in England.

'Man overboard!' a jovial Scot shouted when his hat flew off.

'Whoever commands the sea commands trade.' Captain Buchan looked up at the ragged sails while honking the ship's foghorn. 'We'll have to use the jury mast until we've repaired all the sails, lads. By Jove! They're hanging like ladies' loose gowns.'

'Tedious business.' Duncan looked on, a tad disapprovingly, at two sailors darning a damaged sail. 'Ladies.' His eye caught four young women who had absconded from a brothel in Newcastle. They had bribed an elderly client to hide them in his carriage. Not far off, a few hardy sailors roasted horse chestnuts and shared the hot snacks with the former prostitutes, who had organised a toga party and were laughing and smiling broadly. Duncan found himself admiring a slender pair of ankles peeping from beneath the proxy bride's toga. His eyes lit up until he saw the goats penned in a corner on deck.

'Are you game?' For light relief, Buchan took down a boat and invited Duncan and three hatless Scots to go fishing. Four men in a boat now gazed at an uprooted tree floating on the ocean. 'Hurricane debris. We are surrounded by water with no visible horizon.'

* * *

'Gentlemen, a toast.' The fishing trip was a success. At suppertime, Buchan raised his glass to absent friends, adding: *'To him who came over the water, Charles Edward Stuart.'* The fish supper was followed by a discussion about the economic importance of the Transatlantic slave trade. *'Deus nobis haec otia fecit; we owe all this to God.'* He urged the recovered sailor-boy to play a silver harmonica, belting out, *'As I came thro Sandgate, I heard a lassie sing. O weel may the keel row...'*

'I think you mean, *As I came thro Canongate,'* insisted Duncan, nursing a glass of claret. 'At the risk of sounding pedantic, Sandgate is a street in Newcastle.'

'Anyone been to a bare-knuckle fight at St Giles in the Fields in London?' Buchan imagined nubile young women lunging at each other with their skirts hitched up to their thighs. 'I like those grudge fights between Irishwomen. Perhaps you ought to bed one...'

'Whom might you have in mind?' Smiling, Duncan conjured a faceless redhead. 'As for those bare-knuckle Amazons, there is nothing worse than two women cat-fighting.'

* * *

On calm days, the ocean was littered with a colourful array of marine life which fascinated the female passengers, so much so that they were banned from leaning on the ropes to look overboard. Indifferent to the sight of whales bursting out of the water in their prehistoric ritual, most of the male passengers played chess or cards in their cabins. The deck was the sailors' entire world and often two burly men would let off steam, strapped to a wooden chest. There they sat facing each other, aiming blows at their opponent's ribs and chins.

Before the ship had set sail, Duncan had found a kindred spirit, Evan Brown, who followed him everywhere. Floundering between politics, economics and philosophy, Brown sat in Duncan's fusty cabin discussing the enlightenment until a tall, affable fellow disclosed that he had *gleet,* which he had caught from a doxy in Aberdeen. Soon the wind brought a gale of fresh air into the cabin with news that a ship had been sighted. All eyes immediately swivelled upwards to the ceiling, followed by a mad dash for the deck.

'Privateers, licensed piracy.' Buchan surmised that the unidentified vessel carried no cargo more than what it had captured. 'Ahoy there! What ship are you? We're a British ship sailing under the King's Flag.' Eerily, the *Ballantrae* sailed into a fog and a luminous object appeared on the ocean's surface, soaring upward as if destiny were pointing the way south. The ship's horn pierced the fog but there was no response from the other vessel, which had disappeared like a puff of smoke on the horizon. With his face tense, Buchan sought to calm the anxious Scots by invoking the poet James Thomson, reciting, '*Thy cities shall with commerce shine: All thine shall be the subject main. And every shore it circles thine. Rule, Britannia! Rule the waves: Britons never will be slaves.*'

* * *

'Land ahoy!' Nine weeks later, Pip sighted the Blue Mountains of Jamaica, rising out of the Caribbean Sea like bearded Neptune rising out of the ocean holding a trident. Although most of the Scots hailed from the lower echelons of society, hats were doffed when the Trade Winds brought the ship to its destination. Pip secured the Union Flag's mast pole, hoisting the banner with the red cross of St George. 'Land ahoy!'

'There lies Jamaica.' Duncan's shawl hung from his right shoulder. 'It's a breathtaking sight.' His heart leapt when the *Ballantrae's* anchor hovered above the water. 'Exciting times!' He nodded to the proxy bride but, unfortunately for her, her *Come follow, follow, follow me…to the green woods* smile was not reciprocated. 'The Island of Springs.'

'Guinea gold.' Buchan sniffed when the ship dropped anchor in Kingston Harbour. 'Gentlemen, I see guinea signs in your misty eyes.' He turned when a twenty gun-slaver with a cargo of six hundred kidnapped Africans limped into the harbour. 'This is Jamaica, home to the most belligerent blacks on the planet.' In a friendly gesture, he handed out letters of introduction. 'Take these to Menzies, the Scot auctioneer. *Buy the more docile Papaws from Whidah, and the timid Eboes. No Koromantyns – the fiercest nagas on earth! Oh, and buy the sleek, glossy Congo blacks for domestic use – mild and docile.* Break them in early, gentlemen.'

'Captain Buchan, may I say how much I enjoyed your hospitality on the *Ballantrae,* especially the fishing trip.' Outwardly calm, Duncan left Scotland with seven letters of introduction to prominent families who had fled to Jamaica after the Battle of Culloden. These Scots were mainly Gaelic-speaking with names such as Grandison, Cunningham, Cameron, McDonald, Murray, Campbell and Lindsay. 'I plan to spend five years…'

'Expectations!' The eighth letter came from Buchan, who explained that the potential gains in land and status were immense for those who resisted the temptations of white rum and brown women. 'Keep yer *tickle tails* in yer trousers and avoid those licentious *mulatto* wenches.'

'Caveat emptor.' Duncan held the letter from Buchan, as if he had been thrown a lifeline. *'Let the buyer beware.'* He listened while Buchan said many Scots had arrived with bright ideas that fell apart at the first hurdle. Some were unwilling to soil their hands with blood; others found slave labour gruesomely attritional. Although Duncan carried the Jacobite slogan of *King James and No Union,* he had no qualms about slavery. His views were influenced by David Hume, who had said, *I am apt to suspect the negroes…to be naturally inferior to the whites.* More to the point, Duncan was guided by Aristotle, whom he presently quoted: *'From the hour of their birth, some are marked out for subjection, others for rule.'*

On a sunny November morning in 1765, the more enterprising Scots stepped forward to watch a boat carry a group of Black women selling pineapples. Duncan took a deep breath and prepared to walk down the gangway in a black hat, white frill-fronted shirt and a black morning coat. Feeling somewhat deflated, the less adventurous Scots, including Evan Brown, drew back when an intolerable stench filled their nostrils.

'Go easy on yer sea legs.' Buchan observed Duncan's polished boots. 'It takes a while to get used to walking on land.' For the last two days, a shiver of sharks had been following the ship and now there were two sharks in the harbour. With the elation of arrival, a group of sailors speared and harpooned the female shark. There was a hiatus when Buchan noticed four profligate females flashing their cleavages at the sailors and waving decorously. 'Impossibly flirtatious.' He then quoted Ecclesiastes 7-28: '*One man among a thousand have I found, but a woman among all these have I not found.*'

'Doxies,' remarked Ezekiel Darnley, a red-haired Scot. 'They all behaved wantonly on the voyage.' The male shark was cannibalising its mate who was thrashing about in the water. 'Those mountains are robed in verdure like a hermit's beard.' The carnage enthralled his imagination and he kept his gaze on the landscape until Daniel Defoe's Moll Flanders tripped off his lips, '*With money in the pocket, one is at home anywhere.*'

* * *

With the encouragement of his fellow Scots, Duncan settled in St Ann. The late William Drax, the Younger, who had founded a prosperous sugar plantation on the North Coast, Drax Hall, had influenced this life-changing decision. After the preliminary introductions to the big Scottish planters, Duncan had decided to visit his kinsman, Lewis Hutchinson, who had built a castle on a hillside in a wooded valley and was referred to as 'the Mad Master of Edinburgh Castle.' Hutchinson's two-storied fortress was said to be his own prison. The red-headed Scot was ridiculed by the local whites who had jested that the castle bore no resemblance to its namesake back in Edinburgh. Duncan was just about to leave the castle when a local planter, Robbie Walker, rode by and informed him that Hutchinson was *persona non-grata*. Not having met his kinsman, he was astonished when the enigmatic recluse fired a pistol at him from behind the safety of a loop-holed observation point on the battlement, stating that he himself had been slighted and, *Henceforth my hand will be against all men.*

At forty-five years old, Duncan arrived with books by David Hume, Adam Smith and James Hutton, as well as Johnson's Dictionary and the King James Bible. His first public appearance took place at The Town House restaurant and tavern on Main Street in Montego Bay. With its red-brick frontage and grand staircase, the two-storey hub was a reminder that guests were never far from British hospitality. It was here that he was ribbed by the white elite, Scots who had cautioned that every 'single woman' regarded him as marriage material. Before he left the restaurant, the male diners had jested that one lax moment could see him wedded to a gummy old spinster. The ladies dubbed him 'Our handsome Scotsman.' At soirees, in Montego Bay, Trelawny and St Mary, he was besieged by young women on the more prosperous sugar estates. It was clear that his success hinged on being part of the community life to which he belonged.

'Our handsome Scotsman.' In Trelawny, Mrs Grandison emerged from the big house to stand on the piazza, looking Duncan up and down. She had spent the last two days introducing him to polite society and planned to take him to the neighbouring plantation of Good Hope, with its mile-long cut-stone aqueduct built in 1755. Her advice to the husband-seeking ladies was to, 'Pursue him with vigour.' She would ensure he got their calling cards. She now led a dozen exuberant women into the drawing room, perched herself on a damask sofa, eager to discuss the newcomer.

It was around 3pm on a Sunday afternoon. The Grandisons had hosted a dinner in Duncan's honour. With the women occupying female space, men-talk focused on educating creole children, for it was felt that there were 'no opportunities or culture' for young people in Jamaica. During the meal, Duncan had been conscious of a sense of clannishness and snobbery against the lower-class white men present. The smiling bachelor, sporting a white cravat and black jacket, noticed that haggis, black pudding and bagpipes were plentiful. With so many names to learn, he had told his admirers, who had left their menfolk to enjoy brandy and cigars on the piazza, that he hoped to father a *long-tailed creole dynasty*.

On the voyage over, Duncan had shared a cabin with six Scotsmen, two of whom were present on the piazza. It ran the length of the front of the house where the men were smoking cigars. Taking a pinch of snuff, an ageing planter placed it along the length of his left thumb and inhaled, dribbling mucus. He imagined himself as a tobacco lord in Glasgow (powdered wig, scarlet cloak, black three-cornered hat and a gold-tipped ebony cane) and boasted that he belonged in silk and lace.

'Your success is our success, man.' Puffing on a fat cigar, Jude Cameron Sr smiled. 'You'll soon be a pillar of the community.'

'You must learn to dance,' urged a small Scot with wisps of grey on his hard-boiled egg head. 'Even when we are on our last legs, we whites love to dance.' Ted Murray had fled to Jamaica in 1746 and bore the scars he received at the Battle of Culloden. 'A decade hence, you'll be applying for your own coat of arms as a mark of your status, Hutchinson. You ought to make use of our British symbols, perhaps a griffin or a unicorn.'

'The slaves have a song.' Among the guests was a *walk-foot buckra* named Evan Brown, who went from parish to parish on foot. '*Newcome buckra/He get sick/He tak fever/He be die...*' He gave off a rank smell, complaining that his life was one big disappointment. 'If you could just see your way clear to lending me ten guineas – I'm begging you.'

'Have you no shame, man?' At first glance, it appeared Duncan was not thrilled to see his old shipmate, a shabby man who was considered to be a social outsider. 'We sailed on the same ship, Brown. What happened to your pride, man? Men don't beg.'

'West India *nabobs*.' The Englishman, Elijah Hogg, had a mouth full of misaligned teeth. 'When you are poor, no one wants to know you.' With a heavy heart, he rued leaving Winchester, seat of King Alfred the Great. 'You Jacobites have swallowed up every acre of arable land in Jamaica, though I wouldn't have bought a plantation in the hills: Stirling.' Since the English conquest in 1655, some families had acquired land beyond their wildest dreams. He reflected, 'The slaves have another song, *Massa turn poor buckra away oh! But massa can't turn poor neger away oh!*'

'West India *nabobs?*' Busha Lindsay, who had sailed from England the day after visiting a Lloyd's coffee house in London, advised, 'Take a leaf out of Henry Lascelles's book: go to Barbados and get a job as a customs collector.' He beamed. 'Gentlemen, my lads are fresh from Oxford and Cambridge. I've warned 'em to keep away from *poor buckra ladies*. I refer to the Irish and the Welsh, those half-conquered people. I've assigned the task of running the main estate to my twenty-two-year-old son, Master Ewan, the brain of the family. I could have sent my sons to school in Edinburgh, followed by St Andrews, but the men who run the empire are Eton and Oxbridge educated, their buttocks well-birched.'

'I'm being eaten alive by mosquitoes,' moaned a foppish chap with perspiration soaking the back of his fashionable black flapped coat. 'They're like bloodthirsty midges.' The Cambridge boy, whose face was sunburnt, suggested that his father was pinning his future on slave labour. 'Why are we exiling on this godforsaken rock, Papa? We are civilized white men. Why can't we pay the blackies to work in the cane-fields?'

'Young man, *Jamaica is like a constant mine*,' Septimus McDonald lifted a quote from the Barbadian writer Charles Leslie, '*whence Britain draws prodigious riches*.' He owned three thousand acres of land and regarded his estate as his personal fiefdom. 'I once lobbed off a slave's right foot for daring to run away. I roasted it and forced him to eat it.'

'Nagas must be seasoned: *buck breaking* with a big *tickle tail*; their peers won't respect him.' Busha Lindsay was hardened in his position. 'The next generation is expected to make their mark.'

* * *

Five years later, in 1770, thirty-five-year-old Fiona McDuff arrived in Jamaica on the *Ballantrae*. Within the first three weeks, she and Duncan had planned their marriage. The guests started gathering well in advance of the 10am wedding at Canongate where the rooms were filled corner-to-corner with families. Duncan had met Fiona after his estranged first wife, Morag Watt, and her lover, had drowned on a ship bound for America, in 1757. Thirteen years after some of the darkest hours in his life, he was ready to commit himself to another woman.

Morag: the unknown woman lurked in Fiona's mind. She herself was a crofter's daughter whose people were removed from their crofts during the Highland Clearances. After rising at dawn, she had personally seen to it that the hallway and rooms below stairs were festooned with fragrant branches of orange, lime, lemon and mango; that the fragrant bushes were placed above the doors. As she stepped out the front door onto the lush lawn, she sniffed, walked down the path and regarded the main gate expectantly, waiting with nervous anticipation for the minister and the Redcoats to arrive to complement the wedding guests. The British troops had stopped over at Fort George in the nearby village of Montrose, which was situated in one of the most remote corners of the island.

'What is taking the minister so long?' Fiona, in a plain ivory gown and white satin shoes, succumbed to the demons of doubt. 'He's not coming.' Her patience wore thin, waiting for the second most important man to arrive. 'Today should be a memorable experience…' From the right of the plantation house, she heard a snicker. 'The ladies are impatient, too.' The white elite's arrival marked Canongate's entrance into the plantocracy. 'The wedding will be a non-starter if the parson doesn't show up.'

The main gate at Canongate was left wide open. 'Better late than never.' Duncan was relieved to see the parson arriving on horseback. 'Here he is.' He stood in full Scottish garb, watching the Rev'd McKay dismount. The Church of Scotland minister had been visiting his brother's estate in Clarendon. Duncan stepped around two puppies and told Cassian, his manservant, to kennel them. 'Tether your horse and hurry, parson.'

Presently, a huge ray of sunlight came down on the lawn where the planters, those who had enlisted in the militia, arrived in their finery and dismounted in an orderly manner. There were carriages on the drive and mounted troops dressed in black hats, red jackets with white cuffs and white breeches, too. The soldiers, whom they had been so anxiously awaiting, started to arrive with a pack of barking blood-hounds following behind the horses.

'I didn't count on this.' Fiona blinked when the Redcoats assembled on the lawn. 'Goodness gracious.' Meanwhile, two enslaved African women were given the task of raining rose petals down on their mistress from a bedroom window on the first floor.

'Thank God I can wear Highland dress without breaking the law.' Duncan cracked a smile and stepped forward. 'Welcome, Major.' Being anti-English, he was cautiously cordial with the hollow-eyed, auburn-haired Major who commanded the British Redcoats. Duncan had placed his dirk and powder horn on a chair on the lawn before greeting the Major. He himself was twenty-six during the Battle of Culloden (April 1746) when over twelve hundred men died at the hands of the Duke of Cumberland's force. To a Jacobite like Duncan, the 19 August 1745 was a memorable date. On his birthday, Charles Edward Stuart, the Bonnie Prince Charlie, arrived at Loch Shiel from France. Today, 18 August 1770, on the eve of his birthday, he proudly repeated the words of the charismatic Prince: *'Every man for himself.'*

'I hope I haven't kept you good people waiting.' Rev'd McKay put on his vestment hastily. *'I've come to make Scotland happy.'* The portly Scot's announcement resulted in a few raised eyebrows. *'London is just one-hundred and thirty miles away...'* He liked to tell stories, such as tales of feuding Mackays and Sutherlands, tales of brutal battles, deadly duels and Highland charges. 'The Bruce vindicated us at Bannockburn.'

'Have you forgotten Culloden, parson? I can still hear the drums of war! It is disingenuous to suggest the Scots vanquished us, parson.' The rhetoric was taken up by the half-English Major Herbert Fitzroy-Campbell. 'The Jacobites retreated from London in the snow and the Duke of Cumberland pursued them to the death. I might add that only fifty English soldiers perished at the Battle of Culloden.' Upon hearing this, the Scots planters bristled as the Major passed his eyes over the lawn. *'Are there no Christians to be found?'*

'No, we are only Elliots and Armstrongs!' Rev'd McKay told the rapt crowd, echoing the celebrated Border Reivers and the Elliots's war cry, *'Wha daur meddle wi me?'* The day promised to be long and dry. 'I've been speaking in an inflammatory way.'

'Yes, you have.' Duncan's face hardened at the memory of Culloden. He could still hear the death rattle in his uncle Enoch's throat on the day of the battle. The English had refused to let the Scots retrieve their dead from the battlefield. 'I am so excited, are you?'

Fiona gave him the hint of a smile. 'Excited barely describes how I feel right now.' Surrounded by the Redcoats and the plantocracy, she was in her element as she prepared to make her vows, forgetting the separation from her family back in Scotland. 'Let's begin.'

'Who giveth this woman to be married to this man?' Rev'd McKay hoped and prayed that the golden age of Empire would soon end. He blamed the lack of piety on the fact that there were no trials to prove the Christian faith. 'What! No father of the bride?'

'Happy to step in.' Major Fitzroy-Campbell saw that Fiona had started to fidget. 'Your white knight in shining armour.'

'Good man.' Rev'd McKay dabbed his perspiring face with a soiled, white handkerchief and allowed his mind to wander off. Several years after the Battle of Culloden, he went to the Firth of Clyde and found himself enlisted in the British Army. All it took was a handshake with a soldier who had placed a coin into his right hand, announcing that he had given him 'the King's shilling.' It was only through the intervention of an associate of the influential Rev'd John Witherspoon (who had baptised an African, James Montgomery, who belonged to a Jamaican planter named Robert Sheddan) that the minister, like Montgomery ('Jamie'), managed to secure his freedom. 'Where was I now?'

'Us men want some grog, Major.' Alexander Anderson and several Redcoats drank water from their pouches. The chapped-lipped soldier complained to his superior that if they were in the Navy, they would receive their daily ration. 'Half a pint of rum.' It was all too much for him to resist. 'I want a glass of grog, a wedge of cheese an' a slice o' bread.'

This was met with a long pause from Rev'd McKay, who ignored the complainant. '*Dearly beloved,*' he calmly watched Fiona's face, '*we are gathered here to join this man and woman in holy matrimony...*' He was soon distracted when he spotted a large sundial on the lawn and said absently, '*Those whom God has joined together let no man put asunder.*'

'Money is the curse of all enterprises.' Immediately, a foul-mouthed planter named Guy Stewart ribbed Duncan, jesting that the promise of a more comfortable life proved irresistible for Fiona. 'Bed her and wed her, eh?' This was met with silence while he continued to jest that the marriage ceremony should be shortened in Jamaica where life expectancy for white men was short. 'Where we are is not where some of us want to be, but it's a darn sight better than poverty at home in Scotland. That is the only reason why I'm still here.'

For a time, Duncan said nothing but he felt Fiona's nudge and quickly said, 'Receive this ring as a token of my love.' He had hidden his true self from her and now his back stiffened when he recalled a butcher's shop in Edinburgh. There were slabs of turning beef on the counter. That was where Morag had bought beef for Sunday dinner. 'I think we're done.'

'Not quite.' There was a snickering laugh from one of the ladies when Rev'd McKay forgot his lines and began to stutter, '*To have and hold, in sickness and in health, to cleave to in the flesh.* I pronounce you man and wife. You may kiss the bride, if you so wish.'

'*Tha gaol agam ort.*' A grinning Duncan turned towards Fiona and cleared his throat, repeating in English, 'I love you.' There was the crack of a whip in the morning sun, followed by the sound of a *conch* at 10am. 'I can't promise you wedded bliss.'

'I say, a marriage of female guile and male power in bed.' Major Fitzroy-Campbell threw back his head and laughed. 'Out here, folk do enjoy being together round the campfire.'

'The days of sitting round the fire wrapped in sheepskin are gone.' The off-the-cuff comment did not offend Duncan. 'Think of the ladies, Major. You're supposed to reassure them.'

'We are armed to the teeth,' Major Fitzroy-Campbell cut in. 'Have you been to Port Royal to see Nelson's quarters in the battery? No! You don't get out often enough, man.'

'Agreed.' Fiona's immersion into colonial life began with a visit to Cinnamon Hill in Montego Bay, followed by Seville Great House in St Ann, which was owned by the Hemmings family, who could trace their lineage back to the capture of the island in 1655. During her induction, she and Duncan attended a dinner party at Cardiff Hall in St Ann, then owned by John Blagrove. She had come into herself in this remote village of Stirling, leaving the life of a humble crofter in Scotland. 'So true.'

'Good of you to come, Major.' Duncan beamed at Fiona. 'I realise what a busy man you are.' He had reinvented himself as a sugar planter who kept a methodical inventory of the plantation and did everything he could to demonstrate that he was a lenient master. The sun was brighter than usual, which caused him to blink rapidly while greeting the most prominent families from the hill villages of Stirling, Albany, Montrose and Cocoon. He had explained that Fiona had been reluctant to sail to the West Indies; she believed that two infamous pirates, Henry Morgan and Calico Jack, were still plundering British ships.

'Thank you for giving me away, Major.' Fiona's cheeks rounded into a smile. 'I'm home and dry.' What did it matter that a few ladies were whispering that she lacked their ability to command attention? She thought longingly of home, knowing that unless she could find the regular remittances, her family, crofters working a small plot of land and eking out a meagre living fishing, would become paupers. 'If the tea is not to your liking, Major, we have whisky flavoured with nutmeg. Oh, how could I forget the oatcakes? There's a wide selection of bread and cakes, parson.'

'*The Wedding Feast at Cana.*' Rev'd McKay regurgitated roast pork. 'Hmmm.' The silverware glinted in the sun as he accepted a glass of water. He was reminded of a Veronese artwork when Fiona held up an invisible glass in her right hand. Duncan's dog sat at the minister's feet chewing a bone. 'This must feel like living an opulent life at court.'

'Isolation leads to an element of self-sufficiency.' Duncan picked up his glass, suppressing a medley of childhood memories. 'Friends, if I may have your attention: to my wife, Mrs Foulkes. I also want to thank Rev'd McKay for making this a special day. We'd like you to break bread with us. As for the menu: we have potato scones, Dundee cakes, shortbread and so forth.' After he had drained his tankard, he drew close to Fiona's side when an African dressed in green handed her a glass of wine. 'It's hardly *The Marriage at Cana*. If we do run out of wine, I'm sure the Good Lord will work a miracle today.'

'A papal feast.' Rev'd McKay savoured a slice of chicken and veal pie. 'Ooh!'

Far removed from a life of poverty, Fiona began to reflect. In Glasgow, six months after Duncan had sailed, she was thrown into a filthy jail filled with gin-soaked women and penniless mothers who fretted about their children. There was no room in the dingy, onion-reeking cell where boundaries eroded quickly and quarrels broke out. Her brush with the law came after her creditors had her thrown in jail for non-payment of rent and dry goods which she had shared with her impoverished family. Her father was continually borrowing money and when he renegaded on his debts after falling ill, she had used the money that Duncan had left her to pay her father's creditors and his medical bills. She could not forget her deceased mother, Roslyn, who was half-English. On a visit with her to London when she herself was twelve, she saw an obese woman walking bare-breasted and bare-back behind a wagon in Charing Cross. That was the punishment for failing to pay her creditors.

'Stay a few days, parson.' Fiona thought that his stomach had suddenly grown into a huge belly. 'Are we agreed?' Her dream of respectability, the plantation lady, had come true. After Duncan's first wife, Morag, had left him, he was in no rush to commit to Fiona, earning her the nickname 'Long Wait.' Frustrating though the wait had been, it had turned her initial disappointment into an appointment with destiny. 'I'd like you to take a parcel of tamarind, rum, sugar and chocolate back home for my father, parson.'

'Consider it done.' Rev'd McKay set down his glass, bowed his head and said, 'Lord, bless this house.' There was a sense of uneasiness when an enslaved African, standing by his side, skinned a freshly killed snake and offered him the blood to drink. 'Not for me! I am not one of those white men who turn native in the tropics. No, but thank you!'

'Table theatre.' With his white teeth flashing, Major Fitzroy-Campbell accepted a dram of snake blood and raised his glass to Duncan's good health. 'Energy boost.' The world stood still when he was served up Barbadian monkey meat – said to make men perform better in bed. The ladies were white and nauseous. The Major requested a second piece of kebab snake and monkey meat, garnished with Scotch bonnet pepper. 'You should have got married at St Peter's Church in Port Royal, Foulkes.' He drained his glass of snake blood. 'A wedding is not complete without organ music, Jamaica or not.'

'I want to while away the rest of my days under our tropical sun. When I left Inverkin House on a dreary autumn day in 1731, to attend boarding school in Edinburgh, I had no idea what the future held.' Out in the open under a warming sun, Duncan looked proud and prosperous in frills. 'Why, if Charles Stuart had defeated Cumberland, there's no telling what would have happened to men like us. As it is, we Scots are the backbone of the British Empire.' Nodding, he caught sight of Fiona's disapproving scowl. 'Lizard?'

'We soldiers are used to bush meat, ma'am.' Major Fitzroy-Campbell waved a plate of fried bush meat away and rinsed his mouth clean of snake blood before gurgling rum and water in his throat. 'I hear bat's meat is a staple diet in the Far East.' He knew the effect that his troops had on those present and made it clear that they were simply men in uniform. 'Fill your water pouches before we leave this little provincial backwater, lads.'

'True grit.' Duncan rose from his seat, downed the remaining snake blood and lifted his eyes to a plum tree. 'I'm beginning to view blood pudding as a delicacy.' Perched on a thin branch, a blue and gold macaw with a large black beak looked on, sporting patches of yellow around its eyes. 'Will you take a drop of rum punch with me, Major?'

'Gentlemen, raise your glasses: to the Angel of the House.' Major Fitzroy-Campbell had firmly established his position as the spokesman of the empire. 'Out here in the open, we are surrounded by brute beasts; inside, there is another world dedicated to home.'

'While we are here, living against our will, some would say *in self-imposed exile*, we must adapt in order to survive.' Mrs Frazer, a snooty Scot, got up to enquire what had happened to the fattened goose liver and the fifth quarter. She approached Fiona under a veneer of friendliness. 'Do join us at Mrs Grandison's next week.' They had investigated her family's credentials and knew she had been economic with the truth. 'Keep out of the sun or you'll end up as dark as well-brewed tea. We ladies must preserve the social graces, even if you are a lowly crofter.'

'What!' Major Fitzroy-Campbell cut in. 'I have it on good authority that Mrs Foulkes has an iron-clad pedigree.'

'I got married at Fort Augusta; eighty guns guarding the main approaches to Kingston.' Status conscious, Mrs Frazer smiled. 'Not so long ago, the likes of you marrying a gentleman would have been unthinkable. You don't take my view seriously, do you?'

'Who would have thought you and me, a crofter's daughter, would be hobnobbing over a champagne breakfast?' Fiona replied, throwing out the rule book. 'Having said that, there's enough champagne in the cellar to fill a large barrel.' For a newcomer, who was not a lady of quality and who had yet to distinguish herself as the mistress of Canongate, her response surprised Duncan. 'In years to come, I'll sit beside you in a rocking chair and tell our grandchildren ghost stories in Gaelic.'

'Good-oh,' laughed Duncan. 'And I'll teach 'em ballads about Rob Roy, Robert the Bruce and William Wallace.' He had given his first wife a large chunk of his heart and now there was just a small slice left for Fiona. 'I'll tell 'em about Margaret, Queen of Scotland; King Malcolm and Dunfermline Abbey, burial place of the Scots kings.' He put on the charm and proceeded to toast the pesky Mrs Frazer's health, watching her back as she hastened to her seat after spotting a huge rat darting into the bushes. 'We need a cat, wife.'

'So far, I've seen four great big rats,' Fiona said carelessly, taking his hand and presenting a united front to her critics. 'They're massive. We'll need to set traps under the beds, too.' Where privacy was concerned, she felt that her marriage did not deserve this kind of scrutiny from a group of elite white women, paragons of virtue, who needed a new interest to break up the monotony of their own lives. 'This wedding will enable us to build ties.' She shuddered with delight when Duncan stood up and fastened a rope of freshwater pearls around her neck. 'The creole ladies don't exactly approve of expatriates.'

'Tardy.' Duncan caught sight of a latecomer riding an exhausted steed. 'Here he comes.' By chance, he had met the agent for Denbigh Plantation in Clarendon, which was owned by an absentee Welshman: Richard Pennant, Lord Penrhyn of North Wales. The Patriarch, Gifford Pennant, had come out with Cromwell's army in 1655. The soldier-planter was granted thousands of acres when the English settled the land. Duncan had told the agent that he was due to marry and hoped to have his nuptials blessed by a Scotsman. Luckily for him, Rev'd McKay had recently arrived on the island and was staying in the parish of Clarendon where Duncan had tracked him down. 'I have a feeling Mrs Frazer and her clique of petticoat tyrants are aggrieved because I passed over their daughters.'

Fiona's eyebrows arched. 'I find myself quite liking Rev'd McKay.'

* * *

The wedding breakfast had barely ended when Duncan was obliged to play host to the agent overseeing Denbigh Plantation, which was apparently valued at forty-one thousand pounds when the late Gifford Pennant's son, Edward, died in 1736. Interestingly, Samuel, Gifford's grandson, became the Lord Mayor of London in 1759. Darnley, who had been observing the latecomer, cornered Duncan and brought up the spiritual needs of the mixed-race children whom he himself and the other white employees had fathered.

'Bloody absentee landowners.' Darnley, who envied the Pennants, had ensured that the agent had lost the trust of his fellow whites. From what he knew, the greedy agent had been pocketing some of the profits from Denbigh. 'Nothing at this stage has been proven against him. Changing the subject, I know my half-breed children are a burden on you, boss, but there's an urgent need to save the bairns' souls.'

'True.' Very reluctantly, Duncan agreed to speak with Rev'd McKay. He had changed into a white shirt with eyelets before returning to his guests on the lawn in his treasured kilt. 'I feel like there's a black dog on my shoulder. I must go and entertain.'

'Don't let me keep you.' In a quiet spot by the sundial, Darnley watched Duncan working the lawn. All his adult life, he had wanted to be a money maker. It was like looking through a window into a birthday party from which the spoiled plantation children had excluded him.

'Every happy moment in my life has come from you, husband.' Under a clear blue sky, Fiona stood beside Duncan on the lawn. There was growing excitement and a sense of fulfilment as the ladies waited to catch the bridal bouquet. 'Oh Christ, I've made a fool of myself.' Fiona had spent the last hour freshening up in their bedroom where she had refused to sleep with Duncan without a wedding ring. Her shoulders slumped as she explained to him that she had found a dead rat at the foot of the poster bed and panicked, knocking over the wash-hand basin and a jug of water on the washstand. 'I ran into the arms of your boy, Cassian. Those big eyes and the tribal scars on his face scared me.' This was the beginning of a new stance towards the house servants. 'You should punish him.'

'I'll have to whip him.' About this time, a group of Maroons walked through the open gate, up the path and sauntered onto the lawn. Instinctively, Duncan tightened his grip on Fiona. They watched, astonished, sure that the rebels had come to spy on the wedding party. His face darkened into a mask of anger. 'Who invited them?'

'Here comes *the King of Nubia*.' Darnley smirked. 'Those nagas are trying to force the colonial government's hand by threatening every single white person's safety. It's in the interest of all Europeans for the community to be strengthened before there's another St Domingue.' The chief of the Maroons earned between two and four dollars for each runaway that he returned to the planters. When times were bad, his men were not averse to tracking runaways. 'I'll do a head count of the female slaves before they leave. They're bound to snatch a few and return them so they can collect the reward money. This is a mockery of the rules of the British Redcoats, *protectors of liberty.*'

'Try to act normal.' Psychologically, the day was anything but normal for the newly married Duncan who felt the rising tension in the air. 'If the Redcoats are the engine of the British Empire, how is it that they can't seem to control this guerrilla force? Damn the nagas.'

'Nothing can go wrong today.' Fiona's hair resembled burnt copper. 'Everything must go exactly to plan.' The ladies were all set to lunge for the bridal bouquet. 'One, two...'

'Hah.' Major Fitzroy-Campbell paused while the Redcoats stared with expectant expressions. 'Where is your pass, Captain Kalu?' Wielding his power, the Hand of the King acknowledged the Maroons who strode half-naked onto the lawn. 'Mrs Foulkes, this is Captain Kalu, Chief of the St Ann Maroons, and his men. His cutlass is more of an appendage. Now, ladies and gentlemen, I shall leave you under the protection of the parish militia. They, your spouses, are armed and ready to put down an uprising.'

'Are you mad, Major?' Fiona gave the Maroons a vicious look. 'You ought to put their heads on sticks to deter the field slaves from rebelling.' No one was prepared for her outburst. 'They've sworn blood oaths! For the love of God, do not leave us defenseless.'

'They have us at an advantage, Mrs Foulkes. Best not to do anything to escalate tensions.' The steely-eyed Major Fitzroy-Campbell was direct. 'I'll step up security. To those who are ready to leave, I can offer you safe passage to Trelawny, Ocho Rios, St Mary and Montego Bay.'

'Are you planning to leave us unprotected in the hills, Major?' A keen-eyed planter argued that they, the Scottish sugar barons, were the source of British power and should enjoy the protection of the Redcoats. 'Are we safe with those vengeful nagas on the prowl?'

'If we were talking about the Berbice uprising of 1763, I'd say no.' Major Fitzroy-Campbell exchanged glances with Duncan. 'Right now, we are tiptoeing through history, people, but let me be clear: the Maroons are bound by two peace treaties.'

'You, Japheth.' Rev'd McKay, holding a King James Bible upright, extended his right hand to Captain Kalu until he saw the sixth finger, which was a reminder of the rebel's lineage, stretching back to Africa. 'The unholy one. Put down your weapon and repent.'

'Never!' In that one act of refusal, Captain Kalu had undermined the plantocracy. He slipped into Yoruba, *'Rara!'* To anyone who knew the proud African, it was unthinkable that he would 'bend the knee' to a white man. 'Me, son of Chief Jumoke II of Osun.' The tall, deep-black Maroon stood firm in a faded military coat, breeches and barefoot. Having refused to swear fealty to the planters' God, he brushed his machete against his right thigh and requested a bottle of rum, a sack of yams, salted fish and herrings. Thereafter, the Maroons turned on their heels with the bounty and strode towards the sunbaked road.

'Belligerent! He has a misplaced sense of invincibility.' A merchant named Niall Ayr narrowed his eyes. 'We whites will never accept a two-state solution: Maroon Town and plantation Jamaica!' The Ulster Scot was known as a Scotch-Irish, for his ancestors had settled in Ireland. He had spent his youth raging against the colonization of Ireland by the English, but in the colonies of the eighteenth century, money healed old wounds. 'We are self-made men.' Status sensitive, he argued that their island was been torn apart by the audacious Maroons. 'This is a white man's country. We ought to invoke the Barbados Slave Code of 1661.'

'Aha! Barbados, the cradle of slavery.' Duncan thought of the Slave Code that was set up to exploit slave labour in Barbados of the seventeenth century. 'Caution is needed. St Ann is close to the Maroons' strongholds of Trelawny and Scot's Hall in St Mary.'

'Restraint, sirs.' Mengis Hunter, who had travelled on the *African Empress* from West Africa to Kingston in 1765, allowed Duncan to save face. 'I like what you've done with this place.'

'Aye.' A craggy faced old Scot in his eighties said something about the importance of legislation to intercept the Maroons before they incited rebellion, destroying the tobacco and sugar plantations. 'I hear you set him free, Hunter. That boy is not a patch on Cudjoe, who led a rebellion with his sister, Nanny, in '38. She was mean-looking with piercing eyes. Some say she caught bullets between her buttocks.' His lazy eye closed. 'That Asante woman warrants a page in history: singing songs to the children, preparing the warriors for battle with *obi* and then whipping out her blade. 'I'd flay that boy alive if I were younger. Have you seen the trotters on those nagas? Talk about big feet.'

'Fine swimmers and divers,' Mengis Hunter cut in, recalling the first time he had had a seizure. 'Retaliation can only lead to insurrection.'

'Apparently, in Africa, they sell their wives, children and servants and then cry freedom in Jamaica.' As the afternoon sun faded away, Major Fitzroy-Campbell mounted his horse, looking down at Fiona warily. 'We are the master race, ma'am, ferocious tacticians.' Stern-faced, he offered safe passage to six carriages, explaining the rationale for deserting Canongate. 'Ladies, I regret leaving your families in a state of anxiety; however, my country needs my service. About Captain Kalu, his every move is being tracked. Gentlemen, the biggest threat we face is not having enough troops to fight the Maroons.' He was being urged to invoke the Barbados Slave Code of 1661 that governed slave treatment and control, and had spread to the other British islands. 'The Maroons are a brutish set of people, though some would call them *noble savages*.'

'I am fully aware of the Slave Code, Major. We don't have enough manpower to deal with a skirmish or such a dangerous pride of people,' Duncan argued, though none of this did much to appease the ladies. Others believed the Maroons were a persistent threat and should never gain the same status or access to a white man's property. 'I would caution every man present: less risk taking today. They have the advantage, sirs.'

'What advantage! We have never been afraid to take risks at home and abroad. That is why we have a vast empire, stretching from India's Indus Basin to Africa's Gold Coast.' Busha Lindsay argued that the Redcoats were placing them in danger by deserting Canongate; that given the amount of people present, there was nothing to prevent a massacre. 'After the Tacky revolt in '60, I said we ought to tear up those treaties with the Maroons and deport them to the United States. Those Maroons are spoiling for a fight. They are seeking to pose a threat in the future.'

* * *

There was a distinct shift in the mood on the lawn after Major Fitzroy-Campbell and the Redcoats had left. The sun had already dipped when Duncan was approached by a group of Africans wanting to stage a play. The request was rebuffed, for he was trying to mitigate any anxiety caused by the Maroons earlier on. The enslaved Africans, however, explained that they wanted to celebrate his marriage by re-enacting a traditional play.

'What!' Fiona, meantime, was alarmed when an enslaved man named Kush, who was dressed as an African monarch, rode onto the lawn astride a mule. Flanked by six females, they danced around the mule, gyrating and shaking their breasts and buttocks energetically.

'Och!' Through it all, Duncan kept a steely silence. No one took the drama seriously until Kush dismounted and sat on a makeshift throne with a wreath of bay leaves around his head. He was surrounded by his helpers: one female fanned him with palm fronds, another filled his clay pipe with tobacco and a third defended him with a bamboo spear. This suggested that he was a chieftain. Upon hearing ululating, the white children, who occupied their own play area, rushed from the seesaws and swings to see an enslaved woman pounding the ground between Fiona's shoes, advising her to, *Be a good wife*!

Rev'd McKay made his presence known. '*Woman, know thyself.*' There were two realities on the lawn: a young bride appeared with Fiona's bouquet, wearing one of her old white gowns and matching gloves. Chaos ensued when a puppy ran into the circle and Kush, the owner, tried to catch it. There was more laughter when the bride, Virtue, took off the wrong glove, proffering her right index finger.

'Left glove, you fool,' Mrs Lindsay said glibly, remarking that the enslaved Africans in Jamaica had developed a talent for mimicry. 'You throw the bouquet at the end, idiot!'

'The marriage of the virgin to the aged Joseph?' Mrs Grandison threw back her head and laughed. 'Such whimsical blunders. What a delicious spectacle, Blaine.'

'Quite bizarre.' Mrs Blaine Kerr was equally astringent. 'Come, Jocasta, child.' She headed for the drawing room. 'Mrs Lindsay is going to play the harpsichord for us.'

* * *

'Did you thank Mrs Lindsay for bringing her harpsichord with her?' The celebrations continued in the house where Duncan smiled in appreciation when he heard the sound of clapping. 'A day to remember.' He came up behind Fiona and gave her an unexpected shoulder rub. 'Now you have a chance to turn over a new leaf and to consider the social consequences of your actions. It's a hard world for whites who transgress.' The dialogue changed in the drawing room whose mahogany doors opened into the hallway where the guests had gathered to watch the rhythmical sway of his kilt, clapping with enthusiasm. 'If only I hadn't given Dougal my Targe.' He danced with upheld arms, performing the traditional toe and heel steps to the tune of a lone piper. 'Och! I hope they can't see my knobbly knees.'

'How are we going to keep those dreadful Maroons under control?' If the pep talk was intended to calm the waters, it did nothing for Fiona's anxiety as she watched him dance, his kilt fanning out in rhythm. 'What if they decide to come back in their hundreds, all armed?' Gone was the familiar Scottish greyness and the biting cold. 'To tell you the truth, I was scared something would go wrong when those nagas arrived.'

Duncan's sea-green eyes settled on her face. 'I have nerves of steel, wife.' There was a shift in tone and he abandoned the dance. 'Never show fear in public.' What drew him to Fiona in the first place was her copper hair, heart-shaped face and the fact that she was a hard-working woman. 'We've got a problem with ants, wife.' There was a fat, green caterpillar on the floor being eaten by a writhing mass of black ants.

'Ladies and gentlemen, I would like to thank Mrs Lindsay for playing her harpsicord earlier,' enthused Fiona. 'No more dancing, I'm afraid. It's boiling in here but nothing a cooling breeze outdoors won't heal.' She picked up Kush's playful puppy that had strayed into the hallway and handed it to one of the house girls. 'It belongs in the Negro quarters.'

'Com', Mus-Mus.' Kush, still dressed like an African monarch, stood outside the open door at dusk. 'Sarry, mistress. Mus-Mus too eggs-up.' With arms outstretched, he straightened his back. 'Mus-Mus, yuh *yeye* dem too big.' The puppy barked loudly. 'Com' nuh, Mus-Mus.'

'Get shot of that puppy or I'll have it put down.' Duncan tapped Kush on the left shoulder. 'Mus-Mus? What a silly name.'

Conscious of Canongate's vulnerability to a sudden attack by the Maroons or the enslaved, Rev'd McKay, the planters' spiritual leader, mingled with the women on the lawn. It took a long talk about the peace treaties to convince them that the rebels would not attack. He made a short statement that he had wanted to bring them into the brotherhood of man and was disappointed in his failure to share the glad tidings of salvation with Captain Kalu and his men. Soon after the rebels had left, he had retired to his room and had taken a nap on a full stomach. While experiencing a lucid dream, he had heard a deep voice saying, *Strength grows out of resistance.* Refreshed and revived, he now stood on the lighted lawn exchanging pleasantries with an expatriate name Mrs Rothermere. She was an agnostic whose husband was never seen in public without a full English wig, which was expensive and added to their financial woes.

Rev'd McKay mused, 'I am aware that many Brits have enriched themselves in the tropics. *Ye cannot serve Mammon and God.*' During a recent dinner at the Prices's Worthy Park Plantation in Lluidas Vale, St Catherine, he was accused of trying to humanise chattel, having raised the subject of religion with the Africans. '*Oidhche mhath.*' At the sound of the *conch*, he said goodnight in Gaelic, adding, '*To whom the Goddess thus: O sacred rest/Sweet pleasing sleep…Repairer of Decay/Whose Balms Renew the Limbs to Labours of the Day…*'

'The Scots Bard.' Looking heavily aged and gaunt, Mrs Rothermere was known to say whatever she believed people wanted to hear until she whispered behind their back. 'My husband and I are off to England next week, parson, to see his physician. We'll have to leave our dear old plantation in the hands of attorneys; they're an irritant.'

'They are mavericks.' Rev'd McKay nodded. 'Those parasites are a threat to your livelihood, *swallowers up of estates*. I have just come from Clarendon where my deceased brother's property is in the hands of an attorney until my young nephew comes of age. One impoverished, absentee planter in Dundee warned me before I came out: *Never place trust in an attorney or you'll lose the shirt on your back. They are like driver ants, anchoring down their victims until they devour them.*'

'Don't you just love Mrs Foulkes's hallway?' Mrs Rothermere looked around for her Calinda, a child of four who was her septuagenarian husband's progeny and whom she had made a pet of. 'It is panelled in Jacobean oak.' She considered his sexual incontinence normal, albeit she had whipped his fourteen-year-old bedmate after the child was born.

'"The House of Sleep," from Ovid's *Metamorphoses?*' Rev'd McKay's attempt to edify the lady was greeted with a shrug. In reality, he had no notion of the full extent of the life of plantation women whose house girls were often their husbands' playthings.

Who is Ovid? Mrs Rothermere was lost in thought. 'I must teach my slaves how to use the ash from the fire to wash their clothes before I leave for England. We must economize, parson.'

'I can still recall the smell of boiled laundry in my dear mother's yard,' recollected Rev'd McKay, peering at a wealthy widow nearby whose paper-thin skin was as white as a ghost. 'Mrs Foulkes, how handsome you look tonight. Marriage certainly suits you.'

'It's early days, parson.' There was a mosaic of people on the lawn. The Maroons' appearance earlier had shaken Fiona's confidence. She looked towards Duncan. 'My husband will ensure you have plenty of exercise: fishing, riding; touring the plantation...'

'Exercise! I am in rude health.' Rev'd McKay warmed to Fiona, who had changed into a pastel-peach dress that accentuated her cleavage and had caused him to wonder about her and Duncan. He doubted they were in love, though they were at ease and happy together. 'Ah, Squire Foulkes. I'm looking forward to baptising your people in the river.' He quoted John the Baptist: *Repent, for the Kingdom of Heaven is near.*

'I've had a canoe made for us to go fishing, parson.' Duncan baited a hook with worms inside his head, imagining the minister angling on the River Dee in Aberdeenshire. 'There's a grotto I'd like you to see; it's called Brecon's Cave. The indigenous people, *Arawak Indians*, made primitive pictures on the walls. Their history is written in stone...'

'We ought to take pride in our own stories first.' Fiona was a vocal supporter and a carrier of British culture. 'Don't you agree, parson?' She wondered why the sugar barons and tobacco lords preferred to use slave hands instead of rakes and ploughs. 'Why are farming methods so backward in the West Indies? At least we have the plough at home.'

'Are you finding our methods of cultivating sugar too regressive, ma'am?' Darnley put in, feeling socially inept because he had few elite acquaintances and believed that most of the snobby plantation women regarded the mother of his mixed-race children as lower than pond life. He also felt that Fiona had pretensions, behaving as if she were better than the crofter's life that she had left behind in Scotland.

'Ploughing is no easy task,' Fiona answered abruptly. 'Not in this tropical heat.'

'My dear Mrs Foulkes, one never knows what is lurking under a tropical sun.' Rev'd McKay nodded. 'I feel a verse of Langland's Piers Plowman coming on: *In a summer season when soft was the sun/I clothed myself in a cloak as I shepherd were/Habit like a hermit's, unholy in works...*' He allowed his mind to drift to plump Scotswomen with rounded breasts picking hops in smocks, stockings and bonnets in another age. 'Give me hop-picking anytime, except for Sundays.' He muttered, 'Alas, we are all born corrupted by sin.' Smiling slyly, he stealthily eyed Fiona's plump cleavage. '*Woman! By Heav'ns the very Name's a Curse/Enough to blast and to debauch my Rhyme...*'

'I hear Peterborough Abbey had slaves on its properties in England in the twelfth century, parson; the Church is culpable.' Admittedly, it had been a difficult day for Darnley who was conscious of his lower-class status. He was transported to his schooldays by the minister's voice, when he'd won a prize for reciting *Piers Plowman*. He blinked. 'In Anglo-Saxon England, the ploughman was a slave. The Romans took English slaves to Rome. We're all reduced to different degrees of servitude.' As dusk enveloped the lawn, he cast his flinty eyes at the rich widow's pointy chin and her paper-thin, over-powdered white skin. 'What do they say in Jamaica, parson? What, you don't know? *Marry and bury!*'

'*Golgotha.*' Rev'd McKay noticed the bleached skull of a dead kitten on the lawn, bringing to mind the many funerals that he had conducted, blamed on the flux and fever. 'Without moderation, we risk ruining our health.' Silently condemning the merry widow, he offered a line from one of Dryden's poems, reciting, '*I watch'd the early glories of her eyes, as men for day-break watch the eastern skies.*'

'God damn, this heat has turned my brain to sawdust.' Unfortunately for Darnley, his *Goodnight to you all* was ignored and he felt that he had heaped shame on himself by fathering mixed-raced children with an enslaved woman. He walked off thinking of his shattered dreams, muttering to himself, 'Acht! I've made an error of judgement.'

* * *

Rev'd McKay had retired to bed in turmoil about the conspicuous consumption and the brutality he had witnessed in Jamaica. Sleep brought no relief, for his mind rested on a deceased African named Ariel, a shadowy figure who prowled the corridors and bedrooms at Canongate. Allegedly, the Fanti had stowed away to Glasgow but was soon homeless and alone in North Britain. Two years after blacking boots along the Royal Mile in Edinburgh, he ran back to slavery on a ship named the *Scotch Guineaman*. Upon his return to Canongate, Ariel had been appointed Chief Builder of one of several ponds on the estate, lined with clay and purified with stones to keep the water clean. Ten days after Duncan had had Ariel whipped for refusing to build a third pond, the exhausted Fanti had climbed into one of the soft beds in the big house and had died of wounds inflicted by Darnley. During the night, Rev'd McKay had felt a presence in his room and began to rebuke the spirit: *'In the name of Jesus, I command you to leave this house. Go in peace, go!'*

* * *

The morning after the wedding fell on a Sunday, which was the day set aside for the Africans to cultivate their own provision grounds. To reach the allotments, you climbed a steep precipitous hill, minding where you placed your feet. Occasionally, you came across steps hewn out of the rocky hillside by the indigenous inhabitants, the *Tainos*, only to be replaced by loose gravel and crumbling soil beneath your feet. Once at the top of the hill, the soil was black and fertile from the regular rainfall. Few of the middle-aged visitors to Canongate would have ventured into this pristine terrain. Upon reaching the top, Rev'd McKay stood for a good five minutes, catching his breath and admiring the *lianas* hanging from a nearby tree. With trepidation, he watched an African standing on a looming rocky overhang, calling out his assigned Hebrew name and listening to the echo: *'Eli, Eli; Eli!'*

'The problem with slaves,' remarked Busha Lindsay, 'is they don't value their lives. Who in their right mind would stand on the edge of a mountain dicing with death?'

'Gloria in excelsis deo.' On a windy mountain top, Rev'd McKay looked down into a deep valley with dense tropical trees, translating the Latin words: *'Glory to God in the highest.'* In this mountainous terrain, majestic palm trees grew alongside Blue Mahoe and *lignum vitae* trees. Observing the birds of paradise and listening to their unfamiliar calls, the minister stopped to gaze at a teeming termite mound and to marvel at giant ferns and parasitic vines which clung to the indigenous trees that seemed to be bending beneath the strain. The vines ascended with zeal and descended with a vengeance, slowly choking the host plants to death. 'I'm not sure what I am seeing. Even plants destroy each other.'

'Such a pleasing view.' Duncan studied an ancient indigenous tree. The air smelled of damp earth, tree resin and wild orchids. All eyes were on a massive stone carved into the figure of a man with his mouth open, as if he were laughing. Duncan remarked, *'Laughing Boy.'*

'The tranquility of a rural morning.' Perspiring, Rev'd McKay dabbed his forehead with a handkerchief while negotiating his foot-hold on a mountain pass. 'Awe inspiring.' For a time, he held his tongue until Thomas Gray's voice filled his head and he began to recite: *'The curfew tolls the knell of parting day/The lowing herd wind slowly o'er the lea/ The plough-man homeward plods his weary way/And leaves the world to darkness and to me.'*

The path disintegrated, turning the climb into a daunting task for the ageing planter, Mengis Hunter, who drew back when a boulder dislodged and hurtled into the valley. With the hills behind them, Hunter remarked that the damp stones reminded him of 'licking stones' in Scotland. He described how after the Battle of Culloden some of his relatives were imprisoned and starved so resorted to licking the prison walls.

Upon reaching a plateau, the perspiring planters seemed intrigued by a pile of ancient stones, an echo of what was once there. Amongst the slumbering hills, plots of land were being worked by Africans who stood idly by. They greeted Duncan with the usual query about when they could expect '*a likkle massa*.' Ever vigilant, the planters became increasingly nervous of the rebel Maroons. The tension was palpable.

'Oh, to be young again, traipsing across the landscape, bringing the good news.' Rev'd McKay spotted two carved stones resembling a pair of old shoes. 'This must be the Africans' sacred ground.' He was deeply hostile to any religious beliefs except for Christianity. 'I can hear their ancient chanting reverberating off those stones piled high.'

'This is where the *Arawaks* once communed with the mysteries of nature,' relayed Duncan, nodding. 'Of course, they are extinct now: a dead race.'

'What are those, sir?' asked a creole lad of twenty-one, addressing Busha Lindsay. He had recently graduated from St Andrews with a degree in medicine. Like most creole-born white children, he clearly recognised the papaya fruit but feigned ignorance. 'How exotic.'

Duncan observed the young man in a black tailcoat. 'I suppose this is what happens when creole children are sent home, educated in Britain.' As was customary, he had left the horses below and climbed the steep hill with his hung-over guests. 'At the first sign of spring, the planting season begins on the estate and its provision grounds. Nature provides the slaves with a bounty of free food. It stands to reason that they work harder for themselves than for their masters. I'm sure they produce more up here.'

'Regarding a British education, it has been noted by some visitors that creole girls are intelligent and can hold a conversation on any subject,' objected Busha Lindsay.

'I have found Ponce de Leon's *Fountain of Youth*.' Rev'd McKay halted by a spring of fresh water where an enslaved woman squatted with her skirt lapped between her thighs, washing a heap of shirts. '*The Woman of Samaria*. Your name?' The sour-faced woman looked anything but sweet. '*Sugar*?' On his knees, the minister cupped his hands and sipped water, as if he were drinking from a fountain in Vatican City, picturing Lucas Cranach's (the Elder) painting of *The Fountain of Youth* (1546). '*Dona nobis pacem*.' Then he moved on.

'*Grant us peace*,' Duncan translated the Latin phrase for the benefit of his visitors. 'Your job is to teach the slaves obedience, parson, not Latin or poetry.' He was amazed at how quickly even the freshwater Africans came to regard the provision grounds as their right.

'Watch out – scorpion!' cried the St Andrews boy, bringing his left foot down on a fast-moving centipede and yelling, 'Look out, parson. The scorpion is crawling up your trouser leg.'

Rev'd McKay flinched when an African caught the scorpion and stamped on it. 'Thank you, Jesus.' He said a prayer for the rocks, thorns, and planters and began to view the latter as ungodly; they'd breached the Sabbath day. Fleetingly, he recalled a story from his boyhood: how in February 1322, the bell tower at Ely Cathedral in England crashed down on the central part of the building. When he first discussed this historical incident with his tutor at university, the mentor had explained that it was God's way of speaking to His flock. He bent and dipped his index finger into the ashes from a recent wood fire and made the sign of the cross on his forehead, as if it were Ash Wednesday.

'I daresay we could all benefit from the distillation of the fruits of your knowledge.' Duncan approached the head of the provision grounds. 'How's the family, Gutman? Erm, and how's that sore foot of yours coming along?' In answer to the paunchy African's obtuse response, he nodded vigorously, *'Everybody fine, massa. Foot all right, so-so.'*

'Learned ignorance.' Stirred by the landscape, Rev'd McKay returned to the pool of water where he then proceeded to drink from the spring. 'Chants and dances take place in isolated terrains.' This time, he did not raise an eyebrow when the smiling Gutman said his name was Utopia. 'Ho! Providence has given the unfortunate Africans a dark hue.'

'What is that stink?' asked Ewan Lindsay, who was the apple of his father's eyes and who preferred to be languishing in a cosy armchair at home. 'I'd trade my horse for some cologne water.' A pile of mulching vegetable matter lay nearby. 'What are those nagas doing?'

The hung-over Mengis Hunter was less disciplined in his choice of words, saying, 'Don't waste pity on the nagas, lazy *cunts*.' He observed a Black woman beating cassava in a mortar hewn out of stone. 'They'd sooner kill each other over tribal feuds than work to uplift them-selves.'

'The law of gravity.' Rev'd McKay blinked when a bird dropped a tiny turquoise egg at his feet. 'Aha! My Isaac Newton moment.' Lifting his eyes up to the tree, he noticed the iridescent feathers moving. 'I am constantly surprised by the flora and fauna up here.'

* * *

The dawn was breaking at the start of a new week. Duncan's first job was to meet with his overseer, Ezekiel Darnley, and the bookkeeper, McPhee. At the beginning of a new week, he took the opportunity to brief the two most trusted men on the estate over a cup of black coffee laced with molasses and a dash of salt. It was a challenging time for most of the planters across the island, many of whom had tried to cut corners by not investing in expensive, technologically advanced machinery.

Canongate was awakened to the intrusive sound of the *conch* at 5am. This was the workers' alarm clock. There was an additional challenge today. Duncan had agreed to take a handful of his guests on a guided tour of the estate. Long before the alarm sounded, he had left the marriage bed quietly so as not to disturb Fiona, who had complained before they went to sleep that she disliked his manservant, Cassian. The African slept outside their bedroom door. Duncan wanted Fiona to become more assertive in the midst of his people and enthusiastic about sugar planting. She had replied tartly that she had enough problems nursing two gregarious puppies. They roamed the fields and, consequently, their heads and rumps were infested with fleas and ticks from the livestock – a constant irritant.

Managing a sugar estate the size of Canongate was a huge task. Like a feudal lord, Duncan presided over a monthly court. He supervised his white men and settled grievances. The carpenter, McTaff, and the mason, Smith, were engaged in the building work. As for the Africans, Duncan issued them with the legally required coarse *Osnaburg* fabric and signed their passes to enable them to travel freely on errands. He went the final furlong by meeting McPhee to inspect the accounts, the water wheel and the boiling house. Regular inspection of the latter building was necessary because some of the Africans suffered with dropsy: swelling wrists, fingers and ankles. Oftentimes they found it hard to grasp the large boiling pots and to move speedily, which resulted in burns and scalds, and lost limbs in the machinery. Geographically, it took time to purchase hands for the fields and to transport them to Canongate, so it made sense to look after hard-working Africans who had a detailed local knowledge and whose labour kept Canongate afloat.

In one of three fields, there was roughly an acre of Indian corn that was ground and used to make cornmeal pudding for the enslaved Africans and porridge for the hounds. The shelled corn fed the hens, which kept the plantation in eggs. The dishevelled McPhee was responsible for ensuring that Tyra, an elderly woman, fed the fowls daily. He personally selected the hens for the dinner table; she tucked their heads under their wings. The next job on McPhee's list was to inspect the rats that were caught overnight and to instruct Toto, a superannuated African, to distribute them to the workers. This source of protein reduced their reliance on salt-fish, salt-pork and salt-beef, which contributed to the Africans' newfound diseases of hypertension and oedema.

'There are too many corn stalks lying idle,' Duncan addressed a hung-over white man who was supervising a group of Africans. 'No wonder we're over-run with rats.'

'Put yer backs into it, old *cunts*!' Barking orders in a heavy Scottish accent, the skinny driver had an angular shaped head and fleshy red lips that seemed to crack each time he took a swig of rum. 'If I hear another word, Ditsy, I'll put my *tickle tail* in yer mouth again.'

'About the mosquitoes,' Duncan noticed that the driver, Hague, was sporting a long, unkempt beard, 'I'll get one of the house slaves to burn tobacco and corn stalks in your room tonight, parson.' Riding in the morning breeze, his face was as calm as Sunday. 'We seem to have lost a dozen female slaves, gone walkabout. By the way, parson, I hope to travel to Kingston with you. I need to visit the auction house, to see Menzies…'

'Brought to the hammer?' queried Miss Jocasta Kerr. 'What is a *tickle tail*?' The pale-skinned, curly-haired young lady rode side-saddle. 'I wonder what it's like standing on the block?'

'I haven't a clue, but their punishment is their pigmentation.' Rev'd McKay sat upright on a brown steed, wondering why creole young ladies wore veils at all times. 'Ork!' He watched a large rodent from a distance. 'You need a rat-catcher, Squire Foulkes.'

'Rats?' Miss Augusta Grandison, a young creole lady, lifted her veil to expose her pale skin and pale blue eyes to the morning sun's rays. 'Ugh! Shall we go back, Helena?'

'Not for a moment, please.' Miss Helena Lindsay rode side-saddle towards the sugar mill, sniffing the stench of a dead bullfrog on the air. 'If you're not careful, Squire Foulkes, those rats will spread like impetigo.' She too lifted her veil momentarily. 'Ugh!'

'Alas, the illusion of happy servitude is untrue.' Rev'd McKay spotted an adolescent coercing a mule into walking round and round in a circle, turning a wheel outside the sugar mill.

'Rev'd McKay, what is a *tickle tail?*' Miss Jocasta Kerr picked up the question she asked earlier. 'Is it a feather duster?' She looked across at the minister quite innocently. 'I have a curious mind, parson.'

Stumped, Rev'd McKay began to ramble about God telling man to *Go forth and multiply,* and about bees pollinating flowers. Duncan, who had declined to comment, could be heard harrumphing in the background.

'When you're married, Miss, you'll find out what a *tickle tail* is,' grinned Darnley. His shoulders shook with suppressed laughter. 'In my experience, feather dusters don't give women pleasure, and neither can they make babies.' He spurred his horse. 'Have I said too much, parson?'

The hour wore on with conversation limited to sugar cultivation. Presently, Duncan navigated his way around the estate, putting Miss Jocasta Kerr's naivety aside and the interest of Canongate at the heart of the tour. Impressive as Canongate appeared, it was by no means the most spectacular plantation: Cardiff Hall, Richmond and Shaw Park were contenders. Suspicions had initially been raised that Rev'd McKay was anti-slavery, but Duncan and the minister had clicked. As he became more acquainted with his countryman, the dynamics of their relationship altered. There followed a long discussion about crop rotation and Duncan started to enjoy playing tour guide far more than he had anticipated.

Darnley, perspiring openly, hoisted himself in the saddle and screwed up his eyes in the sun, grinning at the idea of his penis being a *tickle tail*. Aside from his role as a trusted employee, he was responsible for more than a hundred workers who toiled side by side, digging their lives away and getting dust into their lungs and into their eyes. Darnley, who recently shot an unarmed African for refusing to follow orders, believed white women's access to the darker side of the landscape should be limited. Growling and cracking his whip, he got down from his horse and lashed a sleep-ravaged worker for falling down on the job and refusing to get up.

'Mad dogs.' Darnley cracked his whip when two Africans (Yoruba and Ashanti) ran towards the horses, lunging at each other and shouting in their own language. 'Sometimes, a sort of madness comes over them.'

'The working people, eh?' Rev'd McKay guided his horse towards a separate field where twin boys suckled their mother's engorged breasts during her break. 'Good heavens.' He turned his face away when an elderly couple began to defecate in full view of the young white women: the man wiped his rear with corn husks while the woman used a handful of soft broad leaves. 'Look away, ladies.' His horse cantered towards a band of children scratching the earth under the keen eye of an elderly woman nursing a whip. 'Do they have time for spelling games?'

'*Fenning's Universal Spelling-Book* is hardly appropriate reading matter.' Duncan puffed up his cheeks, adopting a granite detachment. 'If we don't put the *piccaninnies* to work, they'll spend hours staring vacantly into space, like happy heads. The whip is a deterrent to stop the little blithers and the lazybones from falling asleep on the job.'

'Ho.' Rev'd McKay studied a boy-child afflicted with hookworms. Duncan's assertion was immediately put to the test when the elderly woman cracked her whip across a girl-child's back. The minister let slip: '*Suffer the little children, and forbid them not, to come unto me...*'

'Oh pray, oh pray for me!' Nineteen-year-old Cleora had been flouting the rules by biting into a piece of sweet juicy cane, which was prohibited and therefore considered theft. 'Du, massa, du!' She had also been caught with a calabash of sugar and McPhee was making sure that the twelve lashes were well-laid in. 'Beg mercy fi me nuh, Clitus. Du, massa.'

'I take it Clitus is her spouse?' Rev'd McKay studied a group of men on oxcarts, delivering freshly-cut sugarcane to the mill. 'It cannot be good for white ladies to see such violence.'

'What a dreary day.' Miss Emelia Murray, a slim-waisted young lady, cantered past three stout females with wicker baskets on their heads, carrying the workers' breakfast. 'I'm off to breakfast.' She galloped in the direction of the big house where her mother was still asleep.

'Why set your face against slavery, parson?' Duncan gazed towards the boiling house. McPhee was whipping a sensible looking man, Clitus, who had assisted two female workers to abscond with a pail of wet sugar. 'I don't hold with theft and pilfering, and carting off my property to Calabash Estate. Are you finding slavery too close for comfort, parson?'

Rev'd McKay spotted a group of basket-carrying Africans in girdles with silver coins jangling as they walked. 'They are getting on in age.' The women walked past the riders and he noticed that they wore their head-kerchiefs turban style. 'Superannuated breeders?' They neared a wooden house fronted with a veranda. Here, a docile looking female sat soothing a mixed-race child off to sleep. 'Your white men's abode, I presume?'

* * *

After a demanding tour of the estate, Duncan returned to the big house. He had been oblivious to the investigation going on into his background and was caught off guard. Nevertheless, he was gracious enough to acknowledge that he hailed from the Highlands; that he had changed his surname for personal reasons. To address some of the personal issues raised by his guests, he explained that his father had died in 1757. Laird Alasdair Ellic Hutchinson VI, born in 1691 (the coldest decade in Scotland's history), had buried the family fortune in a wooden chest on their estate in Argyll. The land was seized by an English aristocrat and his lady. They arrived with sheep and a gardener, enthusing about 'great capabilities.'

'Acht! Idle acres, more like it.' The long-haired, unshaven Aloysius Grandison scooped up a spoonful of sugared porridge. The thought of his host seeing action at Culloden seemed to please him. 'Och! Those English robber barons.'

Fiona's face hardened at the memory of the clearances. 'Gentlemen, we have honeyed ham, cassava bread, eggs, coffee and oats porridge.' Plantation society was a world away from Scotland where there had been wintry nights that left her half-frozen, certain that she would never warm up again. She felt flushed but proud to display her silverware: a tea urn, a sugar bowl; a coffee pot and a tray, all of which were decorated with scenes depicting slavery. 'Chocolate is too heavy on the chest, ladies.'

'Speak for yourself.' Mrs Grandison tapped the arm of a serving house girl, demanding more braised liver. 'I love chocolate tea.'

'Gentlemen.' In a rare departure from the norm, Duncan turned the spotlight on one of his white men. 'Let me introduce my carpenter. He has made canoes for us to picnic on the river.' The shaggy-bearded McTaff grinned. 'Having said that,' Duncan continued, 'some of you may be aware there's another Scot living in these parts: Lewis Hutchinson. As my governess Booth used to say: *There is a common blood tributary somewhere in our pasts.* Canongate is the fulfilment of a youthful dream to turn my life around. I'll not tarnish my reputation. I want to leave my sons' sons a good name.'

'You'd better get started on making sons to carry on your name.' Mengis Hunter balanced his head on a neck grown thick from years of indulgence, imagining a portrait of Fiona gracing the walls of Canongate. 'Make it happen before the empire falls apart.'

'A joyful custodianship,' put in Rev'd McKay, adding that religion followed trade and conquest. 'Your estate is a credit to Scotland, though I for one would never give up my birthright by expunging my father's name.' A once tubercular boy, he had spent his childhood coughing and wheezing in a damp bedroom with mildew around the windowpanes. 'I daresay you'd be criticized and blamed for Hutchinson's crimes if you'd kept that accursed surname. Allegedly, quite a few whites have disappeared not far from Edinburgh Castle. Of course, that butcher has denied any knowledge. He's as barmy as a coot.'

'It won't be long before he kills a white man in public and is brought to book,' prophesied a squint-eyed planter from the quiet village of Falkirk, who had named his plantation Trongate. 'We ought to put together a well-armed party and storm that castle.'

Curiously, a group of hungry-looking enslaved children hovered beneath the dining room window outside, waiting for the leftovers. The figure-conscious ladies ate no more than plain bread with fresh fruit and drank weak tea. Mrs Frazer let the side down, savouring black pudding.

'Mrs Foulkes, please ensure there's a light at the top of the stairs tonight and that my bath water is tepid.' The waspish Mrs Fenella Murray's fair hair was sprinkled with grey. Every aspect of Fiona's life was being scrutinized. 'You need to keep the white children in line, too. They've been going around asking the house girls if they've got tails.'

'Ladies, time for a morning jaunt,' suggested Duncan. 'My wife shall lead the way.' He was aware that relations between Fiona and the ladies had been tense since her arrival. 'Parson, I'd like you to take a barrel of herrings back home for my brother, Dougal.' The younger guests began to spill out of the great house and there was a carnival-like atmosphere on the well-kept lawn. 'Gentlemen, let us join the young people.'

'When I first arrived here after Culloden,' said the patriarch of the group, who resembled an Egyptian mummy, lifting his lazy eye again, 'I hated the auction houses in Kingston. Nowadays, they remind me of the horse markets in Crieff, in Perthshire.' He was being assisted by Duncan's manservant, who helped him into a chair on the lawn. 'Slave-grown sugar is not the only means of prosperity, Foulkes.' Struggling to keep awake, he closed his lazy eye. 'Horses are in demand out here. Our troops need athletic, compact horses. You ought to breed horses.' These sentiments appeared to be mutual among the guests.

'Give me Highland cattle with wide shoulders and dosan fringes anytime.' Even without status, Darnley inserted himself into the polite conversation. 'I could use a dash of rum in this cup of coffee.' The broken capillaries had spread across his nose and cheeks.

'On tropical days like these, you realise how fragile life is,' Rev'd McKay said drily, standing on the lawn. 'Ah, Shakespeare. *Something is rotten in the state of Denmark.*'

'Shakespeare?' Mrs Belvedere coughed. 'Gods stepchildren.' She stood on the lawn, side-eyeing a group of brown children who had cleaned and scaled the fish for the post-wedding breakfast. 'Ninnies.' The younger children stood on tippy toes behind the bushes while the older ones craned their necks. 'You look rather haggard, Mrs Foulkes.'

'How do you like your eggs, ladies?' Fiona strolled along the path, ignoring the put down. 'Cooked milky eggs?' Her early years in Scotland seemed like a distant, bad dream. 'Nice morning for a stroll.'

'This is what I call *walking with Plato* and celebrating Epicurus's joy in the simple life.' Duncan caught up with the women, knowing that Fiona felt outclassed by the plantation ladies. He had woken her around 4am and pulled up her nightgown, putting a hand between her soft thighs until she opened her legs and accommodated him. No words had passed between them, but he was conscious of their creaking bed. 'Maroons!'

'Not again.' Fiona's face hardened when a dozen half-naked females appeared with their arms fastened to wooden poles slung across their shoulders. Advising the ladies to remain calm, she gazed at a deep-black man striding ahead of the captives, carrying a staff with a serpent's head carved on top and looking older than his twenty-six years. She glared at the sixth finger on the Maroon's right hand. 'Wherever he goes, he'll be hunted.'

'Ork.' Duncan's piercing sea-green eyes flashed with anger and the realisation that Kush's wedding charade had created a distraction, deflecting from the real issue of the day. 'How much do you want for them?' During the play, when Fiona was being advised to *Be a good wife*, Captain Kalu's secret army had filched a dozen female workers. 'Forty-eight dollars for my own property? Daylight robbery.'

2

The African Empress

A cloud of red dust rose over the hinterland where a cluster of huts stood in a clearing. The huts were constructed of red ochre mud with thatched roofs and seemed to be silhouetted against the skyline. Just outside the village, which was uncharted and had not been penetrated by European men in search of black ivory, Chief Jumoke's compound occupied a prized area. All around the sixteenth century-built village, spear-carrying young blood, animal skins draped across their blue-black shoulders, went about their business with calculated steps. They were tasked with protecting the village from raiders.

Beyond the boundaries of male society, where the grey beards and high-minded men converged, the women, all shapes and sizes, seemed animated as they gossiped and exchanged pleasantries. For these mothers, grandmothers, wives, sisters and daughters, their history began millennia before the Europeans had marked the year fourteen-ninety-two on The Gregorian Calendar. Theirs was a different world.

Two grey-headed elders, meantime, sat cross-legged under a tree drinking palm wine and frowning pensively. They remembered a day, long ago, when a boy-child named Jumoke was born. Gut protruding outward, one of the men hurled his voice at a pack of dogs, scavenging for food in the dust. Not far off, two heavily pregnant bitches lay under a tree with their tongues lolling in the heat, conserving their energy. Far from human nostrils, tick-infested cattle grazed undisturbed. This was the late King Obalata's territory.

Not for the first or the last time, a sheen of sweat appeared on Chief Jumoke's forehead. On a Saturday afternoon in 1765, the great-grandson of King Obalata was holding court in his compound. Here, he dealt with grievances, collected his rent and levied fines on his people. The honorary monarch took his duties seriously and complaints were dealt with on a case-by-case basis. Today, the communal space was bustling and suffused with the mingling smells of food, plants and animal skins.

On court days, Chief Jumoke allowed for a brisk trade among the more enterprising villagers on the edge of his compound, which was situated away from the bustling village with its smaller dwellings. It was here that the farmers sold their produce, such as guinea corn, maize, cassavas, white yams, millet, plantains, cocoas, cashews and palm wine. This practice enabled the chief to observe who was peddling what, thus increasing the rent on the land that he leased to them. These things done, and having pardoned a few errant husbands, he rose and spread his arms wide. One of his younger wives had recently given birth and he wanted to introduce this gift from the gods to the community.

'My people, this is a moment for the future!' Chief Jumoke's voice rose, beckoning the mother of his second son to approach. His face lit up as he adjusted his ornate headdress of coral beads and gold tassels on red leather. Despite niggling worries, he was at pains to express his joy at having another son. 'He is quite safe with me, woman.' He took the child and held him above his head, introducing the baby-boy to the community. 'My people, I have found joy, a man-son, and I wish to share my happiness with you.'

From all around came a great communal shout, as Chief Jumoke had expected. There was much drumming, women ululating and cheering from the warriors when he discarded the man-child's swaddling cloth and held him above his head again. Warmly applauded by the elders, the chief was especially proud, for this circumcised son had inherited the family trait: a sixth finger on his right hand. A sense of elation was evident, though some of the adults drew back, whispering that the extra finger was a sign that the chief's great-grandfather, King Obalata (Babajide), had returned from the land of the ancestors. A formidable ruler in his day, the late king had been revered by his subjects, who dared not turn their backs on him when leaving his presence for fear of a beheading.

While the elders, whose heads were often bent in conversation and shrouded in secrecy, were heaping good fortune on the latest man-child, ten-year-old Monifa stood beside her rigid-looking mother, Olafemi (or Femi as she was known), on the edge of the compound. Being a girl-child, Monifa was regarded as a burden to her father. Nonetheless, Femi had taught the child to curtsey to her father, a great man, in recognition of his royal lineage, sinking low and focusing on his big feet and his muscular calves. Unsmiling but pleased, he would reach out his hand and help her up. According to custom, he could not show his emotions to a girl-child. This would have been regarded as a sign of weakness.

One by one, the elders congratulated Chief Jumoke. With scarification and full lips, he possessed a magnetism that drew people to him. Monifa, meantime, watched her co-mothers performing a traditional dance involving rapid hand gestures and shaking their bottoms. When she was seven, she sat on her father's knee and asked why she could not inherit his estate. She was silenced when her mother knelt, took the calabash from her father and drank after him. A smile had curved her lips and she got down from his knee to examine a snail, wondering how the shell grew on its back and why it left a trail of silver slime everywhere it went. The present celebrations had triggered anxiety. It was a huge jerk to accept that a girl-child was useless in her father's eyes.

Chief Jumoke, side-eyeing Monifa as he held up his son, was relieved not to be encumbered with another girl-child. He sighed irritably, but a half smile crossed his face. Until recently, she was his favourite child. He had told her gloomily that, according to custom, a girl could not ensure a man's immortality. Bloodline was the key word. She was puzzled until he had explained that one day she would marry and leave his compound to live with her husband, whose blood would flow through her sons' veins, if she produced boys. As for his sons, the eldest was Kalu. He would marry, live in his father's compound and beget sons to continue the lineage. A girl-child would end up in another man's house.

The moment of approbation passed and the treasured man-son was returned to his mother. 'Come hither, harbinger of bad tidings,' remarked Chief Jumoke, who began to fidget when a messenger arrived in the compound. Beads of perspiration ran down the chief's face and he took off his ornate headdress of coral beads in public. 'What!'

Monifa lifted her face, expecting to be publicly recognised but was crushed when her father ignored her. He had returned the child to the mother gently, as if he were as fragile as a butterfly, then dismissed the court and left the village with his bodyguards. There was an urgent matter to deal with elsewhere. He did not acknowledge Monifa or bid her farewell. She, on the point of tears, felt a wave of emotion. There was a fear in her heart that, no matter how hard she tried, she would always be a disappointment to her father. The lack of acknowledgement undid her confidence. She did not love her new baby-brother, who was yet to be named. When the birth was announced, though, she was careful to be seen to jump for joy, to mask her hatred of this man-child. According to custom, as soon as he was old enough, their father would select an antelope and help him to kill it. She talked to her sixth finger, as if it were a listening ear, consoling herself that at least she would not have the obligations which this boy would be required to fulfil.

* * *

Three days after Chief Jumoke had lapped up the adulation, Kalu reclined under the shade of a flame tree and examined the tip of his blood-encrusted spear. Long ago, Chief Jumoke had travelled a great distance to the land called the Gold Coast (which lies in modern day Ghana) and returned with a knife and an iron lance. Being the eldest son, Kalu hoped to inherit the spear. Presently, the shimmering heat scorched the red earth, but he felt cool and dry under the flame tree where the elders often broke kola nuts and drank palm wine.

The previous year, in August 1764, Kalu had taken the carved wooden pole from his bachelor hut, which was decorated with animal skins and contained two wooden stools, wood carvings, his ceremonial loin cloths and a leopard skin robe, and had stood in the centre of the compound. His father had etched the twentieth notch on the staff, which was carved with a lion's head atop. He was over six feet tall and had had a privileged childhood. As was the custom, he celebrated his growth to maturity with a hunting party into the forest.

Days later, Kalu returned home with a dead antelope slung across his shoulders. He had slain it with no assistance from his bodyguards or his boyhood friend, Bami, who was a fierce hunter. There was no denying that Bami was impulsive, often confronting a rival, whereas Kalu was cool-headed. They were notorious for competing in wrestling matches. Full of vitality, the circumcised wrestler had thrown his two bodyguards three times. They had said that he was as sleek as a big cat. Because he was of noble birth, his father had taught him to defend himself for it was hard to recognise the enemy. His late grandmother, a herbwoman, wanted him to grow up strong and healthy. Consequently, she taught him the science of Earthing, connecting his bare feet with the earth's energy. She had also taught him to lay on his back beside the river, covered in leaves, and allow the earth to send her energy through his naked body. She taught him to swim too, and to hold his breath under water for four minutes, breaking his father's record of three minutes.

Unlike his younger sister, Monifa, Kalu did not dislike the long-awaited second son. After all, he was said to be an embodiment of his great-great-grandfather, King Obalata, and was confident that he was his father's crowning glory. Although he did not feel threatened by his new baby-brother, he had promised his mother that he would not place himself in harm's way. Curiously, the errand that took his father away from the compound concerned his safety: a neighbouring kingdom had waged war on another tribe and had placed the young warriors in stockades, ready to barter with the notorious slave traders.

*　*　*

It had not rained for weeks and a sheet of dust rose over the village again. There was a menacing storm brewing on the horizon too. Kalu stood up and took long strides across the compound, passing his mother's hut with the knowledge that she had borne his father's polygamy. She, Olafemi, was weaving a mat for her son and trimming the ends. His bodyguards had speared an antelope and a half-dead zebra for the skin, slitting their throats without a thought for the animals. Already the insects were buzzing around the carcasses, while bloated flies feasted on the dark blood which had seeped from the neck wounds onto the parched land. The dead animals caused Kalu to hawk and spit. He pitied the women; they would have to cure the skins for use as mats or bed covers. Sniffing the hot air, Kalu made a long face when he saw the blue-black flies gorging on the congealed blood of the dead animals. He had returned home late last night so the women had not had a chance to skin the dead animals he and the others had caught. He had remained positive when his father acknowledged the new addition to the family without mentioning his own name. Rather than side with his mother, who had denounced the man-child in private, he had shrugged off her suggestion that the boy was a serious contender. As he left the family compound in Osun, in the north, to embark on another hunting trip, he knew that his mother's eyes were watching him. He had travelled widely with his father, visiting the Yoruba kingdoms of Ondo to the east, Oyo in the west and Ogun to the north. He promised her that he would not stray far from home today.

* * *

Half-hidden in the undergrowth, outside the compound, lurked a python. 'I am old,' Femi began to lament. 'I cannot give my husband another son.' She sat inside her hut weaving and feeling tossed about on the uneasy waters of life. *Ssss!* She heard it first. A menacing-looking python had slithered into the compound. 'Welcome, Great One. You are welcome.' She looked at the threatening mass of blackness morosely. 'If it is ill-tidings, I beg you, take it back.' There were screams coming from an adjacent hut. 'You have been here before, have you not?' The python lost interest in her and moved on, slithering across the compound. Inauspiciously, it stopped in front of one of the huts where it lay and intensely watched the door. Femi swallowed saliva but remained quite still when the python inclined its huge head, made a U-turn with its gargantuan body, left the compound and headed towards the forest.

The woman's screams were loudest on the left side of the compound. Femi sat with her knees apart. Beads of perspiration cascaded down her forehead. A python was the last thing she had expected to see. The sun shone down on the dusty compound while Kalu hacked his way into the forest with a group of men between the ages of fifteen and twenty-five. They were trained in combat and could spear a panther from a hundred yards away, all running like athletes and flinging their spears like javelin throwers. Because she had awoken with a strange feeling in her stomach, Femi was apprehensive about Kalu. To her astonishment, one of the younger co-wives emerged from a nearby hut, shrieking and rolling in the red dirt hysterically. It was rather like watching an unscripted play. Femi dropped her weaving, stood up and moved swiftly when her co-wives came running like cackling hens on a stage. Ululating, the women ran hither and thither, trying to make sense of the situation. Femi was thirteen when a python came into her father's compound. Hours later, one of her mother's co-wives had been put to bed with a stillbirth.

'What is it, my sister-wife?' Gripped by a new fear for her only son, Femi stood in silence while the women wrung their hands and ululated noisily. She, like her sister-wives, was conditioned by culture and aware that they were a part of something much bigger than themselves. 'Where is our man-son, my sister?' Bewildered, she approached the new mother uneasily and tried to calm her down. 'Where is our son, my sister-wife?' Everyone knew that the python's arrival was an omen of coming trouble. 'Where is our man-child?'

White teeth gleaming for a brief second, Aduke, the eldest of Chief Jumoke's wives, said snidely, 'Our man-child?' She was like a blunt instrument piercing Femi's flesh. 'Come.' She recalled how it was when she had lost a son: inconsolable. 'Let us help you to your feet.'

'Go from me, Olafemi!' Abim, a co-wife, refused the hand that was proffered to her. 'You have killed my joy.' Sobbing, she ran past Femi, stopped abruptly and sank to the ground where she sat down. 'My son is dead.' She pulled her knees up to her chin, hugged her thin calves and proceeded to rock back and forth. 'You have killed me.'

While Abim raged, Femi tried to pacify her. 'What are you saying, my sister?' Even so, she found that she was annoyed with her and began to dig the ball of her heels into the dirt. She knew that her co-wives would blame her for the sudden infant death. 'You are upset.' The women enjoyed wading into the catfight as a form of distraction from their own disappointments. 'My sister, I am not responsible for the death of our man-son.'

'I heard your son last night.' Abim was being propped up by Aduke. 'He predicted he would rule as king when his father joins the ancestors. He styles himself Prince Kalu I of Osun and his father indulges him. Foolish man.' There were times when Abim had experienced strange, disturbing dreams which began when she first became pregnant. The day before, she dreamed that a large serpent had fought with a witch to save her own life. The huge reptile had reminded her of a translucent earthworm: it secreted a gooey substance which covered the struggling witch's entire body. When the fight had ended, the giant worm had destroyed the witch and itself in its own secretion.

'Witch!' The chorus rang out across the compound. 'Witch!' The garrulous women battled to out-talk each other while making grotesque faces at Femi. 'Witch, witch!'

'You killed him.' One day on from planning her man-son's naming ceremony, Abim lost the power to stand and collapsed. 'Witch!'

* * *

A short time ago, Chief Jumoke arrived home from the village. Life in his compound was never boring, though it was sometimes hell because of in-fighting, which meant he had to make a diplomatic effort to diffuse the tension. He was straight-faced throughout Abim's tirade. When she had finished, Aduke dished out his food while her co-wives sat on high alert. Abim watched as he mulled over his palm wine. Fifteen women sat on woven mats, eating and expecting their husband to launch an inquiry into the child's death. Femi, sitting on the ground, distinctly apart from the others, abandoned her *fufu* and tried to defend herself when the finger-pointing women began to accuse her of bewitching Abim's son.

'Good evening, Father.' Careful not to address the grief-stricken mother, Monifa's first thought was that she herself had wished the boy dead. She spoke unguardedly, 'Maybe your wives are cursed, my father. People say they are doomed to produce dead man-boys.'

'Who told you that?' In the midst of it all sat Chief Jumoke, listening to the beat of a distant drum. 'My honorary son, how I wish you were a man-son. You speak your mind without fear. Fear is the enemy.'

'If you restored the kingship, Brother Kalu would be a prince.' The look on his face was enough for Monifa to shut up, looking discreetly at his wives and poking out her tongue at them behind his back.

'And I would be a princess.' While the women were eating and Abim had been weeping, Bayo, Chief Jumoke's eldest daughter by his first wife, Aduke, had arrived with Monifa, her half-sister. 'Why is everyone looking miserable?' The sisters had returned from visiting their extended family in the Kingdom of Oyo. At eighteen years old, Bayo wore a string of cowrie beads around her left ankle. 'Why are you weeping, Auntie?' The feisty teenager tightened her tie-dye wrap around her slender waist, knowing full well what had happened. 'Oh, it is only a man-child,' she spoke sharply, pulling a clownishly disrespectful face behind Abim's back. 'I am sorry for your loss, Auntie, but I am sure I would not cry over the death of a man-child. It is only a boy-child.'

'Take another wife, my husband.' Aduke, the senior wife, knelt at his feet and offered him a calabash of freshly made palm wine. 'Drink and consider the future. That boy of yours behaves like a spoilt girl-child. He cares nothing for others, going into the forest with the young warriors and endangering their lives.' She sipped the dregs when he had finished, launching a thinly veiled attack on Femi. 'I think my co-wives know how important it is for you to have another man-child.' Still kneeling, she continued bluntly, 'You cannot pin your hopes on one son. He is a wilful man-son, Jumoke, and not a prince.'

'I love my son and try to correct his faults.' For a long time, Chief Jumoke said nothing. 'Prince, eh?' He sat on a stool covered with animal skin. 'I am in talks with the elders about restoring the kingship.' He chomped on a leg of meat and told her never to address him by his forename. 'I want the monarchy restored. Get off your knees. How many years of marriage did it take for you to give me a girl-child – five or six?'

'You see what you have done to my husband, Olafemi,' Aduke said disparagingly. In the past, they had hit one another with stools. They soon developed a simple rule: *Keep your distance.* 'You are the cause of my troubles.' Chief Jumoke slept with Femi more often than he did with Aduke and the other wives, which made them jealous of her. 'You have bewitched him. You gave him a man-child and stopped my sister-wives from producing sons. Go away and take that daughter of yours with you. Monifa is a bad girl.'

'I would rather die than marry a man who has many wives,' Bayo spoke before her mother could put a hand over her mouth. 'Why can't a woman have more than one husband?' The eighteen-year-old had the longest, most graceful neck her father had ever seen, held high with a copper torque. Because of her mother's status as senior wife, she was well-dressed and her partially shaved head, with a single tuft of hair on top, was an indicator that she was unavailable for marriage. Her father was arranging a union between her and a chief of the Kuramo people. 'Why should a man have more than one wife?'

'Because we wear the crown of authority,' Chief Jumoke said gruffly, pointing to a cluster of trees in the yard. 'Men have natural leader-ship qualities, girl. Fetch me a stick to beat you.' A basking salamander sat completely still on a warm stone in the compound while the chief waited for Bayo's return. 'What is taking your daughter so long, Aduke?' He noticed that Abim had undone her hair to signify that she was bereaved. 'Olafemi, tell me the truth, woman. Did you harm my son, Abim's man-child? Speak truly, Olafemi.'

'Oba, my husband,' Femi made a subtle reference to his status as king in the Yoruba language, 'since the birth of our son, you have become a part of me and our blood-children. I would never lie to you.' Ignoring her co-wives, Femi, who had styled her thick black hair in intricate patterns to make them jealous, sat with her back to them so the patterns could be seen from behind. 'Abim wants me to divide our son. Must I divide him, Oba?'

'There, there.' Chief Jumoke offered a more sympathetic ear than usual. 'Come, no tears.' He scoffed at the idea of dividing Kalu into two halves to appease a grieving mother. 'Olafemi,' his Adam's apple moved when he spoke, toying with the sixth finger on his right hand, 'speak the truth.' He could read how his wives operated and how they were feeling simply by looking at their hairstyles. 'I want no lies.'

'The sacred python came today, Oba.' Femi fell face down on the ground, blowing her warm breath and kissing his feet in a show of humility. 'I was surprised when he came.' She would have crawled on her knees but it was unnecessary because she was not in the habit of doing so. 'Wherever the Great One goes, trouble follows. Remember how Ife, my sister-wife, swelled up and almost died giving birth to a dead son? The sacred python came then. Perhaps the boy was taken by spirit children in the other world, my husband.'

'You are responsible; you killed him.' It was Aduke's job to supervise the younger wives in Chief Jumoke's absence. 'You killed him.' She learned a lot about each wife by observing their constant fights. 'You are cursed to have barren wives and unborn sons, my husband.' Still gurning, Aduke, playing the role of the compliant wife, took the stick from Bayo, handed it to her husband and knelt. 'I may as well be barren. I cannot produce live sons. My failure as a woman has led you to take many wives. Beat me, Oba. I deserve it.'

'I think women should learn to be independent, get involved with market trading.' In what was one of her most disrespectful moments, Bayo forgot herself. Her mind was on Bami. When he last visited the compound, she mooned around with dreamy eyes, imagining the broad-chested warrior spreading his arms and ripping an antelope apart with his bare hands. She often met him in secret by the river; they went no further than holding hands for fear of yielding to temptation. 'I blame the ancestors for making girl-children far less important than boys.' She flounced off. 'It is time to do away with tradition.'

'Forgive her, Oba. I beg of you.' When the words left her daughter's mouth, Aduke wanted to somehow pull them back. Crawling on her hands and knees, she caught sight of Femi's hand-carved wooden comb and got up. Bayo was six months old before Chief Jumoke came to Aduke's bed again. In those days, he was besotted with Femi. 'Olafemi killed your son. I speak the truth.' She did not have a timid disposition and was determined to have her say. 'That witch has engaged a hairdresser to drive you crazy with the power of her hair. See how she laughs at your weakness, flaunting her hair in your face.'

'My wife,' Chief Jumoke gazed upon the basking salamander, 'no one laughs at the great-grandson of King Obalata.' When his father was faced with a comparable situation, his own mother had shouldered the burden of guilt. To his great shame, she was wrongly accused of smothering the new-born son of a co-wife and was beheaded because of female gossip. The boy, Jumoke, never forgave his late father. 'Come! Who is first?'

Aduke sounded disingenuous, 'As the moon of your life, I will bear the scorpion's sting.' Being the highest-ranking wife, it was important to take the lead. 'I am first.' She did not flinch when the stick stung her back six times. A long silence followed until she caught sight of the salamander basking on a stone. 'Hm.' She was furious that it had not bitten Femi (leaving its brittle teeth in her flesh), having earlier placed it inside her hut. 'You need another man-child.'

Known for his measured tone, Chief Jumoke spoke calmly, 'Come, Abim.' He dipped his hand into a calabash and rubbed charcoal on the grieving mother's forehead. 'When your period of mourning is over, I want Olafemi to braid your hair. They say hair-braiding is a time of shared confidences and laughter.' With her engorged breasts leaking, a sweet smell of milk rose from Abim's cleavage as she went off to keep vigil over the dead child. Chief Jumoke mused, 'A woman is happiest with a man in her bed and a man-son in her arms. Olafemi, why do you not braid your co-wives' hair like your own?' He had told his friends that she was the most intriguing and intoxicating woman he had ever seen.

'There is trouble coming, Oba.' Femi was uncharacteristically reticent to reply in case her answer offended him. 'The sacred python brought a message from the gods of things to come.' She touched his hand, longing to groom his thick head of hair but this was a social taboo. The only people who were allowed anywhere near his hair were the griots and his personal hairdresser. 'I had that vision again last night, my husband: men with pale skins rode stripeless zebras straight into the compound. It will not go well if you die. Warring tribes will burn the village and break up your compound, Oba.'

'Let me worry about that,' Chief Jumoke snarled, holding up his right hand and looking around his compound at the lack of strong defences. He had spoken with the elders about building a mud brick wall around his compound but, somehow, they never got around to it. 'Oshun has given you many visions and taught you how to use indigo to dye cloth. Your co-wives are well-dressed because of your skill in dyeing cloth. You have set a fashion with indigo. You should focus less on visions and more on making your sister-wives as beautiful as you are.' Then it was Femi's turn. 'You have beautiful hair.' He dipped his hand into the calabash, smearing her face with charcoal. 'Did you kill my son, Olafemi?'

'I am innocent of the death of your son, Oba.' Femi, who had been pounding millet before her husband arrived home, resumed the task in the yard. 'I speak no lie, Oba.'

'I cannot ignore the fact I've lost a man-son.' Chief Jumoke was blunt. 'I have no shortage of wives to choose from. Come, Olafemi.' He stood up, made his way to his hut and finally slumped in his ceremonial chair. He wanted to protect her from his other wives because he was convinced that life forces flowed through her long hair. 'Ola, I shall marry again – soon. Any woman who has the ear of Oshun and can create such beautiful hairstyles has earned the right to dress my hair.' He asked her gently, 'Your blood, are we expecting it any time soon?'

Femi shook her head – she was late.

* * *

That September, bathed in perspiration and nursing anxiety, Chief Jumoke (who was fifty) married his seventeenth wife: Abeke. At eighteen, the slender girl had walked across his compound with the thirty-two eyes of his sixteen co-wives following her every movement. Abeke was born in the Kingdom of Ondo where her desperate mother, like other barren women, had left sacrifices at the shrine of the river goddess, Oshun. When her flux failed to appear, her husband had drunk palm wine with the elders and pledged that if the expected child was a girl, she would be named Abeke, meaning, *We begged for her*.

For some time, there had been a strange and unsettling feeling in the air. The coming of Chief Jumoke's new bride generated new tensions between his wives, who would have abandoned a girl-child for a man-child. There were over twenty huts in the compound that housed the wives, elders, Kalu and his two bodyguards. The largest hut served as a great hall on feast and rainy days, housing the many artifacts that had come down the generations. Chief Jumoke occupied the adjacent apartment, which he shared with his favourite wives whenever he was in a magnanimous mood.

In this intimate space, the wives slept on pallets and accommodated their husband unabashed in the presence of their rivals. Since the engagement, Chief Jumoke's mind was preoccupied with Abeke, whose slender waist, wrists and ankles he festooned with cowries. Besotted, he neglected his harem and deluded himself that this marriage was not motivated by lust for his bride's youthful body. As for the others, he had told them that he wanted nurturers in his compound, not warrior women who made his head ache.

'I have high hopes,' Chief Jumoke said in the dark. 'You will ensure my immortality.' It troubled him that he was no longer young and agile. 'You shall conceive a man-son tonight.' From the far corner of the hut came the muffled sounds of his five favourites, who were obliged to turn their faces to the four mud walls. In response to his lovemaking, they either chewed on bits of swaddling cloth, stuffed their fingers in their ears or suffered in silence. The jealousy that flowed through each of them reached its peak when he laughed and jarringly declared, 'You are a quick learner, so far. You shall be my favourite.'

'You promised me my own hut when I agreed to marry you.' In her irritation, the young Abeke found herself thinking of her co-wives and tried to move away from her new husband, scratching his bare arm in frustration. 'You are the weakest man I've ever known. You promised to send your first wife away. You are afraid of her – weak man.'

'She is very disrespectful, Oba.' Polygamy had made a kind of tyrant of Aduke as well. 'I will beat her tomorrow.' She lay on her side on her pallet. 'She is a bad girl.'

'Didn't your mother tell you to be a good wife?' Chief Jumoke urged his bride to wrap her gazelle-like legs around him. His hand wandered across her chest, tweaked a pointed nipple and moved down to her groin. Over and over, he swore as he tried to coax his reluctant bride in the darkened hut, which erupted into female laughter. 'Grrrr!'

'You are too heavy, Oba.' Flinching, Abeke realised that she did not feel properly prepared for marriage to such a powerful man with so many wives but kept her thoughts hidden. On the eve of the wedding, her proud mother had taken her aside and had advised her to place a piece of clean cloth beneath her before penetration, to provide proof that she was a virgin. There was no advice about how to deal with the multitude of wives who shared the royal chamber at night. 'Ease up, my husband.'

'Aduke should have prepared her for this moment, Oba.' Sisi, the tenth wife, got up and walked out of the hut in disgust. 'Don't blame the child; she is a virgin bride. Her mother should have given her the talk.'

'You had no patience with me, Oba. I remember how rough you were.' Ayo, discourteous and disgruntled, got up in the dark and stumbled over a foot. 'She needs training in how to take her husband's manhood.'

'You are my wife, not my counsellor.' Chief Jumoke silenced Sisi, threatening to return her to her family for not fulfilling her promise to give him a man-son. 'I do not need advice.' After several unsuccessful attempts to penetrate his bride, he furrowed his damp brow. 'Olafemi, what will survive of me if you do not give me another man-son?'

'Ahem!' went Ayo, saliva filling up her mouth as she left the hut. 'Ptsh!' She spat and returned to hear her husband groaning, thrusting and rising and thrusting, with his buttocks quivering at the thought of Femi's softness. 'Normal service will be resumed after the virgin bride has conceived, my sisters.' Ayo checked her temper and lay on her pallet in the dark, hiding her pregnancy and praying that she was carrying a man-child. 'Tsk!'

From a day of rising bad temper, sitting through the wedding with grace, Femi's sigh was audible. 'She is just a child, Oba.' When she herself had agreed to marry him, he had assured her that he had left Aduke's bed. He had lied to each new wife. 'What is a daughter when she will marry and endure the same fate as her mother and her mother's mothers, too?'

'What is a girl-child to anyone?' Aduke had formed a bond with several of the younger wives, who often confided in her. 'Tomorrow we shall sleep in our own huts, give the new bride some privacy.'

* * *

A week after the wedding, Chief Jumoke placed Abeke in Aduke's care and postponed his monthly court. News had come that forty people had been kidnapped in a village to the east of Osun. He and the elders had held a meeting in the great hall where there was an air of tension. What alarmed them was the news that a king in the north had been captured with his bodyguards. That a man of royal lineage would end up on a plantation in the Americas proved that the emboldened traders did not respect status. In fact, no man under fifty was safe from the raiders, who were determined to acquire shiploads of black ivory for the British West Indian canefields.

Through chairing an early morning meeting, it was left to Chief Jumoke to come up with solutions. He could feel his muscles tensing as he, assisted by Kalu, laid out a plan. The warriors were to fell the tallest trees in the forest to build strong defences around all the compounds. Watchmen would patrol the entrances while the people slept. Chief Jumoke was concerned about the safety of his family, the destruction of neighbouring villages and where this scorched-earth policy might lead in the future. Like his peers, he understood that death was a part of the journey through life, and thus they became obsessed with immortality. With the elders coalesced around a single figurehead, it fell to Chief Jumoke to call for a mind-shift in the way they handled disputes. Try as he might, he could not calm the elders who were beginning to fear their friends, neighbours and even relatives, some of whom had been suspected of participating in the enslavement of their own kinsmen in return for paltry items, such as trinkets, bales of cloth, pots and utensils. While the grey beards discussed how to deal with this problem, Chief Jumoke's wood carvings, stone sculptures and canework stood on display. He glanced at Kalu, who stood beside King Obalata's corona-tion stool with a sinking feeling in his own stomach that spread down to his groin.

'I am no coward, but the thought of my compound being raided is too much.' A look of fear and anger emanated from Chief Jumoke's eyes. When he looked around at what he had achieved, he caught a glimpse of what he stood to lose: his only son and heir, Kalu, his past and his wives and other children, too. The debate heated up and when he finally interjected, it was to stress the importance of working in unity to defend the four kingdoms against a common enemy: the slave traders. 'If we build stronger barricades, we can keep the white devils out.'

'It is too late,' lamented a grey beard who had once ruptured a man's Adam's apple in a fight to the death. 'We don't have time to waste…'

'It is fight or flight, Oba.' The grey beards breakfasted on roasted plantains and yams in the great hall, with its mud walls, where one of the elders, whose great-grandfather was an Igbo and who styled himself *Igwe*, asked cynically, 'What weapons will we be using?' He argued that they should abandon their compounds and flee into the forest until the danger had passed. 'We cannot fight the white devils.' He remarked about the white men's superior weapons, described the methods used to subdue the kidnapped Africans and explained that some captives had died badly; others had longed for death. 'We must abandon this place.'

In moments like this, the heated discussions often escalated into a violent debate, with everyone talking at once. Some expressed disbelief and even denial about the role of their fellow Africans in the kidnapping and trafficking of their countrymen. Very soon the elders, pretending the enemy that they were about to face was a disorganized bunch of ruffians, lambasted Chief Jumoke for his lack of a coherent strategy and drew the meeting to a close, promising to regroup within days.

By mid-morning, the grey beards, with animal skins draped across their shoulders, had left the compound in a hurry. The meeting had become very vocal, each man digging in his heels and insisting he had the best plan of action. Chief Jumoke's family heirlooms had reminded them that they were in the company of history. Except for Aduke, none of the wives dared to enter the great hall in male company. They had gathered outside, at a safe distance, where they argued that an attack would never come. Chief Jumoke emerged into the light, sent them back to their own huts and carried on as if nothing had happened. He was visibly shaking.

'You are afraid, Oba. Go and rest.' Aduke, who saw something in her husband which she had never imagined possible, felt that a memory was being made that day. 'I will bring you some palm wine, Oba.'

'When did you start giving me orders?' Chief Jumoke's hands shook at the thought of his son being taken and carried into unknown and uncharted territory. 'Come, dog.' He clicked his fingers at a fierce black brute that looked at him adoringly and held up a paw for food. The idea of death occupied the chief's mind. Fretful, he joined Kalu beneath the flame tree, pointing to the vultures circling his compound, as if they smelled rotten flesh on the air. Alongside a great determination to live, there was a black sheet of despair in his heart. It was as though he were in his final days. 'You have been misinformed, woman.' He remembered the animal's last kill – the big cat went down kicking. 'Go and feed my dog.'

'You are not yourself, Oba.' Aduke saw the sheet of sweat on his forehead. She lowered her eyes. 'We have been married for many moons. When we were young, you valued my opinion until that witch, Olafemi, came into our marriage and stole your affections from me. Let us go inside and discuss what is troubling you, away from those noisy hens. You look haunted by the ghost of tomorrow, my husband.'

'An ordinary man would not last long with a wife like you.' Early that morning, Chief Jumoke had gone for a stroll with Femi. 'I am no ordinary man.' He felt that if he were to confide in any woman, it would be Femi. 'My contention with you is that you gave me a girl-child and a dead man-child – which caused me to fill my life with a warring tribe of women.' He fixed his eyes on Kalu, sitting beneath the flame tree, but he could not rid himself of history. He was conscious that his shields, tribal headdress, spears and a few artifacts were all that remained of his great-grandfather, King Obalata. 'Go and train your junior wife. Abeke needs guidance.'

'Of all your wives, she is the least compliant.' The idea that he, a king in all but name, was losing his grip on power gave Aduke much satisfaction. Her dark eyes mocked him. 'You are afraid, Oba.' It was an interesting observation and one that thrilled her. 'It is plain to see.'

'I fear no man!' The smile on Chief Jumoke's face slipped when he realised that she was ridiculing him. 'How great a gift it is for a woman to give her husband a man-son. You are barren. You gave me a live girl-child, Bayo, and a dead man-son.' He had by now drifted off to another world where he recalled how, as a boy, his grandfather's compound had been attacked by a rival kingdom. There was enormous relief when the battle had ended. It was a brutal, visceral fight. In a frenzied counterattack, many brave young warriors had perished that day. 'Let us break kola nut and drink palm wine, my son. You are the last of my bloodline.'

'Do not worry, Father. I shall give you many grandsons.' Kalu leaned back against the trunk of the flame tree, watching Monifa's return from the river. 'My honorary brother, good day,' he greeted his sister. Then he dropped his voice, 'Father, I wish to discuss Bayo and Bami's courtship.'

'Welcome, my honorary son.' Chief Jumoke said regrettably, 'You were born in the wrong body.' Monifa was returning from the river with a bundle of freshly laundered clothes on her head. She bent her knees slightly and walked past with her eyes downcast. 'I would give anything to arm her with a spear.' Chief Jumoke believed Monifa's sixth finger was a substitute penis and had said as much to her, tactfully using the word manhood. As he gazed at her, something bothered him so gravely that he wished he had sent his wives and children away. 'She is regal. I want her to marry a prince before I die. No commoner will do.'

'Bayo must marry soon.' Kalu looked from his father to the back of Monifa's head before accepting a calabash from his mother. He nodded after she had poured palm wine. 'This is very good, my mother.' She disregarded gender separation rules and sat on cured skin while he gave an unguarded smile. 'I shall be blunt, Father. We must unite the kingdoms and wage war on those foreign devils from across the great sea. We must drive those white devils from our land. You under-estimate the danger we are in.'

'I never under-estimate danger.' Chief Jumoke's concern was the collateral damage. 'Those white devils think nothing of bringing ancient kingdoms to their knees.' He respected his son's opinions but was also a pragmatist. 'Olafemi, why are you not with your co-wives? I will not have you meddling in men's talk. You are withholding my conjugal rights.'

'I have given you a man-son, Oba.' Seated on cured animal skin on the ground, Femi watched the sunlight flipping off the green leaves. 'You must make another man-son.' She knew that it was not the right time to speak but she wanted to be taken seriously by the two most important people in her life. 'Oba, I did not kill your man-son, your immortality.' She turned her smiling dark eyes on Kalu, knowing that the return of the python had left a menacing presence over their lives. 'My son, I know not what tomorrow will bring you but know that you have my trust.'

'I value it, my mother.' A leaf from the flame tree fell onto Kalu's head, causing him to frown when she said it was a message: *an omen.*

* * *

Nothing unexpected happened for six days, but on the seventh day the python returned. All the children looked on fearfully when it stopped outside their father's hut for the briefest moment before slithering out of the compound while his uneasy co-wives began to ululate. Hitherto, Chief Jumoke had refused to show any emotion, even after the elders had outlined their concerns and advised him to flee into the hinterland with them. After the python had departed with no direct confrontation, the chief sat beneath the flame tree, which was dying, staring blankly. It reminded him of his late mother. Before she was beheaded, she had gone on hunger strike; her clothes had hung loosely on her skeletal frame.

Even the most pessimistic of the elders could not have predicted what followed next. On the dawn of the eight day, a dozen white men, and six Africans, forced their way into the compound without the need for a siege. Chief Jumoke's great black hound stood outside his master's door, howling while the intruders set fire to the defences around the compound. The enslavers had used a heavy log, which was carelessly left outside, to ram the wooden structure until the stout door collapsed inwards. Ever vigilant, the ramming of the outer fortification had awakened Kalu and his bodyguards, as well as his friend, Bami, who had slept over.

'The end has come, my husband.' Femi awoke with a start in the dark. 'Wake up, Oba.' She shook her husband, a deep sleeper, until he sat up. 'This is it.' Thereafter, she stood in silence in the great hall. There was a sudden realisation that their lives would never be the same again.

The first sound Chief Jumoke heard was a barking hound. Before he could get dressed and whistle for the dog, he heard Aduke beating at his door, screaming that the young women were being kidnapped. Most of the young people had been pinned down with their arms and legs bound to prevent them from escaping. Chief Jumoke spat as he emerged from his hut half-dressed and hurried towards the flame tree. In a scene of panic, he threw his hands up in the air when a pistol was discharged in his direction. His blood ran cold. There was a searing, agonising pain in his chest, which felled him beneath the flame tree where he loved to sit with Kalu. Nearby, Aduke lay dead with one leg folded beneath her where she had fallen in flight.

'Shurrup!' Among the raiders was a white man in wide-brimmed hat and white clothes. 'Shut yer effing mouth!' He fired a volume of phlegm and dragged Kalu by the legs. 'Kick an' I'll shoot you, *nigger*!'

Chief Jumoke came to his senses but everything was black. 'When I can see again, I shall hunt down the white devils and burn their boats.' He loved the rush before a kill but the power of sight had been taken away and he was startled by a stray musket ball. 'Stay alive, my son. Do whatever you must to stay alive – live another day. Use your head, not your hands. Do not fear what lies ahead.'

'I shall live to fight another day, Father.' Shocked, Kalu watched his father sinking into dazed oblivion and heard the raiders laughing, having their fun. He had not expected his father to die so brutally and vowed revenge. 'I have the will to live. I promise you that, my father.'

'Tame your heart, my son.' Femi threw herself forward to save Monifa. 'Yemaya, Mother of Mercy!' When she was young, the *Igwes* had celebrated their history and culture by blessing the land and its citizens. She had been looking forward to this year's festival in December and the New Year. 'They have killed me.' In the confusion, a musket ball had hit her in the centre of her back. She stumbled over a dying hound with a gaping hole in its side. 'My son, remember me to your children's children.' With her life-blood draining away, she called after Monifa, who wrenched herself away from her captors and ran to her. 'My honorary son, do what you must to survive. You must not let our story die with you…'

In the compound, pandemonium had broken out. The familiar sounds of habitation had been replaced by the screams of children running after their mothers and the groans of the maimed and dying. Meantime, Monifa flung herself on the ground and tried to shield her mother's body while the kidnappers burned the huts and destroyed her father's ceremonial masks, his headwear and his tortoise-shell warrior shields. In the pale light of dawn, the raiders had smashed most of the clay pots and had looted the stone sculptures, elephant tusks and the bronze busts that were so proudly displayed on feast days. Six of Chief Jumoke's co-wives, with heads down and shoulders hunched, had been captured. There were long lines of young people wailing and loud voices barking orders all around them.

'I said move it!' Walking briskly, a prematurely grey Englishman cracked a whip when he saw Kalu looking back at his parents' bodies; the flies were already hovering. Ned Weekes, a former coal miner from Durham, had never forgotten stepping into a cage at dawn and hurtling down to the hot and filthy coalface every day. 'Move it!'

* * *

The thing that Kalu regretted most was that he had been lulled off to sleep by palm wine the night before this calamity. He could not help thinking that if he had not been tipsy, he might not be a captive with his father dead. For a while, the leg irons on his ankles chafed and his temples throbbed while they made their way through the forest. He longed to comfort Monifa, Abeke and Bayo but when he tried to speak to his sisters, no words came. The memory of his parents' corpses would remain with him forever. They had all woken up to find their freedom stolen, their very way of life taken away from them.

Everything about the raid seemed cloudy to Bami, who'd also woken groggy from too much palm wine. He had not seen his father, a chief in another village, since the day before the attack. He himself was afraid of death and frightened that his mother would think him dead; it would break her heart. The pain in his legs grew steadily until he was in agony, limping along on bleeding feet. The rattle of chains, the crack of whips and the cries of many made him think he was on the route to madness.

At first, they moved quickly with the morning sun on their faces. The traders decided to take an extra precaution by cutting pieces of heavy wood, which they forked at one end so that the wood could fit around the necks of the more belligerent Africans. On the second leg of the journey, they walked slowly, picking up more captives until the line stretched out like an ancient caravan in the desert, on its way to Mecca. For the sickly, the ordeal was too much; they lay where they fell and awaited death. As for those who had the will to go on, there was a long way left.

Following in the footsteps of those who had gone before them, hoping to escape at an opportune time, they had not spoken to one another since they were taken. Silently, they marched through the hinterland, envying the big cats and wild boars their freedom. Fraught, they tried to memorise the grasslands and forests they had known since childhood. At last, their faces contorted when they saw the hordes of perspiring Africans and the boats and overcrowded canoes. They had reached the great River Niger.

'You must obey orders, my sister.' Kalu was about to assist Monifa into a canoe when she was unceremoniously pushed into the vessel that would take them on the next leg of the journey. 'If we are separated, try to stay alive. Try to stay close to the women. Do whatever it takes to survive. Yemaya, Mother of Mercy, keep her safe. Yemaya!'

* * *

Having lost all hope of seeing their loved ones again, five Africans had dropped dead from fatigue before the captives were taken by boats to a fortified stronghold by the sea: Elmina Castle. Inside the dungeons, ten-year-old Monifa and the others had been held in the dark for three weeks: it was pitch black. Ironically, the castle also boasted a Church of England chapel. Here, they were imprisoned at Elmina where the stench of humanity, the smell of death and the rattle of chains caused Monifa to chafe her malformed sixth finger with her thumbnail. In less than an hour, the time it took to destroy her family, her destiny had changed. Going into a frustrated fury about the loss of freedom, she hollered along with many others, who rattled their chains. The air of confidence which she exuded in her father's compound was gone.

* * *

It had been a hot and torturous night before the day of departure dawned. When the sun rose over Elmina Castle, the *African Empress* made ready to sail from the coast of West Africa with a cargo of two hundred Africans and a crew of ruthless sailors. In addition to Captain Finlay, a talkative Scot, there were two officers, a surgeon, cabin boy, cook and five returning European merchants. They were listed as a Dutchman from Surinam, a Portuguese from Brazil, a Scot from Glasgow, a Spaniard from Cuba and a Frenchman from St Domingue.

The men were united under the Treaty of Utrecht, 1713–1714. The signing of the *Asiento* gave Britain's South Sea Company a monopoly on the Transatlantic slave trade, to transport five thousand Africans annually to the Spanish colonies for each of the next thirty years, which in turn enabled Britain to make use of several Spanish Transatlantic seaports.

Captain Finlay and the five European Merchants all shared a belief that they had a clear mandate: black ivory for the sugar plantations in Jamaica. Once this part of the bargain had been completed in Kingston, any unsold captives were scrambled in Port Maria in the parish of St Mary. With these jobs done, the crew cleaned the ships before going 'wenching' in the Kingston taverns. In the case of the *African Empress*, Finlay would collect his cargo of sugar, molasses, coffee, rum and tobacco. When the ship returned to the Port of Glasgow, in the Firth of Clyde, it had completed the Triangular Trade.

For a wishful moment, Kalu hoped that he would wake from a bad dream. With a sense of foreboding, he and the others were ferried in boats to the waiting ship which was lolling on the wild Atlantic Ocean. When they were taken through the outer wall at Elmina, built by the Portuguese in 1482, Chief Jumoke's six co-wives had refused to enter 'the door of no return.' Petrified, they wailed as they were being lowered into the boat that would take them to the ship. With an utterly graceless gesture, the crew dragged them, kicking and screaming, onto the deck before removing the chafing leg irons. On this voyage of no return, there was bitterness, anger, hatred and mistrust of every white man.

'No weeping.' A faceless Yoruba man began to dance and sing, urging, 'Show no fear, my brothers and sisters. Shango, the most powerful of all our gods, is with us. He will not forsake us. Shango!'

Glad for the diversion, Bayo had been reliving the terror of seeing her mother shot in the forehead. Aduke's life had expired instantly. She had tried to shield her daughter from the truth of the external threat they faced. Bayo's own sad life, manifested by the breaking of artifacts in her father's compound, left her feeling like a tree without roots. Of course, the real ordeal was just beginning for her and the others. They had been herded into a cramped space and crammed cheek-by-jowl in the fetid hold.

'You have your orders, lads. I want no mishaps on this journey.' Captain Finlay was a ruddy-faced, stocky man in his late fifties whose skin had refused to tan under the African sun. 'I specifically told the factor I wanted no children. This ship is not a fucking nursery.' Perspiring and irritable, he was inspecting the vessel and was displeased to see a group of terrified, shitty children. 'I hope we're carrying enough salt to cure the meat for the blacks.' On his last voyage, a dozen half-starving Africans had been lowered into the sea because the meat had rotted. There was not enough supplies to sustain their healthy country-men. 'I hope we've got enough snakes in those baskets to feed the brutes when the meat runs out. Snake meat tastes like chicken, a delicacy in these parts.'

'Welcome to your doom, nagas.' Wally, a brawny sailor, held a bullwhip in his calloused right hand. 'Quick about it. Move it, whores.' Mouthing off profanities, he stood with his legs wide apart, wearing a wide brimmed hat, pale blue shirt and white baggy trousers stuffed into calf-length leather boots. This was the standard dress for the ship's crew. He had once bullwhipped a mutinous African to death. 'On the double.'

'On yer feet, girl.' Gussie, a bearded sailor, jerked his thumb at a child with breasts starting to form and pubic hair just beginning to sprout. 'I'll see yer later.' It was a well-worn maxim on the ship that young flesh was *as tender as veal*. 'This one will do me nicely.'

'What are you talking about, man?' Dr Sawney Bridges, the ship's surgeon, cleared his throat. 'Captain, in the name of compassion, we ought to supply the girls with something to cover their pelvic girdles.' Almost immediately, the child used her hands to hide her pubic area. Bridges turned bright red. 'The crew must restrain their eyes and hands.'

'You are a strange one. I ought to take you down into the hold. I want to get it over with.' It had been some weeks since Captain Finlay left Scotland and any attempt at civility had been tossed overboard. 'Right, lads! I hope we've got enough limes to prevent scurvy.' He glowered at a child who was short of breath and suffering with double incontinence. 'No more talk of the rights of man. We do not live in a halcyon world.'

Hanging back, Abeke and Kalu were the last to board. When they looked over the side of the ship, they saw the corpse of a naked woman floating in the water. Kalu blinked, trying to avoid looking at Abeke's nakedness. In his father's compound, he was used to strict rules about decency and gender separation, but he did not dwell on this because the leg irons had left him with painful, suppurating sores around his ankles. Once or twice along the journey through the forest, he tried to struggle whenever the traders whipped Bayo and Monifa for refusing to cooperate. To compound matters, he had wrestled two of them to the ground – middlemen who spoke his language and who were Africans from the Gold Coast. He had left his father's home with bitter memories of death and destruction.

Glancing around with her hands bound and her ankles chained, what struck Abeke about the crew was their lanky greasy hair, rotten teeth and biscuit-tan skin. She staggered forward, frightened and trembling, when she was shoved from behind by a scrawny sailor. Quick to react, she turned around and lifted what her mother had called 'the foot of pride.' Meanwhile, her pert breasts caught the attention of a sailor with a bent nose who grabbed her hand and placed it on his crotch. She and Kalu were both naked and had lost their dignity cooped up in a dark dungeon at Elmina Castle where they had been tormented around the clock. She shook her head, silently pleading with him not to retaliate as he had done at Elmina whenever the guards had fondled her breasts. Two years ago, sitting by the river, they had longed for the day when they would marry and raise a family of man-sons. Ruthlessly dispatched across the deck with a kick up her rear, she descended into the abyss.

'Get below before you start shitting yourselves all over this deck, nagas,' ordered a black-nailed sailor with receding hairline and bogey in his left nostril. 'You filthy pigs.' This gaunt-looking Scot had an eye infection and a recurring dose of the clap, which he had caught from a prostitute in a brothel in Glasgow. 'My gut is turning with the smell, you dirty dogs.' Unabashed, he scratched his crotch while complaining, 'They should have washed 'em down before sending 'em aboard, effin' fart arses. Shit-holes.'

'Everything up to scratch?' Finlay, feeling the beginning of a head-ache coming on, dug his right ear with his index finger. 'Oh good. Then we can get a move on, can't we?' A decade ago, he had been thinner. Years of plenty had widened his girth and now his breeches were held up with a wide leather belt. He dreamed of owning a Highlands estate with yew trees in all directions. 'No candles below deck.' Still picking his ear, he gave the order for the ship to sail. 'I want to avoid the Trade Winds when we reach the Tropics.'

'Anchors away.' Rocking on his heels, Jim, a googly-eyed joker, could feel the ship moving. 'Westward Ho!' The mast pole began to creak. At precisely 8am on 24 October 1765, the *African Empress* left West Africa with two hundred Africans, including a dozen pregnant women. On this voyage, half the children would sicken and die. 'Westward Ho!'

'Get a bucket of water and clean that shit away, lad.' Finlay stood on deck with his right foot resting on a wooden crate, watching a languid sailor. 'Come with me, Bridges. Let us go and examine the cargo.' He looked at the soles of his leather boots. 'Shit!' A nervous captive had defecated when his leg irons were removed on deck. Ten days into the voyage, he would become psychotic and tossed overboard to the sharks. 'I am a man of scruples, Bridges. Still, I cannot prevent the crew from fucking the more attractive wenches and the more physically appealing bucks. Oh, while we are on the subject of tars, some of our men are cut-throats and highway robbers; others have been pressed into service. Now that everything is settled, Dr Bridges, I'd like to discuss your duties.'

'Let us dispense with my title: Bridges will do.' Openly perspiring, Bridges did not care about the backgrounds of the sailors whose ailments he would treat on the voyage. 'What do we do about the women's monthly flux, *menses*? What about their dignity? I suggest we separate the men and women into different quarters for hygiene purposes, Captain.' He rubbed the heat rash at the nape of his neck while one of the women in the hold began to raise a racket, sobbing that death was preferable to being shackled with her countrywomen like wild animals in captivity. 'They'll suffocate under their own bodily fluids, Finlay.'

'All right, all right. Steady the boat. Please don't bore me with trivial matters. It's very tiresome.' Finlay descended into the hold and gazed at a one-breasted woman chained to a child. 'Ah, this one must be the black Spartan, a warrior woman. According to legend, they slice off the right breast so they can throw spears and shoot arrows on horseback more effectively. Folklore.' With his hands folded behind his back, he implied that the one-breasted woman was unattractive and would have no problems with the crew. 'Before this voyage is over, you'll be used to the stench of shit, death and disease. Ork! I've got turd on my boots. Hm. We've still got space to squeeze in a few more nagas.'

'Oh God, the smell is really bad down here. Oh Christ, it stinks to high heaven.' Bridges screwed up his face and wrinkled up his nose in the confined space where there was no light during the night. 'Oh Lord! Jesus, it's disgusting.' More than a little claustrophobic, he began to feel everything closing in on him and longed for green cornfields, woodlands and squawking birds. 'Look at that enormous rat. We ought to bring a cat or two on the next voyage. You do know rats have fleas? Those vermin carry the bubonic plague.'

'Nevertheless, blacks enjoy eating rats. I always encourage the captives to eat whatever moves on four legs down here in the hold.' The filth-hardened Finlay came straight to the point. 'Let's be clear, I'm not interested in any theory about rats and fleas as vectors of diseases. Nagas are a poor specimen of humanity. Don't give me that look. Compared to where they're coming from, the jungle, those blacks are in seventh heaven down here.'

'Now I get the phrase *filthy lucre*.' Gagging, Bridges came close to being overwhelmed by the oppressive heat and the odour of human waste. 'This is where Britain's interests lay. Before we sailed from home, I brushed up on my history and discovered that the trade was initially started by John Hawkins, whose three voyages were sponsored by Queen Elizabeth I, beginning in 1564 (and later King James I became involved in the trade). Did you know that, in 1662, the Royal African Company (RAC) was founded by the Royal Stuart family and merchants in the City of London?' Although Bridges had done his research, nothing prepared him for the overpowering stench and misery in the hold. It was the first time that he had seen human suffering on such a vast scale, which caused him to remark that he had wittingly entered a world that was not for the faint-hearted nor the weak-stomached. 'I can hardly breathe with the foul smell of excrement in my nostrils.'

'While you're busy pointing the finger at our British Royal Family for enriching themselves, let's hope we've got enough scraps of rags to wipe my arse.' Finlay, amused by Bridges' reaction to the traditional smell of a slave ship, reminded the surgeon that Africans were property. 'There's something soft about you. You look like you're shitting your breeches, man.' He emerged from the hold and halted on deck, giving his first officers a displeased look. 'Get one of the lads to open the portholes and the gratings.' He liked his ship to be ready to receive the cargo and wished not to be bothered with mundane things like portholes. 'I want no more shit on this deck.' Perched on a mast pole high above their heads was a white gull. 'I must make a start on my logbook and journal right away.'

'What about their *menses*?' After being given a quick tour of the hold, Bridges came up gasping for air and expressed his concerns. 'The least we can do in these awful conditions is to keep them apart. What! You don't suggest they bleed all over themselves?'

'I can't worry about that.' Finlay threw up his hands in exasperation and said, slightly tartly, 'I am not interested in your platitudes, man. It's your job to seal all their orifices until we reach Jamaica.' His face was jowly and stern as he too studied the calm Atlantic waters. 'At home, lower-class wenches bleed into their chemises day after day.'

'I wonder whether you ever realised for one second that those blacks in that airless shithole are not just cargo.' Bridges inhaled and exhaled fresh air greedily, trying to imbue the Africans with a sense of humanity. 'It's very sad and demoralizing to see them cooped up in such insanitary conditions.' He inhaled the fresh air slowly. 'On the next voyage from Glasgow, we must bring enough fabric to cover their pelvic girdles.'

'A pragmatist as well.' Amongst other things, Finlay began to suspect that he had hired a thought police and this made him suspicious of Bridges. 'Some of the younger wenches will be fucked senseless before we reach Kingston. I might just take a turn among the cabbages. In any case, I am more concerned with water infiltration in the hold, which is a common problem on long sea voyages.' A few years back, he would not have heeded his surgeon's suggestions. This headstrong attitude had led to a sense of impermanence on the *African Empress*. Consequently, every voyage saw the captain engaging a new surgeon. 'Leave me. I want the sea breeze to caress my cheeks.'

* * *

When Kalu had first gone down into the hold, he had tears in his eyes as he pictured the distorted faces of his dying parents. His will to live had become stronger than it had been when he was first taken. The stench of suppurating sores on legs and the misery around him turned stronger stomachs than his, yet he did not feel unduly disturbed by it all. Motionless, he lay in the dark worrying about where they were headed while still mourning his parents. His body ached with grief and physical pain. As the coast of West Africa receded in his mind, he could hear rattling chains, wailing women and children, and waves lapping outside the ship. What troubled him most was not the sight of his parents dying helplessly but that the slave traders had been aided and abetted by some of his own countrymen. This left an indelible image on his troubled mind: Africa was becoming a depopulated continent. Bayo, meantime, needed to be protected from the salacious sailors and Monifa talked to her hand as if she had lost her grip on reality.

In the interim, a chain reaction of events was unfolding before Abeke's eyes. 'This is not a dream,' she called out in Yoruba, making no effort to adjust to the darkness. 'Mama-o! A rat is nibbling my toes.' It was as if something had broken in her mind. 'I feel like a caged animal.' She looked around in the darkened hold. 'Am I dead? Where are we?'

'We are where we are,' grunted a big-bellied African who had a habit of holding out his hand regally to be kissed. 'I am a king.' He turned, as imperially as he could, to his two crestfallen bodyguards. 'Tell them, I should not be here. I am of royal lineage, a king.'

In the adjacent area, Monifa was disturbed by yelling and screaming which kept the exhausted children awake. Chained together in the dark, they banged their heads and drove themselves to the edge of madness. Several hours had passed since they'd packed into the hold like canned sardines. Feeling disconnected from everything, the vastness of the sea had frightened Monifa into believing the ship would sail off the edge of the world. She screamed inwardly.

The creaking ship and lapping waves affected the men's morale. They rattled their chains and yelled constantly. While the incessant noise was going on, Bami reached out and took Bayo's hand, cautioning her not to fight back because the sailors had no respect for black womanhood. She had woken from a lucid dream in which she was surrounded by men with hooded eyes. She had panicked, pleading with the ancestors to rescue her from the depths of hell. Sobbing, she saw a big, gaping hole in the centre of her late mother's forehead where a musket ball had entered it. Body odours reeked from every corner in the hold. Nearby, a particularly putrid smell of flesh sickened her. Gradually, Bami's soothing voice calmed her until she inclined her head towards him.

* * *

Several days into the sea voyage, just as the captives were becoming accustomed to the rats in the hold, the sea began to crash against the ship's hull. Almost immediately, the howling wind rose to a powerful storm: petrified women and children hollered, lightning flashed and thunder rolled as if it were the Last Judgment. When the sea's fury had died down, the sun broke through the grey clouds and the Africans were brought up to the deck for fresh air and exercise. The relief on their unwashed faces was evident, even as they were forced to walk the deck to the drum's roll and whip's crack.

Kalu, afflicted by Montezuma's revenge and wearing a hangdog expression, had decided to accept his fate. His main priority was staying alive. He, according to custom, was an accomplished warrior who had been used to giving orders, not taking them. Beaten down by hunger and weariness, he understood that they were simply flesh to be sold at the end of the voyage. They had been chained up in the hold for three days and many of his countrymen were morose, depressed and suicidal. For those with irritable bowels, like himself, the excrement caked onto their bodies and their shame increased when the crew doused them with seawater, sending a stream of effluence running across the deck.

* * *

On the fifth night at sea, Captain Finlay had enjoyed a fish supper with his two officers, Dr Bridges and the five European merchants. They had spent the last month waiting for the cargo and being entertained by European agents in the upper-storey at Elmina where they had bedded more than a dozen young women. Relaxing in his quarters after supper,

Finlay whipped out Laurence Sterne's *Tristram Shandy*. Although he was not a literary man, he had a well-stocked library and enjoyed reading. He spoke about Tristram Shandy, the importance of conceiving without interruption to produce a well-favoured child and the need to have a big nose – a prerequisite for a man to succeed in the world.

'I disagree.' Senor Xavier de la Vega, a Cuban merchant, who was in his early thirties, looked doubtful. 'A man is in charge of his own destiny.' He stroked his goatee beard with his index finger and argued that he was well-placed to comment because his father had left Spain penniless to become a self-made man. 'A man makes his own path.'

'Evidently so.' The Dutchman, Willem Wolff, had recently visited the graves of two of his forebears (buried in the Dutch cemetery at Elmina) and the Dutch-built St Jago Hill Fort. 'I find myself in agreement with you.' He watched Finlay close *Tristram Shandy* and open a copy of Samuel Richardson's *Pamela*. 'A library on a Scots ship?'

'This is an English bottom,' said Finlay, getting scarlet in the face and closing the text abruptly. 'The owner of this vessel is an Englishman from Berwick, a border town. He's a cultured gentleman with a good business head and a half a dozen slave ships.' There was something learned about the Dutchman, who made Finlay feel undereducated and insecure. 'Has anyone been to London, a city of sceptres and church bells ringing?'

'You should see Lisbon, city of culture.' The Portuguese merchant, Senhor Cristiano Azul, felt pride that his countrymen had built Elmina and was still marvelling at the colonial buildings in the town. He was already missing 'the placid Benya Lagoon' on the opposite side of the castle, which had the Atlantic Ocean on its other side. '*Pamela or Virtue Rewarded*? Speaking of virtue, those sable wenches in the hold may be savages to us, but to their men they are virtuous sisters, cousins, wives and daughters.' His olive skin stretched over his face while he spoke, relating the story of the biggest slave revolt in Brazil: the rebels had left the plantations and founded two towns of five thousand Africans in Palmares. 'Take care, Finlay. You don't want a revolt on your hands.'

'A slave revolt at sea? Not on my ship! That will never happen, not over my dead body.' Finlay dismissed the cabin boy when the crew let out a whooping on deck. 'Palmares?' Upon hearing the story, he inferred that the Portuguese cocks had spent too much time crowing and tupping too many black bitches. 'Africans must be disciplined.'

'The only reason we can master them is our superior weapons.' Monsieur Alain Fontane, the Frenchman, dispassionately observed the captain's musty quarters. 'Africans are divided by language and culture and cannot communicate with each other.' He believed that slavery was far too complex and sensitive an issue to focus on the treatment and control of slaves. Some of his superannuated slaves struggled with age-related illnesses and had begged him to end their lives. 'In my opinion, what the blacks want is to be treated as humans, not lesser beings, and then they will cooperate. Though some would say the Negro is like a black bear, having a natural instinct to climb trees.'

'The Negro is like a jungle plant.' Mengis Hunter, a greasy-haired Scotsman, winced as he scratched his itchy scalp with his right index finger. 'I take it you'll be the first to fall on your sword and give them your property, Monsieur Fontane?' He told the group with a smile, 'It seems likely that the dark continent, Africa, has bewitched him, gentlemen.'

'I put it down to sunstroke, gentlemen.' Finlay puffed on his Havana cigar, filling up the cramped cabin with smoke. 'Monsieur Fontane, those of us at the sharp end of slavery know the real work that goes into keeping slaves alive on the high seas and treating them humanely. I am a rational man. Nonetheless, I am persuaded you've fallen between two evils: black magic and the *black pussy*. Of course, we seafarers enjoy the perks of the trade: *black veal*.'

'You have the best-fed crew, Finlay.' Willem Wolff, the Dutchman, fantasized about girls with milky complexions and fat blonde plaits in Holland. 'All talk of slavery should be tempered with humanity and compassion.' He turned his head towards the cabin door and unwittingly showed the creases in his dirty neck where he had not bathed for weeks, instead only sponging his important bits. 'Where is the entertainment? I've been on ships where they tie the wenches to whipping posts for sport, though there are times when the fun gets too boisterous. I prefer my blacks on their backs, young and frisky, doing the same exact movement every time. What I love is the way they move in rhythm with you.'

While the merchants convulsed with laughter, Dr Bridges appeared ill at ease. 'I find slavery repugnant, so should anyone who calls himself a gentleman.' After a short stint working at Bedlam in London where he witnessed unimaginable cruelty, the lapsed Quaker had turned his back on the Church. 'Yesterday, a wench leapt overboard after being ravaged by two ruffians. Almost all the adolescent girls have been raped by the crew.' He accepted a mug of coffee from a chubby cabin boy, who had put down his oat biscuit when an insect crawled out. 'There's weevil in the flour and this coffee is undrinkable, boy.'

'Hasn't anybody told you that compulsive honesty is a vice?' The overly talkative Finlay continued to puff on his cigar, insinuating that they should discuss slavery in a spirit of tolerance. 'I tell you slavery is a positive good, Bridges. There are a few misinformed and malevolent elements who'd like to see the trade abolished. That will never happen, never. Gentlemen, the road to hell is paved with good intentions, even for well-meaning Quakers like Bridges. Of course, men like us do not have consciences.'

'I don't believe in dividing generations, separating families, in the name of commerce.' Bridges was often moved to compassion by the sight of those who were in distress or dying. 'I have given my life to medicine, to helping the weak and vulnerable. As a surgeon, taking life is the antithesis of my training.' He remembered the hopeful atmosphere in which he had trained and the personal experience of a surgeon who had influenced him. Initially, he greatly admired Dr Jonas Undercliffe, a bearded physician who believed that terminally ill and depressed elderly people should be euthanised. Undercliffe had a negative attitude towards old age and was fond of reciting from *King Lear*: *O, let him pass! He hates him much/That would upon the rack of this tough world/Stretch him out longer*. Invariably, Undercliffe fell off the pedestal in Bridges's head. 'I am deeply concerned about respecting human rights, whether black, yellow, brown or white. That also includes Red Indians, though I daresay they are savages by nature.'

'I am not without sympathy. My mother is of a delicate constitution, delicate as a flower in bloom.' The Scotsman, Mengis Hunter, argued that most planters were not in the business of torturing their slaves. 'Take off yer war paint and put down yer tomahawk. Yer red skin blood brothers would gladly take yer scalp and gouge out yer eyes. As for the Africans, they often go in for ritual cannibalism in the jungle.'

'Those poor souls are fair game for any white man.' Bridges was trying to raise human rights issues on a slave ship where the main pursuit after dark was wenching or a spot of cock fighting until blood was drawn with feathers flying. Seeing Finlay's scowl, he hastened to inform the group that his great-grandmother had been hanged in North America for being a Quaker. This piece of information was met with silence until he added that her persecutors had checked her body for marks to indicate that she was a witch.

'What, they found no cauldrons?' Finlay cast an eye on the officers.

'Oh, good Lord.' Bridges changed the subject, revealing that his great-grandfather had been incarcerated for holding illegal meetings and was persecuted for refusing to support the established Church and swear oaths. 'I am a Unitarian now: Unitarian. I reserve the right to develop my own religious opinions. I believe social evils are manmade, not God inflicted.' Surprisingly, there was a modicum of sympathy for Sawney Bridges because his forebears were vilified in North America for their religious beliefs. 'In the end, my great-grandfather was deported to England. Not one to mope, he went north and married a Scotswoman; she raised my grandfather in Fife.'

'This voyage is full of promise, gentlemen, new beginnings. I'm diversifying from dry goods to cane sugar.' It was Mengis Hunter, the erstwhile merchant, who now spoke. He had recently diversified into sugar planting and was frightened that, if the slave laws changed, this would mark the start of the dismantling of slavery. 'If there's a heaven, planters like me are shut out. I daresay I could bribe St Peter to let me through the gate.' He shuddered dramatically, as though he were about to topple off his chair with a minor seizure. 'I like the way you permit the cargo to dance on deck, exercise. They don't know it, but they're securing our financial future, gentlemen, as long as they're fit and stay alive.'

Finlay chomped on the cigar, which the Cuban merchant had given him, and downed a glass of Madeira, gifted by the Portuguese. 'Bridges, when I gave you the job, you assured me I'd not regret my decision. For a white man to question slave treatment and control is tantamount to social suicide.' He placed a bottle of brandy on the table, courtesy of Monsieur Fontane. 'Clean glasses, gentlemen?' Unexpectedly, the men felt a judder when the ship began to veer off course, as if going round and round in circles. 'If you're not careful, Bridges, you'll have to find another berth when we dock in Kingston.'

'I'm to tell you the ship has sprung a leak, Cap'n.' The lad who came barging in on male conversation was a twelve-year-old, illiterate cabin boy named Barnaby. 'Wot shall we do?' Panicking, he flung the door wide open and relayed that the vessel was teetering on the edge of a whirlpool. 'We're about to capsize and the lads are scared. The slaves are hollering and rattling their chains like caged animals. Say suppen, Cap'n.'

Senor de la Vega rescued the bottle of brandy, which was rolling on the table. 'A crew should know how to cap a leak.' He heard the captives screaming that water spirits were trying to sink the vessel. 'You ought to appease their African gods, Finlay. If I were you, I would select the least healthy of the cargo, the Jonahs, and jettison them overboard – flotsam? Call it divine inspiration from the biblical story of Jonah…'

'Something pongs in here, like a rancid camel.' Finlay rose to his feet and sniffed. 'You need a wash, lad.' He rounded on the two senior officers who dragged themselves away from civilized company and the bottle of brandy, but only after he ticked them off. 'Get off yer fat backsides, sirs.' He followed them and the cabin boy out the door, unwisely carrying a candle, while the ship continued to lurch. It was not long before he returned. 'I have a rule about candles, gentlemen, but rules are meant to be broken.'

'Given that everything is back to normal, I think I'll go for a stroll.' Curious, Senor de la Vega stood up to look out the porthole. 'I want to feel the wind in my face.'

'Should you decide to select a high-bosomed virgin to play with her brown orbs of pleasure, you are required to take three crewmen into the hold with you for health and safety reasons. Those savages are not to be trusted. Well, gentlemen, be my guest. If they happen to fall pregnant, then that's even more hands for the canefields. The more the merrier.' A grin crept across his face when two captives were ushered into the cigar-scented cabin with their heads bowed and shoulders hunched. 'A fine specimen.' He examined Kalu's gums, teeth and oval-shaped testicles. 'Take your pick, sirs, boy or girl?'

'Really.' Bridges reproved Finlay for behaving as if he were running a floating brothel. 'I do not approve.' For the lapsed Quaker, this was immoral. 'Good God.' He watched Finlay tugging at Kalu's phallus like a milkmaid. What compounded the antics was the fact that Kalu reacted by using his hands to shield his erect penis while Abeke's hands hid her pubic hair. 'With all due respect, Captain, your behaviour is abhorrent.'

'The way to punish blacks is to take their women.' The Dutchman leered at Abeke's naked breasts and fondled an erect nipple until he himself was aroused. 'We're both prisoners here, girl; me out of choice and you, well.' He gently fondled her breasts and his thoughts were stimulated by her resistance to him. Chuckling, he felt inspired to tell the men about the Bush Negroes of Surinam who had founded highly developed societies which they vigorously defended. 'As for the Maroons of Surinam and Jamaica, so long as they have women, bush meat and can worship their African ancestors, they are happy.'

'Once they accept their fate, life gets easier.' Monsieur Fontane eyed Abeke's hardened nipples and Kalu's erect penis. The sea suddenly seemed calmer. 'Amused, gentlemen?' A light breeze came through the porthole. 'We don't have all night.'

'I can feel a philosophical chat coming on,' grinned Mengis Hunter. 'He's hung like a horse.' He dredged up an alleged conversation between Samuel Johnson, the compiler of the English dictionary, and his friend, Boswell, by asking: *What right have we to make unhappy people happy? Why should we make these star-crossed lovers happy?*'

Senor Xavier de la Vega came and knelt by two black bodies on the floor. 'Faster,' he spoke with urgency. Kalu tried to perform, trembling with pent up rage. Abeke was nervous, too, making a strange sobbing sound which was interspersed with her tears. 'Faster.' The Cuban sipped Cognac and his eyes widened, as if to say, 'I know you are suffering, but we all must suffer.' Soon he was deep in thought, saying absently, 'Take Francis Barber, a happy Jamaican slave: I hear Dr Johnson plans to send him to school and will no doubt provide for him in his will. The most a white man can expect when he becomes a tenant of the grave is a pauper's burial – no funeral dirge for him.'

'I have no desire to be remembered when I fall off this mortal coil.' Finlay killed the subject of mortality and turned his attention to Kalu and Abeke. 'Let us make the most of the entertainment, gentlemen.' The double-talk continued when he bent and placed his right index finger in Abeke's mouth. 'Suck on this! A little encouragement is all you need. We don't have all night, wench. I've not tried her for size, gentlemen, but I wager she's a virgin – nice and tight.'

'I am not going to be sorry for anything tonight, Dr Bridges.' The Portuguese, a sly man with a bony face, smothered a laugh when Abeke began to sob. 'If you'd rather not look, why not go on deck? I think the problem for you is that slaves cease to be humans to us whites and are valued as commodity. There are some obvious benefits for master and slave: pleasure for one; rewards for the other.' Leering at Abeke's legs spread wide apart as she lay on her back, he recalled how one of his slaves had deliberately starved herself to death. He was still furious, having lost a fortune when his best sex worker took her life. 'I like my wenches to be buxom, sweaty and sensuous. Ooh! I shall let you enjoy.'

'I'm sure I shall,' Finlay said, while the merchants ignored Bridges. 'Let's not over-dramatize things, Sawney.' He urged Kalu and Abeke to move slowly, sensually and expressively. 'Gentlemen, like the arrival of frost, they are bound to come, eventually.'

* * *

The challenges that the captives faced had overwhelmed Bayo. She was terrified of the crew, whose job was to provide the Africans with two meals per day: breakfast and supper. They were being fed on deck. Bayo glanced at Bami, whose leg irons were removed from his festering ankles. She had been raped repeatedly and had given up all hope of freedom. On her sixteenth birthday, she had rejected a good marriage proposal that her father had arranged with a wealthy chief. She had been waiting for Bami to approach her father.

They were six weeks into the journey. Bayo was doing her best to obey orders, but every piece of instruction simply liquidized in her head. Before her lay a mighty wilderness of sea and a never-ending sky whose fluffy clouds occupied those who were locked in a prison of despair. They barely had enough to eat and it was a constant battle to stay awake on deck. Bayo missed her father's commanding presence and rued the way she had questioned his authority in the presence of his wives and her mother, who sometimes used to chide her husband, *What would you do if I were a dog, Oba, kick me?* While she was reflecting on her parents' polygamous marriage, two bare-chested sailors got into a fight and were egged on by the crew. Even as they threw punches, the hard-drinking sailors kept an eye out for trouble, accustomed as they were to fights.

'Feeding time in the monkey house.' An eagle-eyed sailor with pierced ears spat while handing out stale biscuits. 'Varmints.' The ship was low on food and part of his duty was to feed the captives, who were brought on deck in small groups so as not to overwhelm the crew by sheer force of numbers when their leg irons were removed to allow for a bout of physical activity. 'Lift yer effin' feet 'fore I take the whip to yer black backs. Go on, show us yer titties 'fore I put a hot poker up your arse, girl. You there, come here. I want a quickie.'

'Keep your hands to yourself,' admonished Bridges, pausing to look at a group of underfed children being force-fed grain to bulk up their bodies in preparation for the auction block awaiting them beyond the ocean crossing. Faltering, he stopped to examine an adolescent rape victim who was haemorrhaging in agony. He said absently, 'This is inhumanely cruel, but it will come to an end, one way or another.'

* * *

The weeks of abuse had left Bayo feeling worthless. Staring blankly into the vast ocean, she made her way to an unmanned area but was accosted by the eagle-eyed sailor who began to grind his groin into her. Not for the first time, he threw her down, straddled her and grabbed her crotch. She had longed for the day when she and Bami would marry but could not meet his eyes now. Sated, the known paedophile pulled up his breeches and moved on, not noticing that she had climbed the ropes. The 'quickie' had been witnessed by the other captives, some of whom were alerted by her screams and wished it was a figment of their fevered imaginations.

'We shall meet again in the next life, my love.' On the verge of tears, Bami's eyes flashed anger when he saw the crew pointing. Surrounded by sharks that were in no hurry to begin the feeding frenzy, Bayo thrashed about in the water frantically when a whale began to circle the sharks. Seeing this, Bami's lips trembled, for he had suffered the indignity of being forced to watch her being raped repeatedly and now, powerless, her screams caused him to turn away. 'Devils.' In recent days, he had barely slept, reliving the rape scenes in his dreams. 'I shall avenge you, my love.'

'Don't try anything or I'll cut you down, naga.' Finlay stood at the helm of the ship. 'That is an amusing sight, gentlemen.' Curiosity got the better of him and he leaned over the side of the ship, observing the unmistakable outline of a woman thrashing about in the water. A shiver of sharks began to fight over their prized possession. This scene triggered a sequence of events that would cause chaos on the deck. 'Gentlemen, please go below for your own safety. If you remain on deck, it is at your own risk.'

'Yemaya, Mother of Mercy, help her!' Bami, advancing slowly across the deck, cried out in Yoruba, 'Blood for blood!' For a moment, Bayo's voice caused him to stiffen. Furious, the other captives flew into a rage when they heard her blood-curdling screams. Ever since they were taken, Bami had thought of his father and hoped to return home one day. 'If I must live, let it be as a free man or die a warrior's death.' Without hesitation, he broke away from a group of young men, still in chains, and sprinted across the deck at full speed. 'I am a dead man, my brothers.'

'I want that naga strung up,' Finlay thundered, whipping out a pistol. Deftly, he whirled round and fired a warning shot into the air while Bami was frogmarched across the deck. 'String him up at once, lads.' A few minutes later, a bullet nipped Bami's left ear. The scene turned even uglier when the rebel was placed on a wooden block and a noose put around his neck. Finlay kicked the block aside, for he sensed that the threat against the ship's crew was about to get worse. Bami's pink tongue seemed to be lolling. 'That naga was a leading light.'

'This is a tragic loss, Captain.' Bridges pointed out that tensions between the Africans and the crew had reached a plateau. 'Tragic.' There, the matter might have ended, except that Bami took on a heroic dimension: he challenged his white oppressors and was in no hurry to depart this world, hanging from the gallows with his eyes bulging. 'For the love of God, there must be another way to punish the poor soul, Captain.'

'Gentlemen, make your way below deck!' Finlay returned the pistol to his belt, looking up at the figure of the half-dead rebel. 'I ought to put you on latrine duty, Bridges. I never thought I'd see the day when a white man on a slaver would take the side of the nagas. That savage on the gallows is a benign influence. I must make an example of him. It wouldn't surprise me if he encouraged that stinking whore to jump overboard.'

'Shut yer effin' cake 'oles, nagas.' The bent-nosed sailor was taken aback when a loud roar rend the skies. 'The blacks are up in arms!' Quite quickly, panic gripped the deck when the captives banded together and began trading blows with the crew. 'They sound like a bunch of warring chimpanzees, Cap'n.' A pistol was discharged and the bang caused the women to scatter. 'Stand back!' The bent-nosed sailor spat. 'Nagas.'

Anger and disbelief gripped the one-breasted Layla, who was no longer the young firebrand she once was. 'Show no fear, little ones.' Her face had been scrubbed clean and her cheeks resembled an orange peel. Something like pandemonium broke out when a knife-thrower flung a blade at Bami's chest. Always quick to hug a fretful child, Layla calmed the gathering children. She sat down and cradled a small boy-child whose mother had died of gastroenteritis during the night. 'Hush, my son.'

'If you say another word, I'll kick you so hard you'll never get up, whore.' Very rapidly, the scene escalated. 'Back them into a corner, lads.' Finlay now armed the crew with cutlasses, clubs and pistols. 'I want that Amazon whipped for insolence.' This had a dramatic effect on the young warriors, who raised their fists in defiance of their oppressors. 'I'm taking that naga out!' A musket ball hit Bami in the right temple. Everything went quiet when the lynching rope broke under his weight and the hanging post toppled. 'What is this? The revolt of the ape-men?'

'They are obviously in shock, Captain.' Bridges, the peace-maker, found himself pitched headlong into the mayhem of a revolt. 'The girl committed suicide and her lover was, understandably, upset.' A large proportion of the Africans had wanted revenge but he had talked them into calming down. The day before, he had gone down into the hold to examine a sickly female; she had slipped out of the world during the night. He was conscious that the sailors feared being overpowered; hence, they kept the physically stronger males shackled and manacled.

'Feckin' fool.' Finlay spun round on his heels to face Bridges. 'I ought to put you in irons, idiot. Those nagas are listed as commodities; they have no rights.' He whipped out his knife as an extra precaution. 'Feed that big black buck to the fish, lads. Let me gut him first. I want that one-breasted *cunt* flogged to put the fear of God in those *piccaninnies*.'

'I'll 'ave yer guts for garters.' An ill-tempered sailor, sporting two panda eyes from a drunken brawl the night before, approached a group of young warriors whom he thought might be about to rush him. 'I'll bash yer feckin' 'eads in, nagas. Oi, you! Get on yer knees, you feckin' *cunt*.' The ugly mood spread across the deck when the backlash began. 'String up that one-tit cow, lads. She's the ugliest *cunt* I've ever seen. Get 'er, lads.'

'Have no fear.' Layla stared back at him and her eyes were filled with contempt. 'Hush.' The children bunched into a desperate circle around her. 'Show no fear.'

'Aieee!' cried a small man, Little Titch, holding a club in his right hand. The Africans, chained at the ankles, watched while Finlay gutted Bami. Incensed by this violence, five men refused to back down. They rushed Finlay but the crew bludgeoned them to death. Blood splattered across the deck and the children were terrified. Bewildered, Monifa's shoulders slumped and she peed herself. Meantime, Little Titch spat at Kalu. 'If you know what's good for you, monkey-man, back away or I'll ram my club up yer arse. Hey, lads! Fancy a piece of black arse?'

* * *

After the incident on deck was contained, the captives were subjected to intense scrutiny and strict discipline. Jittery, Captain Finlay exercised greater control over the kidnapped Africans, for he and the crew were convinced that the captives were plotting another shipboard revolt. The changes involved forcing them to stand in silence on deck for up to eight hours. Then, for ten days, during persistently heavy rainfall, they were confined below deck where the men were made to clean the hold daily. This decision caused apoplexy among the Africans and further demoralisation. Meanwhile, the adolescent girls and boys were abused on deck at nightfall.

* * *

On the eleventh day, they returned to the deck under supervision. Moving to the sound of drumbeats, the starving captives were forced to throw their arms above their heads, run up and down and jump at the crack of a whip. Their hunger pangs increased and the children could no longer stand up. Most of them fainted where they stood; others crumpled into heaps. While this was going on, the clouds gave way to a gust of wind and rainfall, which appeared like a supernatural storm. After several stomach-churning hours in the hold, the adults lay trussed up in the bowel of the ship where they tried to stay calm. The more optimistic fantasised about land, or seeing the morning dew or hearing birds singing at dawn.

'Their lives were cut short.' Layla had felt helpless whilst watching Bami die in agony on the day of Bayo's suicide. 'But we are survivors.' The hold seemed divided on the issue of mass suicide, causing her to argue, 'If we take our lives, who will tell our story? Today we could be planting a seed that bears fruit in the future. Remember the children.'

The storm had abated and there was an energy in the foul air, coming from the seawater and seeping between the planks in the belly of the hold. 'What are we?' asked a former middleman (slave trader) who was keen to stage a mutiny. Not thinking through the logistics of seizing a ship and navigating it back to where they had come from, Kalu's bodyguards were enthusiastic until he himself opposed the idea. In a heated exchange, he argued that Finlay was never without a pistol and they were ill-equipped to overthrow the crew. Not enjoying poetic justice for his part in the enslavement of his fellow Africans, the former slave trader muttered, 'I should have killed you when we were on the road.'

'You should have.' The violence on deck exacerbated Kalu's anger; he had seen family and friends murdered and abused. Pensive, he found himself in disagreement with his peers who planned to seize the ship. In the stinking hold, the built-up effluvia gave off an obnoxious smell, causing the children to vomit. The pregnant women were in danger of being asphyxiated. With flies laying eggs in sores, the men raged that the excrement was bad for their health and plotted to seize the ship. 'They are armed,' Kalu said, trying to placate the young men. 'Listen.' He rolled his eyes upwards towards the deck where the sailors were firing random shots into the air. The irony was that threats of physical violence no longer terrified men who were dispossessed, caged and easily aggravated. 'If we seize the ship, we cannot navigate our way home,' Kalu argued in Yoruba. 'The whites are fully armed and equipped to defend themselves.'

Ayo, one of Chief Jumoke's wives, sobbed. 'Even the rats have more freedom.' She was now in the second trimester of pregnancy and kept scaring the children by insisting that those who had sickened and died were being sacrificed to the sea gods. 'Where are we?'

'Somewhere at sea,' replied Layla, who was born in Saudi Arabia where she had lived in a mud brick house within a courtyard. Harking back to her harrowing past, without divulging too much, she tried to lift the children's morale by telling them stories from the *Arabian Nights*: Sinbad sailing the Seven Seas to find his lost money, meeting one-eyed Cyclops and fire-breathing dragons on the journey. As the night wore on, she embellished her stories to strengthen the weak and the dying, telling them how she had defied her Arab master who sold her twelve children and hired her as a wet-nurse to a rich family. In protest at being used like a dairy cow, she deliberately cut off one of her breasts and ran away. Unluckily for her, she was captured and sold by Arab slave traders. 'Our children must live! Some of the sickly ones have been thrown overboard, eaten by sharks. The others must live to tell our story in their own words.'

Kalu tried to pacify the aggrieved voices. 'We will not die,' he insisted. 'If we are to survive this ordeal, we must accept this new reality.' The air was punctuated by the shrieks and screams of those who could not manage their emotions. 'We must not be impulsive.'

'You are wise, my son.' Coughing up phlegm, Layla reflected, 'We are like ghosts walking in the footsteps of other ghosts, those who have gone ahead of us.' Their physical reality was intolerable and, for her, one of the most alarming things was the daily violence. Despite the stench and cries of despair, she kept telling the children stories. 'I shall tell you the one about Mansa Musa, the richest man who ever lived.' She could vividly imagine the African ruler on his way to Mecca with gifts of gold. 'He was Emperor of the Mali Empire some four hundred years ago...'

'*How the mighty have fallen.*' Ayo, not caring to hear about a dead emperor, tried to resurrect the rivalry between her and Olafemi. 'My Oba and his favourite wife are dead. Their son has lost his *oko*, the man with an *obo*.' The allusion to the loss of Kalu's manhood touched a chord. 'You have become a woman, *obo*; you are like a barren woman.'

'My mother,' Kalu spoke softly, reflecting on how quickly the fabric of their lives had been ripped apart, 'you have a man-child in your belly. Do not distress yourself on my account. I am weak today but, one day, I shall tell the white devils how much I despise them.'

'My sister,' Layla tried to offer Ayo a glimmer of hope, 'you will have a man-child to hold, a son to cherish you when you are old and grey. You will be remembered.'

This idea of Kalu being an *obo* was met with derision by the men. They began to attack Ayo verbally, grunting, muttering and flinging insults at her in their floating prison. Even as they silenced female anger, they could not, however, forget for long that Bami and six of their shipmates had been murdered and thrown overboard to feed the sharks.

'You are a leader of men. You were born for this task.' Layla looked across at Kalu in the dark, saying the voyage had gone from crisis to crisis. 'One day, you will become a legend. Your name will be on many people's lips for generations to come.' She bowed her head and wept, releasing the tension. 'Whai-o! They are sucking Africa's breasts dry.'

'You are a strong woman.' Kalu returned the compliment. 'You must not break down.' He reminded her that even after a long day

106

cooped up, she still had a story to tell them and a smile for the children, especially the younger ones. 'Who will keep us from misbehaving? You are doing something important for others, my mother.'

'My son, you are wise and humble for your age and stature.' Layla reflected, 'You kept your head and dignity under extreme provocation from those white devils.'

'There is always a guard loitering outside this prison, my mother.' The unelected leader, Kalu stared at the darkness all around them, sniffing the nauseous odours of excrement and bodily fluids. 'Stay alive, my brothers. We shall live to fight another day.'

'You are pitiful.' Ayo, who had a severe form of nausea, vomited over the person next to her, and not for the first time. 'They have taken away your right to enjoy your life with your family and you talk about restraint!' After the rant, she became hysterical and began to invoke Chief Jumoke. 'Oba-o! Come see! Your son has a coward's heart.'

'My mother, you will live to deliver a live boy-child and to see your grandchildren,' Kalu said encouragingly, dropping a hint about her last miscarriage. 'What if I were to die?' He reawakened her secret desire to see him killed on a hunting trip. It was a reminder of how lethal the rivalry between his own mother's co-wives had been. 'Tell me, who would carry on your husband's name?'

'Why would any woman want to bring a child into an unknown world, fool?' The speaker was Sisi, Chief Jumoke's tenth wife. 'My sisters, I would rather feed salt to my babies before I let those white devils chain them up like animals and sell them to anyone.' The disgruntled woman made a gesture that those around her understood, rolling her eyes up to the deck. 'Kalu, my son, your sister will become a wandering spirit.'

'It is a lie,' Kalu replied defensively, experiencing flashbacks of a hysterical Bayo being circled by a shiver of sharks. 'You lie.' He loved his half-sister with an affection that was otherwise reserved only for his parents and Monifa. The white slavers had decimated his family and with it, a lethal lesson had been learnt. 'It is half-true. I am certain she is with her mother, Aduke. She is no wandering spirit.' All he could see was the road behind him strewn with black bodies chained together: innocent victims killed, maimed or injured. 'Yemaya, Mother of Mercy, will guide her steps to the ancestors.'

'You talk like you know everything,' Ayo said with spirit. 'You know nothing, boy!'

'He is his father's son, Ayo.' Just days ago, Sisi dreamed of a tyrant with two hairy testicles for cheeks. 'Our Oba was a stubborn man.' The images of Chief Jumoke, Aduke and Olafemi in former days haunted her. 'The *agbalumo* never falls far from the tree.'

'You are right, my mother.' Kalu swallowed his pride with a smile. 'I do not know everything.' Fortunately, he was accustomed to his father's wives disparaging his mother, who would politely ignore her rivals and go about her business with humility. 'Better give your mouth a rest before you bite your tongue.' He was no longer in his father's compound and was not obliged to be a gentleman. 'Once you stop feeling sorry for yourself, you might want to help the girl-children.' He sniffed the foul air in the dirty hold and thought then that he would never be clean again. 'They have lost their innocence, poor things.'

* * *

When day broke in December 1765, the pale rays of morning belied the fact that a roasting sun would soon penetrate the clouds. Within the hour, the *African Empress* had sighted a large bank of sand, which was known as the Pedro Keys. A host of birds and frothing waves indicated that they were approaching the coast of Jamaica. At 6am, the vessel sighted land when what had resembled low-lying clouds in the early morning light turned out to be the Blue Mountains. Soon the mist thinned and the anchor chain rattled ominously. Expectant tropical birds and vultures circled the stinking ship as it sailed towards the Port of Kingston, which boasted fourteen piers with numerous ships berthed there. The journey from West Africa to the West Indies had taken ten weeks.

'Land ahoy!' Jim, the googly-eyed joker, shouted at the top of his lungs, feeling important in bringing his tidings. 'The land of wood and water: Jamaica.' It was usually a treat for him to go ashore and drink a tankard of English ale upon arrival. 'Land ahoy!'

While the captives were dozing in the hold at dawn, for none among them ever slept deeply or for more than three hours, a slither of light came through the portholes into the floating prison. At the mention of land, Monifa awoke and turned her face to the light. She sniffed the distinctive smell of faeces on the air around her person. In the half-light of morning, it was possible to see the pain, anger and sadness etched in the faces around her as she listened to a babel of voices, moaning and groaning. Even before they had reached Jamaica, a bilingual community had sprung up around her in the hold.

'A man's time on earth is short but his influence lives on in his bloodline, if he is lucky.' After being cooped up in their floating prison for weeks, Layla, who had completed her morning prayers in Arabic, lay on her back in a dry-eyed state of misery. 'Land at last.' She had developed respiratory problems and breathed erratically, saying, 'Allah be praised.' After the shipboard revolt, she had taken Monifa under her wing and now she proceeded to mull over a fortuitous dream. 'Monifa means I am lucky,' she spoke softly. 'We all grow up and change, my daughter. Never lose sight of who you are. Some day, you will meet your brother again, by chance, *inshallah*. Remember, some people see further than others.'

'I see the past. They came like thieves in the night and have brought us to this strange land with only what we carry in our heads.' Kalu tried to focus on the future. 'My father's bloodline is all that matters.'

* * *

Whooping and huzzaing, the sailors were in high spirits on deck when they spotted the Blue Mountains rising out of the blue sea. They had given this moment a great deal of thought. In their imaginations, what occupied their internal lives was the prospect of setting foot on dry land and wenching in the waterfront taverns. Rays of sunlight came into the portholes below the scrubbed deck of the *African Empress*. As the vessel approached the harbour after weeks of death and degradation, the air of anxiety among the Africans intensified when they imagined the horrors that awaited them. A delirious Carib grackle bird, meantime, collided with one of the sails and dropped dead on deck.

As the ship's anchor was lowered, there was a sense of anticipation in the air. When the first fifty Africans emerged from the hold, their black bodies had gone through a rapid transformation in a matter of hours. Scrubbed clean with loofahs, which Captain Finlay had kept for that very occasion, and shining with palm oil, six half-starved warriors immediately, but unsuccessfully, tried to jump overboard. Quick on the draw, Finlay had fired his pistol into the air. Terror and panic overwhelmed at least a dozen pregnant females, who were bodily carried off the ship; their muscles had atrophied in the cramped hold and they could barely walk.

When Chief Jumoke's six co-wives had recovered from the shock of the pistol shot and discovered that there were no man-eating giants in Jamaica, they began to ululate with their tongues moving rapidly in their mouths. The elation of arrival had overwhelmed Ayo, who stood on the deck spitting and cupping her pregnant stomach with both hands. Her first glimpse of Jamaica was to be her last, for she was in transit to Cuba.

'Jamaica once belonged to Spain.' Senor Xavier de la Vega smiled. 'Columbus named it Isla de Santiago.' The Cuban, having reserved Ayo and fifty Africans, turned to the Frenchman. 'Come to Havana as my guest. If you think this is anything remarkable, wait 'til you see the ships sailing between the Pillars of El Morrow and La Punta into Havana Harbour. You will see the fortress of rock topped with its scarlet and gold banner, welcoming you to Havana, and slaves being marched through the street.'

'I shall find myself a tavern and a pretty mulatto wench,' said the Portuguese to the Dutchman, urging him to visit Brazil at the earliest convenience. 'Be my guest.' He had earmarked Layla and five of Chief Jumoke's co-wives. 'Come to Brazil with me, Senhor Wolff. Who knows, you might decide to buy a silver or copper mine and settle there.'

'You're finally in your place, Bridges, and I'm keeping you there.' Finlay, in good spirits upon arrival, believed that the surgeon had healed himself and would pose no further trouble. 'Gentlemen, I advise you to invest your money in stocks and shares in the City of London. I have a great deal of respect for stockbrokers.' He kept his eye on Bridges, who had ceased to preach about the rights of man since the unsuccessful slave revolt. 'Your investments will be *as safe as the Bank of England*, gentlemen. Why, some of the governors have invested in the trade.'

'I shall take another look in the hold, Captain.' Monsieur Fontane extended his right hand in friendship. 'Don't forget to ask the agent to let me have a bill of sale.' He peeped through the grate down into the hold where Kalu was consoling a child in fetters. 'There's something quintessentially African about that buck. He is proud, handsome and has the advantage of a good, strong body. That child, she has the same manner and bearing.'

'Are you sure you want to buy her, Monsieur Fontane? She does not follow orders.' Wrinkling up his nose, Finlay peered into the hold and cast an eye over the stragglers. 'I'm quite happy to scramble her in Port Maria with the other rejects. She is trouble, a wild one.'

* * *

'Mama-o!' Seeing Kalu's face, Monifa began to yelp in the hold. 'Mama-o!' Between sobs, she tried to recall and memorise every tiny detail of the life she had left in Africa, including the last time her father had called her his 'honorary son.' From an early age, she had looked up to her big brother and had expected him to become a king one day. She remembered the day their father presented a man-child to his people; it was a market day. She was grateful for the memory and longed to see him. 'Babajide, help me. Baba-o!'

'You are behaving like a weak girl-child.' Kalu crouched down, patted her head and said, 'If you are to survive this ordeal, you must behave like my honorary brother.'

'I am not a man-child!' Monifa sank to her knees in chains and clasped her outstretched hands, as if to say to the world and those watching, *Am I not a girl-child and a sister*? She continued staring up at him, weeping and wailing. 'Will we ever see our home again, my brother? We must remember not to forget what they have done to us.'

'They will try to rid us of our past.' Kalu attempted to memorise every detail of his life at home. 'But our children's children will avenge us.' When he was a boy, his father told him stories of the sturdy mounted warriors of Mali and the sinuous bronzes of the Ivory Coast. He had been indoctrinated into the clan and would have been fearless in battle. 'Oh, why did I not hear them come?' Though many had foreseen the coming of the white men, they struck with speed and precision when they came; they had identified a weak point in the defences around the compound. 'Stay strong, my honorary brother.' Taken by surprise, the warriors were unable to respond quickly enough and had lost their freedom. A woman laughed hysterically in the hold. Kalu stood upright. '*Odabo.*'

For the stragglers left behind, there was despair and despondency. 'Come back, Auntie Layla. Help me!' Still kneeling, Monifa's heart thumped with fear. 'I want you to be my other mother.' The light had gone out of Layla's eyes when she told Monifa that she herself would not live another year in the West Indies: her lungs were filling up with' fluid. Grief-stricken, the child rattled her chains. 'Don't leave me here, my brother!' The scene of their parting seeped into her consciousness. 'They have killed us, Babajide.'

'He is with the ancestors.' By now Kalu was burning with rage. The raid on their father's compound had happened so fast. On the field of battle, he would have fought with skill, courage and determination. 'The great Yemaya will not forsake us, my sister.' Looking over his shoulder one last time before making his way up to the deck, he realised that resistance was futile and surrendered to his fate. 'Keep our stories alive. Tell them to your children and grandchildren. We will meet again in this world; that I promise you.'

The triumph that the crew felt, mastering the waves, was not shared by the Africans whose ordeal, for most of them, would persist until the day they could no longer work. The vengeful sun hovered ominously over the harbour, which stood on the brink of a bustling bay at least a mile long. The seafront was teeming with European ships coming from Africa and *Jamaica packets* sailing to Britain, some taking expatriate planter families back home.

'This flesh for cash business makes slaves of us all, boy.' Finlay had spent three weeks studying Kalu's gait and mannerisms because he was conscious of his great inner strength. Standing on deck beside Bridges, he turned his voice on Kalu, 'Move it, boy! You were the last to board and you're the last to disembark. You there, eff off, whore!'

'Toosh!' Half-naked and sapped of energy, Layla spat in the air and walked down the gangway. Meanwhile, five of Chief Jumoke's wives began to weep on seeing the ship that would take them to Brazil, away from the fictive kinship which had sprung up on board between the captives. Cooped up in a slave ship for so many weeks, Layla's legs buckled. They were all ill-prepared for this stretch of the journey and sat down, following Layla's lead. 'Toosh!'

'Get up, monkeys,' came the order from a cock-eyed sailor on the ship's deck. 'Move it.'

'They own us.' Layla got to her feet, bizarrely imagining frothing snails. 'We are property.' Dehydrated and deteriorating, she stood for a second on the gangway, looking back at the ship. The anguished mother of twelve children, all sold to Arab traders, knew from the moment they arrived that her purpose had been fulfilled: she had been their surrogate mother and storyteller, too. 'Your friend Bami came last night, my son; he said you shall gain your freedom very soon. You will get three opportunities to win your freedom on the road, and very soon: water, snake and…'

'I hear you, my mother.' At the end of the slippery gangway, Kalu was surprised to see how fast she had declined. 'You must look after yourself, my mother.' She seemed delirious, laughing with the kind of lunatic laugher that the kidnapped Africans had grown used to in the airless hold. 'If I had not fallen asleep that night, the white men would not have invaded my father's compound and I would not be a slave. That was my costliest mistake.'

Weeks of living in the squalid hell had taken its toll on Layla's health. 'Your time will come, my son.' A shattered and hailing Layla breathed heavily, straining every nerve to keep body and soul going. For days and nights on end, she had barely slept and was near collapse as she allowed her eyes to wander. Kingston Wharf was a hive of all kinds of activity: scores of brown prostitutes had come down from the outskirts of the city to make money for their white mistresses. A few carried wicker baskets of livestock on their heads while others carried granadillas, pineapples, papayas and flowers in neat baskets. 'It takes one man with self-confidence and determination to lead an army.'

'He was almost a godlike figure in his father's compound.' Sisi, Chief Jumoke's tenth wife, interrupted Layla. It was then that she saw Monifa walking the plank to board another ship. 'My honorary son, you are a weak girl-child.' For a fleeting moment, she recalled how she and Aduke, the first wife, had conspired together to poison Abim's only son. Laughing out loud, she cackled, 'There he is, eh-eh-eh-eh, Prince Kalu in chains.'

The crack of the whip sent chills through Kalu, whose eyes met Abeke's beyond the gangway. 'Stay connected to our source, my sister.' Last night, he had dreamt of hundreds of black flying insects; they resembled ladybirds without red spots. They had flown out of the ship's portholes and scattered in all directions. He took one step at a time before walking on shaky legs. 'I will find you, Abeke.' Aboard the *African Empress*, a sailor tread carefully across two planks and boarded a French ship waiting to take its cargo on to St Domingue. Kalu called to Monifa, 'Remember me, my honorary brother.'

* * *

'Thank God we're back to a safe position: dry land.' Finlay walked down the gangway, cocking his pistol out of habit; he was being extra cautious and was ready for an assault. 'Bridges, you and I are going ashore to sit on the cushion of advantage at The Catt & Fiddle and drink our fill of ale.' The stench around him was intolerable. 'Well, this is *the whore of Babylon*: Jamaica.' He walked slowly, advising Bridges not to rush things but to find his sea legs slowly. 'King Sugar is her master.'

'Jamaica, the fairest isle.' Bridges fished out a handkerchief and wiped his perspiring face before blowing the rising dust out of his nostrils. 'This heat is intolerable.' They skirted through the throngs of shackled Africans, unemployed sailors, well-dressed planters and prosperous merchants. 'Aha! The upstart Kingston, new capital of Jamaica.'

Finlay replied without hesitating, 'When we get to the Catt & Fiddle, don't go spouting rubbish about Spanish Town being the old capital.' He gave a perfunctory wave to the storekeepers outside their shops along the wharf. 'There's a bath waiting at Mrs Limehouse's inn. I smell like a ram goat.' He waved when a prostitute approached with a child in her arms, calling him *Good-time Finlay*. 'Tell Mrs Limehouse I've got company. I want a cool bed, two bunks and a blowsy wench to wash our dirty socks and underwear. Off you go, Evadne.'

'Good heavens, a half-breed.' Bridges turned his gaze to a johncrow perched on a horse's rump, attracted by the stench of fish guts and horse dung. 'It's hanging its head as if it's ashamed of its filthy ways.' Presently, a carriage pulled up by the quayside, depositing Duncan Foulkes and two associates: Messrs. Grandison and Cameron. The men were teaching him the ropes, eager to be in the thick of the scramble. Bridges squinted. 'Why are they hurrying? They don't look as if they're sailing today.'

'You'll understand the upstart Kingston better when you're at your most selfish. They're off to the auction house to get the best blacks before they're carted off to the hinterland, rugged terrain.' Finlay licked his lips in the burning sun. 'Jamaica is a bed of vice: wenches! I advise you to grab a beaver and eat some bearded clam before we sail.'

'A beaver?' Bridges observed two elderly ladies stepping down from a British-made crested carriage. 'I say, that *Jamaica packet* is ready to sail.' The ladies' small companion put his head outside the door, showing his dark face and the white of his eyes. 'If I had their money, I'd have my portrait painted with a Negro page posing by my side.' He watched the well-dressed boy boarding the ship. 'He has a Glaswegian accent.'

* * *

On the afternoon of 31 December, the *African Empress* had sailed from Kingston to St Mary to offload the last of the captives, along with the merchant Mengis Hunter and his chattel: Kalu, his bodyguards, Abeke and a caravan of Africans. Having left Port Maria, they made their way into the rural landscape. There, Layla's message from Bami was put to the test when Kalu was faced with the first of three opportunities to win his freedom. They had stopped to rest by a river and witnessed a white man's near-drowning. Without thinking, Kalu had dived in at the deep end. Beneath the surface, he searched frantically until he got hold of the man's collar. Mengis Hunter's new overseer was now sprawled on the bank of the river. Chained, Kalu's bodyguards had dived into the water to assist him. Uncannily, three Africans and a white man lay side-by-side on the bank of the river, bringing up water and gasping for air.

'Why did he save him?' a white man in an old straw hat and boots grunted. 'Never trust a blackie.' Red-faced, he cracked a whip and the heroes stood up, spitting out water. They would soon enter the parish of St Ann, on their way to the plantation of New Hall, which would later change hands and be renamed Lafayette. Dismounting, the white man, a driver, casually walked over and coolly held a large knife to Kalu's throat. 'This one is a mountain, lads. We ought to kill him, black bastard.'

'Let him be.' The new overseer, presently drying off in the sun, urged restraint on the driver after reflection. His voice seemed to come from deep within him, hoarse and croaky from swallowing too much water. 'Don't be a fool. It's almost supernatural, isn't it?'

'Put away that knife, you idiot.' Mengis Hunter, the ruddy-faced merchant-turned-slave owner, had recently acquired the New Hall plantation, which was some miles away from Duncan Foulkes's estate, Canongate. Now, he stood on the edge of the river counting heads: this lap of the journey was a perilous one. St Ann shared a border with Trelawny, a Maroon stronghold. Hunter's eyes were everywhere. 'He's a hero today.' He gave an exasperated eye-roll. 'Help Phineas up, you fool. Can't you see he saved his life?'

It was the custom of ships' captains to fire sickly sailors and trouble-makers as soon as they arrived in port, then hire a new crew for the return to Britain. Mengis Hunter had hired six of Captain Finlay's crew. One of them was Billy, whose eyes the Africans had called hard-boiled eggs. Another had the pox and was unabashed about scratching himself. As they journeyed into the hills, the second opportunity presented itself to Kalu. Billy had picked up what resembled a twig and was instead bitten by a snake. In agony, he rolled on the ground. None of Hunter's men knew what to do. Kalu had stepped forward. Using sign language, he told Hunter to slit the hand with a knife. He then proceeded to suck out the venom. Within the hour, Kalu had saved two white men's lives.

* * *

The third incident occurred not long after when Hunter was over-whelmed by the heat after leaving the market town of Claremont. Having taken the wrong route, which took them off the beaten track to a sparsely populated village named Friendship, he stopped to allow the Africans and the horses to drink water from a spring. The old Kingston merchant took off his straw hat, washed his dusty face with the cool water and shuddered dramatically, though it was not the first time this had happened. Perspiration poured out of his bare head and he began to convulse, sending the Africans and the former sailors into a panic. At the end of a much-needed break, Kalu took this incident as a sign that Yemaya, Mother of Mercy, was guiding his footsteps as his dying mother had requested. Even though his legs were chained, his hands were free so he shuffled over to Hunter and threw himself across the convulsing Scotsman, holding down his tongue as Aduke had done. One of his father's wives had been an epileptic, so he had experience in the matter.

'Go from me, Jonah.' Mengis Hunter, now recovered after the uncanny mishaps and the seizure, bawled, 'Go!' He waved Kalu's bodyguards away too. He was disturbed by the fact that Phineas, the ex-sailor with the bent nose, had also had a near-drowning experience. The freshwater Africans believed Mami Wata tried to drown Phineas and give Mengis Hunter a seizure. Hunter replayed again the image of Kalu, legs chained, jumping into the river where the still water ran deep. His jaw had dropped when, after five minutes, three Africans emerged from the water with Phineas. Clamping his mouth over Phineas's lips, Kalu had blown into his lungs. The others took turns giving the white man a heart massage. Hunter had never seen any man hold his breath under water for that long and still manage to revive another person. He turned to Kalu, 'What manner of witchcraft is this? Go and don't come back, and take those black devils with you. Oh, go away.'

After a week of grey clouds over the *African Empress*, the sombre mood gave way to a fleeting smile. Kalu's brow furrowed. Like a collage painting, grey images brushed onto a canvas of the *African Empress*: Finlay with a pistol drawn; Bami swinging from a whipping post; Bayo climbing the ropes and jumping; crewmen beating Black men with clubs; and women and girls with their legs spread wide. He could not see Abeke in that picture.

'I will find you. I shall follow at a safe distance,' Kalu said to Abeke in Yoruba, toying with the sixth finger on his right hand. 'Yemaya, the great river goddess has answered my mother's prayers.' It was inconceivable that after so many weeks caged like a filthy animal on a stinking slaver, with a life of toil ahead, that he should gain his freedom within hours of his arrival in Jamaica. Having suffered for weeks, he fell on the ground by the river and was aware of his reflection on the water. Since the raid on his father's compound, the cascade of events had seemed unreal, and now this. He did not take his freedom lightly because others had lost their lives on the voyage and some had even lost their minds.

'Don't follow me!' Abeke spat saliva into the sky and the wind blew it back in her face. 'I am dead to the world.' On the voyage, Finlay had forced Kalu to rape her repeatedly until she had pleaded for mercy and had longed to climb the ropes and join Bayo, but she was terrified of the sharks' white teeth. For the merchants in Finlay's cabin, it was about size and stamina. The rougher Kalu performed, the more satisfying the night's entertainment. 'Go!' Abeke and Kalu looked at each other one last time, noting the sores around their ankles: the chains had cut into their flesh. 'They have killed us. I am a dead woman walking. You are a dead man. Don't look back. Don't come after me. You are a spirit. Go back, go!'

'No, we are not in the spirit world.' Powerless and relieved to be free, Kalu watched the caravan of enslaved Africans shuffling along in chains until they disappeared from view. He hardened his heart when a vision of a warrior surfaced, hanging from a whipping post on a ghost ship. 'I shall avenge you, Brother.' He stood in the sun, remembering that his friend, Bami, had said he and Abeke were made for each other. Cut adrift, Kalu sat down by the roadside: 'Yemaya, Mother of Mercy, you have guided me this far.' He picked up a handful of the red soil of St Ann, rubbed it between his palms and threw it to the wind. 'Show me a sign.' His eyes lit up and he sprang to his feet. 'Yemaya never fails.' Out of nowhere, an aged African in rags approached them at the crossroads, heading towards the parish of Trelawny: 'Welcome, Papa Legba.'

3
Canongate

Fiona was in the kitchen garden when Duncan returned from the canefields at one o'clock. For once, he was on time and this troubled her, for it often seemed that she was an option rather than a priority. Despite the initial lack of experience, she had rolled up her sleeves and dug in planting flowers, herbs and vegetables. Holding a watering can, she directed water to the soil at the base of the plants but looked up when she heard footsteps.

'That damn Lewis Hutchinson is nothing but trouble.' Duncan's success had been hard-earned. He was in a rage, stepping around a crawling caterpillar while informing her that his kinsman had assaulted a retired doctor in a boundary dispute. He was neighbourly with the English expatriate, Dr Jonathan Hutton, who had been on his way to Kingston to set sail for home when he had, it would appear, been set upon by Hutchinson.

'You're not his keeper.' Fiona, putting down the watering can, sniffed the sweet tropical flowers in the air. 'Neither are you responsible for his behaviour.' She pulled down the sun bonnet on her face and picked up her herb basket. 'Forget about that madman.' Sleep-deprived, she looked at him from lidded eyes. 'All this fuss about boundaries.'

'That Scotsman is a disgrace.' Far away from the bustling crowds in Edinburgh, Duncan admired spinach, tomatoes, lettuces and cabbages in the salad patch. Ever since they were married, he had agreed that they would work together to survive on a plantation the size of Canongate. He knew that not every woman in Scotland would choose to leave the civilized world to live in the wilds of Jamaica, even if she had grown up in a house with wet laundry hanging across the kitchen on rainy days. 'Are you really happy, wife?'

'*My cup runneth over.*' Fiona did not mean to sound patronising. 'I'm hot.' Since building the slave hospital, she had been cultivating worm grass which, when boiled, worked as a laxative, expelling oodles of worms from the children working in the fields. After receiving a bite from a black spider, on her arm, she was advised to use a poultice made with Indian arrow root. Within a week, the swelling had disappeared; hence she now cultivated Indian arrow root. She also planted velvet-bur, which was used to treat bleeding wounds and sores. 'I'm not a gentle-woman. All that tittle-tattling, sewing, embroidering and riding side saddle. Give me herbaceous borders and a vegetable patch any time.'

'You ought to wear gloves and a veil like a proper lady,' suggested Duncan, dampening her enthusiasm. 'Oh, we've been invited to a ball at Grandison Hall. I'd like you to make a special effort: perhaps a new dress and some white powder and rouge? Ask the ladies where they buy all that war paint that they put on their faces. I'm not criticising you, wife, but we must keep up appearances.'

'I need to prune those climbing roses.' Fiona, who recently had a miscarriage, noticed an army of sugar ants crawling up the side of a glass on the path. 'Please remind me to set the feet of the dining table in pans of water. These ants are everywhere.' A creole lady had suggested suspending an old wig for the ants to climb up. As they climbed, they got entangled in the hairs and exhausted themselves during the never-ending fool's errand. 'I hope you're hungry. I've made a fish pie for lunch. I've set up a table on the lawn.'

'Ah, happiness: doves and wood pigeons cooing softly in the trees.' Suspended at eye level, on a climbing rose trailing on a bamboo post, was a golden silk spider. 'Its bite is harmless,' said Duncan. At his feet, the ants carried off the carcass of a croaking lizard, whose *acccking* sound kept many people awake. 'We're missing a dozen slaves.'

'I'd like to know what Major Fitzroy-Campbell plans to do about Captain Kalu and those Maroons,' Fiona grunted and placed the basket in the crook of her right arm. 'Every couple of months, they arrive with runaways and expect you to pay up. I bet they're using the money to buy arms.' The first miscarriage had happened while she was bending down to plant a South Sea rose bush in the garden. The pain was unlike anything that she had ever known. Later, when her personal maid took the bloody pail away, she had lain in bed picturing a wobbling blob that resembled liver on a silver platter. Delirious at the time, she was convinced that it was staring at her. 'You should see the crust on that fish pie.'

'You are letting yourself go,' Duncan said insensitively and perhaps a little more forcefully than was usual, despite being conscious of his manservant in the background. 'Your place is in my bed, entertaining my guests, or presiding at the dining room table like a plantation lady.' He saw that she had gone through a recalibration of priorities but the change was not enough. 'We are part of the aristocracy of sugar and slaves, which means spending precious time with friends: hunting, fishing; shooting…'

'Sorry to cut yuh, massa.' Cassian, standing in the far corner of the garden, sniffed the aromas of thyme, mint, rosemary and escallion. 'Di *conch* blowin'. Is t'ree blow. It tellin' us t'ree slave pull foot.' The Fanti thought to himself: *What's di use of servin' di massa faithfully an' dyin' a slave?* A decade ago, he had been kidnapped and taken to Cape Coast Castle, roughly six miles from Elmina Castle. He had walked through 'the door of no return' and ended up at Canongate. As he stood there listening to his master and mistress in their private moment, he pictured the orange-tiled roof, the brick courtyard and the huge black cannons facing the Atlantic Ocean at Cape Coast Castle, a vision which he memorised the day before the ship had sailed. 'Maas Darnley callin' yuh, massa.'

'Dammit!' Duncan's voice changed tone, becoming manly and virile. 'Can't I have an hour's romp without that redhead tracking my every move?' He studied Fiona's hair: burnt copper. After all the effort she had put into baking the fish pie, he smiled when she turned and her breasts pressed against his chest. They now walked in single file along the footpath in the kitchen garden. He raised his eyebrows. 'Siesta?'

'I'll ask Happy to bring up a tray.' Fiona, caught off guard, hid the surprise on her face, looking around for her dogs and then up at the sky. The puppies were fully grown and wiser now; they kept away from the tall grass and tick-carrying animals. 'Look at those clouds. They remind me of snow heaps in the garden at home, waiting to thaw.'

'Yuh nuh 'ear di *conch*, massa?' The private conversation lasted a few minutes with pauses before Cassian gained Duncan's attention. 'Maas

Darnley callin'. It soun' urgent.' Turning away and looking subdued, he could not forget that after the wedding his master had hit him in the face for scaring the mistress, leaving him with a blackened front tooth. Since then, whenever Fiona approached him, he kept his distance from her for fear of losing his front teeth entirely. 'Yuh 'ave yuh lunch an' a nap, massa. I'll 'elp Maas Darnley an' di odders search fi dose runaways, freshwater Africans. Dem nuh season yet.'

'You have my permission to take up arms against them, Cassian.' It was reassuring to know he could take a siesta, leaving his valiant overseer and manservant to capture his runaway property. 'I've earned an afternoon off.' Duncan dismissed Cassian, though he was still concerned about his kinsman, Lewis Hutchinson. He knew that the white community operated on tribal lines and functioned like a tree root system, producing shoots with extreme views. 'The clock has started ticking, wife. It's time for our siesta.'

'Yes.' Fiona, eager to let go of the past, agreed but remained silent. Her transformation from impoverished Scottish crofter to wealthy plantation mistress seemed complete.

* * *

Duncan had changed his surname legally, but there was no denying that the name Hutchinson could not be easily effaced. As reports began emerging that the retired Dr Jonathan Hutton had returned from England with a metal plate fitted to his skull, after being brutally assaulted by Lewis Hutchinson, the sugar barons rushed from plantation to plantation, spreading the news that Hutton had pressed charges against Hutchinson. By this time, every mishap in the hills was blamed on the reclusive Scot, who had no precious bond with the four-nation union: Britain. Even though the authorities had known of his crimes, no one dared to venture into Edinburgh Castle for fear of being fired upon by the insane Hutchinson and his enslaved people, forced to do their master's bidding.

To make things worse for the planters, there was a general feeling that Lewis Hutchinson was invincible. Ironically, he was not a large man and no one was on first-name terms with him. The nagging question in the domestic quarters, as well as at the manly *tête-à- têtes,* was who would subdue the 'mad master of Edinburgh Castle' and finally put an end to his eccentricities? The prominent planters in the hill villages, of course, were anxious about their individual safety and fantasised about burning down the castle. At this time, Major Fitzroy-Campbell had returned home: there was talk of unrest and famine in India, where Britain had been trading since around 1600, so a lay person would have to apprehend Hutchinson. One disastrous attempt was made by a soldier named John Callendar after a group of planters had decided to serve him an arrest warrant. Strategically placed within his fortified castle, the Scot had deliberately shot and killed the young Callendar from behind a loop-holed wall.

Almost at once, with vultures swarming over the body, the planters fled Edinburgh Castle to convey the news of John Callendar's murder, spreading it all the way to Kingston. Even though Duncan was never slow to take an active role in community cohesion, he had refused to play vigilante. On the contrary, he got straight to the point when the militia had stopped at Canongate to muster support. He maintained that he would have no part in the death of a blood relation. He was now in his fifties with an angular face, though not unfriendly, and a confident stride. Most of the militia had attended his wedding and knew he had changed his surname. They disagreed with him but always enjoyed his hospitality and praised him as a model expatriate. He had made a significant contribution to the small, white minority community by hosting dinner parties and attending homecoming feasts across the island. He was also known to offer British travellers 'a cool bed' for the night.

In response, the militia accepted Duncan's recusal and agreed that Hutchinson had placed him in a difficult situation by taking up arms against the world. Besides, there was a fatalism about the whole affair. History would record that Lewis Hutchinson's reign of terror ended when an armed party stormed the castle and captured him alive.

Fiona, meantime, had quietly placed herself in purdah. At dinner parties in the lowlands of Jamaica, several theories were put forward for Hutchinson's behaviour: that madness ran in his blood; that the social leper had gone insane in an isolated corner of the empire; or worse, that he had aligned himself with the Gothic movement. Misguided ladies, who had read Horace Walpole's novel, *The Castle of Otranto*, held dinner parties where there was much theorising that Hutchinson's behaviour and his sinister fortified home mirrored the novel with its dark hidden passages and elements of madness and terror. Tales of the uncanny details of Hutchinson's home were shared by the militiamen who had ransacked the castle.

Swift to shift the blame, some readers of British literature, who had immersed themselves in graveyard poetry and Edmund Burke, argued that Lewis Hutchinson was influenced by the Gothic architecture in Edinburgh's Old Town and notions of the sublime. To relieve the boredom, the more literate and informed ladies made Hutchinson their conversation piece at their dinner tables, letting their words hang in the air for the sugar and tobacco barons' amusement. It was said that Hutchinson tormented his victims to discover if there was something more to life; that the rational victims died because they could not endure the pain inflicted on them; and that the irrational Hutchinson had gone insane, living out his life amongst ruin, decay and death. Behind this tragedy, it was easy to forget that John Callendar, a soldier, was murdered, thus avoiding the nasty business of slavery.

Although he was not easily embarrassed, Duncan appeared ill at ease wherever he went. Socially, he could not withdraw from the country club called polite society because each member depended on the goodwill of neighbours, especially during slave revolts. The last time Duncan saw Hutchinson in the overflowing courthouse, he did not feel any anger towards his flame-haired relative. While Hutchinson no longer seemed threatening, there was no mistaking the malice in the murderer's voice. Duncan had taken in every account of the trial and could not deny that his kinsman had helped him: he'd given him enough reasons to reinvent himself and strive toward respectability as a sugar baron.

When Duncan returned from the trial, he breakfasted with Darnley, the overseer, and his white men, explaining that Hutchinson had had several accomplices and was not influenced by the Gothic movement or the Edinburgh school of thought. One farmer, James Walker, had been implicated in the crimes and was tried for the murder of a yeoman named William Lickley. Over coffee, Duncan explained that dozens of watches and handkerchiefs had been found within the castle. Ironically, Hutchinson was only charged with the murder of Timothy Callendar. During the lively discussion, Duncan stated that he himself made no connection between Hutchinson and Edmund Burke's treatise on the sublime, albeit Edinburgh Castle was found to have a subterranean labyrinth. There was also talk of supernatural occurrences; that his enslaved Africans had used the skulls of the victims in *voodoo rituals*. This news did not sit well with the planters whose forebears had rejected superstition and relied on scientific facts to reach the truth.

'I wonder if anybody would care if he'd killed a naga?' Darnley, the man responsible for keeping the plantation in some semblance of order, lifted the cup of sugared coffee to his lips. 'I daresay, like most of us who've faced challenges, he left Scotland with big dreams.' He confessed that he had hoped Hutchinson's capture might provide him with a chance to lease the Edinburgh estate. '*One man's loss is another man's gain.*'

'Nagas are half-humans with light fingers; a sort of warm-blooded animal. They wake from their daily torpor to eat and shit. Sometimes they remind me of black bats huddling together in a cluster.' McPhee, the bookkeeper, resented being a lower-class white, and so he looked for subordinates to belittle. 'Take that naga, Clitus. He thinks it's okay to steal molasses from the boiling house and hates being whipped for thieving.' When McPhee arrived in Jamaica, he was the skinniest Scot in the hills. He had flesh on his bones now, but his dreams of marrying a wealthy creole heiress had withered on the vine. He dipped a hunk of bread into his sugar-laced coffee and bemoaned the fact that he was, like so many adventure seekers, a failure. 'If I wasn't needed here, I'd be at that trial every day.'

'You say they found gold watches and handkerchiefs?' McTaff, the carpenter, was in the act of lacing his black coffee with unrefined rum. 'I think I'll ride over to Bonville Pen later, to see how Dr Hutton is doing. If he's not there, I'll ride over to Lebanon Pen, the rich bastard. He owns acres of arable land but spends most of his time at his club in London.' Leaning back in the chair, he yawned widely, reflecting that Hutchinson's real crime was not inviting the lower-class white men on Canongate to the alleged all-night orgies, which were attended by a select group of white yeomen and their womenfolk. 'I hear he gave Hutton, English *twat*, a good hiding and took his sword from him. They say he boasted, *You can give my compliments to Dr Hutton and tell him I've got his sabre.*'

'They say he killed one wretch who went looking for a cool bed at dusk,' Darnley added, amused. 'When he finished with the poor sod, he put his head in the hollow trunk of a cotton tree and left it there for the vultures.' This piece of gossip had come from Minah, the mother of Darnley's children, a field hand who sat in the corner awaiting orders and cradling a feverish brown child. 'I can't say I believe all this hearsay. A year ago, he stopped me by the roadside, a stone's throw from the castle. We talked about rearing Highland cattle with wide shoulders and dosan fringes. He seemed sane enough.'

'Why should a forty-year-old, Edinburgh University-educated doctor with a sound mind go mad?' McPhee glanced with a slight grimace at the unkempt McTaff. 'If you ask me, his lazy slaves have a mistaken sense of duty. After he butchered the first white man, they should have killed him and reported it to the authorities. I blame the nagas, imbeciles.'

Darnley grunted, 'Why would any slave report his master when the law doesn't recognise him as a human? All human beings have inherent dignity and resent losing their freedom.' He picked up his hat and walked over to where his woman sat with the feverish brown child. 'Don't move.' She shook her head and he reached up, catching a spider in his hat, still picturing a lonely turret at Edinburgh Castle. 'In years to come, people will sing ballads about Lewis Hutchinson and his happy nagas, but we'll be forgotten. Remarkable.'

'I doubt it.' Duncan stood up and ignored the enslaved woman in the far corner, inured to a pervasive smell of body odour and stale cabbage. 'They'll be talking about those blasted Maroons instead.' He had tried to befriend Hutchinson without success and had been an eyewitness to John Callander's murder, which was mentioned in the court papers. 'McTaff, you need to bathe. We are having guests and I want you there. You've been commissioned to make barrels as an extra income for me. Be sure to use soap and a loofah. Need I say more?'

Darnley brought his foot down on the spider. 'If he has a commission to make barrels, he should be paid.' All of a sudden, the *conch* sounded outside. 'Oh no, not those bloody Maroons again. They're the ones carting off our slaves to Calabash Estate. If I may speak frankly, your reputation is on the line each time you welcome those animals.'

'Acht!' Canongate was not just a plantation: it fuelled Duncan's life and, as a self-made planter, he wanted to deal with the Maroons in his own way. 'Let me handle this myself.' Outside the barrack-style dwelling, about two hundred yards away, stood a group of Maroons who were adept at bush camouflage and unobtrusive withdrawals. They often snuck into Canongate at night and carried off a clutch of young women and foodstuffs. Darnley argued that a trap should be set and all female slaves should be branded with Duncan's initials: *DF*. Duncan's tone was final. 'Smile.' Walking down the steps, his own smile was firmly in place. 'What can I do for you, Captain Kalu? Do you have any tobacco, McPhee?' The captives included two wasted young men with cracked lips and bleeding bare feet. 'Are you sure they belong to Canongate, Captain? I don't recognise them.'

'I find dem in di bush.' Faced with four angry-looking white men, Captain Kalu squatted down to talk to a small boy who resembled little more than a bag of bones. He communicated in Yoruba, gently pushing him forward. 'Dis one belong to New Hall. I find 'im on di road, sick an' abandon.' Hiding behind the strapping bodyguards, a barefoot woman with bloodshot eyes seemed to have a stitch in her left side. 'Dis one is yours: Cleora.' He accepted a mug of water and fed the bony-faced boy, thinking, *Dis slave-master livin' di white man's dream at di expense of di African.* He vowed that he would never give up his freedom. 'Me nuh wahn nuh money fi 'im.' The peace pipe was being passed around. 'Maroon sign treaty 'fore mi time. Dose unjust treaty weaken di Maroon 'ands.'

'Our laws are made in England, at the Houses of Parliament. I don't expect you to understand that.' Duncan accepted the peace pipe and handed it to Darnley. 'Captain Kalu,' he began, loath to become complacent, 'on principle, I do not accept stolen goods. I will make an exception because these nagas are likely to die and are valuable property.'

'Me is a man. Me value mi life. Me wahn liv' in peace an' 'ave a *fambily* an' lan' like di white man.' Captain Kalu was relieved to find a planter like Duncan with whom he had a sort of *ad hoc* arrangement.

'Tobacco good.' He inhaled smoke, a habit that he had acquired in Jamaica. 'Me wahn a bundle of di dry leaf an' two 'ooden pipe. Me nuh like clay pipe; dem bruk too easy. Me wahn 'errin' an' saltfish 'fore me go. Weh me com' fram in Afrika, man nuh depend on white man fi supply 'im wid fish an' salt. We teach a man fi fish fi 'imself.'

'You got a lot of confidence, naga.' It wasn't long before McTaff, speaking in Gaelic, started complaining that Duncan had flung the door open to the Maroons. 'We should get some Cuban hounds and *sick 'em* on those filthy nagas.' Carpenters were in short supply in the hills, which gave him a sense of self-importance. 'You ought to send for Major Fitzroy-Campbell, or whoever is in charge at Fort George, boss. The law says nagas are property. Hop it. Go away, naga.'

'Me wahn Scotch 'errin'.' For twenty adrenalin minutes, Captain Kalu bartered with Duncan, knowing that he could not afford to show any sign of weakness. 'Me seh me wahn 'errin' an' tobacco, too.'

'I think we ought to kill 'em all,' McPhee said in Gaelic, watching anxiously. There was a suspicion that many more Maroons were waiting in the hills around Canongate for the signal to attack. 'Those nagas are half-dead and he wants us to make them better. Then, they'll runaway and he'll bring them back for a price.' There was dissatisfaction outside the unpretentious barracks, referred to as a cottage, that was built at a discreet distance away from the great house. 'This *piccaninny* here, he wants us to believe Mengis Hunter abandoned it. He takes you, an educated white man, for a fool, boss. I ought to run him down.'

'There's an Irish overseer running New Hall.' Darnley accepted the peace pipe, feeling as if he were standing between an eye-witness and an actor who refused to play *The Grateful Negro*. 'Hunter diversified from merchant to sugar and, damn, he's back home in Glasgow, parading up and down Trongate like a West Indian sugar baron.'

Without wishing to reveal his intentions, Captain Kalu addressed the skinny boy in Yoruba: 'Be patient, mi son. Stay an' dohn pull foot. One day, w'en yuh big an' strong, me will com' fi yuh.' He detested Duncan and the other whites and would have burnt Canongate to dust, but he knew the consequences. 'Yuh will be free soon, son.'

'That boy has yaws,' Smith, the mason, muttered under his breath, plagued with the sense that they were dealing with a father in the skin of a malevolent black spirit. 'This Cleora wench, why should we pay for her, boss? She's our property to buy and sell.'

'Our property?' Duncan seemed to be filtering the information. 'The big difference here is that I am the owner.' Glancing at Cleora, whose skin looked dry and ashy, he had a serious expression. 'I will not be undermined in front of a naga, carting off my property to Calabash Estate.' When he had first bought the serial runaway, Cleora, his guests remarked that there was *a certain ripeness of womanhood* about her. In the early days, he found it difficult to talk about the enslaved, as if they were property, and could not explain his distaste of blackness. Matching Captain Kalu's stare, he harrumphed, 'If she runs away again, do not bring her back. When she is better, take her as your woman; a gift from me.'

'Yuh mus' be proud o' all yuh achieve since yuh com' out 'ere, buyin' an' sellin' Black man an' ooman an' *pickney*.' Squatting on his haunches, Captain Kalu passed the pipe to Duncan and cast a flinty eye over Canongate where no one dared to say no to this wealthy Scot planter. He longed to return to his homeland; instead, he was cast adrift in a strange land. Last night, he dreamed that he was raking seaweed on a beach on a tropical island where a storm had washed his house away with Abeke trapped inside. The shame and dishonour that she had suffered at the hands of the crew on the *African Empress* lived with him day and night. Then there was his half-sister, Bayo, who was still haunting him. There were days when the journey seemed remote and unreal, especially when he pictured the leering white merchants on the *African Empress*, gratifying their cravings as voyeurs. Sneezing, his manner was distant, and the conversation abruptly died. 'We go.'

'That one is a tough, surly naga. There's no chance of separating him from his followers, boss.' McTaff, who had come to feel at ease with his black bedmate, stared at Captain Kalu and his bodyguards, long rifles and arrows slung across their backs, picturing the dirt-encrusted soles of their big feet. 'That Maroon is not just a free naga; he's a revered leader. Their rules are different from ours, boss, and that makes him dangerous.'

'I disapprove of his very existence,' Duncan said, as if to confirm the thoughts of the white men present, with his eyes still on the road. 'The way to beat your enemy is to kill him with kindness – show no anger. That's why I keep extra supplies and set aside enough petty cash. Blast! They left without the reward money and the dry goods.'

'It's a ploy, designed to lull you into a false sense of security. They'll be back.' Darnley, standing outside the cottage, blew his nostrils with his right index finger and made a guttural sound in his throat, spitting phlegm at the captives. 'Look at 'em, useless nagas. They'll die without food and medical attention. Have you seen the trotters on that Maroon leader?'

'Yes, big feet.' McTaff was anxious about the consequences if the Maroons were to raid Canongate. 'I'm going over to Edinburgh Castle later.' He watched a dozen goats chewing down the grass mechanically. 'I want to remember the real Edinburgh Castle, if possible.'

'I'll come with you.' McPhee, who still pined for home, hated the wild and inhospitable terrain surrounding Canongate. He often dreamed of initiating a love affair with one of the planters' daughters, too. 'When I was a lad, I'd stand for hours looking at Edinburgh Castle in *Auld Reekie*, marvelling at how those monarchs managed to build it on that rock.' Before he found work as a bookkeeper, he had been a fiddler, playing at weddings and parties in the lowland parishes, lustfully listening to the young ladies reading John Donne's poem, "The Flea."

'You're not thinking about those nubile young ladies' white flesh, are you?' McTaff was known for his interrogations whenever a molasses theft occurred. He'd brandish his whip and insist the Africans recount their movements until the weakest link gave up the culprit. In his drunken moments, he goaded McPhee into reciting Donne: *Mark but this flea... It sucked me first and now sucks thee...* His mind drifted to Scotch pines at home, reciting, *'And in this flea our two bloods mingled...'*

'I don't give a fig for this poetry malarkey, nonsense verse; that romantic stuff is for perfumed men with silk handkerchiefs.' Smith scratched his scalp with his dirty fingernails. 'I'd rather shag a brown wench until she oinks like a pig than listen to poetry. I'm shattered. I didn't sleep a wink last night. I can't sleep without a drop of rum.'

'Poor you. Sleep is for the righteous.' McPhee's greasy hair hung around his ears and his unshaven face was unwashed. 'Och.' Alone at night, after he had thrown his black sleeping companion out of his berth, he would lay awake waiting for sleep to carry him off but sleep often evaded him. His legs and arms were covered in tattoos of mermaids and seahorses. 'There's plenty to do today.' He had spent some time in Canada, where he met a young native woman and fell in love with body art. She had spent time at an English mission and answered to the name Maria Teresa. He missed her smooth skin and had promised her that one day he would return to find her. 'What were you saying, boss?'

* * *

As was to be expected, when Lewis Hutchinson's trial began Duncan noticed a change in the planters. He, unlike the creole planters, had come to believe that Hutchinson was affected by the dark moods that sometimes came over eccentric newcomers who tried hard to retain their individualism in a tight-knit society based on ethnic and cultural unity. This, for him, was the case with Hutchinson, and thus he made peace with the fact, even informing his brother Dougal in a letter, that their surname had been tarnished, and that Hutchinson had left one hundred pounds in gold to have a marble monument inscribed with a record of his death. The Scot even composed a pithy quote before he was hanged at Spanish Town in 1773: *Their sentence, pride and malice, I defy; Despite their power, and, like a Roman, die*

The name Lewis Hutchinson is still ringing in everyone's ears across the island, even though he went to the gallows on 16 March...I am busy planting herbs and potions to cure the slaves. Most of their ailments are due to superstition or bad habits, like gorging on worm-infested fruits, or digging holes with their bare hands and getting worm eggs under their fingernails. I cultivate wormwood grass, which is a useful medicine at Canongate. When it is boiled and used with senna pods, it sends the slaves off to sleep in the hospital.

As for the vessels I use, the calibash tree bares a fruit resembling a gourd. They are plentiful and come in various shapes and sizes. The slaves make carvings on these vessels, which they use to hold water and to drink homemade palm wine. My chief nurse is Agar, a Gold Coast old girl. She has shown me how to use the gourds as cups, bowls, plates, saucers and ladles. I'm trying to be economical and calabashes are a cheap supply of utensils. They are plentiful in the slave village, Pimento Walk. As a matter of fact, the slave quarters are surrounded by avenues of pimento, also known as allspice.

The plants in Jamaica are mostly native to the island, but some were introduced by the first colonists, the Spanish; others were added by us British. There is a plant called branched horsetail which, when dried and ground into a powder, is used to stop haemorrhage. The slaves are clumsy and accident-prone, which means they are in and out of the hospital with open, running sores. We also grow a plant called winter cherry, whose berries are yellow when ripe. This is given to the old women and pregnant slaves to reduce swelling in their hands and feet. Agar does most of the work with an assistant named Cresentia.

The watermelons are something to behold; they are giant fruits with red pulps. Agar and Cresentia squeeze the pulp, which reminds me of pink water laced with sugar. The juice is given to pregnant women in labour as it loosens the bowel. I am told that it can chill the stomach, allowing tapeworms to multiply. We have an abundance of guavas, whose outer skin is hard but the fruit within is pink with numerous seeds. Agar and Cresentia use the seeds to cure patients suffering with fluxes, or 'run belly.' They use the granadilla to cure fevers too. The white pulpy fruit cools the *patients down and relaxes them. There's also the broom weed. It functions as a broom to sweep the yard in the slave quarters, but the larger top-roots are used by the slaves as toothbrushes. The women make a bath of the leaves to cure their children of scabs – they are prone to sores that suppurate and fester.*

As for the pickney gang, they dread a reptile called a galliwasp. This scaly creature resembles a miniature crocodile and lives in rocks or in the bush. It doesn't bite unless you disturb it. The slaves go barefoot, which means they are always stepping on something. Last week, a half-drowned boy was brought into the hospital. His father explained that if someone is bitten by a galliwasp, they must reach water before the reptile or the person will die. The child was in terrible pain. We gave him a wormwood and senna draught to induce sleep. Agar cut out the teeth, which were embedded in the flesh, and used horsetail to stop the bleeding. Can you believe it? Me, Fiona McDuff, a doctress.

I will instruct our attorneys in Kingston to make continued regular payments to cover rent and expenses. I enclose £120, the proceeds from the sale of two female slaves. In future, I will send a note via Dougal in Duncan's letters (I hate writing). He will see you get it.

All my love,
Fiona.

Ten years had passed since Fiona arrived in Jamaica. Over the years, she had been put to the test on many occasions, but none more so than when she threw a glass of water over a house girl named Happy. Despite her name, Happy was anything but cheerful. She was in fact Abeke, and her son, Akin, lived with his father, Captain Kalu. The child was conceived on the *African Empress* whilst they were providing entertainment (in Captain Finlay's cabin) for the lascivious merchants, who had returned to their respective homes and were getting on with the business of making money from black ivory. When Fiona whipped Happy for insolence, the African had wagged a finger and told her to do her worst. She had said that as long as she was alive, Fiona would *never carry a child full term.*

On the day of Happy's suicide, a brass bracelet and a pottery dish filled with white stones from the riverbed at Little River were found under her bed. In her lucid moments, she had gone into a fury over being kidnapped, walking through the bush in chains with her ankles seeping blood. At times, she wished she had committed shipboard suicide. In the end, she had stolen Duncan's treasured dirk and slashed her own wrists with it. Unlike Bayo, who had spared herself the ordeal of becoming one of *the living dead*, Abeke was traumatized by the slave ship experience and had stockpiled her wounds inside her head.

'Good riddance,' Fiona said dismissively. 'Mad as a coot.' She stood in Happy's room which doubled as the attic. 'She was a strange one, creeping around, murmuring to herself at night.' She looked out at the rich canefields to the horses grazing, a view lost on the three over-worked enslaved African women who occupied the space. 'Simple, pack that fool's belongings into a sack and give them to the elderly slave women.'

'Yes, mam.' Simple, whose real name was Abutu, was an Igbo who had travelled through wooded pastures and thick forests to reach Cape Coast Castle, leaving West Africa via the 'door of no return.' She did not care for the deceased Happy who was a Yoruba. She grew tired of hearing her repeating the same old story of how her stepdaughter, Bayo, had committed suicide at sea and how a large shark had risen out of the mighty ocean and snatched the young woman away, leaving a snapping shiver of sharks in a foaming swirl. 'I gwine beg yuh *Appy* frocks dem, mistress. Poor Cleora is 'alf-naked an' she really in need of clothes. It not nice to see such a *preety* gal 'alf-naked, mistress.'

'She's troublesome, always breaking things.' Fiona, having grown up in poverty, was eternally tight-fisted and known to watch every shilling. 'She's kept naked to teach her a lesson, Simple. Next time Captain Kalu brings her back, I'll see to it she loses four toes.'

'Oh, mistress! Cleora not bad; she sick in di 'ead like Appy was.' Simple, placing her fingers over her mouth, pictured a skinny woman in chains, refusing to obey orders, wailing: *Dem kill us; we nuh 'member wi name or who wi used to be.* Simple swallowed. 'Cleora good girl. I giv' 'er *Appy* dead-an-lef' draaz dem. I was 'opin' yuh'd understan', mam.'

'Be quiet or I'll slap you.' Amidst the dust and female clutter, Fiona had a sense of self-fulfillment. 'Idiot.' She turned from the window and surveyed the room. She was optimistic about this pregnancy and felt as though her dreams were about to come true. Although she was still recovering from the shock of Happy's suicide, she felt uneasy with a new life growing within her. That morning, she had awoken from a dream: two African children stood on a ship holding money bags and anchors, weeping, *Mama-o!*

'Afternoon, massa, mistress.' Simple bowed her head and made a dash for the door. She did not fear Fiona but was usually dumbstruck in Duncan's presence.

'Where's my lunch?' Duncan stood in the doorway, playing up to Simple's fear of him and knowing that, in Fiona, he had a pair of strong female hands to help him climb his way up the social and economic ladder. The rhythm of their days was simple and largely contented. They both took pride in cultivating the land. However, he desperately wanted a son to fulfil his dreams. 'You have to draw the line. That girl is too over-familiar with you.'

'I was thinking the exact same thing.' Fiona, her eyes misting over, had told him at breakfast that she was pregnant. 'Before I went to jail for debt, I almost joined a gang of cockle pickers in Argyll. Me, mistress of Canongate. This feels like a happy dream to me.'

Dear Dougal,   *7 June 1779*

I hope this letter finds you in rude health, Brother. You will soon hear the news: HMS Glasgow caught fire in Montego Bay on the 1 June and burnt down the next day. No doubt they'll end up naming a street in Glasgow in her honour. I was, however, overjoyed to hear that you have had a letter from Cousin Iain. He did not have a good start in life, what with his mother being illegitimate. I am sorry to hear that he was transported to Tasmania for life: petty larceny and battery of his employer is inexcusable. I wish him luck with those Tasmanian devils.

Last month we had a 'petticoat rebellion' on the plantation. Fiona was overwhelmed but not harmed (she is blooming – pregnancy suits her). Six spitfires, the most troublesome wenches I have ever seen, plotted a go-slow at work. First, Rosetta, a fiery one, lost two fingers in the sugar mill. Venus, a vixen, was rendered speechless after eating dumb cane before she could be questioned about the incident. Her tongue was numb and dilated, causing her mouth to fill up with saliva. Ketty, a hot-tempered Koromantyn, set fire to the rubbish outside the boiling house and burnt her hands badly. Dido, who rarely washes her dirty feet, has chigoe under her toes and can barely walk these days. Lizzy, who ate the pulp of the green calabash fruit to induce her third abortion, stepped on shards of glass when she was questioned and has been laid up ever since. That troublesome girl is hell-bent on self-destruction. And finally Myra, whose children are riddled with the contagious yaws, walked into a wasps' nest with her arms exposed. Her lips and eyelids puffed up and her arms ballooned in size. I had them put in the stocks for malingering – viragos!

With all this talk of abolition of the slave trade, I have introduced a new initiative called 'breed and rear.' Last week, Doll, who has seven children and was given a special tartan coat, reported that a group of field slaves were planning a revolt. Darnley rounded them up and whipped them severely. Meggie, mother of seven, whispered in Fiona's ear that some of the men were planning to burn down the mill. She has been given extra food and clothing for her loyalty to us. Oh, the joys of plantation life.

Some of our superannuated slaves are burdensome and bothersome. Goldie, a hunch-backed wretch, has encouraged all the girl-children to perfume their bodies with the powdered bark of the musk wood tree, leaving them smelling like civet cats. No man will go near them – that is, our white workers. Benina, who has tribal marks on her sagging breasts and facial scarification, flew at Darnley for whipping her grandson. Piss-a-bed, who has a bladder problem, drops his trousers anywhere, anytime. His wood has shrivelled to a kernel. He seems to derive a great deal of fun from exposing himself. These troublesome old people cannot endure the whip. In any case, we need them to do the weeding.

As for the children, they are frightened of the yellow snakes that were introduced to reduce the rat population. At the first sight of a snake, the girl-children are reduced to tears. The boys catch them for their mothers, who fry the flesh as a treat: they make a good chicken substitute. I have given orders that children are not to be whipped. Doing so makes them nervous and they wet themselves. They are the future of Canongate. We need strong slaves, not weaklings.

Finally, I enclose a note for Fiona's parents; please see that they get it. I have also arranged for my attorneys in Kingston to make regular monthly remittances to you. I also enclose 20 shillings to be given to the Kirk of St Giles – my conscience clearer!

Your same,
Duncan.

There had not been a white birth in the hills since Fiona's arrival. Although she was thirty-five when she and Duncan wedded, old for a first timer, she had several miscarriages before a last minute baby arrived on 3 October 1780. The sky was overcast, buildings swayed in the south-western parishes, fires raged out of control and waves from the sea swept the coastal villages. On the day Jamaica experienced the worst hurricane of the eighteenth century, Christopher Lachlan Foulkes was wrapped in a swaddling cloth.

Unlike the neighbouring estates, cowering under threats from the Maroons who were in the throes of their last war with the Colonial Government, no fires burned on Canongate when Duncan finally christened his son in mid-December 1781. The white elite turned out, including an English planter named Thomas Thistlewood, whom Duncan had met in Westmorland. He was the talk of polite society, for he lived with an enslaved African named Phibbah. He was in the act of sharing gossip: a Mrs Blake had allegedly said that, *Mr. John Rodon's mother is kept by a Negro man and has several Mulatto children.*

'I'm afraid this must be a terrible bore for you right now,' Darnley said laughingly. 'So, you've got a marble-covered diary, or two? I daresay they're full of dark secrets.'

Thistlewood, whose mixed-race son, John, died mysteriously on 7 September 1780, raised a glass. 'One day, my diaries will provide a first-hand account of slavery.' The tall Englishman offended the ladies present when he spoke unguardedly, disclosing that a planter named Mr Cope had kicked his wife out of his bed and slept unabashedly with *girls of 8 or 9 years...*

Duncan cut a dignified figure at the table. 'Gentlemen, there are ladies present.' But despite his clear disapproval, Thistlewood was unfazed. 'Reporting bad behaviour is crass, man.'

'Perhaps it's because he's lived with nagas so long.' Mrs Grandison put on her shoes beneath the table. 'A wee bit of gossip never hurts.' Years ago, she had suspected that her husband had been sleeping with a thirteen-year-old house girl but did not have the courage to confront him. 'Oh dear, let us not dwell on the domestic manners of West Indian plantation houses. Mrs Foulkes, shall we retire to coo over your beautiful little boy?'

'When I first came out, a slave girl borrowed my razor to shave her private parts,' continued Thistlewood, who had arrived in 1750 on board the *Flying Flamborough*. 'Some wenches in Jamaica are very sensual, sirs.' Like so many expatriates, he was escaping a crisis at home and had come to Jamaica seeking a West India Fortune, taking advantage of the opportunities open to colonial men. 'Gentlemen, I take it you've heard the recent story of the *Zong*? All that free labour thrown to the sharks by the captain. I daresay the *Zong* will go down in history, unlike other ships.'

'I've been meaning to visit Black River to see where she docked.' Duncan regarded Thistlewood as a jovial extrovert. 'It's one thing throwing sick slaves overboard, but I daresay Captain Collingwood regards all Africans as property.' He was glad Fiona and the ladies had retired to the drawing room. 'Acht! Talk to us about the Tacky Revolt.'

'Contrary to belief, the revolt was not confined to St Mary only; Westmorland bore the brunt of it.' Thistlewood, sitting on the edge of his chair, pictured his treasured marble-covered diary in which he had recorded the event, as he always did whenever anything notable occurred on the island. 'I don't like to boast, gentlemen, but I found myself in the thick of the battle. At least fifty white people perished and 500 slaves lost their lives in the uprising and retribution that followed. Fortunately, Col Cudjoe sent his men to hunt down Tacky…'

Darnley smiled at Thistlewood, who met Duncan in Westmorland some time ago. 'Nice watch. If only I could turn back time.'

'You could try winding it up again.' Thistlewood kept a jealous guard on his watch. 'I had it cleaned by Mr John Urquhart, a watch-maker in Kingston.' A magistrate, Thistlewood was not wealthy but was at the peak of his prosperity and he also loved to entertain. He had faced his share of economic problems, which would be worsened by a series of hurricanes in the next few years (from 1781 to 1786), destroying most of his property and beginning his financial decline. 'I hope you're keeping a journal, Foulkes?' Most days, he wrote in his diary and was on the way to amassing thirty-seven journals in his thirty-six-year stay. 'Even if you don't keep one, write letters home on a regular basis. Leave a record of your sojourn in Jamaica.'

Dear Dougal,   *22 December 1781*

I hope this letter finds you well. I am sorry you've not heard from Iain again. Perhaps he is dead? In August just gone, we had another hurricane, uprooting our cedar trees, flattening banana and plantain trees, and destroying the corn and a great deal of cane. The Colonial Government has only just paid out £500 for my share of the damage back in '80. Meat is scarce. Last Christmas, we had to substitute it with saltfish, distributing roughly 2 1/2 lb to each person, along with rum. The slaves are angry, but we must work them twice as hard due to the devastation.

This hurricane was a blessing for some of us. Although the canefields were damaged, the rat population has dramatically decreased: most of the little blighters drowned. I recently sold 30 troublesome slaves for £2,200 to planters in Savannah-La-Mar where seventy whites and 500 slaves perished in the hurricane last year. I sold 15 male bucks for £85 each and the females for £75 each, being weaker vessels, of course.

Ezekiel Darnley is the best overseer a planter could have in Jamacia; my right-hand man. He rallied the slaves and we are now up and running. However, the fields were water-logged in August and we are preparing for inclement weather in the years ahead. Thankfully, it is the coastal parishes that bear the brunt of these destructive hurricanes – towns like Falmouth and Montego Bay that are right on the sea. Incidentally, there is a hurricane-damaged plantation selling in Hanover for £10,500, with 1,650 acres of land. I am not a bragger, but Canongate recently expanded to 2,000 acres! If you were the adventurous type, I'd encourage you to buy it – come to Jamaica.

Some trouble and worry to report: Shamboy, a Mandingo, refused to bill the guinea grass pasture. He ate green cassava and almost died, choking on his tongue and fitting. His jaw locked and his teeth clenched. Edwin, a member of the holing gang, ate cane trash and his stomach puffed up like a big-bellied wench. He was in agony and had to be purged. The last time we had a dinner party here, he played the banjo and Shamboy played the fiddle. Those little rascals had earlier sprinkled cayenne pepper on the floor. As soon as it got hot in the room, the ladies' thighs were, allegedly, set on fire, 'driving them mad with desire.' The following morning, at breakfast, none of the ladies put in an appearance.

That slave, Shamboy, is nothing but trouble. His sable wife, Ancilla, ate 'poison crabs' and tried to hang herself. She ran away and was 'disordered in her senses' for two days. I branded her left shoulder with my initials: DF. I chopped up Shamboy's banjo and burned it for his insolence; he had kept playing it under my bedroom window.

By the way, I recently had a second letter asking me to reconsider becoming Justice of the Peace for the parish of St Ann when the present holder steps down. I'll never take the King's shilling. I'm not surprised they considered me though. Not a week goes by without news of a sudden death in our community. Jamaica is 'the white man's graveyard,' so many of us buried on lonely hillsides and in churchyards. Thankfully, I am in rude health.

In the next box, please could you send the following items via Captain Buchan: two dozen tartan headkerchiefs, a pack of needles, two dozen straw hats, 1 bale of linen, 2 rolls of Osnaburg, 12 yards of checked slave cloth, 1 pair of leather boots (for myself) and 12 lead pencils. I enclose 20 shillings in silver to be given to the parson at the Kirk of St Giles as a Christmas offering.

I have instructed my attorneys in Kingston to make the usual funds available to you promptly. By my calculations, you have five years remaining on the mortgage for your property in Edinburgh. Please manage the remittances. Those do-gooders in England, Wilberforce and Granville Sharpe, are stirring up trouble, so we cannot be sure of anything. I must remind Fiona to tell the slaves to burn effigies of Sharpe, Pitt and Lord Mansfield. He outlawed slavery in England and, as you no doubt will be aware, has started the bleat for abolition of the trade in the British West Indies. I enclose a note for Fiona's father.

Your same,
Duncan.

With the infamous Lewis Hutchinson exiting a mocking world, Fiona and Duncan were now consummate optimists. Even if there were plenty of reasons for pessimism, including the dark shadow of the Maroons, they spoke often about the needs of their slaves (clothes and nutrition) and their monetary worth. They recognised their important role in tapping into slave psyche by alienating them from their fellow tribesmen, getting the best from them in the canefields and the sugar mill, and preserving the *status quo*. Canongate was everything; it was their creation and they hoped to pass it on to their son.

'I never understood how difficult things were for my mother when I was growing up.' They stood in the polished hallway where Fiona held Christopher. 'She should have explained things to me.' Yawning, she had had another sleepless night because the child was grouchy and refused to be put down. 'Let's hope he doesn't grow up to be an ungrateful son. He'll have a lot of responsibility heaped on him. I don't want to spoil him.'

'Excessive indulgence.' Duncan was not prepared for the niggling jealousy that he felt towards his son and heir. 'Any worse weather and the cane will be ruined.' They were expecting another hurricane, just when he thought they had seen the back of the last one. 'We'll batten down the hatches and rope off the paddock with the horses.' In that moment, he had more hope than he'd ever had: he had a son and heir. 'We'll weather the storm.'

'Acht! My kitchen garden will be ruined. Thankfully, I can pickle and preserve the vegetables.' In a pensive mood, Fiona handed the child over to a nursemaid and followed Duncan out onto the lawn. 'What are you doing there, Amina? You're idling away the time while the others toil in the fields with their backs bent.' She waved the work-shy house girl away. 'She does this daily, mopes around the house complaining that she has a backache. She has set her eyes on Cassian. What are you waiting for, girl? Get on with it, imbecile.'

Walking across the lawn, away from the great house, Duncan stopped under a lime tree and bent to kiss Fiona's head; a rare public display. Instinctively, she lifted her face to him. Since the birth of Christopher, he had been full of jealousy and guilt, escaping to his study because he disliked demanding babies. Nagging away at the back of his mind was the thought that he might not live to see his grandchildren. He had reached the age of sixty-one years and his younger brother, Dougal, was married with three children older than his son, Christopher. He was pleased that the Hutchinson name would live on through Dougal. He had promised to educate his nephew and ensure that his nieces were financially provided for so that they could enter the marriage market with reasonable dowries and *trousseaus*.

'These days I can't afford to relax, what with the grass in the lowland pasture taking a scorching and not enough hay to feed the horses.' Duncan suggested they turn in early for the hurricane was imminent. 'Most of the cattle will starve to death and the rest will perish, but we'll be in meat for weeks.' Upon reaching an apple tree, he picked a red fruit and handed it to her. 'I've come to realise that most plantation owners wear four faces: master, husband; father and lover. With you, I wear two of them: husband and lover.'

'Lucky you. I always wear three faces: wife, mother and mistress.' Fiona chewed the apple, listening while he discussed plans to develop a second field of tobacco. 'Since the last hurricane, we've had an infestation of caterpillars. They are attracted by the smell of the tobacco leaves in the field. Incidentally, I'm thinking of breeding puppies.'

'Oh God no, not another Port Royal quake!' The tender moment of planning together was rudely interrupted when the ground shifted beneath their feet. 'Did you feel that?' Duncan looked up when he heard a rumbling noise. The sky appeared turbulent. For a fleeting moment, he was reminded of the aftershocks from the earthquake in Cuba in June 1770, felt all the way in Kingston where a few chimneys and walls had been thrown down. 'Make sure Christopher is safe while I go see what Darnley and our people are up to. Christopher is your priority.' The wind blew hard, whipping up the leaves until he was forced to abandon the ride to the canefields. He had followed Edward Long's suggestions in *The History of Jamaica*, instructing his carpenters not to use bolts or iron bars on the estate's buildings. 'Good grief, lightning has struck the apple tree. We've had a lucky escape.'

'The birds seem to have gone.' There was a series of deafening bangs. 'Oh Lord, no.' Fiona turned ghostly white and was dashing indoors when a coconut tree was struck not far from where they were standing minutes ago. Windswept, it was as if they were caught in a storm on canvas.

'Mistress, mistress,' the frantic call came from the back of the house. 'Lightin' kill Ovid, di new saltwater *African bubu*.' An elderly slave was returning from the long pasture; he carried a scythe and an iron-bill hook on his shoulder. 'Two of di chilvren shelter under a tree an' lightin' burn dem up.' He had been billing the grass. 'It fry dem up.'

'Get to your hut, you fool,' Duncan said irritably, entering the hallway and ordering Amina, the house girl, to shut all the jalousie windows. 'The problem with Jamaica is that a perfectly clear day can turn at any moment into a drizzling shower, heavy rain, strong winds or a deadly hurricane. With Christopher here, we must ensure there are no metal conductors anywhere near the house.' He gave his usual eye-roll, mounting the wide stairs to the master bedroom. 'It's no use protesting, wife. We planters must snatch our food and pleasures when and where we can. Thank God for storms, hurricanes and rainy days.'

'What, in this weather?' Grimacing, Fiona abhorred the sight and sound of lightning and thunder, which reminded her of Judgment Day. 'You should sleep in a hammock, alone.'

'Did you know that there are male and female trees, and barren trees too?' Duncan stared into the empty cradle and undressed hurriedly, taking his mind off the lightning and thunder, saying he hoped the house girls would have the good sense not to light any candles tonight. 'They say the earthquake in Hispaniola swallowed a whole mountain...'

'You and your double-talk.' Fiona poured brackish water into her bidet, a European chair with an enamel basin seated within it like a commode. She lifted her workday skirt and petticoat and placed her left foot on a chair, washing her *punt* – Duncan's nickname for her privates. 'I daresay this wind will blow hard for a couple of hours.' Ignoring the thunder and lightning, she completed the ritual and produced a hummingbird's green plumage. 'At least the house is built of stone, so there'll be no damage to the building.'

'I can see myself in Venice,' Duncan held the plumage, 'enjoying a cigar in a gondola. Had my father not lost our Highland estate, I would have done the Grand Tour of Europe.' He felt a pang of guilt when he saw the hummingbird feather. A Madagascan on the Camerons's estate had taught him certain tricks. Enjoying their downtime, he was still thinking about the light-skinned Madagascan as he tickled his wife's inner thighs. 'I'm pleased you've retained your good looks in this harsh climate. Your face is still smooth and line-free. Some women's faces seem to collapse under the pressure of plantation life.'

'Get on with it.' Fiona had lain awake for most of the night, listening to the child's breathing. 'I'm exhausted.' She was afraid that he would die in his sleep like several creole white babies. 'Och.' A gasp escaped and she shivered. 'Christopher is crying. I'd better go and see to him. He's a very demanding baby. I can't break the habit of feeding him on demand.'

Duncan tossed the plumage aside and ran a hand through his hair. 'You're putting up a wall between us.' He hinted at her dark past. 'If we were back home, you'd make time for me. The prospect of a respectable life in the West Indies appealed to you then.'

'I can't believe you said that.' Fiona slipped into her clothes and her boots. 'I knew you'd bring up my past one day.' With tears coursing down her face, she said angrily, 'It's always sugar and slaves, or my white men are slacking off; it's always something else.'

'I trust you're not offended.' Duncan, his neck turning red, added coldly, 'I may as well take a naga bedmate: Amina. There's an idea.' He was tired and felt that the time was right for her to come into herself. 'That is, until you've stopped chest-feeding.' She bustled out of the room at this. Frustrated, he flicked a small caterpillar off the pillow and stood up, stomping around the room and looking out the window at the trees, which were bending in the direction of the hurricane wind. He heard Rev'd McKay's voice, cautioning, *Know what bridge to cross and which one to burn, man.* 'What is it, Cassian?' In the yard, a tree had uprooted and was carried away by the wind, along with numerous banana and plantain leaves. 'Kindly don't interrupt me.'

'Dere's a white man at di front door seekin' shelter.' Cassian, standing at a safe distance outside the bedroom door, turned away from Duncan's nakedness. 'I sarry, massa.'

'Who left the gate open?' Standing in the centre of the room, Duncan made no attempt to cover his nudity. 'Who is this stranger? For God's sake, boy, fetch my clothes.'

'Him seh 'im com' to instruct di slaves in religious principles, massa. Is a Englishman.' Cassian had a dead pea-dove bird hidden in his trouser pocket. It had been killed by a flying object and would still be fresh enough to roast that night. 'I show 'im into di big 'all 'cause is white man, massa. But 'im sure look 'ungry, sah.'

'You should have shown him into the stables, clod,' Duncan snapped, accepting his trousers. 'Help me with my boots.' He had heard that Cassian and one of the house girls were sweet on each other and planned to make a match between them. 'And my shirt, idiot.' He controlled his people's sexuality and had told Fiona that Cassian had proven himself to be loyal and, thus, worthy of such a reward. 'If you were a centaur, which part of its body would you prefer? You do know what a centaur is, don't you? Good-oh. Which part would you prefer, the top half? For God's sake, answer me. You're not a mute.'

'Arhm.' Bewildered, Cassian stalled, giving himself time to respond because he was unsure of where the question was leading. 'If I was a ooman, I'd prefer di ches', massa.' He knew that his master did not take kindly to clever remarks that diminished him in stature. 'I'm a man like any odder man, so I'd choose di bottom part, fi sure.' He found himself genuinely smiling. 'White man seh naga man 'ang like a horse dung to di floor.'

'Careful or you'll step on your own wood.' Duncan buttoned his shirt and seized upon the Greek legend of the Battle of the Lapillis and the Centaurs. 'When I was at school, I learned about the Greek myths and legends.' He listened to the howling wind. *Once, there was a wedding and the Lapillis invited the centaurs along.* The jalousie windows rattled and the warm air made his skin feel damp and clammy. *'During the festivities, the centaurs got drunk and tried to carry off the women, stupid, but the Lapillis gave chase and sent them packing.'*

'I was tryin' to do di rite t'ing, massa.' Almost choking with laughter, Cassian knelt and helped Duncan into his polished leather boots. 'We cahn sen' white stranger packin' in a 'urricane.' Still kneeling, the Yoruba looked up at his chameleon like master, knowing that he himself was considered his master's subordinate. 'Besides, di man is a missionary.'

'I want you to bed Amina.' Duncan had strongly held views about the treatment and control of Africans, views he expressed at social events where he described Jamaica as *a hotbed of gnats* and the missionaries as *misguided fools*. He knew Cassian well and that, given the opportunity, his bodyguard would choose freedom over bondage. He wanted to tease it out of him. 'Tell me about the strong gang. Some of those bucks are physically superior to us whites, albeit not mentally. I heard someone call me a pig this morning. I could have been mistaken. About Amina, I might break her in myself.'

'Arhm,' Cassian said hesitantly, knowing that his master could either get angry or become charming in a flash. 'She savin' 'erself fi me, massa.' There was a plaque over the front door, saying: *Nemo Me Inpune Lacessit – No one harms me*. He remembered the shame of having to recite it while hacking away at brambles after he had dared to say 'howdy-do' to Captain Kalu, who had just returned Cleora and a dozen runaways.

'You're tupping that little wench, Amina, aren't you?' After asking this question, the smile slipped down Duncan's face when Fiona walked into the bedroom with the child in her arms. 'I've just had a post-coitus conversation with Cassian since that part of your duty is non-existent nowadays.' He stood there looking at the child with a mixture of guilt and pride. 'You must get a wet-nurse.' Cassian bowed, wanting to make a quick escape. 'You've had a hard day.' Duncan urged, 'Put your head down until the hurricane passes.'

Fiona curled her lips, 'What about this little one?' She held the child possessively, sitting in an armchair in the darkened room. 'I'm not letting a naga wet-nurse near him. It's unhealthy and unnatural, not when my breasts are leaking. These days, I feel like a milking cow in a dairy.' The shutters had been lowered due to the lightning. 'A wet-nurse? No.'

'Please yourself.' Duncan paused. 'If this weather continues, the canefields will be water-logged. We're bound to lose some of the cattle, too. When I was a boy, our cook used to say, *Brains and boiled eggs make a nourishing meal for babies – weaning food*.'

'Cows' brains!' Fiona gave a smirk, adding, 'We feed that to the *piccaninnies*.'

'It is good weaning food.' Duncan calculated that their food supplies would be depleted, too. 'At present, we have sufficient dry goods for our needs but if this weather continues, the slaves' provision grounds will be destroyed. They are in the mountains, situated on a flat bed, and will be flooded.' Because of how remote they were, the Africans could not be given time off to visit their provision grounds. There was the danger of being killed by fallen or flying objects, and the fear that they would abscond to Calabash Estate if there was insufficient supervision. 'Given that they're still recovering from the last hurricane, there'll be a shortage of meat. I'll have to issue extra saltfish. Staples like flour, milk, eggs (the hens are exposed in their coops) and sugar will all be in short supply. As the less well-off would say, *We'll have to mend and make do.*'

'Massa, yuh forget seh yer guest waitin' dung stairs?' Cassian stood outside the door and followed up, stating, 'Yuh cahn leave 'im on 'is own. Wat mus' 'e be t'inkin', massa? Yuh comin' wid me?'

'Let him wait.' Gently, Fiona guided a fat teat into the child's mouth and pressed her lips together, pondering. 'I'm all for boiled eggs, but there's no way I'm feeding my son brains; that is poor people's food.' She continued, 'Hopefully the hurricane won't damage all the pumpkins and *chochos*. Those are good weaning food.' The child stiffened and a flush crept into his face when a thunder bolt fell outside the house. For a moment, Fiona was startled. It seemed that the bolt had hit the great house. 'Ouch! He bit me again.'

'He's over-indulged, woman.' Duncan glanced at his son fleetingly, disappointed that Fiona had refused to use a wet-nurse, the custom in plantation society. 'You refused to marry me in Scotland until I could provide you with the means to improve your life. Now that I'm a rich man, you say I must wait in line behind my son.' He strode away, partly because they had a guest below stairs and partly because he was disgusted with the idea of breastfeeding a toddler with teeth. 'Cassian, tell our guest I'll be down in a minute.'

* * *

Duncan's ascendancy in plantation society had been an ongoing struggle. He was a man against the elements. On this turbulent night, Cassian stood behind him, ready to defend his master to the death and keeping silent so as not to undermine the two white men present.

He resembled a eunuch in the "Arabian tales," heeding the chatter in his head: *We is di victims an' our cries go unanswered.* A hare's breath away, Duncan, unaware of his manservant's other self, played host to a stranger. The man at the fireplace in the drawing room was a huge, pasty-skinned, avuncular figure with a long chin and bushy eyebrows. He stooped, picked up a coin and addressed his host without being invited to do so.

'My wife sailed from Leicestershire with me but, alas, she has entered her eternal rest. There was an accident in a four-in-hand carriage. We travelled through wooded vales, barbarous nooks and quiet glens to bring the good news of salvation to the heathens but, sadly, our carriage went off the road into a gully. Alas, I am currently on foot.'

On foot? thought Duncan, heeding the stranger's voice. 'You came here on foot, today of all days?' He looked astonished. 'In this weather?'

'If I were you, I would shut the curtains – shut out the lightning and other acts of nature.' The traveller extended his right hand. 'You're the master of Canongate. I'm a horseless *walk-foot buckra*, a nobody.'

'I think not.' For a while, Duncan did not speak, though he took the big man's hand and pumped it. His sea-green eyes met a pair of blue ones that stared into his soul. 'You've been evangelizing in the hills? A thankless task, I'd think. Would you care for a drink?'

'Good heavens!' The traveller raised his voice when a thunderbolt fell, hitting the stables and catching fire. 'Please don't trouble yourself on my account. A stone bed is all I require. If it's no trouble, a draught of worm grass with sugar and a dash of lemon juice will suffice. I've been spending time with a poor white family in MacDowell, the source of Little River, and I suspect I have worms. The pork was off, but there was little else at the dinner table. Could I trouble you for some chaw sticks to whiten and preserve my teeth? Alas, I spent two days with a free Negro family in Ty Dixon, eating Charles Price rats roasted on a spit.' He looked up at the candles in the cut-glass chandelier and blinked. 'My feet are sore and tender. I've got corns and bunions. If your cook could rustle up a meal for me, that would be good.'

'Cassian, go and see to the horses.' Duncan, railing about acts of God and nature in his mind, felt unchristian that day. 'Do a spot check and come back as soon as you can. Off you go.'

'The dark night will pass,' said the traveller, warming his hands over an imaginary glow in the fireplace, as if he were toasting crumpets. 'The best thing we Christians can do in these hard times is to live life the best way we can – alleluia!'

There came a loud thunderclap from outside. Cassian appeared, informing Duncan that the stables were ablaze. Powerless, they looked through the window, watching the flames rising from the roof of the stables. A tree had fallen and the winds were fanning the flames. A dozen horses were trapped in the stables, thrown into a panic.

'Tell the house girls to prepare a tepid bath and a cool bed for our guest.' Duncan felt his heart sinking.

* * *

The arrival of the Rev'd Robson Ellis marked the beginning of a new chapter in Duncan's life. At daybreak, he found himself fully clothed on the sofa in the drawing room. He had slept through the vengeful hurricane and his manly urges, plaguing him for days, had dissipated. As he got up, he called on all the resources that his body had to offer, bracing himself for bad news. The Rev'd Ellis, meantime, likened the hurricane to *a proud shatterer of men's dreams*. Grateful to find himself in the presence of such opulence, he had taken off Duncan's boots and watched over him while he slept. He looked around the room enviously.

'I don't know what shape I'd be in if you weren't here last night.' Duncan could not recall taking off his own boots. 'I can't thank you enough for your company, Rev'd Ellis.'

'We're not letting it rain on your roof.' The big man stood by the fireplace, watching Fiona carry the sleeping child into the room, thinking, *He's heir to all this. They live in complacent splendour and wealth from that inhuman trade.* The rain fell on the roof and the traveller's voice bounced off the walls, 'Last year, I caught a fever from a lady of ill-repute in Port Royal. I was trying to exorcise her demons. Parsons' wives are above the flesh.' He had an innate ability to make those around him feel pangs of guilt. 'What I wouldn't give for a cool bed.'

'You will stay a few days, won't you?' Duncan was the perfect host.

'Alas, I'm a nobody,' Rev'd Ellis repeated and Fiona looked at him in surprise. He was the strangest visitor ever to have knocked on their door seeking shelter. 'I go where the Lord leads me.'

'When I first came out, I was confused by the term *a cool bed*,' yawned Fiona. 'Ah, the call of the road.'

'Whatever happens after the storm, I will be here to lend a hand, dear lady.' Rev'd Ellis spoke before Fiona could finish her sentence. 'I shall roll up my sleeves today and earn my keep.' He believed that he had a moral duty to save sinners and boost morale wherever he went, taking care not to offend the plantocracy whose hospitality he enjoyed on his travels across Jamaica. The forty-something-year-old missionary had visited many British plantations. He often wrote letters home about the comfort and sense of solidarity he had witnessed between sugar barons in the mountainous regions and those in the lowland parishes. 'If it is no trouble, I would appreciate a bath in tepid water, as well as a back-washer. Just imagine if I had slept in the stables with the horses.'

Jonah himself, thought Duncan, slipping a strong protective arm around Fiona's waist. 'I can give you a loofah but, I'm afraid, you'll have to wash your back yourself. The house girls are busy today,' he spoke firmly and with a sombre expression. Immediately, Cassian limped into the room with further bad news. Duncan's heart sank when he heard that most of the slave huts were in ruins and almost all the cattle and poultry had perished.

'Meatless days,' Rev'd Ellis said under his breath. 'Alas, life is short and sad in the West Indies, a paradise lost.' The disgraced parson, defrocked in England for lewd conduct with minors, hastily added, 'The Lord has shown his people hard things over the generations. You, Squire Foulkes, shall drink *the wine of astonishment* no more.'

'I daresay the dark clouds will soon be lifted, Rev'd Ellis.' Fiona did not agonize over exactly what he meant but was quick on the draw. 'While you're here, it would be good if you could visit Pimento Walk and baptise our slaves, please.'

* * *

In the years that followed, the preternaturally self-possessed Rev'd Robson Ellis would appear at Canongate out of the blue as if he were

Jonah sent to warn Nineveh. Duncan, who had credited him with lifting the plantation's mood after the hurricane, poured his energies into sugar planting and raising his son, whom he taught to ride and swim as soon as he could walk. Quite often, the boy accompanied him to the Cave Valley market where traders bought and sold horses. Despite well-meaning and probably sound advice from Rev'd McKay in 1770, Duncan did not diversify into breeding Highland cattle. The trips, however, enabled him to socialize and buy the odd mule or horse. He valued these outings to Cave Valley where he spent quality time with his son. These away days also gave the boy an opportunity to meet other white boys his own age. Once business was over, they spent the night at the Camerons's second home, Rain Penn, on the fringes of Alexandria.

Although Christopher's creole childhood was relatively smooth and untroubled, he was isolated. Consequently, Fiona constantly worried about how few close white friends he had. History would show that she had set a precedent for the women who came after her by producing last-minute babies before the menopause. From the moment her son was washed and wrapped in his swaddling cloth, she behaved like a marsupial carrying its young in its pouch. She had rebuffed Duncan's advice to send him to boarding school in Edinburgh, where he could be in the company of male teachers and white boys.

Throughout the pregnancy, Duncan had discreetly doused himself with cold water, as advised by a male friend. After the birth, the child's temper, constant crying and refusal to sleep in his crib drove Duncan to distraction. With growing frustration, he admitted to himself that sex was the bedrock of his relationship with his second wife. A demanding baby meant that if he did not do something, his horn would hang around all day. Reluctantly, he caved in and slept with the occasional brown house girl, but only when he visited the Grandisons and the Camerons, twice a month. He credited his men friends with keeping his secret.

* * *

When Christopher turned fifteen, he killed his first wild boar with his father's help and smeared the blood over his body before bathing in

Little River. The kill was not easy: the boar took them both on a wild goose chase for over an hour. Determined, they tracked it on horseback through the hills until its back was against a rock.

Duncan began to take stock. He was surprised to learn from Darnley that he himself owned roughly three hundred Africans, nine horses and four fields of sugarcane, corn, tobacco and coffee. That same month, he had dined with the Grandisons in Trelawny. In a show of pride, he had predicted that his beloved son would father the *long-tailed dynasty* of which he dreamed. He now observed his son from a discreet distance.

For the moment, Christopher languished on his back gazing up at the cloudless blue sky. Sunday was a day of rest for the family, which meant visiting their circle of friends in the mountains and lowlands. For the longest time, Christopher had not seen his boyhood friends, Jude Cameron and Josiah Grandison, who were enjoying boarding school back home in Edinburgh. They had been there for the past four years, writing to him and joking that his father had exiled him in Jamaica. Duncan denied it, explaining to Christopher that there were other considerations: chief among them was that he did not need a grand education in Scotland. What he needed was agricultural knowledge, practical experience of running a sugar plantation from an early age, an understanding of the planting seasons, and sound knowledge of the law in relation to slave treatment and control in the British West Indies.

After spending the morning watching Darnley's brown boys muck out the stables, Christopher had returned to the house to get ready for Sunday lunch. Ever since he could remember, a feisty African named Seraphima had lived in the great house. She was eighteen, three years older than he was. In his memory, she had knelt by his bed every night and taught him to say his prayers. Presently, he chewed on a blade of grass, skulking under the wall, lying in wait. He intended to have her: nothing would stand in his way.

A tall, good-looking fifteen-year-old, Christopher was often moody and secretive by nature. When he was four, he had woken up screaming because there were caterpillars crawling all over his bedcover. Before a past hurricane, Seraphima had hidden a bundle of tobacco leaves under his bed, not realising the leaves were infested with insects. Amina had asked her to hide the tobacco leaves for her. At the time, she was seven and spent her days in the kitchen. Impatient to have his way with Seraphima, Christopher lay on the lawn with his hands folded behind his head, waiting for her to bring him a sandwich, for he did not wish to eat with his parents. He had secretly taught her to read and had sent her a note via Cassian, begging her to meet him there. He tried to be careful because his mother policed Seraphima's every move. But he was determined, and had told his father that he wanted her for Christmas. Duncan had reluctantly agreed.

'Gweh, Lachlan.' Seraphima waited until he had eaten his tongue sandwich and had drunk a glass of lemonade before telling him that she had work to do. 'Me busy today.'

'You took your time coming.' The simple lunch over, Christopher was determined to delay her. 'I've asked Father to let me have you as a gift. He's all for it.' All the while, he was sinking downward in the quicksand that had trapped so many lascivious white men and boys before him. His leisure time was mainly spent in the lowlands with the Camerons and the Grandisons. Here, the expatriate and creole girls with their oval faces or round cheeks and smooth white foreheads also caught his eye in their pretty afternoon dresses and beautiful evening gowns. Conflicted, he leaned back against the wall. 'Father says I can have you for my birthday, in October, and at Christmas.' Her dark eyes were looking piercingly into his, causing him to add, 'If you say no, I'll tell him we did it. I'll say you forced me. I must see you tonight, Sera. Say you'll come to my room after midnight. Promise.'

'*A promise is a comfort to a fool.*' Seraphima was anxious to prevent any discussion that would lead to her receiving punishment from Duncan for flirting with his son an heir. 'Gweh, bwoy.' She chided this man-boy, who started to make demands on her when he turned fourteen. She remembered how his face used to look pale and sweet when he was a baby, with his pink fingers tugging at her. Then, as soon as he entered his teens, she felt a warm hand wandering up her skirt. 'Me busy.'

'Well?' Christopher lifted his audacious sea-green eyes, tugging at her hem. She had looks and she made him feel grown up. 'Midnight?' He watched her striding towards a flourishing annatto tree, carrying a wicker basket. 'Yes,' he said triumphantly when she returned to his side with a basket filled with annatto pods. 'I won't go all the way this time.'

'Why yuh nuh go an' get som' *white punny* in Trelawny, Lachlan?' Seraphima turned her roaming dark eyes upon him. 'Yuh is a likkle bwoy, Lachlan. I wahn a real naga man.'

'Father says that, *There are no real men except for white men*,' replied Christopher, reciting a mantra that he had heard repeated often. Having followed her around for several days, he was stalking her by now. 'I give you something you want; you give me something I need.'

'Me *naah* giv' weh mi *gold mine* fi free. Me wahn t'ree yard o' muslin,' Seraphima answered, 'and two-an-six. Me value miself.'

'Two shillings and sixpence for a piece of *black pussy*?' The value that she had placed on herself drew laughter from Christopher. 'It's not worth it. One-an-six.' He got up immediately when he saw his father, whose left arm was in a calico sling. 'Hullo, Father. How goes it?'

'Christopher.' Duncan walked towards the wall where a John-to-wit bird answered from a Seville orange tree. 'What have I told you about sniffing around that naga wench?'

Stirrings of a sexual awakening had begun to plague Christopher. 'I'm not doing anything, Father.' He clung to the promise that the object of his desire, Seraphima, would receive him at midnight. His Adam's apple bobbed. 'I'm just bird watching, John-to-wits.'

'Don't act the monk. That wench is not the path to enlightenment. If you have an itch, scratch it yourself.' Out of the corner of his eye, Duncan observed Seraphima, who curtsied and scarpered. 'Whites are rational beings, cerebral thinkers; nagas are non-intellectual, hyper-emotional children. They have stupendous energy, brute strength and no sense of decency.' Before long, the sound of hooves distracted him and he let out a sigh, adding, 'Here comes that Frenchman, Pierre Fontane. Oh good, he's got his wife and his pretty niece with him.' He grinned wickedly. 'If you want that itch scratched, we could marry you off at sixteen. In case you haven't noticed, pure white women are in short supply.'

* * *

In the late afternoon, Duncan, Christopher and the Fontane family stood outside the stables. After the hurricane of '86, the artisans had constructed a weather-proof building in which they stabled the horses.

They had built a henhouse and a pigsty too. Although the hospital was destroyed, Fiona had had her hands full with Christopher, whom she breastfed for three years. In those nursing days, she and Duncan had said things they later regretted but he never could resist her rosewater scent before a siesta. At such times, she had grudgingly handed over Christopher to Amina and played the dutiful wife.

'I recently bought Christopher this white stallion named Peppa.' Duncan watched the adolescent nestle his face in the horse's mane and stroke its neck. 'I could have bought him any old nag for seventeen pounds but, of course, he had to have this one: twenty-five pounds. There was a time when good horses could be had for ten pounds.'

'These are dark days.' Pierre Fontane toured the stables with his hosts. 'Speaking of dark days, it seems there is no end to the revolution in St Domingue. We French are, how you say, *wanderers of the earth*.' A sudden movement of the horse's tail caused his niece to squeal. 'I'm afraid Lydia is not keen on horses. She's the musical sort who would have enjoyed the grandeur of Versailles where Marie Antoinette played a harp.'

'Her mother was half-English, so she was educated in England.' Edessa Fontane, the Frenchwoman, proudly added, 'Come and visit us at Lafayette anytime, Christopher. Your father says you're a keen horseman and a good shot. Lydia is a keen horsewoman.'

'A good shot, perhaps, but I'm not sure about the horsemanship.' Christopher stroked Peppa's mane. 'Whatever you do, don't visit the pigsty.' The horse turned her head and whinnied loudly, startling Edessa. Christopher said, 'You'll be ankle-deep in manure, I'm afraid. Don't go near the kennel either, ladies; those dogs will rip your dresses apart.'

'Should we risk it?' Edessa regarded her niece's muslin dress, which clung to her slender frame in all the right places. Lydia, meantime, looked uneasily at Christopher, whom she regarded as a boy. 'I think not.' Edessa peered anxiously down at her own feet and up, smiling across at the handsome young man. 'If only you were five years older.'

'I am sure Mademoiselle Fontane has lots of suitors,' Duncan said teasingly. 'Why, she is the fairest flower in the Garden Parish.' As he laughed, he felt a sharp pain in his left wrist which he had broken two months prior. 'If no suitor comes calling for her hand, in two years' time, I expect Christopher to do the gentlemanly thing by proposing marriage.'

'My horse is more of a friend than a pet, aren't you?' Christopher allowed the white mare to rub her nose against his shoulder. 'I've got your wet sugar.' He held out his hand when the horse whinnied again, pawing the ground and begging for her treat. 'Show off. Don't be afraid, Mademoiselle. Her name is Peppa, as in bird-pepper. She's a gentle soul.' The animal's eyes followed Lydia, shaking her mane as if she could hear a deafening roar somewhere in the future. 'Shush.' Christopher fixed his eyes in Peppa's direction.

'This is Diamond.' Duncan approached a brown stallion. 'Hullo.' Simultaneously, his gaze flicked regularly back at Lydia, whose clingy muslin dress had aroused him. 'He has two strong back legs. I wouldn't stand too close, ladies.' He coughed. 'I plan to sell him to the British Redcoats. They need studs to breed.'

'They say horses have an internal compass that allows them to find their way home.' Edessa tried her hand at small talk, desperate to steer the conversation away from horses, when Peppa farted and Diamond dropped a wet, steaming load of dung on the ground. 'Or is it birds? Oh yes, so it is. Apparently, birds use the earth's magnetic field to navigate their way home. When I was a girl, my French tutor was an amateur ornithologist.'

'*Taisez-vous,*' Pierre Fontane snapped at his wife, before reaching out to the horse. 'He measures up well,' he said unguardedly. '*Le cout total?*'

'Twenty pounds.' Diamond's eyes flared when Duncan said, 'If you're interested in a spot of horse trading, I'd rather sell him to you than to the Redcoats.' He gave the horse's enlarged scrotum a sidelong glance then moved on to spare the ladies' blushes. '*Stud, par excellence.*' On exiting the stables, he harrumphed, 'I'm looking forward to the dinner table; so is Christopher, I am sure. I hope you have a good appetite.'

* * *

In August 1795, while the second Maroon War was raging, the 83rd Regiment disembarked in Montego Bay. Duncan was seventy-five and still energetic. Adjusting his sling while entertaining his Sunday guests on the lawn, he listened to Lydia sing in French. Meantime, one of the house girls served red wine, decanted an hour ago, from a Waterford glass decanter. Laughter filled the air when seven aged Africans began to dance in honour of the master's birthday: some with their backs stooped while other bodies crooked, bent, dipped and leapt. One elderly African leapt into the air to catch a ball, which was thrown by an old woman who had started to jig to the sound of a flute.

While this went on, Cassian stepped forward and announced a change of scene: a re-enactment of the Battle of the Lapillis and the Centaurs. He had planned and choreographed a play to honour his master's milestone birthday. This was his moment to outshine the previous act. Duncan, whose attention had been waning, gave his manservant a withering glance and narrowed his eyes when at least twenty Africans sat down to eat at a wedding feast. Ten 'human' guests, Lapillis, appeared in white masks, emulating their master and mistress. The other actors wore old hessian sacks intended to transform their rear ends into centaurs. In keeping with the legend, the Lapillis and the centaurs sat down to eat. An enthusiastic Seraphima played the bride while a fractious African named Ocean played the groom, offering his bride a freshly cut pink rose.

'We have arranged a spectacle for the amusement of Mademoiselle Fontane.' Duncan was lost in thought: *I can see her raising her face as the snowflakes fall in Paris.*

'*Je ne comprends pas.*' Lydia gazed in amazement, wishing her voice would not tremble when she spoke, 'Oh dear, I don't quite understand what this is all about.' A seemingly drunken Lapillis sat on the floor with her legs wide apart, putting a glint in the Pierre Fontane's eyes, all of which made Lydia blush furiously. '*Je ne comprends pas.*'

The play received a less than enthusiastic review from Edessa. 'Of course, the Battle of the Lapillis and the Centaurs is not meant to be staged by slaves. No culture.'

While the drums were beating faster and faster, and the Lapillis were getting drunk, an amorous centaur's hand rested on the bride's arm, sliding down to her wrist. There was a great rush when the centaurs picked up the females and carried them off. Ocean, forgetting that he was a Lapillis, tried to capture Seraphima. Duncan and Monsieur

Fontane laughed until they could hardly take a breath. No sooner had they composed themselves than Christopher bristled up, incensed, and unfurled his horsewhip.

'Good gracious.' Fiona watched Seraphima surge past, chased by Ocean. She leaned back in her chair, looking at the enslaved Africans in white masks, and her face flamed. 'Stop this nonsense.' Protesting and struggling, Seraphima caught Christopher's eye. He turned his head away when she passively allowed Ocean to throw her over his shoulder. In hot theatrical pursuit, the Lapillis threw themselves into the drama. 'That is enough!'

'Mimicry and mockery.' Edessa sneered at the seemingly drunken Lapillis men and centaurs. They were in character, pretending to ravish the women in white masks whom they proceeded to carry off. 'Such infantile behaviour. Lydia, you are trembling like a whippet. God knows why nagas like play-acting at socials, disrespecting white ladies.'

'I'll teach them respect if I have to write it across their black backs with my whip.' Christopher, who was miserably jealous and finding Ocean's bold attempts to flirt with Seraphima intolerable, flipped his hair back from his forehead. 'Savages.' Everything about the performance's playful artifice fell apart at the sound of his whip. 'What was the point of all that carrying on?' A black insect crawled to the top of one of the glasses and fell back into the red wine, too exhausted to try a second time. 'Cassian and those decrepit dancers made a fool of you in front of your guests, Father. I don't like all that chanting and dancing.' Minutes later, he galloped away on his white horse, Peppa, threatening to thrash his father's manservant later. 'I mean it. I'm going to whip that Cassian – blockhead.'

'Oh dear.' Juggling her role as wife, mother and plantation mistress, Fiona's smile vanished. 'Arguably, Cassian should be punished for putting on that awful play.'

'I have received some heart-warming birthday messages from old friends.' Masking his annoyance at Christopher's behaviour, a still energetic seventy-five-year-old Duncan stood up, remarking that there were days his body refused to obey his commands. 'We Scots do things differently in the hills, Madame Fontane; we're more insular. Sometimes it appears that our slaves take liberty with us but, alas, they must have their entertainment. We must mollify the irater workforce because free muscles, which provide the hard labour in the fields, don't come cheap. Are you enjoying the entertainment so far, Mademoiselle Fontane?'

'I am speechless.' Trembling, Lydia's expression was instantly replaced by her habitual coyness, as though by a long-practised habit, but she liked the way he dragged out her surname: *Fontaaine*. 'Please don't punish them on my account.'

'Welcome to the realities of plantation life.' Fiona bent and picked up a discarded mask. 'Christopher is fifteen going on thirty – there are not enough suitable young people of his own race for him to socialize with.' Until that moment, she had barely realised that he was changing. 'I must have a word with him later about the way he turned out this evening, shirt not tucked in and hair loose. I do apologise on his father's behalf.'

* * *

'Come here.' The following morning, Fiona stopped Seraphima in the hallway. 'How long has this thing with Christopher been going on?' A door opened along the corridor, causing Fiona to glance away, but this did not deter her from scolding Seraphima. 'Don't play deaf with me, hussy.' She had suspected, for some time now, that the house girl and Christopher were lovers but had turned a blind eye to his antics. She had seen for herself, during the play, how overwhelming the situation had been for her son. 'Don't think I'm blind.'

'Me nuh know wat yuh mean,' Seraphima blurted out, running a hand over her stinging right cheek. She was not prepared for the imposing appearance of her master, too. 'I was only playin' a part, massa.' Her voice sounded like a squeak. 'I swear.'

'Christopher,' Duncan said sternly, standing in the hallway with worry lines criss-crossing his forehead, 'when Peppa galloped onto the lawn ten minutes ago, I was sure something bad had happened to you. Where have you been all this time? I was worried.'

'A yellow snake slithered into the road and startled Peppa; she bolted and threw me.' Shamefaced, Christopher tried to worm his way out of a tricky situation. 'I'm sorry.'

Fiona, looking at him quizzically, came straight out with it. 'Are you sleeping with Seraphima?' She watched him turning his handsome face towards his father, completely ignoring her. 'If I find out you've slept with that slut, I'll sell her.' The only other sound was a drum beating outside in the distance; the Maroons were talking in the hills. 'I mean it, Christopher.'

'Acht! He's had a wee bit of slap and tickle.' Duncan smiled. 'Keep out of it, Fiona.'

'May I go to my room, Father?' Christopher grimaced. 'I'm not saying anything.'

'Have you seen your blood lately?' Fiona eyed Seraphima's stomach suspiciously. 'How worried are you about that, Christopher?' she asked him directly. 'Is she carrying your child?'

'I done nutten wrong, mistress,' Seraphima's lips trembled. 'Mercy!' She placed her hand on the emergent baby bulge, which she had hidden in layers of fabric during the play-acting. 'Mercy!' Dragged along the floor by Fiona, she screamed and appealed to Duncan, whose face seemed to be carved out of stone. 'Mercy, massa! Mercy, massa!'

'He is a minor, strumpet.' Fiona's hands were around Seraphima's throat and her right knee rested on the girl's swollen stomach. 'You told us you've had vomiting sickness since eating unripe ackees two months ago.' Before Duncan could intervene, she took off a shoe and, battering Seraphima with the heel, she would not stop until her hand was stained with blood. 'You are not having this child, a half-breed, not over my dead body. You should mate with your own kind, naga.'

Christopher dropped his eyes to the floor when he saw the seat of Seraphima's plaid dress. It was, by now, soaked with blood, which was seeping down her inside legs when she stood up and tried to walk. Tears hovered behind his adolescent eyes when the dress was ripped off her body. He knew that this moment would alter his life.

'Cover her nakedness with your shirt and take her up to the attic, Cassian. Put her to bed and tell Amina to fetch that slave midwife, Monifa, from the Fontane plantation.' Duncan watched the poker-faced African take off his shirt and cover Seraphima, who had fainted. 'Go, Cassian.' He eyed the blood-stained floor with a mixture of anger and remorse. 'You have let me down, Lachlan.'

'Stay where you are,' Fiona, her voice flat and affectionless, went to fetch the Bible from the study. 'Your father wants you to swear on the Holy Bible that you will never ever father a half-breed child.' They remained standing where Seraphima had miscarried. 'You are white, superior to her, a barefoot naga. You do not value your whiteness, Lachlan. Swear on the Bible that your father's bloodline will remain pure.'

'Nagas and half-breeds want what we value, our white skin.' Duncan was beginning to find his son's obsession with Seraphima an annoyance. 'Och! The family Bible is a record of our history, Lachlan.'

* * *

Twenty-four hours later, after speaking with Amina, who had been sent to Lafayette to fetch the midwife named Monifa, Fiona shifted on the mat by her bedside. She was not a praying woman, albeit there were times when events changed a person's life: aborting her first grandchild in front of her son and husband was a symbolic act. She could not have been the only white plantation mistress to have faced such a situation. She tasted the salt on her lips, wiped her eyes with the back of her hand and roused herself, convinced that she did what she had to do for Canongate's sake. Yet, she could not understand why Christopher was so volatile. She could only draw on her own adolescent days, growing up with two boisterous brothers, for comparison. The mood swings and the rows with their father became frequent and the tantrums usually ended in fisticuffs between the menfolk.

'My knees are getting creaky.' Fiona was fighting for the survival of her husband's bloodline. For a split second, Seraphima's pain flashed in her eyes and, with something like a sob in her throat, she again felt her knee pressing down on a rounded stomach. 'In this house, we have a double standard. You kill a slave and that's all right.'

'I would have taken her to the Grandisons's place until she'd had it. Then, I would have sold her and kept it,' sighed Duncan. 'You could have made a pet of it.' He ignored her tears and walked out of their bedroom, stopping on the landing outside Christopher's door. He knocked quietly and then said, 'Son, may I come in?' There was no response. He turned the handle and entered, only to find the boy sprawled over his bed, face down. 'In the great scheme of things, nothing happened yesterday. There is a big clock ticking behind me, son. I am relying on you to take over Canongate.' Duncan, wearing a hangdog expression, noticed that his son's knapsack was packed. There was a gun resting on top of the bag. 'Now see here, Lachlan. Take a good look around. Everything I have belongs to you. It's Monday morning and we've got work to do. We need to check the fields and see to it that the sugar mill is running smoothly.' He began to fiddle with his sling. 'All right, all right. You can have her for your sixteenth and at Christmas. I did promise.'

'Don't expect me to act as if nothing has happened.' Christopher cut him short, but in a distracted way, as if he were trying to make up his mind about something. 'Leave me be, Father.' His eyes were stinging and his lips twitched, 'All right, all right. I started seeing Sera when I was fourteen. You have your brown whore, Father. Please don't deny it because Josiah told me. If you sell Sera, I'll tell Mother everything. You can't stop me from seeing her or I'll join the Redcoats. Don't you dare treat me like a child. Everybody knows that all white men in the West Indies have their black and brown concubines. You're a hypocrite.'

'We won't bring it up again.' Duncan held out his right hand, wearing a reluctant smile. Suddenly, the boy's hands rested on his father's shoulders and pushed him down on the bed. 'You pushed me, Lachlan! I broke my wrist the other day and you just pushed me.'

'You killed it.' Christopher brushed past his mother at the door, bounded down the stairs, only halting when he saw Amina scrubbing the floor with a brush. He stood rigidly; his shoulders were very straight. 'Tell Sera I'm sorry.' He heard a crash at the end of the Hallway. Cassian had dropped Fiona's bloodstained leather shoes. Babbling to himself in haste and renewed anger, he ran out of the house and down the path. 'This is your fault, Father!' he barked back at the house. 'You should have sent me to boarding school in Edinburgh. If I behave like a grown man, I'm only following your lead.'

Suddenly, Monifa, who was an indispensable midwife on Lafayette, collided with Christopher on the path and came to an abrupt stand-still. The forty-year-old Yoruba woman had come, as instructed by her master, to nurse Seraphima. Christopher, furious with his parents, looked surprised to see the African woman on the ground. Nothing was said for a few moments, no apologies, but he did something that would have raised eyebrows in plantation society. He dropped his knapsack and gun on the ground, stretched out his hands and helped her to her feet.

'*Merci.*' Monifa wiped one hand against the seat of her plaid dress before picking up her calico bundle. The last of the morning dew now glistened on the grass and the smell of damp earth hung in the air. She studied the adolescent with his wheatish-brown hair, knapsack back on and a rifle in his hand. 'Nice day fi a ride to Lafayette, Massa Foulkes. Mademoiselle Fontane (Miss Lydia) could use di company. *Vous allez?*'

'I don't take orders from nagas,' Christopher snarled. 'Who are you?'

'I am Monifa, dawta of Chief Jumoke II of Osun.' She waited for his temper to cool. 'Weh Serafima deh, massa?' She was directed, with a gesture of Christopher's right hand, towards the front door, which she approached without hesitation. 'I not usin' di back door, sah.' Not unlike a sentry, Cassian stood guard in the hallway where he drew himself up and told Monifa to use the back door. She hit back, 'Yuh nuh see massa in front o' me?'

'Get lost,' Christopher said, telling Cassian to push off. 'Go away.'

* * *

'A word, boss.' A reticent man by nature, it took Ezekiel Darnley all his courage to broach the subject of his children with Duncan over breakfast a week later. He was anxious to support his three boys and two girls, who were between the ages of five and fourteen. Slurping rum-laced coffee, he murmured something about their mother, Minah, being a slave but that, because he was a white man, they should take his status. He looked directly at Duncan. 'They belong to me,' Darnley insisted. 'They're my bairns.'

'Those children are my property, man.' After a few minutes of feet shuffling, Duncan reminded Darnley that under British slave laws, children took their mother's status, which meant that the children fathered by his white men were classed as chattel. Darnley had produced five offspring, McPhee had fathered three girls, Smith doted on his six daughters and McTaff had two sets of twin boys. 'They belong to Canongate.'

In reality, there were now eighteen brown children on Canongate. Unlike their African counterparts, who toiled in the *pickney* gang daily, they were not 'hands for the canefields.' With nothing left to say to his old shipmate on the subject, Darnley sliced into a piece of black pudding and chewed, trying his best to separate friendship and business.

'Acht! Now is a good time to lay things bare, Foulkes,' Darnley said petulantly. 'It's no use avoiding the subject.'

Beyond the boiling house, Smith's daughters could be seen playing with their rag dolls beside a treehouse which McTaff had built when his first set of twins were born. Beneath the blue mahoe tree, innocent and exempted from field work, the girls played a ring game while giggling and singing aloud: *Ring-a-ring o' roses, a pocketful of posies...*

It was common knowledge on Canongate that if you needed money urgently, you could bribe the mixed-race children by giving them useless gifts, such as beads and shiny things. During the working hours, when their mothers were in the fields, they were left to their own devices due to their white fathers' status. This meant that they craved attention and bullied the Africans, especially the enslaved children, threatening to have their black heads bashed in like coconuts.

'That son of yours is a liability.' Darnley stood up and pulled his hat down on his head. 'He bribes all the girls behind the sugar mill. It's groping alley down there. He's like a bulldog tracking down the scent of *black pussy*. He should do himself like other boys his age.' Looking gaunt and dispirited, he watched the older boys baiting his prized cockerels. 'Oh, stop looking at me like a shocked parson in a brothel.' He slung the horsewhip over his shoulder. 'The Welsh shag sheep; your son mounts anything on legs. You've done nicely, man, but you won't let me have the one thing I've asked for: my children's freedom.'

'If I offered you their freedom on a silver platter it would still not be enough.' Duncan watched a brown girl stretching up on her toes, trying to hang a rag doll from a young orange tree. 'The law is the law. Am I to presume you're the mouthpiece for the others?'

'I'm my own man.' Darnley walked down the steps and was aware of three men watching him from afar, like mongooses. 'You grab life and squeeze until you make blood flow out of stone.' It was hard for his children and their mother, Minah, who felt the sharp edge of his wrath whenever he spiralled into depression, usually after a night of excessive drinking. 'When I was young, I had plans to retire to the Scottish hills: a white cottage in the woods, surrounded by lots of heather, and a loch teeming with salmon.'

'Youthful dreams.' Duncan stepped back and admired the green landscape, walking around a brown child making a mud pie. 'We've been called to muster at Fort George tomorrow.'

'Och! I'm too busy to muster anything except pissing in the breeze.' Darnley lashed out with his whip when a croaking lizard crawled towards his daughter, Wannaca, whose red hair was a family trait. 'When I was a boy, my mother used to say: *When we're gaun up the hill of fortune, may we ne'er meet a frien' comin' doun.*' Back in Scotland, he would have shown Duncan far more respect but, in plantation Jamaica, he believed that the age of deference was well and truly over. 'My daughters will soon be grown and if your tom cat comes sniffing around, I won't be responsible for my actions: I'll neuter him myself.'

'I hear the Fedon Revolt ended in June.' Duncan changed tact. 'That *mulatto*, Julien Fedon, wanted to massacre all the whites in Grenada. That is why we can't give the free coloured people full citizenship. Thank God for Henry Dundas – our man in Parliament.'

'Dundas, "The Great Tyrant." That reprobate has Prime Minister Pitt's ear; he sent Redcoats to Grenada to quell a storm in a teacup.' With his heart divided between Scotland and Jamaica, Darnley ambled off. 'There was a time when I wanted to send for a lassie. Acht! A man should have some place to belong to, a place to call his own.'

'Stop acting like the ostrich, burying your head in the sand.' Duncan walked in the morning sun, chewing his gums while a group of brown boys head-butted each other like antelopes. 'Your Minah, from now on, is exempt from field work. Best I can do.'

'Not good enough.' Darnley wished that he had enough money to return home. 'I'm still hoping to go back to Glasgow and take the children; they'll be free there.' He had heard of the James Somerset case in England in 1772, when Lord Mansfield had ruled that Somerset should be free. He also learned of Joseph Knight from Dundee, whom the high court in Scotland ruled was a free man in 1778. 'If I were to return home with my children, there is the possibility of a good future for them.' He mounted his horse while a brown boy clung to the tail, shouting, *Go, Daddy, go*! A feared figure among the *pickney* gang, he whipped the animal's rump, though still stationary. 'Sometimes I wish I could leave this place.'

'My only wish is that the 83rd Regiment would destroy the Maroons in Trelawny and in these hills.' Duncan noticed two brown girls catching grasshoppers and stringing them together to make a necklace. 'I will draw up a codicil and send it to their godfather, Rev'd McKay. Acht! He sold his brother's plantation, joined the anti-slavery movement and has raised his voice in support of the abolitionists. He had the gall to send me a copy of *The Interesting Narrative of the Life of Olaudah Equiano...the African*.' With Darnley galloping off in a fit of temper, Duncan's voice was hard, 'McPhee, McTaff, Smith – a word!'

'We're one step up from poverty, boss,' defended the unshaven McTaff. 'Ain't that right, boys?' He was an alcoholic and a heavy smoker. 'Didn't you hear me, Phee?'

'I'm not deaf.' When he first left Scotland, McPhee had had high hopes of marrying a creole heiress. 'Boss, we mean you no disrespect.' With a smile and a polite gesture, he took off his hat and bowed. 'But what if something happened to us? What of our children?'

'I lead by example and to uphold the law,' answered Duncan, noting that McPhee's face had an odd droopy eyelid and he was completely bald. 'If you don't want any more brown bairns, half-breed children, get rid of your sable wives or arrange to be castrated before your *bully sticks* swell up and get too big for your breeches. We white men must exercise restraint. You men do not value your whiteness, wenching with nagas.'

'And your son?' McPhee hit back with a loaded gun, refusing to be trampled by the *status quo* to which Duncan belonged. 'He's like a dog pissing up the nearest tree stump. You ought to have him neutered, tom cat.' He looked around, hoping to see Christopher on his horse, Peppa. 'There's nothing demeaning about sleeping with a naga wench.'

'Who would have thought it would have come to this.' Duncan was eager to leave, for he wanted to inspect the strong gang and the sugar mill. 'All my white men have taken naga wenches and fathered *mulatto* children.' He did not mean to sound unfeeling. 'Perhaps a game of cards over a dram of brandy tonight?'

Dear Dougal, *6 August 1795*

I hope this letter finds you well. There is much to tell you. First, the 83rd British Regiment has arrived in Trelawny Town. We shall soon be rid of the Maroons, thanks to Henry Dundas who has sent troops to crush the rebels. When I came out, I had no interest in the House of Assembly and the British Parliament. Alas, that has changed. In England, that wretched William Wilberforce has found an ally in Prime Minister Pitt and has put forward a petition to prevent the transportation of Africans in British vessels ('Hooray!' shout the French and Spanish planters). They say Dundas, "the Uncrowned King of Scotland," has Pitt's ear; that he is responsible for sending hounds to hunt down the Trelawny Maroons. Dundas is my man.

My fellow planters and I will be meeting to discuss the abolition of the slave trade. If this bill is passed, it would affect our sugar colonies. Financially, it will be the ruin of most of us sugar planters. Naturally, the lazy blacks will simply 'down tools' and cause more unrest. The Negroes are not dumb; they eavesdrop on our conversations in the great houses and are aided and abetted by those worthless Methodists telling them that 'all men are born free,' that 'all men are equal in the sight of God,' informing them of their rights.

You may recall that I wrote back in '89 when Wilberforce made his now infamous speech about the abolition of the slave trade, backed by his good friend Pitt and their allies. It seems that the British Parliament wants us to make bricks without straw (a nod to the Pharaohs of old). If you cut off the source of labour, where will we get the hands to work in the canefields and in the sugar mills? Given the new duty on sugar (a source of income for Britain during this long war with Napoleon) and the vigorous debate about the slave trade, if this were to happen it would be the ruin of Canongate: the price of sugar would decrease due to competition from elsewhere. I can imagine the Portuguese and the Dutch rubbing their hands in glee, mopping up the surplus Africans who've been denied to us.

What is more, I believe the House of Assembly wrote a report about the financial benefits of the trade to Britain back in '92. Pitt should hang his head in shame for losing the American colonies. Instead, he and his anti-slavery advocates are doing their best to ruin us Scots, backbone of the empire. Pitt and Wilberforce don't care a farthing about us. They want to go down in history as saints, painting us as sinners. If Wilberforce has his way, who is going to compensate us for our losses? Worryingly, the tide is now turning against us West India planters (oh, those green-eyed monsters). I blame the absentee planters who are swaggering about Merchant City in Glasgow and the English sugar barons swallowing up the Fitzrovia estate in London. It's hard to imagine a life without slavery. When the trade is abolished, I sincerely hope we can acquire slaves from Cuba.

Since that free Negro Toussaint L'Ouverture led a revolt in St Domingo in '91, we have had constant musterings of the militia. We are on high alert, as there could at any moment be clashes between the free people of colour and their white overlords. Jamaica has opened her doors to French refugees, though most are in Kingston. We have two French plantations in the hills, owned by friends of mine: Lafayette and Ginger Hall. Pierre Fontane and his wife Edessa own the former; René Dupont and his wife Giselle recently bought the latter (I am sending you a sack of ginger from Dupont's estate). The Camerons are hosting a dinner in Montego Bay and I have invited our French neighbours.

I have instructed my attorneys to make the usual payments to you in Edinburgh. I also enclose a note for Fiona's father. He is ill at present and has medical expenses that I am obliged to pay via my attorneys, etc. I look forward to hearing from you.

Your same,
Duncan.

At the end of July 1797, the morning after 'crop over' celebrations, Darnley went missing from his retirement home in the sleepy hamlet of Brown's Valley, as if he had vanished off the face of the earth. Prior to this, he and his woman, Minah, had drunk a great deal of rum punch and danced the *tabrabtah*. Her mother was a Koromantyn and had taught her the rope dance. Whilst smoking her tobacco pipe, Minah told their children *abarra* stories: how evil spirits lured good people to their deaths, appearing in the form of deceased friends and relatives. Darnley was very drunk by this point and had spoken of a dream in which he had met Lewis Hutchinson on the road to Hutchinson's Hole. According to Minah, he had promised to erect a stone at Edinburgh Castle in memory of the mass murderer. Squirrelling away the money that he had saved in the early days at Canongate, Darnley had managed to buy three acres of flat arable land before his aspiration was thwarted. After a thorough search of his estate in Brown's Valley, his sons had widened the search to Edinburgh Castle. It was not long before they found Darnley's black boots, horsewhip and his green militia uniform in a neat pile at the edge of Hutchinson's Hole.

On the ninth night of Darnley's transition, the day before the funeral, there were loud shouts of huzzah and ululating on Canongate. One field worker, who once flew at Darnley's throat in a bid to cut out his tongue, was heard beating a goatskin drum, saying the tyrant was dead. Locked in conflict with Duncan, the retired white men put it about that their friend had been distraught after a quarrel. Duncan had flogged two of Darnley's sons for drumming beneath his bedroom window, disturbing Fiona. Darnley had argued with Duncan, who refused to legally free his children. In retaliation, he committed suicide.

Darnley was the first white man to be buried on Canongate, thus assuring his place in the plantation's history. A month ago, whilst he was out riding with Duncan, he had had an apoplectic fit under a cedar tree with its deeply fissured branches. It was three hours before he could speak. He had requested pen and paper to make his will. He had lost the use of his left arm and his only request was to be buried beneath the tree.

Over the years, Duncan had watched many expatriate white men come to the island only to be buried six feet under. During the funeral, something unexpected happened when a gust of wind ripped through the stout cedar tree. One of the branches had snapped, followed by a commotion when Darnley's woman flung herself at the cedar coffin. Duncan had told the wailing Minah to behave with dignity. Darnley, a former Colonel of the St Ann militia, was always ready to hunt the Maroons and was therefore highly respected by the well-heeled mourners from as far afield as Savanna-La-Mar and Hanover.

'*Rock of ages, cleft for me...*' Duncan halted when Minah defied him and jumped on top of the coffin in the grave. 'Slaves aren't buried alive with their masters these days, wench.'

'Why, if we were in India, she'd be throwing herself on the funeral pyre. *Suttee,* or is it *sati*?' old Mrs Grandison said wryly, looking around and remarking on all the sudden deaths of white men. 'I daresay most plantation ladies would sooner dance on their husbands' graves.'

'Ork.' Amid the leafy surrounds, for there were many cedar and citrus trees around, Fiona waited until Minah had been fished out of the open grave before continuing, 'Oh look, it's Monsieur Fontane.'

'Christopher, go and keep Monsieur Fontane's company.' Naturally, Duncan could not help smiling at the image of Minah jumping into Darnley's open grave. He also thought of his neighbour, Pierre Fontane, who had offered to make his Lafayette plantation house in Albany available for guests to stay overnight if Canongate could not accommodate all those who had attended the funeral. 'I want you to mingle and get used to the older folk. I don't like it when you stand on the sidelines with the Grandison boy and that Jude Cameron, smoking at seventeen.'

'When this is over, you need to talk to him.' Fiona leaned in and whispered in his ear, 'I hear Jude Cameron and Josiah Grandison have been bedding slave girls on their fathers' estates and going to taverns in Montego Bay, Lucea and even in Savanna-La-Mar. Have a word with Christopher, please.' There was a smile on her face as she stretched out her hand to greet Edessa Fontane. She did not care for foreigners and generally kept her distance from her French neighbours wherever possible. 'That boy is defying you, Duncan.'

* * *

'Christopher, a word.' A week later, while standing in the wood panelled hall, Duncan pulled his son aside. The hall was his attempt to create a replica of Inverkin House, his childhood home in the Highlands of Scotland. 'I know we had a tough time after that incident with Seraphima, awful situation, but we came through it.' He walked the length of the hallway, keeping in a straight line as if he had been blind-folded. 'Look here. Jude Cameron and Josiah Grandison are used to bedding tavern wenches back in Edinburgh. I'd hate to think they're leading you astray, son. Are they?' Pacing the hallway, he looked up to the landing where, for a split second, he imagined he saw Miss Euphemia Booth, standing there in her austere black dress. 'I think you ought to take a trip back home. You need a change of scenery.'

'This is the only home I know,' countered Christopher. 'I am going nowhere.' Holding his saddle and looking dapper in a lightweight camel jacket with tails, black riding breeches and buckled black shoes, he had one thing on his mind and his fuse was lit. 'After years of mother keeping me in a marsupial pouch, you want to send me home now? I'm certainly not staying with Uncle Dougal in Edinburgh, not unless he has a stately pile with chambermaids and stables.' The elegant, long-haired young man deliberately sat on his saddle, crossing his legs. 'There's no need to worry. I've not caught the clap, not yet.'

'I hope you're not tupping Darnley's girls.' Duncan felt like a moose locking horns with a young bull. 'The biggest mistake I ever made was allowing you to play with those half-breed boys, the Darnleys. You must not know them. Do you hear me?'

'I have exclusive mating rights to the females on Canongate, Father. Then again, they're technically my property. Well, when you're gone.' Christopher glanced languidly at the family Bible, unread on a table in the hallway, placed alongside a copy of JH Lawrence-Archer's book, *Monumental Inscriptions of the British West Indies* (1775). 'May I go? We've been invited to the Fontanes for Sunday lunch. Oh God! I've got a horn, Father, but at least there's no danger of me tupping any of the naga wenches there. They're really ugly.'

'Once you've seen one cuckoo's nest,' Duncan snorted, 'you've seen them all.' There was a time when he thought he had lost his son and thus he was in no hurry to draw the conversation to a close. 'I shall require you to swear on the Bible that you'll not father any half-blood children.' Despite the tussle, his face shone with pride as he discovered and enjoyed his son's company. 'I want my bloodline to remain pure, Christopher.' He was now in his late seventies and had gone through dramatic physical changes, losing muscle tone, and his silver hair was wispy. Standing at the foot of the stairs, looking at his strong-willed son, he pictured Dougal trying to pacify the headstrong Duncan of his childhood. 'Ezekiel Darnley got tangled up with bindweed and paid for it in his old age.'

'When I was a boy, I was afraid of falling asleep, scared that you wouldn't be there when I woke up and I'd be all alone in this big house with mother.' Christopher stood up and was conscious of his father's gaze. 'Some nights, when there was not a sound in the house, I'd imagine you suffocating in a coffin in the ground, trying to dig your way out.'

'I wish you'd been born when I was a young man.' Duncan opened the door to his study, hoping his son would grow out of his predatory ways against women and girls. He was eager to return to David Hume and his other reading matter. 'You'll have to escort your mother tonight. I cannot bear those Frenchies. I bet they're in league with Napoleon. Those bogus Frenchmen are overrunning Kingston, leaping about like jumping frogs.'

'It's not the kind of thing we normally say,' laughed Christopher. 'I think I can hear Mrs Cameron and Mrs Grandison's carriages rolling up outside. Why did you have to invite those old windbags along, anyway?' He deserted the saddle, held his riding crop close to his right leg and took the stairs two at a time. 'Mother, are you ready?' He paused to look out the window on the landing. 'Good-oh. I can hear Jude and Josiah's horses. At least I shan't be stuck with two old biddies. Are you ready, Mother?'

'Fasten my pearls, please.' Irritated, Fiona came out onto the landing, murmuring that she had caught ringworm from one of the workers in the new hospital which she had founded when Christopher stopped needing her at fifteen. 'It's £2.10s to call a doctor. Still, it's worth it. I am not putting bush medicine on my skin – far too delicate.'

Standing on the landing and looking down to the quiet hallway, Christopher's bravado vanished. His heart pounded and his mouth was dry, seeing Seraphima standing on the spot where she had miscarried their child. Fired with a deep hunger, he was like a predator devouring any meat it could find. *Tonight*, he thought, *she'll be seeing Ocean.* She had been spending time with him and was deliberately leading him on, though they had not slept together. Today Christopher did not care what plans she had made because his friends, Jude and Josiah, had come to spend the weekend. He longed for companionship, age mates, and could hear them on the lawn.

'I hope you're not associating with Darnley's brown girls,' said Fiona, opening her mouth wide like a lion before it devoured its smaller victim. 'Beware of brown women. You are a young man from a prominent white family. You cannot take your whiteness for granted; it is your badge to society. If you get entangled with those brown girls, you will end up having quadroon children – not over my dead body.'

* * *

Even as Darnley's body was being laid to rest at Canongate, his seed was multiplying. Five months after the burial, rumours began to swirl that Darnley's daughters were both pregnant. Fiona had summoned them to the hospital to get to the heart of the matter, threatening to flog them for refusing to name the men who had impregnated them.

Please, God, let them not be Christopher's. Fiona had kept all her fingers crossed. That was in early 1798, when two quadroon baby-girls were born on Canongate. She had kissed their pink cheeks and carefully examined their faces for signs of her son's features.

'Lachlan, a word.' Duncan summoned Christopher to his study and braced himself. 'I should have had this talk with you sooner.' After all, he told himself, Christopher had played with the Darnley girls in his childhood and was still fond of them. 'How would it look for a highly respected Scotsman like me to have brown, illegitimate grandchildren?'

Christopher stood by the bookshelf. 'You worry too much, Father.' He remembered the discussions they'd had in the study-cum-smoking room, especially on New Year's Day, when the plantocracy celebrated Hogmanay and argued about the merits of philosophers such as James Hutton, David Hume and Adam Smith. 'What do you take me for?'

'You must realise, son, that you are vulnerable to exploitation by brown and naga wenches.' Duncan breathed a sigh of relief, sitting back in his leather-bound chair, where a few minutes earlier he had been dreaming of the Highlands and the sound of rain battering the roof at Inverkin House. 'I wish you'd gone to boarding school at home. You could have gone to any of the old seats of learning: Edinburgh, St Andrews or Glasgow.'

'If you miss Scotland so much, why are we exiling in this place?' With a pensive look, Christopher gave him a glance before selecting a book from the shelf: James Grainger's *The Sugar Cane*. He proceeded to recite, '*Who sees, with grief, they sons in fetters bound; Who wishes freedom to the race of men…*' His sea-green eyes were suspiciously shiny. 'I hope you're not still tupping those sultry brown whores at your age?'

'Shh! I am entitled to at least one secret.' Duncan uncrossed his legs and got up out of the leather chair. 'I know you're seeing Seraphima.' With his back to Christopher, he looked out the window. 'I want no brown babies in this house. Your mother carries the guilt for your first bastard. As for Darnley's girls, we'll have to wait and see the colour of the babies to determine the fathers. We've clearly had foxes in the henhouse.'

Needless to say, a pack of ageing Scotsmen, having spent several days at Canongate celebrating Darnley's life and mourning his demise, had gained access to the henhouse. McPhee's three daughters and Smith's six grown-up girls were all 'big with child,' according to the house girls Venus and Flora. Fiona had tried to elicit the names of the culprits. But because Duncan was a discreet soul, his female workers knew it was unwise to accuse a white man of misdeeds. No number of threats from Fiona could bring the mixed-race girls to name the white men who were responsible for their present conditions.

* * *

Between late March and April 1798, Fiona stopped threatening to put the young women to cutting the grass when fourteen quadroon children were brought up to the big house for inspection. Fiona said a silent prayer: *Thank you, God.* She was relieved that Christopher had not

176

been fooling around with the brown girls on Canongate. Fiona, now sitting in the hallway, had given each mother a guinea and recorded the names of the quadroon babies in an inventory of the workers on the estate. Compulsive *tongue-waggers*, Venus and Flora were soon removed from the great house and dispatched to the canefields. This demotion occurred when it was discovered that they had been gossiping about the brown girls setting their caps at the elderly white men and using sexual favours to obtain better conditions and even, it was hinted, their freedom.

Before banishing Venus and Flora to endure labour in the canefields, Duncan had ordered their husbands (in the strong gang) to flog them: six lashes each. They had started a rumour that the master was a tyrant who had allowed the Darnley girls' virtue to be 'trampled underfoot' by a handful of elderly white planters; that the grandchildren of the man who had made Canongate a success were to be branded with the entwined initials: *DF*.

'It's a difficult business.' Duncan chewed his gums, as he did whenever there was a nagging issue that needed his careful consideration. 'The babies are almost white and cannot be treated like slave children, Fiona. You should not have recorded their names in the inventory.' He was determined to get to the bottom of their paternity out of respect for Darnley, who had been his right-hand man. 'If it's the last thing I do, I'm going to whip them 'til they break, or else I'll set them to work in the fields. What do they want now?' He stood inside the open door.

Standing on the lawn, wearing their customary torque bracelets which their fathers had bought them to constantly remind Duncan of their unfree status, Darnley's sons and the three retired white workers' sons complained to Duncan that their mixed-race sisters had been abused by a handful of elderly planters. By night, when they were off duty, the brown men played cards and drank together and kept their distance from the enslaved Africans. They were, after all, the head drivers and overseers on the estate, walking in their fathers' shoes.

'Yer visitor use we sistas like 'hores,' said a sulky youth accusingly, balling his right hand into a fist behind his back. 'Mi blood boil.' Twitchy and agitated, Perseus was prone to sleepwalking in childhood and his mother, Minah, had resorted to tying his feet to his two brothers' feet while he slept. 'If mi faddah was alive, dis couldn't 'appen, massa.' He waited for Duncan to emerge from the house.

'If my father were alive,' corrected Duncan, holding a jug of grog. 'I have an idea who fathered your nieces and nephews. There are at least three carpenters and two masons among you. Pollux, your father left three acres of land in Brown's Valley, which is now a retirement home for McPhee, Smith and McTaff. I want you and Perseus to take a dozen sawyers and go and cut down some cedar trees. Castor, build a dozen cottages for your sisters and their bairns on the edge of Brown's Valley where the slaves used to plant Guinea grass. We'll call it Flamborough. It's the name of a ship, the *Flying Flamborough*.'

'Yuh whites always namin' t'ings.' Castor, big and burly, walked up and down the line of brown brothers, keeping their tempers in check. 'An' financial support fi di *picknies*?'

'If I had my way, you'd find yourselves on the auction block.' Fiona came out of the house in a sun bonnet and a high-neck yellow dress. 'Less of your lip.' Holding a riding crop, she approached Castor. 'Last year, three octoroons were brought to the hammer in Kingston.'

'Be quiet, wife.' Duncan drained the jug of grog and handed it to Fiona, saying the brown men were getting above their station. He had planned to travel to Kingston with Christopher to hire a dozen out of work European sailors and to install them in the barrack-style building which had recently been erected. It contained six bunk beds and the usual table and chairs. There was an outside latrine and an outdoor kitchen with a mortar and fireplace. 'Fetch the branding iron, son.' Duncan was being shadowed by eighteen-year-old Christopher. 'You there, I don't want you to go hog-wild with that whip, naga.'

'Me not a naga.' Pollux, brimming with bravado, had inherited Darnley's job as overseer and had followed his predecessor in applying the whip in biblical fashion. He did not warm to Duncan though, and focused instead on Christopher. 'Yuh cahn bran' us.'

'Wat about we sistas?' Still feeling jittery and agitated by the sight of Duncan, big-boned Perseus objected to his sisters' children being branded. 'Dose babies almos' white. Yuh cahn bran' dem like seh dem is naga-man *picknies*. Dem daddies white like fimme daddy.' He had felt betrayed by his father, that his childhood had been a lie, for he was led to believe that he was superior to all Africans. 'Yuh cahn bran' mi sistas, too.'

'If yuh put yer mark on dose babies an' dem maddahs, massa, yuh gwine liv' fi regret it.' Pollux, who was affectionately known as 'Bigger' by his siblings, demanded a monthly allowance to help his sisters with the upkeep of the children. 'Ten shillings…'

'You boys ought to be grateful for small mercies.' Fiona accused the brothers of being utterly indifferent to their sisters until they realised that the arrival of the quadroon children could be used as a bargaining tool to elevate their status. 'I wouldn't give you tuppence.'

'If I were to free your sisters and they decided to leave the safety of Canongate, they'd be taken by unscrupulous white men and sold to brothels in Kingston within six months.' Reasoning came naturally to Duncan, who chewed his gums. 'I'm giving you lads and your sisters a piece of land in the name of Flamborough. I'm feeling generous.'

'It wohn wuk, not widout an allowance fi tek care o' di chilvren,' said Castor. 'No, massa, no.' When they were children, he had told Christopher often enough that white men and women did not scare them because their white father had raised them to, *T'ink a lot of weself*; that they were half-Scottish and not African. 'Dose babies almos' white, massa.'

'But not quite!' Fiona handed Duncan's jug to Amina, nursing her riding crop, while recalling an enormous shark flouncing as it followed the *Ballantrae* outside Kingston Harbour. 'We ought to put them on the auction block.' More than two decades later, she could still summon up the Scots' cries when lightning struck the pole of the ship's main top mast. A sailor had fallen overboard and drowned. 'Christopher.' The hovering clouds seemed pleasant and serene when suddenly there was a deluge of warm rain, just as had come that day onboard the *Ballantrae*. 'You must get used to branding our slaves, son.'

'Get out of the rain, lads. I cannot make any promises, except for the land.' Duncan signed to Fiona, hurrying towards the great house and dismissing the disgruntled young men. 'Tomorrow, if this inclement weather changes, I expect you to brand your first slave, son.' He was about to embark on his last project: building a self-contained village named Flamborough. 'You will accompany me to Kingston to recruit at least a dozen white drivers. I want a mason, bookkeeper and an overseer, too. Those brown boys are trouble.'

'If I were in charge, I'd put the bastards to the rack.' Christopher noticed how frail his father had looked during the confrontation with the three strapping mixed-race men on the lawn. 'You leave those work-shy boys to me, Father.' His long hair was dripping wet.

'I have become old, Lachlan.' Duncan's wide-brimmed hat sailed off with the dried leaves when a gust of wind lifted Fiona's dress, showing her thickening ankles. Upon reaching the front door, he wiped his feet on the mat and turned to Christopher. 'Brandy, son?' He was satisfied that, when the time came, Canongate would be in firm hands. 'Come into the study. There is much to discuss with you. I want you to oversee the building of Flamborough. You are just the man for the job. You have my trust.'

'Yes, indeed. When the time comes, Canongate will be in safe hands.' Fiona returned to the hallway with her wet bonnet drooping around her face. 'Stay away from those half-breed boys, Christopher. You have what they, and all half-breeds, really want: your whiteness.'

Dear Dougal, *20 November 1798*

I have received the box with the list of goods I ordered, including the 2 dozen Scotch checked handkerchiefs of 28″ square. They will be distributed to our female slaves for good conduct. I also received the blue coat, black waistcoat, 7 white shirts, 2 night caps, black top hat, 2 pairs of boots and 3 cravats. I gifted Christopher the watch and the telescope. Last week, I had a female slave, Seraphima, flogged for fiddling with my watch.

I have gone into the hiring business. My French neighbour, René Dupont, is short of labour, so I have hired out 20 of my laziest slaves. The fee will be paid annually, but I have asked for a deposit of 25%. I charge £20 per annum for each male slave (10 x £20) and £10 for 10 females. They cut wood on the estate, hoe and dig, plant ginger, etc. We have 14 quadroon babies on Canongate. My neighbour, Pierre, sold a mulatto infant for £5; I could get £10 for a quadroon. I sold a naga child for £35; he likes to eat dirt and has yaws scars on his knees. I sold an impudent wretch for £70. Two years in a row she planted potato slips the wrong end up. She refused to suckle her new baby and it died because we had no wet-nurses at the time. Acht! Her legs are swollen with guinea worms.

By the way, I am an attorney. A widow, Mrs Beckford, from Hanover (no relation to the ex-Lord Mayor of London, who was born in Jamaica and whose son William is the author of Vothek), pays me £230 per annum to act as her attorney. She lost her husband in the hurricane in '85 and so returned to London to live in St John's Wood. I recruited an Irishman as overseer. I would give anything to see Edinburgh again. Alas, I cannot spare the time, at least not yet.

Thank you for Jean-Jacques Rousseau's Emile: or, A Treatise of Education, and Sir Thomas Brown's Vulgar Errors. I lent the latter to a planter in Cave Valley. He has my Robinson Crusoe. These days, when Christopher and I go to Cave Valley to buy horses we stay at his place, play cricket (on Sundays) and cards, and discuss the war with France.

Incidentally, we had a minor fire after I 'made a match' between two slaves who fight like cat and dog. I suspected the wife was the arsonist. I put a chain and collar about her neck. Two wenches are locked in the bilboes. Since April 1782, when Admiral Rodney took 5 French ships and sank another, these firebrands have not done a week's work. I flogged Nalla for deliberately swallowing cane trash, which made her belly swell. I whipped Tully for drinking grave dirt, slitting her ears and claiming her neck hurts. Some of our slaves suffer from colds, chills and recurring bouts of the clap. Please could you purchase the following medicine for Fiona: 100 Mercury pills, 100 Ward's Red Pills and James' Powder, salt physics (Epsom salt). I would also like a pair of spectacles, a new walking stick, a white top hat and 28 yds of Osnaburg fabric. I enclose a note from Fiona requesting flower seeds and vegetable seeds, including rhubarb and Battersea asparagus (which she got from Thomas Thistlewood when he attended Christopher's christening).

I have instructed my attorneys in Kingston to ensure that your son's school fees are paid annually and on time. I hope that one day your son will make you proud, perhaps by going into medicine. I think Father would be proud of me for supporting you, always looking down and smiling at the way I've turned a bad hand into a success. If I say so myself, Jamaica has the means to turn a barrel boy from Scotland into a sugar baron. Given that Fiona's father has passed away, I have told her that she must collect the fees for the six seamstresses she hires out at 1s. 3d per week each; that is all I can spare. This money must be reserved for her family's upkeep rather than digging into the estate's coffers. I have enclosed the plumages of two long-tailed hummingbirds for your wife's hat, which Fiona has kindly sent her. My wife has been a godsend – 'a helpmeet.'

Your same,
Duncan.

The annual work cycle on Canongate began again in October 1799 with fieldhands trudging off to work at dawn, heads down, yawning, or already deep in conversation about their hopes and fears. The new white drivers, implanted with racial attitudes, were themselves despised as poor whites but proved to be an asset. There were a dozen erstwhile sailors, who had been walking up and down Kingston Harbour waiting for ship captains to hire fresh hands for the return journey to Britain.

Reaching for his whip, bareheaded Christopher mounted his white horse outside the stables. He acknowledged Fiona without the customary salutation of, *Good morning, Mother.* She was heading for the kitchen garden with Seraphima, who had turned twenty-two. Looking over his shoulder, Christopher made a lewd gesture, showing her his long finger. He and his father were to inspect the 'great gang,' that is, the strongest workers. The enslaved Africans had cleared the ground in preparation, transforming each section into squares in which they would soon be planting pieces of cane stem.

* * *

On 31 December 1799, Canongate came to the usual standstill. Four days of celebrations were planned, including a Hogmanay dinner for the plantocracy. After fifteen months of back-breaking work, the cane had been harvested and crushed in the sugar mill. The juice from the cane was boiled meticulously until it crystallized. Christopher was up early throughout December, inspecting the boiling house to ensure that the new white men were being properly supervised and the fieldhands were not shirking. The sugar was secured in barrels, ready to be ferried to Kingston, from where it would be shipped to Britain.

'I can just picture the scene.' Duncan rode proudly with his son at his side. Although he was enjoying the company, he was discomfited by a creeping sensation up his left arm. 'Robbie Burns working on a slave plantation and composing poetry to his lover, an Edinburgh beauty: Agnes M'Lehose, Clarinda. They say that, *He was on his way to Jamaica to take up a post on a sugar plantation when his literary career took off.*'

'I need a lump of coal for tonight.' Christopher was more interested in the traditional Hogmanay celebrations than about the literary output of Robert Burns. 'I'll do the first footstep into the house, Father, after midnight. If I get bored before then, I might ride over to the Fontanes.'

'I'm too old for that sort of caper.' Duncan was conscious of a dull ache in his chest. 'It's a daunting job, stepping into your father's shoes, but you've risen admirably to the challenge. I cannot tell you how proud I am of you, Lachlan. You've finally grown up.'

'I'm sorry I was such a troublesome adolescent. It was a frustrating time for you. Father, I would prefer it if you didn't call me Lachlan.' Christopher smiled contentedly. 'What?' There was a small brown boy standing rigidly staring at them as they passed on horseback. 'You needn't look at me. He's not my sprog. I stopped poking wenches when I got the clap for the fifth time. Those mercury pills made me ill. Father, there's something wrong with Sera's bits, too. She's not fallen again, even though I refuse to withdraw, not that I'm complaining.'

'Where did he go, that strange child?' Duncan rode with slackened reins, embarrassed by the mention of his son's sex life. 'If I didn't know better, I'd say we've just seen a ghost.' The boy had vanished. From then on, he rode at a slow pace, carefully and subtly mooting the idea of a proxy marriage between Christopher and a Scotch lass from Aberdeen, whom Dougal had said was an educated young woman. 'Oh, very well! I shan't mention it again, not until you turn twenty-one. Erm, we need to talk about making financial provision for Cassian. He's been with me for years and should be freed when I go. I've drawn up papers. Seraphima is to be made housekeeper. I loaned her to you for your eighteenth. When you marry, you must free her. It won't work, having your concubine under the same roof as a respectable white woman. It's not about what you want.'

'I can't give her up, not ever.' Christopher held the reins with his left hand, cupping his forehead with his right hand. 'Oh God, it's that other French planter, René Dupont, and his wife, Giselle, isn't it? He's been after Sera for ages. If he chooses her at midnight, I'm going to have words with him. Why must you keep up this outdated tradition, providing each man with a wench on New Year's Eve? Why can't he sleep with his wife?'

'Don't be a fool. You know what white women in Jamaica are like; they won't lift their skirts once they've given their husbands a son and heir.' Duncan, composing his face to greet his guests, suddenly felt irritated. 'On the stroke of midnight, whoever chooses that naga wench is entitled to shag her. Perhaps I might consider it myself.'

'You think of everything, don't you? Well, she's not catching the clap off any randy old goats tonight.' They got within sight of the French planter's retinue. Christopher noticed that his father looked tired and pale. 'Why don't you ride back to the house with the Duponts and have a lie down? I must have some *pussy* tonight! I've got a bone.'

'You think you're the only dog that's got a bone?' Duncan smirked at Christopher's wink, having made his son his confidante. 'When I first saw Mademoiselle Fontane, quivering from the stirrings of unspent passion, I said to myself, *Damn, I've got a bone.*' He often found himself thinking about David Hume's ideas but always decided that abstract theories about reason and passion had no place on a slave plantation. 'You need a bodyguard and a fierce hound for protection; go ahead and train one of your mother's puppies. Cassian has a bodyguard in mind, too. He's a eunuch and a member of the strong gang. They castrated him in Africa where he was a royal household slave.'

* * *

The evening guests began to arrive and Canongate was transformed into a traditional Scottish community, populated by kilt-wearing men, and women with tartan shawls draped across their shoulders. Lanterns were strung up on the lawn for decoration. Planters from the mountains and lowlands were present, many of whom had built retirement homes in Scotland and looked forward to handing over the reins to their plantations to sons, overseers or attorneys. Although he was not feeling tip-top tonight, Duncan heard the skirl of bagpipes and could not help but throw himself into the Jacobite Sword Dance. In the meantime, the Africans lit a bonfire on the lawn to keep the mosquitoes away and see out the old year in style.

'These are perilous times.' Fiona smiled politely, making small talk with the Camerons. 'How good of you to come.' With the plantations located in remote hill corners and with the threat of a sudden uprising, even a dinner party was an expedition. 'We feel fortunate to be able to share another end-of-year thanksgiving with our dear friends and neighbours. Pity the Fontanes can't join us tonight.'

'Yes, nothing beats a Hogmanay knees-up with good neighbours.' Beaming with pride, Duncan watched Christopher and old man Grandison finishing the traditional dance. 'I don't like to bring it up, wife, but that incident with Seraphima was probably a saving grace.'

'Hm.' Curiously enough, this was Fiona's day and she wanted it to be a success. She found herself wiping a tear while watching her son's kilt fanning out as he danced. 'If I say so myself, I've raised him well.' Almost three decades after her wedding, she cared far more about how other people perceived her son. 'He's a charming, good looking young man. I can't wait for him to get married and give us grandchildren.'

'Relax.' Duncan was on excellent terms with Christopher. 'Do nothing to upset him tonight. Remember what happened when Cassian staged the Battle of the Lapillis and the Centaurs? He went into a jealous rage when that boy, Ocean, carried off Seraphima.' Duncan stood up, holding out his hand. 'Monsieur Dupont, Madame Dupont, I trust you are well-rested after your nap.' He nodded when René and his grinning wife, Giselle, approached them on the lawn. 'I have a feeling this might be my last Hogmanay, people.'

Into this gathering of sugar barons stepped another French planter, René Dupont, whose manner and bearing indicated the arrival of a social equal. He and his wife, Giselle, had fled from the uprising in St Domingue and had brought their stories of the massacre of French citizens. Tonight, the glitter of jewellery and the talk of a bygone world in the Scotland of yesteryear, when most of the British planters were young men, was over-shadowed by the sudden and unexpected arrival of a horseless and extremely shabby white man.

'I'm off to see a wench about a bone.' Christopher slunk off. 'Och! I'm popping over to Lafayette to see in the New Year with the Fontanes.'

'Mrs Foulkes, I must apologise for my appearance and my tardiness.' The Rev'd Robson Ellis had come uninvited and was on foot, again. 'It is so tranquil here, Squire Foulkes, and yet the hills can be so unloving and unwelcoming. Oh dear! I hope I haven't driven your son away.'

4

Casualties of Empire

On an overcast August day in 1795, five years ago, Duncan went to Trelawny Town with Cassian, his manservant, to collect horses from a Welshman, Dai Hughes, who made a career out of rescuing horses that were emaciated and *worm burden* due to fly grazing. The day before, Duncan had been delighted when an enthusiastic Christopher knocked on the study door, saying he would accompany him. A trip to Trelawny, sandwiched between the parishes of St Ann and Montego Bay, would allow them to visit the Grandisons and Camerons. Although Duncan's heart was racing, at seventy-five years old, he was no longer fazed by unforeseen events. Upon their approach to the border milestone, they came face-to-face with a jostling crowd.

'Whoa.' Duncan's horse was nervous and edgy. 'Stay close to Cassian, Christopher.' Chosen for his physique, the African was a huge bulk who could break a man's neck with little effort. Various shouts and cries from the crowd were directed at Duncan. 'What? The Maroons are on the warpath and the 83rd Regiment is in Trelawny Town?'

'Wah 'appen, *braah*?' Cassian sat on his horse behind Duncan. 'Aww! I see. Ascordin' to di talk, massa, two young Maroon roughneck t'ief two pig fram a plaanta in Montego Bay an' di court convict dem o' stealin', sentencin' both o' dem to t'irty nine lash each…'

'It looks like there's a bit of a chase going on,' Duncan said over his shoulder. 'I don't like this.' He made a U-turn, weaving through a mass of freed brown men, enslaved people, anxious planters, horses and carriages. 'What the hell is that?' There was a dead dog dumped on the sidewalk with his tongue sticking out of his mouth. 'Ork!' Duncan, too tired to gallop in the sweltering heat, simply allowed his horse to trot while listening to Cassian, who informed him that the two Maroons had been previously lashed by a Negro prison overseer in front of a crowd of freed and enslaved Africans. 'Where are the Redcoats when you need them? The road to Fort Dundas is blocked. What now?'

'Di man ober dere seh four 'undred militia gone to Trelawny Town to meet wid t'ree 'undred armed Maroons fi discuss di situation.' At sixty-two years old, Cassian still resembled a man in his early fifties due to his air of strength and health. He had a bad feeling about this uprising. 'Dem seh martial law declare, massa; all di Trelawny Maroons mus' go to Montego Bay an' surrender by August 12, sah. I cahn see dat 'appenin', can yuh? Di Maroons a free *peeple*, so why should dem giv' up deir freedom?' He kept turning and staring back over his shoulder, expecting to be ambushed by the rebels. They would, in the future, burn the town of Trelawny to the ground and defeat the British Redcoats and the militiamen. 'I sure dose Maroons who refuse to surrender gwine 'ide in di 'ills of *Sint Ann*. Dem cahn expect 'elp fram di Windward Maroons in di eas' rite now or di Leeward Maroons in di Cockpit Country.'

'Well, Cassian, for a man who never puts his thinking cap on at home, you know a lot about the Maroons.' Duncan spurred his horse on, remembering how different things were when he was a boy. The first time he saw the Redcoats was while riding in a carriage in Edinburgh with his father. 'All we need is for those brutes to defeat the might of the British Army.' This prophetic statement came true not long afterwards, when the Maroons killed a British commander and began raiding isolated plantations and murdering the white planters living on them. 'Those blasted Maroons have a fearless ability to surprise us.'

'Damn! Where are the Redcoats when you need them?' Inwardly, Christopher flinched. Outwardly, he sat upright in the saddle between his father and Cassian. He had no interest in the sea, whose foam washed the shores on the North Coast, and kept his eyes on the road: ten white drivers and a chained gang of Black men were heading towards Richmond Plantation. As they rode, his father's voice was inaudible and he stared anxiously ahead. They did not know it yet, but by the end of the year over one hundred bloodhounds and forty Cuban dog handlers would be drafted to quash the Trelawny Maroons. 'Father, my stomach is turning at the thought that we could have been killed earlier on.'

'Dat's 'cause yuh ridin' fi yer life, Maas Christopher.' Cassian looked across, seeing the foaming sea on the left side of the road and dense green vegetation on his right.

'It's not safe to travel today.' Duncan rode past Drax Hall Plantation where he halted to read a road sign, pointing in the direction of Shaw Park Plantation in Ocho Rios. 'I'll wager the disturbance between the Maroons and the military will spread among Captain Kalu and his men.' His voice quavered with the first sign that he was concerned about Canongate. 'Those rebels are members of the Trelawny Maroons.' He and Christopher fell silent for the longest time. 'Whatever happens, stay close to Cassian.'

'With any luck, the Maroons will calm down.' Christopher kept an eye on the road. 'You should have bought somewhere like Richmond or Drax Hall, on the coast, or even Greenwood. It's not far from Trelawny.'

'I don't rely on luck. We are going to Fort Stewart for safety,' Duncan replied, but only because it kept his mind off Canongate, which was in no immediate danger. 'I rather fancy Shaw Park.'

'Richmond Plantation nice an' flat, massa,' remarked Cassian. 'So is Drax Hall.' They rode towards the town of Ocho Rios, passing the entrance to Dunn's River Falls. 'Yuh should buy a nice piece o' flat land by di coast, massa.' The African's straw hat flew off while the horses galloped along the coastal road, putting distance between Trelawny and St Ann. 'Is much easier to transport sugar fram 'ere dan up in di 'ills at Canongate. Pity Greenwood plantation not fi sale or Seville Great House in *Sint* Ann's Bay.'

On the opposite side of the road, away from the sea, the cluster of fadeless green trees and blooms seemed to be looking down on them from the hill. There was a strong breeze and the leaves appeared to tremble on the trees above. Along the road, a group of women appeared ahead with *cottas* on their heads resembling head-rings that had been woven with grass or cotton. They carried stones to repair the main road not far from the Turtle River. Curious, they stood on the verge watching the riders. Soon, a rickety carriage sped past the stone-carriers, heading towards the parish of St Mary, away from St Ann.

* * *

Each day brought a set of challenges for Canongate. Sweating in a black wide-cuff jacket, white knee breeches and a wide-brimmed hat, Evan Brown, who had arrived in Jamaica with two guineas in his pocket, appeared on the horizon wearing his worldly possessions. With him came three white children on a mangy donkey that he urged to giddy up. They approached the newly installed iron gates which led up to the great house. The old-timer was unimpressed when Cassian approached and ordered him to wait outside the gate.

'Sanctuary, children.' After thirty years, struggling to forge a life in plantation society, Evan Brown had given up trying to better himself. 'Squire Foulkes is an honourable, decent man. He's a goodun. Everyone in these parts says you can rely on him to provide a cool bed for the night and a solid meal. The starving times are over.' He walked alongside Cassian, leading the donkey up to the great house and launching into a 'woe is me' tale about being 'a whisker away from death' in Trelawny Town where the Maroons had gone on the rampage. He left the story hanging in the air when Duncan appeared to greet him. 'Foulkes, I met the Redcoats in Trelawny. There was nothing that they could do to help me with the children; they are orphans. Their parents were two of the first whites to perish at the hands of the Maroons. I must tell you, Foulkes, there is going to be a meat feast in Trelawny soon and in these hills too. The Maroons have scattered, man; they've fled to the Cockpit Country and beyond.'

'And who might they be?' Fiona, coming from the kitchen garden, sneered at three unkempt children who were being helped down from the limping donkey by their guardian. 'Why are you walking about the countryside with three white children in rags?' She looked towards the stables, relieved that Christopher had gone to Lafayette. 'Well?'

'Give the man a chance to catch his breath, woman.' Duncan looked across the children's heads and exchanged a glance with Fiona. 'Judging by their accents and broken English, they are poor whites,' he said flatly. 'Casualties of the empire. There was a time when I was desperate for an overseer, Brown. You are too late, man. I can put you up for a week, maximum; that's the best I can do. What do you know about their parents? Are they English or Scots?'

'The mother, a brunette with eyes like the fishpond of Lebanon, very

190

beautiful, was a proxy bride.' Having arrived with an air of optimism and alert caution, Brown spoke hesitantly, 'She parted company with her husband after five years of beatings and worked all night, slept all day, until she took up with an overseer in Falmouth. He made her an honest woman when she turned forty and gave her the three children you see before you.'

'A woman of the night?' Fiona felt the blood rushing to her cheeks, where two pink spots appeared. 'We are at full capacity – no room at the inn. Put them in the stables.'

'Set four extra places for lunch, girl.' Duncan beckoned Amina, who had come out of the house when she heard raised voices. 'What are you gawking at? Tell cook we have visitors.' Years ago, when the Rev'd Robson Ellis had first turned up on foot during a destructive hurricane, Duncan had inquired in the neighbouring villages about the *walk-foot buckra*. No one knew anything about him except that an Englishman had been seen in the hamlets of Ty Dixon and MacDowell. At the time, Duncan had promised Fiona that he would never accommodate another *walk-foot buckra*. 'Before we go any further, Brown, we need to talk. Amina! What is keeping you, imbecile?' The house girl came running, almost skidding to a halt. 'These children need to bathe – today. That child's hair must be thoroughly washed, combed and inspected for lice.' He turned around to face his manservant. 'Cassian, see to it that the boys bathe and inspect their horns for ticks and crab lice. I cannot expect the house girls to bathe two white boys. How old are they?'

'The boys are fourteen and sixteen, and the wee girl is only thirteen,' Brown said sheepishly. 'They're a wee bit small for their ages; they're undernourished.' Peeking from behind the thin-shouldered *walk-foot buckra* was a hollow-cheeked, precocious girl who clung to his jacket tail. 'We slept in a *rude* hut last night.' Though the girl-child was tired, her cheeks were flushed with the prospect of a meal. 'Go with the naga house girl, child. You've been on the road for two days and nights. You need a female's touch, lass.' He turned appealing eyes on his old shipmate, continuing, 'She'd be an asset to your dear wife, Foulkes.'

'I cannot be responsible for a girl-child on a sugar plantation, not with so many nagas running around.' Duncan steered clear of any discussion about filling his house with three impoverished white children, one of whom was already kicking Amina in the shins and calling her a 'filthy naga' on the lawn. 'See here, she is like a feral rose sprouting in the bush. You cannot make a silk purse out of a sow's ear. She is too old.'

'Too old for what?' Brown allowed his tongue to run away with him before adding, with a hint of humility, 'I do appreciate your hospitality. She's like a white rose blooming among thorns.' He grudgingly offered an apology wrapped in a proverb, '*Bend the tree while it is young*, my mother used to say. The child is a wildling, motherless daughter.'

'Com', missy.' Amina got hold of her wrist, coaxing the wild child along. 'Com' nuh.'

'She knows how to flick a duster over furniture.' Brown, clinging to an air of humility, followed Duncan and Fiona into the house where he hoped to be shown into the drawing room. 'If I don't find her a home, my lotus flower will continue to grow in the mud.' Today was the usual Fish Friday, a practice that was observed in the hills, especially at Easter. 'Go, lads, go.' He slapped the boys upside their heads, forgetting about the braying donkey on the lawn. 'You do as you're told, scamps. Wash your hands before lunch.'

'Cassian, when you've settled the boys, put that donkey to pasture,' said Duncan, recalling how optimistic Brown had been, doffing his hat when the *Ballantrae* docked in Kingston Harbour all those years ago. 'Um, you seem to have a way with them.' The family that he had hoped for, two boys and a daughter with an angelic face, had instead been given to this feckless failure of a man. 'Fiona, why don't you go and change your workday clothes while I have a word with Brown in the study.' He marvelled at the way his former shipmate had marched onto the lawn at Canongate like a long-lost brother and stood boldly between his sons, displaying his arrogance and ignorance of life on a slave plantation. 'I cannot have my workers distracted by a motherless girl-child who is used to male company and appears to be mistress of her own virtue at such a tender age.'

'You were so professional and kind on the *Ballantrae*.' Brown, swivelling his head to look around, entered the study with its floor-to-ceiling bookshelves filled with leather-bound volumes. 'All I'm asking is seven days. They'll soon be off your hands. Trust me.'

Fiona stood inside the door. 'Trust is in short supply today.' She enjoyed a standard of living that she had not experienced at home and did not want the disruptive children to associate with her son. 'You say seven days?' She walked out the door. 'Three days.'

'You are disingenuous, Evan Brown.' Duncan closed the study door and sat down. 'I wager you married the proxy bride you spoke of earlier. You are clearly their father, man. I saw the way that you looked at those children, heard the tenderness in your voice.'

'How things change.' Despite his poverty, Brown went from shelf to shelf reading familiar titles and keeping up the pretence he had created. 'What a difference a few years make.' The air reeked of old books. 'No one cares a fig for poverty cases and poor whites can't help poor whites.'

'Defeat is not an option. I am self-reliant.' Contemplative, Duncan listened to the man's ramblings for a while longer. Then he spoke, even more decisively, 'You dare to come here with three motherless children and no belongings and expect me to welcome you into my home. A man is master of his destiny. You are a fraud and a liar: flim-flam artist.'

'I admire your honesty, Foulkes.' Cross-eyed, looking upwards and sideways at the books, Brown felt humiliated. '*Jacula Prudentum* (1651),' he read, selecting George Herbert's proverb collection. 'They say to achieve status in the West Indies you must be ruthless. I can't break a man's spirit or break up his family and sell them to make money. It should be unlawful to make a slave of others against their will.' He took a breath, then theatrically dropped to his knees, apologising for his anti-slavery rant. 'I'm nothing on this accursed rock, just a *walk-foot buckra*. We sailed on the same ship and you done good.' Pleading, the supplicant crawled on all fours before stopping to kneel and beg, with his hands in a prayer position. 'In the name of God, help me! I don't have a chamber pot to piss in.'

* * *

'Redcoats!' Joy, a freshwater African, was beating the dust out of a floor rug on the lawn at Lafayette plantation great house. 'Redcoats, mistress!' It was a sweltering August morning in 1795 and her face was covered in goose bumps, undoubtedly caused by anxiety. The column of soldiers advanced slowly. She ran towards the house, singing a song of resistance to calm her nerves: *Fire on di mountain, run, boy, run. Yuh wid di redcoat, fire wid di gun. Di gun shall lose an' yuh shall win...*

'Colonel Hemmings here? How wonderful.' Upon hearing that the Redcoats were approaching Lafayette, Edessa Fontane rushed to the open window in the empty nursery, grumbling that the troops had arrived at a time when food supplies were getting low. 'Go and open the windows and dust the rooms, halfwit. Then go to the kitchen and tell Cookie to prepare to feed the five thousand. Hurry up, silly girl.' Louvered doors opened onto the encircling veranda where air entered the rooms through shutters. 'Do hurry up, imbecile.' She always gave her house girls plenty of work to do. 'Pierre! The British Army!'

'At ease, gentlemen.' Out of the shimmering heat came a carriage escorted by a troop of soldiers resplendent in their red coats, white breeches and black hats. 'Captain Eaton, please help the ladies from the carriage, but not yet.' The Redcoats were under the command of an Englishman, Colonel Orlando Hemmings, who had an unmistakable aura of power and authority. 'Monsieur Fontane, it is I.' He alighted from his white horse and removed his gloves. 'Squire Foulkes, I called at Canongate. It appears you have deserted your post.'

'Not I.' Duncan corrected the Colonel, who had gone to Canongate seeking fresh horses, which the army was authorized to seize if the owner refused to sell. 'I am not bound by the King's shilling.' He was not about to second-guess what the Colonel was thinking. 'An army marches on its stomach.' Prior to the troops' arrival, he had been advising Pierre Fontane on building a new slave village. The last one had been destroyed by the hurricane in '86, when the plantation belonged to Mengis Hunter. The huts were so low that they were practically caves with thatched roofs. 'So, you are after horses, Colonel?'

'*Qu'est-ce que c'est?*' Pierre Fontane, the French creole owner of Lafayette, was startled to see two runaways with their hands tied. Neither was he expecting to see twenty Redcoats and six militiamen heading for the stables. Lafayette had been taken over by 'the olden days poster boy' of the British Army: Colonel Orlando Hemmings. Pierre said, 'A libation for the regiment, Colonel?'

'Something to wash the dust out of my throat, Monsieur,' answered the Colonel, dusting a pair of military gloves against his right thigh.

'Where is that house boy?' Unlike Duncan, who was anti-English due to the Highland Clearances and the Battle of Culloden, the Frenchman welcomed the British Army at Lafayette, which stood as a symbol of economic prosperity. The Lafayette plantation house looked down on its sugar mill, slave village, white artisans' cottages, stables and the outhouses. There was a chapel, far removed from the watchful eye of the Catholic Church, but the hill planters were not overly religious and were averse to Bible thumping. 'What news of St Domingue, Colonel?'

The repercussions of the Haitian Revolution were being felt in Jamaica, too. Being neither English nor Scottish, the French planter was even more fearful of slave revolts and had tried to align himself with the British Army for maximum protection. Pierre Fontane had argued with Duncan that the rebels in St Domingue, once the richest colony in the French Empire, should be buried alive to deter others from destroying the remaining sugar plantations. The Frenchman despised the revolt's leader, an African named Toussaint L'Ouverture.

'What news of St Domingue, Colonel?' Trying to ingratiate himself into Hemmings's confidence, Pierre was keen to hear the latest news of the rebellion. 'I hear Dundas wants to seize St Domingue and…'

'Ah, Dundas, Secretary of State for War.' Hemmings removed his black three-cornered hat and tucked it under his armpit. 'The discourse of war should be left to soldiers.' That August in 1795, Jamaica was in the grip of its second Maroon War. Hemmings said, 'I am thirsty.' France and England were at war and he was loath to share intelligence with someone he considered to be an enemy. 'Confounded war.' Walking with an air of authority, he side-eyed three Cuban dog-handlers who were struggling to keep six bloodhounds at bay. 'Corporal Birch, you are slacking in your duties: keep those hounds under control. Monsieur Fontane, I need watering: black coffee, if you please.'

'Certainly, Colonel.' Forty-five-year-old Pierre's greying hair, steel-grey eyes and his French accent commanded attention. '*Café noir.*' As he sat on the veranda observing Hemmings approaching, he noticed that the Englishman's chin was as smooth as a baby's bottom and that he looked to be a bit of a dandy. 'Might I ask how long you plan to stay?'

'Captain Eaton, have you forgotten the ladies? They are stifling in the carriage.' Hemmings's immediate concern was to organize sleeping arrangements for the troops. 'Pitch my tent when you're done. Monsieur Fontane, we may be camping here for some time.' From then on, he turned his attention to Duncan. 'How many horses do you have on your estate, Foulkes? We checked the stables and there are six steeds there. Emperor Taizong and his six horses, eh? I cannot believe a sugar baron stables six steeds on a grand plantation. You do know I have the authority to clap you in irons for hindering the war efforts, don't you?'

'Colonel, I've been informed that fifteen hundred Redcoats will be deployed to rid our island of the troublesome Trelawny Maroons,' Duncan relayed, getting up to stretch his legs on the veranda. 'Is it true that the Earl of Balcarres intercepted a warship bound for St Domingue to rescue French citizens and to put down five hundred rebels? I hope he manages to settle this Maroon trouble soon.' The sun was blazing down, but there was a stiff wind blowing. 'How is it that a veteran of the American War of Independence, serving under Balcarres, allowed a band of nagas to lead him on a wild goose chase? Apparently, Balcarres met six Maroon chiefs in Llandovery on their way to Spanish Town to parley with him, and then arrested them. Jamaica is becoming a garrison like the Highlands were when I was a boy.'

'You, sir, are a Highlander, not a soldier! Balcarres imprisoned those Maroon chiefs in Montego Bay and ordered us to burn their provision grounds. They burnt the grounds themselves and retreated into the hills; an invisible enemy.' Standing on the bottom step of the veranda, Hemmings added, 'There was a Scotsman in the Regiment in North America who was forever regaling the powder-monkeys and the bugler. After the battle, we found him dead in his tent, scalped by Red Indians for telling too many tall tales in times of war.'

'What is General George Walpole doing?' Duncan asked.

'What news of the rebels in St Domingue, Colonel?' Pierre, who felt his outsiderness in this British outpost, pressed him for an answer.

'If I were a French citizen in Jamaica, where you yourself have been welcomed with open arms, I'd forget about St Domingue.' Hemmings looked in the direction of the stables. 'The priority, Monsieur, is to secure fresh horses for the British Army. St Domingue is the last thing on my mind. We, my men and I, were on our way to the French colony when Balcarres ordered our ship to turn back. That said, I should emphasize that we are fighting to defend the British Empire only, Monsieur. *Vous comprenez?*'

'One can only assume that when the Maroons are vanquished, you'll be on the next ship to St Domingue to rescue those poor French ladies.' Duncan observed a Black scout conversing with a young corporal. 'Indigestion.' He regretted the fried egg on his plate earlier. 'Have you had the pleasure of meeting Mademoiselle Fontane, sir?' His voice was low as he listened to two wood pigeons cooing, adding haltingly, 'My son is too young for her liking but, if you don't mind me saying so, you look like you could be a proverbial handsome stranger.' He had gained the impression that the Colonel, whose furtive look made him curious, had not just come to Lafayette to procure horses.

'By Jove, the ladies!' Hemmings glanced at the carriage, conscious that Captain Eaton had gone off to the stables and disobeyed his orders. 'They'll parboil in there.'

'Ladies, what ladies?' With the heat shimmering in the grasslands, Edessa Fontane appeared at the door. 'Colonel Hemmings! Thank God, and just when I'd given up all hope. Lydia, *ma petite fille chérie*.' She lifted her grey dress off the floor. 'Welcome, Colonel. If I had known you were coming, I'd have prepared a feast and a cool bed.'

'No ceremony.' Smiling and craning his neck to look inside the house and up the stairs, Hemmings informed her that the troops were tracking a band of Maroons who had recently raided several planta-tions in Trelawny and murdered a white planter. The search had been abandoned and they were presently escorting two young ladies and their chaperone from Fort George to Fort Dundas. 'A plate of something hot will suffice.'

'My wife would not dream of giving our guests plain fare, Colonel.' Pierre queried why the ladies were dithering in the carriage. 'They will faint in this stifling heat, Colonel. There is nothing to fear in these parts.'

'There is always something to fear.' Returning to stand by the crested carriage of a military family, Hemmings gave a light-hearted account of the journey so far. Like most Europeans who travelled through the hills, they enjoyed the ruins and the untended scenery. 'Come along, ladies.'

'Is it safe, Colonel?' From within the carriage came the matronly voice of an Englishwoman, a Miss Regina Bidwell. It transpired that the troops and the ladies (Miss Portia Freeman, Miss Flavia Hastings and their chaperone, Bidwell) were en route to Edinburgh Castle but a sudden fog, which often happened in the hills of St Ann, had obscured their view. 'Come along, girls,' urged the jovial Englishwoman. 'The coast is clear.'

'*On a clear day you can see forever.*' Clicking his heels, the Colonel helped the ladies from the carriage. 'What the hell!' Then, in a terrifying burst of speed, a big, fierce, broad-chested hound rushed forward and something close to pandemonium broke out when the ladies began to panic. The hound smelled fresh blood: one of the young ladies was menstruating. With a flash of steel and quick-thinking, the Colonel gave a taste of what he was capable of, after which the dog's entrails spilled onto the ground. 'Scout! Get shot of that carcass now and clean my blade. I want all the hounds muzzled – pronto.'

'I hear General Walpole had to run for his life after one of the brutes chased him.' Duncan shuddered, watching two peacocks shake their enchanting tail and eye feathers on the drive. 'Where is Mademoiselle Fontane?' He called for Lydia to appear. She was being dressed by her Black mammy, Scribbles, and was in no hurry to come hither. 'They say Wilberforce and Clarkson are fighting to end slavery. Those do-gooders are gambling with my livelihood.'

'*Alas, Queen Anne is dead,*' Hemmings said mockingly, handing his sword to a Black scout sporting a brown suede tassel jacket. 'Stale news, I'm afraid.' In a scathing attack on the Clapham Sect, he went on to disparage the abolitionists as a handful of idealistic men who were ruled by blind faith rather than a desire for racial equality. 'We can't hold back progress. Alas, free labour will eventually give way to paid labour.'

'I am still reeling from the revolution.' Pierre vividly imagined the faces of vengeful Africans hacking their masters to pieces. 'If only Henry Dundas's troops could take St Domingue and hold it for England. Has Dundas ordered you to burn those Maroons alive?'

Hemmings growled, 'General George Walpole is now in command.' Forays into the Trelawny Maroons' enclave was reaping rewards; the rebels were kept on the run. 'And what have we here?' Presently, two females, wearing steel collars with links of chain, threw themselves face down in the dirt. Their necks showed signs of clotted blood and the skin on their legs was marred by multiple lacerations. 'By Jove!' Po-faced, the Colonel rubbed his right index finger against the thumb absently while the women ululated their distress. 'How on earth can a human being make such a horrid sound?' He frowned when Pierre attempted to ask a question. 'I think you'll find I was speaking, Monsieur.'

'They are livestock.' Duncan noted that, along with the females, the troops had also captured a male runaway, Kuki, whom he himself had sold to Pierre. 'Would you care to see the floggings, Colonel? That miscreant is a habitual runaway. I urge you to teach him a lesson, Fontane. Mind you, I would caution: moderate whipping.'

'Put his severed head on a pole to deter absconders,' Hemmings said in his clipped English accent, withdrawing a lace handkerchief from his sleeve. 'Oh, I am feeling generous. Cut off his ears.' Sniffing, he blew his nose and stated that a leader should be severe. 'It is your right to flog him, Fontane, but I have the power to put him to the question, drawn and quartered. Cut off the boy's left ear as a punishment. By Jove! I beg your pardon, ladies. I have offended your sensibilities.'

'You ladies must be parched, travelling since dawn.' Edessa, who had jeered when Louis XVI's death warrant was signed in France in 1793 and squealed with delight when Marie Antoinette was executed, objected to Hemmings's suggestion. 'A flogging should suffice.'

Hemmings replied, 'We English Protestants like to set an example.'

'Cookie is preparing a meal.' Edessa lowered her accented voice, 'I expect you ladies would like to freshen up. Joy will assist.' As the news of France's reign of terror spread throughout its empire, she had devoured old newspapers which carried caricatures of French children eating the intestines of decapitated aristocrats. 'Come along, ladies.' She returned to the hallway to call her niece. 'Lydia, why are you not here to greet our esteemed guest, Colonel Hemmings? Do you suppose it is a coincidence that he has arrived on the eve of your twenty-first birthday? He has looked at all the military daughters on the island and has no shortage of young women to choose from, *ma petite fille chérie.*'

Upon overhearing this, Duncan let his guard down. 'If I were you, Colonel, I'd snap her up. She has a fine figure: Venus de Milo.' He had not felt this invigorated since Lydia had visited the stables with her guardians, twitching when Wet-Sugar swished his tail. They now stood on the veranda. 'If I were you, I'd whisk her off to a remote castle.'

'I am no libertine,' tished Hemmings, entering the colonial house which featured *lignum vitae* wood beams in the ceiling. 'They say whisky is a panacea for all reticence, boy, but I am sure I requested black coffee.' Bleary-eyed and fatigued from a night with barely an eyewink, he accepted a crystal tumbler from a vacant-looking African named Juno, who proceeded to serve the ladies tamarind juice. 'A simple meal will do, Madame Fontane. We soldiers are used to plain fare on the hoof. I require hot water and soap, too.'

In retrospect, on his last visit to Lafayette in 1793, the then nineteen-year-old Lydia and her fiercely protective mammy, Scribbles, had accompanied Hemmings on a tour of Little River. Looking back on that afternoon, he remembered a stout Black woman walking behind two horses and a young lady with delicate skin riding deftly along the edge of a precipice, down to the banks of a roaring river. He had separated her from her over-protective mammy and escorted her to the mouth of Brecon's Cave, smiling, *Why so reticent, Mademoiselle? Oh, I say, it's good to see familiar country again.*

'I never thought Lydia would see you again,' said the pear-shaped Edessa, alarmed when her niece appeared at the foot of the stairs. 'Let us retire to the dining room and wait for the ladies to join us.' She respected Hemmings and was pleased to see him because there were no eligible men in the hills. Quietly seething at her niece, she wished Lydia, isolated from civilized company, was one of those accomplished young ladies who were not only eager to escape from their walled-up palaces, but also disposed to talk. 'We have no cow's milk, I am afraid. Will coconut milk do for those who take milky coffee?'

'Coconut milk?' grimaced Hemmings, handing Juno the cup and producing a pair of teardrop pearl earrings wrapped in gold paper. 'Mademoiselle Fontane.' He approached Lydia, whom he admired because she was positively radiant and not one of those simple, normal-minded, creole creatures. 'A gift for you.' He proffered, asking, 'Did you miss me? I heard you were indisposed.'

'I was not aware I'd kept you waiting.' Lydia stood on the last rung of the stairs. 'Don't crush me, Orlando.' With a short, straight nose and dark eyes hidden behind long lashes, she was known for her quiet disposition. 'Thank you for the gift, but my ears aren't pierced.' She flushed rosily. 'May I go outside, Uncle? I feel hemmed in.'

Wearing an anxious expression, Edessa said, 'Keep your views to yourself.' Lydia had made her nervous by keeping the Colonel waiting for fifteen minutes. Speaking harshly to her niece, she had called her an overgrown child and told her to sit beside Hemmings in the dining room and to serve him in a delicate cup. 'Don't spoil things, Lydia.'

'Ah, the dining room.' Pierre had waited and waited for the fighting soldier to return. 'I don't know what we should have done without Colonel Hemmings's visits, I am sure.'

Duncan admired Lydia's long white neck, which reminded him of a Botticelli nymph. 'Women should curb that natural desire to explore the world.' He wished she had a head of thick burnish-gold hair, square white shoulders and a long waist. 'Mademoiselle, why are you wearing elbow-length gloves and a bonnet indoors like a pantomime dame?'

'Ho.' With his black three-cornered hat secured under his armpit, Hemmings appraised the two sniggering young ladies making their way into the dining room, thinking, *No tetons*. Blinking, he eyed Lydia's off the shoulder black dress, ogling her cleavage. 'Charming ensemble. If I may say so, you look ravishing today, Mademoiselle Fontane.' Smiling, he conjured up the placid image of Vermeer's painting, *Girl with a Pearl Earring*. 'You ought to pierce your dainty ears, Mademoiselle. And you are stinting with your praise, Foulkes.'

'I have been gently rebuked.' Duncan sat down at the dining room table where he fiddled with his cutlery. 'Alas, I am too old and rickety to flirt with beautiful young ladies.'

'Pearls, wonderful,' Edessa exclaimed in her French accent, praising the dashing Redcoat as a man of gallantry. 'There is a pitcher of tepid water in your room, Colonel.' The ladies were left to find their own seats. 'Oh, and Joy has drawn you a soothing bath.'

'The bath can wait.' From the dining room window, Pierre observed the then fifteen-year-old Christopher Foulkes with the Redcoats on the lawn. 'You know, Colonel, if young Foulkes was a bit older, he and my niece would be wedded. He seems to be taking a lot of interest in the troops. I do hope he's not thinking of enlisting, Foulkes?'

'I hope not! My family tree would be chopped down,' Duncan said, imagining Lydia melting into Hemmings's arms and immediately feeling ashamed of the thought. 'Don't wait too long to have a son, Monsieur. I was sixty before he was born and I have rightly made a companion of him.' He gesticulated vaguely, adding, 'There are three suitable young ladies here but, alas, my son is not of marriageable age. Don't be fooled by his height and intelligence, Monsieur.'

'Captain Eaton,' Hemmings put his head out the window, 'I would like you to join us, pronto. You too, young Foulkes.' He then placed his hat on a sideboard nearby. 'That is an order. I am not a patient man.'

'You are a leader of men, Colonel.' Grinning from ear to ear, Duncan was right about his son's intelligence. No sooner had Christopher entered the house than Hemmings began to engage him in a discussion about battles, citing Agincourt and Thermopylae to illustrate his points. Christopher, who had read most of the books in his father's study, interrupted Hemmings several times, making some informed arguments.

'Leonidas blocked the only route by which the Persian army could pass…the Greeks eventually defeated the Persians at the Battle of Plataea,' Hemmings said, pleased that Lydia was not one of those society belles who liked to be fussed over and to be made love to. Blinking, he was completely controlling. 'I am yours 'til the end of time.'

'That is a promissory note, Lydia.' You could see the desperation in Pierre's grey eyes. 'I warn you, Colonel, my niece likes to listen to the birds singing in the trees while she drinks her tea. Thankfully, she is free from the spites and envies that come so naturally to creole white women in the West Indies. Um, we shall have lunch on the lawn later.'

* * *

Lafayette without visitors was a melancholy place, though not tonight. Despite Christopher's knowledge of the ancient world and warfare, Hemmings had lost interest by suppertime: the boy did not have the glamour of a sophisticated young man about town. Nevertheless, he was the apple of his father's eye and Duncan was relieved that he no longer showed interest in becoming a Redcoat. Duncan had a theory that women, blinded by men in uniform, could not see past their gold buttons and muscular thighs in white breeches and leather boots. Side-eyeing the Colonel as they all tucked into braised liver, he thought, *No wonder then that when they marry such men, they are made unhappy.*

After a sumptuous supper of chicken, pork and fish, Edessa and her guests retired to the drawing room. The ladies had had a siesta while the Colonel had pitched his tent outside the stables with the officers. Edessa was busy tonight, organizing the evening's entertainment. She had gone to her niece's room at sunset and told Lydia, who was still looking a little listless and pale, to keep smiling with her back straight because tonight there would be a silvery moon shining in the sky. She and Pierre had no intention of burdening themselves with a spinster; they wanted her to marry before the flush of youth left her face. She wished the Colonel had given warning of his arrival so that Pierre could arrange a shooting and hunting party to entertain the officers, freeing up the Colonel so that he could spend time flirting with Lydia. A faint sigh escaped her lips. That morning she was hopeful, but by the evening she wished that Lydia had adorned her neck and arms with some sparkling ornaments, which had come from France via St Domingue.

On the stroke of 8pm, Pierre, seeing that Christopher was not enjoying female company, had organised a cockfight for him and the troops in the barn. In the great house, the night's entertainment for the rest was bound to revolve around the charismatic Colonel Hemmings. Duncan had been wondering why he was still unattached at his age. The Colonel was a handsome figure of a man, who had no time for what he himself called the clever ones. He observed that Lydia tended to flush whenever Hemmings looked at her.

'You must be very lonely here, Mademoiselle Fontane?' Hemmings remarked that music was the white man's social salvation in Jamaica. 'That brown satin dress, it does become you.'

'I am sure we could prevail upon Mademoiselle Fontane for a song or two.' Smiling, Duncan sat cross-legged in an armchair, noting that Hemmings had an air of what he wanted. Duncan was stimulated when Lydia began to play a Christopher Marlowe poem-cum-love song on the piano, "The Passionate Shepherd to His Love."

'I couldn't have chosen a better title, Mademoiselle Fontane,' smiled Hemmings. 'I am just not sure passion and rustic shepherds go together. My preference would be for a song about drinking and good fellowship.'

'I apologise for my niece, Colonel.' Edessa's eyes flashed. Lydia had been struggling to be heard, singing, *And love cannot endure without its youth*...Edessa wore a fixed smile. 'Tomorrow we shall have a picnic on the lawn, Colonel, embowered in trees. Lydia shall wait on you.'

'I think not!' Hemmings roared with laughter. 'A young lady of good-breeding and social standing does not wait on her guests, Madame,' he sounded amicable enough. 'My ears are starved of good music.'

'I am not musical,' Lydia replied. 'I am out of practice.' Her aunt's words went round in her head: *He would be a great catch for any girl in England*. At all events, in Kingston, where the Fontanes had spent the first year in Jamaica, Lydia had kept out of the way and had met no eligible suitors. She had made one false start and now she applied herself, singing, '*Who is Sylvia...What is she that all our swains command her?*'

'Charming thought,' Hemmings teased her. 'But, alas, Shakespeare was not meant to be read in the bush, not *Two Gentlemen of Verona*.' The classically educated Colonel was unaware of the quiet rivalry between the well-travelled Portia and Flavia who, with adoring expressions, hung on to his every word. 'Are you ladies enjoying the entertainment?' They shrugged their collective shoulders and he promptly ignored them. 'I prefer *A Midsummer Night's Dream*, a play within a play.' He recited coolly, '*Ill met by moonlight, proud Titania! What, jealous Oberon? Fairies skip hence. I have forsworn his bed and company...*'

'Go on, go on!' urged an exuberant Miss Bidwell, filching a line from Leontes in Shakespeare's *The Winter's Tale*, gesturing furtively, '*Go play, boy, play...*' She disliked those seventeenth century alehouse drinking songs that Hemmings had referred to but appreciated good fellowship.

Lydia was pressed for yet another song until her voice crumpled, singing, '*Drink to me only with thine eyes...*' Predictably, she flushed when Hemmings picked up her gloves, which had fallen off the piano. '*Or leave a kiss within the cup and I'll not ask for wine.*'

'Are you musical, Miss Bidwell?' beamed Edessa, who had been angered because Pierre refused to drag himself away from the cock-fight, preferring Christopher's company. She wanted to present the image of a unified French creole family. 'Miss Freeman and Miss Hastings, do they play the piano? Oh dear, Captain Eaton is falling asleep, bored.'

'"Greensleeves,"' Hemmings cracked a smile, admiring the gloves. 'O rather.' He was a ruthless soldier who had given the order to kill and whom no one dared to challenge. 'A keepsake to remind me of you, Mademoiselle.' He inspected the gloves. 'You have small hands.'

'Ahh, you came, Colonel,' Edessa repeated, and not for the first or the second time. 'We thought we'd never see you again.'

'Wild horses couldn't keep me away, Madame Fontane.' Hemmings instantly pictured horses running wild in medieval England, dragging a prisoner along and stretching him as a form of torture. In his saddle bag, he kept a journal in which he recorded world events and his sexual exploits, using Latin words such as *mulier* (prostitute) and *cum* (sexual relations) as his code. In 1786, for example, he noted that *King George IV was stabbed in the chest outside St James's Palace; a Margaret Nicholson arrested.* Two years later, he observed, *George III delirious and in great pain; the King's madness is in his mouth. William Pitt rules the Empire.* In February 1793, he wrote, *HMS Providence docked at Port Royal; consignment of breadfruit plants, Capt. Bligh is a hero.* In the same year, he referred to the war between Britain and France: *French spies in Kingston; WI vulnerable to attack by France; a cache of weapons and ammunition stored in the gun-room at Lafayette.* In April 1794, the diary entry was more personal: *Cum mulier in Cheapside… ménage à trois at Miss Felicia's, Covent Garden.*

'"Greensleeves" is challenging at the best of times, Mademoiselle Fontane.' Duncan, his heart now pounding, could barely meet Lydia's gaze when she looked up at him. 'It takes the voice of an angel to reach those high notes. Perhaps a round: *Dona nobis pacem?*'

'*Dona nobis pacem?*' repeated Lydia, giving a bashful smile under Hemmings's gaze and dropping the music sheet. 'Oh dear, I can't find the right page.' In her mind, it was still two years earlier – 1793 – and all her mental roads led back to Little River where Hemmings had said that he wanted to start a new life with her in Bombay. She sang a long-forgotten song, '*Alas, my love you do we wrong/To cast me off discourteously.*' Unaccustomed to the male gaze, she was conscious of Hemmings's intense blue eyes, Captain Eaton's cold brown eyes and Duncan's playful sea-green eyes. '*For I have loved you well and long…*'

'I am sorry the entertainment can't be a little more cheerful.' Poised at the piano, closing the music sheet, Hemmings said with an appreciative eye, 'I am surrounded by beauty.' A teasing smile spread across his face and he began to regale Portia and Flavia with a legend; they were hanging off his every word. '*Long ago in the kingdom of Lydia, Asia Minor, there lived a king called Cambletes who had a voracious appetite. One night, overcome by a great hunger, he arose and unconsciously ate his queen. In the morning, he woke up to find one of her dainty hands in his big mouth: hanky-panky.*' Smiling enigmatically, his attention turned to Lydia. 'Mademoiselle Fontane, one day music and life will merge into one for you. I plan to be there to see that it happens.'

'How prophetic.' Miss Bidwell broke into a laugh. 'She'll make a good wife for a merchant or a country parson. Do regale us with a story or a song, Squire Foulkes.'

'*Come follow, follow, follow, follow, follow, follow me,*' sang Duncan, picturing the proxy bride on the *Ballantrae*. '*Wither shall I follow… follow thee?*' He stopped abruptly and began to tell the fable of Hercules wrestling with Cerberus, the three-headed dog that kept the living from entering the gate of Hades, to the conclusion in which the Greek hero slew the beast and dragged it out of hell back to earth. This was followed by another song, "The Spanish Merchant's Daughter." He began to sing: '*On yonder hill there stands a creature/Who she is I do not know/I will court her for her beauty/She must answer yes or no…*'

'*Oh no John, no John…*' Over-exuberant, Miss Bidwell and Duncan smiled at one another, enjoying a shared foot-tapping moment.

'*Oh no John, no John, no John…*' Duncan laughed out loud.

'I am mildly entertained, Squire Foulkes.' Captain Eaton was a tad preoccupied with thoughts of imported British culture, which dictated what songs were sung in drawing rooms in the great houses across the British West Indies. 'You are leading Miss Bidwell up the garden path.'

'Ha ha ha.' Miss Bidwell heard a titter and joined in, unaware that the joke was in fact on her. 'Manners, girls.' Dressed in white satin and ringlets, Flavia and Portia shook with suppressed laughter when she gave a thorough-cough and let slip, *'O tempora! O mores.'*

'Oh the customs,' laughed Duncan. *'Oh the times.'*

'Oops! I forgot you Scots do not like toilet humour.' Miss Bidwell covered her blushes with a riddle. *'Miss Nancy go to market in 'er fine yellow gown but it tear. No tailor in town could mend it.'* Infected by Hemmings's sense of humour, her smile widened. *'Wat am I? Me is ripe plantain wid broken skin.'* The toxic mood of cheerfulness returned as she admired Hemmings's long ponytail and its dashing black velvet bow. 'Why do men wage wars of aggression and lay claim to vast tracts of land that nobody in England will ever see, Colonel? The wanton killings and destruction are surely a high price to pay?'

'Women should not meddle in war games,' remarked a bored-looking Captain Eaton. 'Don't you agree?' This message acted as a provocation, designed to silence the over-talkative chaperone and to elicit a response from male company. 'Why should we be saddled with three helpless female passengers? We are fighting a war, not baby-sitting little girls.'

'War is a necessity.' Hemmings glanced slyly at Captain Eaton, who was leaning against the piano. 'Storytime, methinks.'

'Do regale us with a story of military exploits.' Miss Bidwell clapped her neck where a mosquito had landed. 'Oh, I do admire men in uniform: Redcoats!'

'Ditto!' Chortling, Hemmings proceeded to recount the tale of an ancient Greek woman hitching up her skirt and asking her cowardly soldier-son if he intended to crawl back up to where he came from. 'Your turn, Captain Eaton – a story.'

'I am partial to the odd alehouse song about beer drinking and good fellowship, but storytelling is not my forte.' Eaton's narrow eyes screwed up with suspicion. 'You are setting me up to fail.' He began, 'Twenty years ago, I was a member of a troop of Redcoats who raided a Maroon village. Funnily enough, there was an old woman there named Nanny. Allegedly, she used magic to render the Maroons invincible in battle. She wore a leather holster with two daggers, too. The leader of the raiding party, Colonel Wessex, turned in his saddle and said, *When anything doesn't please me, I take it off.'* He was aware of furtive glances between Lydia and Hemmings. 'Do you always stare so boldly at ladies, Orlando?'

'Mademoiselle Fontane, you and I are to be married imminently.' Hemmings, getting down on one knee without difficulty, took Lydia's hand and kissed it. 'I bind myself to you by *the Promise of Odin*. Once we are married, you won't find me ungenerous as a husband.'

'Oh, I'm delighted for you both, Colonel.' Miss Bidwell gawped. 'What is she bringing to the table? She has a nice straight back, if I say so myself, but one cannot make a lady out of a creole-born person.'

'Hang on there.' Duncan pictured a full-bearded Odin astride his eight-legged horse, Sleipnir, entering the gates of Valhalla. 'My son is creole-born and he is a gentleman.' Despite the grudging responses to the marriage proposal, he was acutely aware that Captain Eaton offered no congratulations. 'Good-oh.' Embarrassed, he realised that he, a man of seventy-five, had come close to declaring his personal feelings in public. 'We ought to drink to your health, Mademoiselle Fontane.'

'I am ecstatic, Colonel.' Edessa's eyes lit up. 'Lydia being a French creole, she is simple and unspoilt; she brings her virtue to the table.'

A week beforehand, an African named Peninah had approached Pierre and sank to her knees: *Save me, massa.* To make matters worse, she was clutching a brown child. Her man, Boaz, later strangled her because the child was fathered by Pierre. Despite the threats of punishment made towards him, the murderer, Boaz, had maintained his innocence. The Africans had sung dirges at Peninah's funeral, saying with relief, *She free at last.*

'Wonderful news, Lydia.' Edessa's mind was elsewhere. She seemed so distant and yet so ecstatic that it was almost worrying, especially when she turned to Hemmings and said cheerily, 'Could I possibly lure you and your dashing Redcoats to a picnic at Little River tomorrow, Colonel?'

'You lucky hog.' Duncan's smile slipped and he sounded less than effusive in his congratulatory remarks. 'No doubt she'll inspire you at jousting tournaments.' Almost choking on the words, he took Lydia's hand. 'Mademoiselle Fontane, what a nice old ring.'

'Perfectly splendid.' Tearing herself away from Pierre's constant indiscretions, Edessa watched Joy dishing out tamarind ball sweets. 'First pearls and now rubies.' She admired Lydia's antique engagement ring, an heirloom. 'I am impressed.' There was an underlying unease in the air and a fierce look on Captain Eaton's face. Joy left the room with an empty silver platter. 'Now that you are spoken for, Colonel, I daresay you won't be needing a groom of the stool or of the wardrobe to dress you once you have a wife for those tasks.'

'How good of you to say so, Madame Fontane,' Miss Bidwell said snidely, towards the end of the evening's entertainment. 'Crikey! A brown baby servant: mulatto.' She fixed her gaze on a plump mixed-race child crawling across the room. 'Whose is that awful, half-breed child?'

'Sheesh!' Edessa's thin lips curled when the curious child sat still, watching the guests like a chameleon crawling up a cedar tree in silence. Meanwhile, the sour-faced ladies ate their tamarind balls, looking on as if they were all sucking lemons collectively. 'Go away, child. Shoo.'

'How civilized of you to make a house pet of her, Madame Fontane.' Keeping up a running commentary, for Edessa was tight-lipped, Miss Bidwell sucked her tamarind ball. 'Wise to incorporate her into the domestic sphere, keep her out of the hands of those ruthless slave traders. I have seen quite a few of these brown children in St Mary. Shoo, child!'

* * *

In the morning, at 9am, the troops decamped to Little River fortified with a hearty breakfast of oat porridge, boiled eggs and pigs' liver. They were under strain, scouring the hills in search of the rebels, and had found refuge and restoration in this secluded spot. Hemmings prided himself on his appearance and was a stickler for personal hygiene in the camp, so the bolthole served its purpose. Before bathing, the soldiers had washed their clothes whilst sitting by the waterside like washerwomen. Stained shirts, discoloured drawers and grubby socks lay drying on branches and on hot boulders by the river. Three months ago, some of these young men had marched through the Scottish Highlands, looking dashing in their red coats and shouldering muskets. At home, they had been waved off to sea by their mothers, wives and anxious fiancées with tear-stained red cheeks.

'*Heart of oaks are our ships...*' Standing up and swaying on their feet, a group of men with lily-white skin jumped into the river naked, enjoying the manly camaraderie and raising up a song that was popular in the Navy: '*We always are ready, steady, boys…*'

While these words echoed across the hills, Hemmings bathed further down river, using the aloe vera plant as a substitute for soap. He had wanted Lydia to accompany him, but she had slept in. The soap was a gift from Edessa, who had instructed Monifa (Captain Kalu's long-lost sister) to supply the troops with homemade soap. Surrounded by indigenous trees, whose low branches hung over the river, the troops frolicked in the water in the sunlit morning. Since his surprising engagement, Hemmings had gone to great lengths to distance himself from a po-faced Captain Eaton. He felt that he had embarked on a journey from the sublime to the ridiculous when a young soldier, whooping and punching the air, climbed a misshapen tree and fell into a bed of prickly cacti. He howled in agony while his comrades sang "Rule Britannia."

'Must you wreck my happiness?' In a thinly veiled swipe at Eaton's jealousy, Hemmings cleaned his teeth with wood ashes, which he kept in his saddlebag, and chewed sugarcane to cleanse his mouth. 'Do stop sulking.' He waded into the water and was transported back to London where he and Eaton had once taken a boat down the River Thames to Blackfriars. From there, they travelled to Bank and picked up a bisexual prostitute in Cheapside, under the sound of the Bow Bells, and enjoyed a frenetic weekend as a threesome. Fresh out of Fleet Prison for not paying his creditors, the laughing Larry had given them a disease and they were obliged to see a doctor. Lost in a reverie, the incessant birdsong in nearby trees and bramble clumps caused the Colonel to snap back into reality and swim towards the bank of the river. 'Do you still love me, Jason?'

'You won't let me,' quipped Captain Eaton, who had been willing to debase himself on numerous occasions to keep his lover. There was the time he had had sex with a prostitute up against a wall near Petticoat Lane because Hemmings wanted to watch, even though Eaton disliked women. 'I am too old to change my habit.' Nearby, a snake lay still, camouflaged on a boulder beside the seething captain who made it clear that their personal relationship could not be so easily erased. 'So then.' The surprise engagement had floored him. He spent the night sleeping with one eye open, hoping that Hemmings would come to his tent. 'I've never been unfaithful, *semper fidelis*, not even at home. London is full of laughing boys who'll go with any man for a phial of opium, but not me. I risked my life for you, Orla, only to be thrown over for a shivering little girl.'

'Please don't let us fall out, Jason.' Water dripped from Hemmings's hair. He stood on dry land with a shiver down his spine when he saw a snake lying in the dirt with its head lobbed off. 'Don't nag me.' He suggested that it was time for a fresh start, and one that he took gladly. Some distance away, a soldier with chronic diarrhoea defecated with a protracted groan in the bush. 'As for my intended's age, psh! They say Margaret Beaufort was twelve when she married Edmund Tudor and thirteen when she became mother to Henry VIII.'

'The best way to boost morale in the camp is to capture the Maroons.' Eaton looked around to ensure that they were not overheard. 'For days, we've been one step behind the rebels.' It was noon and he had spent the morning with the Cuban dog-handlers: one of the hounds had turned aggressively on the scout. He knew well that if his lover were to marry, he would become surplus to requirements and therefore unwelcome in his life. 'This engagement, what about us?' Stepping into his damp but clean breeches, he felt the full awkwardness of the moment. 'We should be mobilizing the troops.'

'We both know that tracking the Maroons is mind-numbingly tedious.' Hemmings winced, as if to emphasize his discomfort. 'I wager I've got a boil on my backside from sitting in the saddle all day.' In the searing heat, two sets of eyes narrowed, watching a mud-caked bullfrog being carried down river on driftwood. It would suffocate in the heat unless it escaped. 'Let me go, Jason.' Torn between his love of Eaton and desire for Lydia, there followed a dance of carefully chosen words, for he knew that his lover was prepared to do anything to stay in his orbit. 'Please release me.'

'We had an agreement: *quid pro quo*.' Eaton had been left reeling after the surprise marriage proposal. '*You scratch my back and I'll scratch yours*.' The mud-caked frog leapt into the water and was carried off by the current while two soldiers bludgeoned a wild boar they had caught and fed it to the hounds. '*Acta non verba. Deeds, not words*.'

'So, we're talking Latin now, eh?' Hemmings hit back, having gone to great lengths to conceal their relationship. *'Veni, vidi, vici. I came, I saw, I conquered.'* Irritated by this exchange with his lover, he heard the roll of drums and pictured soldiers clambering over broken bodies. They had experienced active service together in St Domingue where they had travelled in a warship to rescue French citizens during the first wave of the revolution. Dressing with haste, he recalled the time he took Lydia, who had told him to drop the Mademoiselle, on the river in a canoe made from a hollow cotton tree. While they were paddling, he put down the oars and caressed her left ankle until he noticed a scar on her leg. She was embarrassed by the blemish and quickly covered her legs before explaining that the injury was sustained in St Domingue during the revolution. After two decades with Eaton, he knew well beforehand that his lover would not accept the engagement, yet he could not bring himself to sit down with him and talk about their situation, even though he felt that it would be right and proper to do so. 'I know you as well as I know my right hand, Jason. However, I have a duty and I must follow the dictates of my own heart.'

'Confucius?' Eaton began to spar with his lover while the troops were up to their necks in river water. 'I should have left you to die in the American War of Independence.' Although he too was handsome, he lacked Hemmings's charm, style and panache, and was too direct, verging on rude. 'St Sebastian was with you that day, lucky hog: an arrow through your side.' There was a feeling of betrayal. 'Well, it grazed your side.'

'Blasted Mohawks.' Hemmings made a show of crossing swords with his constant companion, for they were being watched by a group of men upriver. He remembered being accidentally shot by a friendly arrow from an over-zealous Mohawk who had fought on the side of the British. Eaton had removed the arrow and cauterized the wound with hot tar. 'You've known for a long time that my father desires a grandson. You also know fine well that my brother died in a freak accident and, as the sole surviving heir, I have an obligation to marry a fertile bride, beget sons and pass on the family seat at The Warren.'

'Your lack of contrition is insulting, Orla.' The bond between them had been fundamentally broken. 'Oh, very well. If you must, you must.' Eaton continued his rant, 'I shan't take this rejection lying down.'

'Perhaps you ought to take the cowl and remove yourself from female company,' Hemmings hit back. 'Why must you always pick a fight with me, Jason?'

'Look about you, Orla. We're in the middle of a war with the Maroons and you spend your time seducing young women as if you were Casanova, or a snake charmer. You are no longer capable of making decisions.' When he was a boy, Eaton had been sent to The Warren in Kent to learn the ways of the gentry. His father was a self-made man who owned a cotton mill in the town of Lancashire. At the Warren, the then baron had presided over a large estate and led a lavish lifestyle at his manor house where an extended social circle of friends from the landed gentry visited constantly. 'We promised to be honest with each other.' The word 'bounder' came to mind and his voice cracked with emotion, 'Cad.'

'Given your dislike of civilian life and pretty young women, Jason, you might consider joining the Cistercians.' Hemmings, still putting on a show for the troops who were some distance away, clashed swords with a humiliated Eaton. 'What do you think of young Foulkes, our handsome West Indian? Which way does his cock hang: left or right?'

'You are impossible.' All eyes swivelled in their direction, causing Eaton to bellow, 'King Richard is dead!' A curious group of Redcoats stopped to listen when he shouted, 'We are re-enacting the Battle of Bosworth. Long live the King!' The troops, grunting and roaring, began to spar. He picked up a pair of scented gloves and slapped Hemmings on both cheeks before throwing them down. *Esto quod es; be what you are.'*

'*Sum quod sum.*' Hemmings stared at the gloves on the riverbank. '*I am what I am.*' Meanwhile, two ensigns stood on the riverbank ready to dive into a shallow part of the water. One word was enough from Hemmings to stop their recklessness. 'Attention!'

A hundred yards to the right, Monifa (who had bathed with dried patchouli leaves, chili peppers and citrus leaves to keep her safe) hid in a clump of bamboo plants, clutching a sack of herbs and spying on the Redcoats, thinking: Man love, *Lettuse and Mordecai.*

'We had a bet, Orlando.' Eaton, putting the soldiers out of his mind, wielded his blade in true swordsmanship. 'See here, there are plenty of other girls out there, Orla. I wager she is an enchantress.' A charm of hummingbirds – flower-kissers – flew upside across the sky. 'Damn you!' He looked up momentarily when a flock of crows flew overhead, making a cacophony of noise, and reacted to the squawking by bringing his blade crashing down on a boulder beside the dead snake. 'This is my fault.'

'*Mea culpa*,' Hemmings said, almost to himself. 'The last time we had a similar showdown over a woman, you slashed my arm.' The sabre fell from his hand with memories of the American Revolution: the sound of cannon fire and musket shots. One soldier's head was split open; another's guts had spilled out. In the middle of the carnage, he had been wounded but a Black Loyalist, Jack, had carried him off the field. By chance, he and Eaton ran into Jack, busking on Hampstead Heath where they had been admiring the view down to St Paul's Cathedral and across the City of London. He had immediately offered Jack a position as a scout. 'She, my fiancée, is everybody's ideal, don't you think?'

'I am lost in admiration.' Eaton skinned the snake which he had killed earlier. He swung it in a circular movement above his head before releasing it. 'I am sick of the sound of your smug portentousness.' The headless reptile landed with a thud, adjacent to the warring hounds. 'To kill a snake, you must first chop off its head.' Growling, they pulled their prize to-and-fro in a savage tug-of-war. 'What do you see in that girl?'

Hemmings made it clear Lydia was no ordinary woman. 'She is my intended.' After a minute's silence had passed, he plunged his hands into the river, coming up with a piece of gold carved like a fish. In fact, this token was *Taino gold*, lost by a young maiden way back in the fifteenth century. 'Oh, I love exotic plants from the outer edges of the empire.'

'You've fallen under two evils: a lace petticoat and a pretty face.' Eaton slid his sword into its sheath. 'I suspect that old man Foulkes, lecher, is under her spell, too. She has bewitched you, Orla.'

'That randy old sire can barely piss straight from his shrivelled todger.' Hemmings laughed at the thought of Duncan being infatuated with his fiancée, recalling his own first homosexual encounter at Oxford: a middle-aged master had grabbed his crotch and winked, *How does your cock do, sirrah?* He had feared the worst and the grooming came quickly. He had been asked to bagpipe the hairy-legged, fifty-something master.

'Old lecher.' Eaton recalled his tenth birthday: an ageing master had put a furry tongue into his mouth. 'I think it's odd that young Foulkes hasn't given your exotic beauty a green gown.'

'Stop it.' Hemmings tried to turn the talk away from Lydia. 'You're being impossible, Jason.' He wanted Eaton but had to restrain his sexual urges. Instead, he was obliged to marry a young woman and to father a son and heir. 'Don't look, Jason. We have company.'

'I take a different view; they are unwelcome interrupters,' Eaton lowered his voice when he saw five glowing ladies riding side-saddle and two donkey-riding Africans, with picnic hampers, trotting at a safe distance behind. 'Good of you to join us, Squire Foulkes.'

'Should unmarried young ladies ride astride a horse at home or abroad, Colonel?' Duncan, on horseback, approached the two military men whose resilience he admired. He sensed that something was amiss, for Hemmings and Eaton seemed deep in hushed conversation upon his approach. 'Married women, yes, no risk of rupturing the maidenhead.' Dismounting, he watched while Pierre assisted two button-nosed young ladies to dismount: Flavia and Portia. 'I've brought my son along. He doesn't have much of a social life in these hills.' He smiled warily. 'For a moment there, I thought you and Captain Eaton had come to blows.'

'We were restaging the Battle of Bosworth; the exercise was useful,' remarked Hemmings, observing Christopher and the riding party approach. 'Nice of you to join us, young blade.' He buttoned his red coat and proceeded to help Lydia to dismount, admiring the shapely contours of the nubile young woman in a white muslin dress. 'So then.'

'Your left cheek is almost purple, like a star apple's inside.' Duncan suspected something. Curious, he observed the discarded skin of a snake on the ground, frowning when he saw the Redcoats gathering their clean linen. 'White men washing their own cotton drawers? I hazard a guess you don't get a chance to change them often.'

'Needs must,' Hemmings said, eyeing a clump of African marigolds flowering their hearts out in the Jamaican wilderness. Although he had assured Eaton often that there would be no other man in his life, a woman had come between them. 'This is for you, Lydia, a gift from the gods on the banks of the River Tiber. *Arawak gold: memento mori; a keepsake.*'

'*Memento mori*! How delightful.' A timid fieldmouse darted into the bushes. 'Did you know the humble dormouse was a delicacy in ancient Rome?' Miss Bidwell volunteered. 'Once fattened, dormice were ready for the dinner table. Petronius recommended sprinkling this small edible with poppy seeds and honey.' She smiled wryly. 'Did the *Arawaks* exist?'

'They have vanished off the face of the earth, extinct,' said Duncan, explaining that the old town of *Seville Neuva*, on the North Coast, was an original *Taino* settlement, though he had used the word *Arawak*. Seizing his chance to tell the first story of the day, he said that the *Arawaks* had died of European diseases; that the Spanish had built a city on the site of the encounter, including a cathedral, churches and a well-laid out town. 'Oh, they existed all right. I have a copy of Bartolomé de las Casas's book, *A Short Account of the Destruction of the Indies*. It is a rare copy, so I shan't offer to lend it.'

'Oh, for summer days in an English country garden in merry olde England,' Miss Bidwell sighed wistfully. A glass of punch was swiftly drunk before she plucked a random subject out of thin air: that in ancient China, there were over seventy-thousand eunuchs, destitute men who self-mutilated to improve their lives and gain access to the inner sanctums of the Imperial Palace. A plague of mosquitoes descended to complaints over the heat. 'Oh, for summer berries: blueberries and strawberries are my favourite fruit.'

'We must not excite the young ladies' senses with plants and passion-fruit that fill the air with summer's sweet scent.' Duncan watched her fuss over Flavia and Portia. 'Having said that,' he eyed Hemmings who was scanning the horizons with a spyglass, 'nothing beats a picnic by the river to watch the day fold around you.'

'I concur. I say, I love the flush of verdant green leaves.' Hemmings, fiddling with his saddlebag, returned his spyglass to its lair. 'Scout, there is a person in the bushes over there. She has been spying on us.' His eyes rested on the scout, a Loyalist who had fought on the side of the British in the American Revolution. Having enlisted in the Army in return for freedom, he later settled in England. Whilst there, he and many homeless Black Loyalists had swelled the streets of London, only to be removed en masse to Sierra Leone in 1787. 'Scout, cut out the buffoonery, at once!' One glance from Hemmings and Jack, who had been entertaining the men with a riddle (*What runs but has no legs? A river.*), went off with two ferocious hounds in tow. 'Scout, fetch that Negress who has been spying on us for some time; bring that spy to me at once.'

'They say the American Constitution states that, *One male slave counts as three fifths of a white man.*' Miss Bidwell chomped on roasted corn on the cob, chewing loudly. 'We shouldn't have given our infant colony independence in '76.' In London, she had seen hordes of Black vagrants sleeping in doorways and even a homeless Black man with a ship on his head, traipsing through the streets. 'Eyes closed, girls. The horses are relieving themselves.'

'*Vulgaire.*' Edessa's disapproving eyes fell on Miss Bidwell's square white shoulders, around which the Englishwoman had draped a white lace shawl. 'I cannot abide bees and wasps,' she complained when a swarm of bees began to buzz around a pot of honey on the gingham tablecloth. 'Bees are like swarms of locusts, one of the ten plagues of Egypt.'

'That is not edifying.' Hemmings flashed Lydia a flirtatious smile and pressed the golden fish, which he had previously offered Eaton, into her palm. 'Come with me to England.' With a fleeting smile, he noticed again how her white muslin dress clung in all the right places. 'I am fond of eating mangoes, dearest. I shall show you how to eat them without making a mess.' First, he softened the mango's flesh until the pulp had turned to juice. He then cut a hole in the top of the mango and sucked, savouring the juice. 'What in the name of God is that awful noise?' A melancholy warbling filled the air while the scent of ripe mangoes titillated his taste buds. 'Take.' Holding out the pulverized fruit, he offered it to Lydia. Unhappy as the object of his admiration, she withdrew into herself. 'Might I tempt you to some mango juice, dearest? They say lust and mangoes are the best sweeteners.'

'Here, doggy.' Christopher cut pieces of gristle off his meat and fed a quiet hound.

'Wiser men would let that naga go, Colonel.' Duncan observed a hound baring its fangs. 'Without her, half of all the births on Lafayette would end in death – lives may depend on her being kept alive. You have no idea how well she has served the Fontanes, and even on Canongate.' He watched the hounds back away from a rigid Monifa. She had approached them with a sack of herbs, reeking of a concoction of patchouli, crushed chili peppers and citrus leaves, which was a dog-repellent. 'Might I ask how long you plan to dilly-dally here? Should you not be out there fighting the Trelawny Maroons, Colonel?'

Pierre's French accent escaped, 'Last week, a wench was savaged to death at Fort George. She shooed a hound and it went for her throat. Let her live, Colonel.'

'Jack, that Negress is wearing a pungent smell, irritating the hounds. See how they back down. Get her out of here.' Hemmings turned to Christopher with a poker face. 'Sirrah, shouldn't you be at school in North Britain or perhaps in Barbados?' In his head, a winged goddess of Victory descended in her war chariot. 'As for the Maroons, it's only a matter of time before we have them cornered.' He threw the mango into the river. 'I am the King's Hand, Foulkes, and I hold his authority to punish Negro insurgents.'

'*Ave Caesar!*' proclaimed Eaton, thumping his chest and imagining an enormous alabaster hand sitting loftily on a marble plinth in the ancient world. '*Saluto Romano.*' He chortled, 'Oh, those defenders of Rome!'

'Might you be thinking of Pompey the Great?' Well-versed in antiquity, Miss Bidwell imagined a laurel wreath, the Emperor and his ignominious end: a head being pulled out of a jar. 'Isn't this the most divine spot? Not exactly studded with classical ruins,' she said jovially to titters from her girls. 'If not for the mosquitoes, I'd swear we were in Arcadia.'

'Arcadia?' There was an easy rapport between Duncan and Miss Bidwell. In a strange way, she reminded him of his boyhood governess, Miss Booth, who was fond of taking sideswipes at his male forebears. 'I fear you have no knowledge of the British Army's might.' In his mind, he saw a bearded bust of the Emperor Commodus. '*Ave Caesar!*'

Hemmings, who was known to exercise authority over those beneath him, said, 'Corporal Birch, you are remiss, sirrah.' Instantly, a soldier with a pineapple-shaped head slipped into a red coat and placed a reverential fist over his heart. Satisfied, Hemmings put on his black three-cornered hat. 'The hour belongs to us, Lydia. Let us walk and enjoy the scenery.'

'There are two lazy white lads at Canongate. They'd be useful as drummer boys.' Duncan, sniffing the odour of patchouli, felt the heavy burden which Evan Brown had placed on his shoulders. 'You'd be doing me a favour by taking them off my hands.'

'Fetch them.' Hemmings slipped an arm around his intended's waist, looking at Eaton through half-closed eyes and knowing full well that his lover was not going to allow him to claim his trophy fiancée unopposed. 'Today, sir. We don't have the luxury of time.'

'There's a young girl needing a berth, too.' Duncan half-pleaded with Hemmings, who was engrossed in conversation with Lydia. She herself was under intense scrutiny. Not far off, an army of black ants marched across a fallen tree trunk where a colony of spiders fed off their dead mother's flesh. 'Colonel,' Duncan said with exasperation, 'I need another favour. The man in mind is getting on in age and he has an adolescent daughter...'

'What in God's name is she doing traipsing across this island like a barefoot naga?' Hemmings asked. 'This is no place for a female-child.' Even with the tension easing, he knew there could be no certainty that Eaton would not cause a commotion. 'As we speak, secretive plans are being hatched by the Maroons. I sympathise with you, Foulkes, but we are fighting those troublesome rebels on the go, eyeball-to-eyeball. Can you honestly see an adolescent girl around the campfire with a group of randy young men?'

'The poor child would have been pretty, if not for the fact that she is so emaciated.' Duncan's response raised a few eyebrows, causing him to add, 'Had she been fair-haired and pretty, she'd probably elicit far more sympathy from the average plantation lady.'

'*Espèce de maladroit!*' Edessa's voice pierced the air, chastising Joy, who had dropped a glass, and ordered her to pick up the pieces. 'Black fool!' She whacked her with Lydia's white parasol. 'Alas, the white child is motherless. Perhaps Miss Bidwell could take her.'

'You ladies have clearly forgotten how to be kind,' Hemmings said accusingly. 'Walk with me, Lydia. I do admire the island's dense forests and breathtaking mountains: eerily atmospheric.'

'I am an enthusiastic rambler and observer of nature.' Miss Bidwell watched Joy picking up a shard of broken glass. *'Black is the badge of hell. The hue of dungeons and the style of night. No devil will fright thee...'* she recited a line from Shakespeare again, *Love's Labour's Lost*, before adding, 'I cannot be responsible for a redleg child.'

'Neither can I. She needs supervision, a chaperone.' Edessa looked across at Miss Bidwell and asked, 'What happened to her mother?'

'How should I know? Her presence, a poor white girl running around on a plantation, will only cause confusion and disruption. She is a *redleg*,' Miss Bidwell said unkindly. '*Redlegs* are white Negroes.' This was the derogatory term for lower-class whites in islands such as Barbados and St Vincent. With that, she rejected Edessa's idea outright, instead asking, 'Have you heard of Jack Mansong, or Three-Fingered Jack, Squire Foulkes? He was a notorious Negro from the parish of St Thomas who tried to incite the slaves to revolt. Governor Dalling put a price of £100 on his head in 1780...You would do wise to learn his story, Monsieur Fontane. I'd hate to be stuck on a plantation with so many Negroes.'

'Can't say that I've heard of him.' Duncan likened the plump English-woman to a whale, dubbing her 'Royal Fish' because whales belonged to the Crown. 'If you'll excuse me, ladies, Captain Eaton. I must return to Canongate to fetch three idle hands for the Colonel. Come along, Christopher. I want those tearaways off my property today.'

* * *

Having faced down Eaton earlier, Hemmings strode forward, noting that bamboos and giant ferns had intertwined to form an archway into Brecon's Cave. 'I'm not one of those fiendish Faustian friends, getting fresh with you.' Striding into the grotto with Lydia, he told himself that she would be the perfect mother to the sons he hoped to have. 'Don't be frightened.' He took her hand and assured her in a calm voice, 'You are quite safe with me.' The scene changed when they entered the grotto:

scorpions, centipedes and spiders scurried for cover in the gloom, as though they had heard the footsteps of giant creatures from above. 'You made quite an entrance in that bonnet yesterday, rather fetching.'

'It smells awful in here, Orlando.' Lydia, drawing back, took in every detail in the rank-smelling cave where she spotted a colony of ratbats whose droppings gave off a pungent odour. In camouflage, a sandstone-coloured crab the size of a saucer scurried for cover while a huge spider dangled above her head. Her large white hat with its lace frills became enmeshed in the spider's intricate web. 'Why did you bring me here?'

'Why did you come?' Hemmings drew her close.

'Awful place.' Inevitably, their second outing was awkward. Lydia was reluctant to go any further but she could not take her eyes off the slow-moving crab with its huge claws. 'I don't like it here, Orlando.' In the semi-darkness, she caught sight of a snake veering to the left. Unchaperoned, her main concern was for her reputation, even though they were engaged. 'I don't like it.' She was petrified of snakes. 'Let us return to the picnic.'

'I have been riding for days. I need a break.' Hemmings was close behind, gazing at a rock sculpture that resembled a she-wolf nursing two feral cubs. He named them Romulus and Remus: *A receptacle for the bones of the dead.* There before their eyes was the sculpture of a coffin hewn out of stone. Holding her close, he was unaware that the cave was, in fact, decorated with shells dating back to the time of the *Tainos*, who had named the site around Little River *Ku*: sacred ground. From the apex of the cave came a ray of light, illuminating the drawings on the wall of crabs with pincers.

'When I agreed to walk with you, Orlando, I had no idea it was to be a clandestine meeting.' Disturbed by the squeaking ratbats, Lydia thought of the scene she had witnessed with Monifa and the bloodhounds. That morning, the enslaved woman had pierced Lydia's ears and instructed Mammy Scribbles to bathe them with salt water daily. There was a small rise of water in a pool nearby. 'There's something crawling down my back, Orlando. Get it out.'

Hemmings, noting that she was on the edge of hysteria, undid her dress to bare her smooth back. 'An ant.' In the gloom, he spotted a sculpture of a couple in an intimate embrace with their dark rock eyes staring into emptiness. 'How I've longed for this moment with you.' He was aware of the foul-smelling droppings all around them, too. 'I never drop my guard in public, Lydia. Do not forget it, not for a minute.' He mused, 'Do you like the earrings?'

'It's been two years.' Lydia recalled a recent incident in which an enslaved woman cut off her own ears, believing the voices in her head had told her to pierce them, which she had already done a dozen times. 'You promised to write, but you didn't. Did you think of me?'

'I've thought of nothing else: kissing your soft lips.' Hemmings took her in his arms. 'Last night, you reminded me of Vermeer's tronie, *Girl with a Pearl Earring*, albeit you have only just pierced your ears. You smell delectable. What are you wearing?'

'Monifa, our indispensable slave, made up a phial of scent for me using frankincense, jasmine, rosewater, cinnamon, vanilla and myrrh.' Lydia stood close beside him, allowing him to kiss her neck. 'You are taking liberties.' She moved away and her voice quavered when he walked into the shadows. 'What would I have done if the dog had killed Monifa?'

'Life goes on with or without your Negress.' Hemmings could not banish an image of Eaton in a dingy room in London's Moorfields, eating cheese and stale bread after they had made love. 'Negroes are a kind of sub-human species; they are primitive beings.' He longed to tell Eaton that he was tired of sneaking off to the seedier parts of London to pick up a gammy leg old bird, their regular cover. Eaton's face receded to the back of his mind. Only then did he approach the silent Lydia and fastened her dress. '*Nous allons.*' He took her hand and walked into the sunlight.

* * *

'Hold yourself straight, Corporal Birch!' Hemmings returned to the picnic scene where the enslaved Joy and Juno were clearing up the leftovers. He made a show of inspecting the mounted troops while Eaton's horse pawed the ground. 'Good man.' Edessa, meantime, remarked that it was a relief to see Lydia back in the open, to which the

Colonel replied, 'What are you implying, Madame? We have made no Faustian bargain. I will not have you, a lady of leisure, cast aspersions on my fiancée's virtue, the next Baroness Hemmings.'

'We must not forget etiquette,' Edessa's lips moved. 'An unwed young lady of quality does not wander off without a chaperone.'

'Contrary to belief, I do value myself.' Lydia, who had no idea of the battle being waged between Hemmings and his lover, pointed to the ground where the gloves had lain since Eaton had slapped his face with them. 'Your gloves, Orlando.' Her gaze moved to a redhead, Sergeant Benbow, picking up the Union Flag. 'What a lovely day, Orlando.' Her dainty white shoes were soiled with ratbat droppings. 'I'm so happy.'

'We may never again be as happy as we are now.' Hemmings helped her onto her horse and told her to cherish the gift, which was *Taino gold*. 'Fetch my gloves, Captain Eaton.' A soft breeze swept through the hills. 'We are waiting.' He took the reins of his white horse, Munda. 'Lydia, I await your orders,' he said playfully, his eyes like a dead fish. Eaton knew him well enough to dismount and retrieve a pair of riding gloves. It was clear that Hemmings would tolerate no dissent as he slipped on the gloves and sat astride his horse. 'Our orders are to march.' Sitting ramrod straight in the saddle, he cantered off with Lydia by his side. 'Those Redcoats are going to dance at our wedding in Kingston.'

'You'd do best to keep your eyes on the road and leave the courting until we are safe, out of danger.' Eaton over-smiled. 'She should ride with the ladies. She will distract you from your duties.' He and Hemmings had spent years at boarding and military schools together. He watched Lydia with growing anger. 'Orlando, your first duty is to your men. I blame Foulkes for this distraction.' They rode on in silence.

'Orlando, Miss Bidwell is keen to see Edinburgh Castle,' Lydia said, following the Englishwoman's gaze. 'Do you mind taking a detour?' Ten minutes had passed and now they made a slow ascent up to a ruin perched on top of a steep hill. 'You do know the history?'

'It will keep, Lydia dearest.' Hemmings, hoisting himself in the saddle, looked over his shoulder. 'Hold the Union Flag high, Sergeant Benbow.' His senses were alerted to danger when the hounds began to bark. 'I wager there's more to this place than giant ferns. Captain Eaton, I want a thorough search of that ruined castle. In my opinion, we...'

'That is not my opinion,' scoffed Eaton, who felt that Hemmings was making a rash decision to amuse the ladies. 'Let us continue on our journey to Lafayette, Orlando.'

'I do so like Roman ruins and medieval castles.' Miss Bidwell said agog, 'The castle is in ruin!' She brought her horse to a halt, gazing at a decaying fortress that stood as a distant metaphor of Scotland's royal heritage. 'I can see Rapunzel at the window above.' Having read Friedrich Schultz's short story, she pictured the young girl with long golden hair as her prince called out, *Rapunzel, Rapunzel, let down your hair.*

'Poor Rapunzel.' Lydia, who had attended boarding school in England prior to the revolution in St Domingue, knew Rapunzel's story. She sat up in her saddle, craning her neck to see what was so fascinating about a pile of bricks and mortar whose macabre history gave her the shivers. 'When you write up your account of today's events, Orlando,' she said teasingly, 'say you rescued me from the castle by my hair.' She too called out, 'Rapunzel!'

'Scout.' A movement caught Hemmings's eye, causing him to look cautiously across to where the castle stood and to scrutinize its semi-ruined fortified walls. 'Take two of the hounds into that ruin and check it for signs of activity. Something about this place disturbs me. I always trust my gut instinct. By Jove, I am not about to be ambushed today.'

'We are wasting time, Orlando.' Eaton spurred his horse back down the fern-strewn path. 'Let's get away from this wretched place. There's nothing here but ghosts. It's rumoured that you can still hear Hutchinson crying out for vengeance at night.'

'It's all nonsense.' Miss Bidwell wished they had travelled in the carriage, which they had left behind at Lafayette.

'Captain Eaton, see that Fontane rides alongside the ladies, flanked by the main body of men.' Hemmings led his horse back onto the main road. 'We must find out where the Maroons are hiding. I can smell the brutes.' A lush green valley opened in front of them and, with the ladies under heavy guard, he rode on in contemplation. Although there was a pang of guilt, he felt certain that Eaton had put rejection behind him temporarily, and therefore he ordered him to escort Lydia while he and Jack doubled back. Last night, at dinner, Lydia had been seated beside him and her unusually white skin had glowed. The two people who made his life complete cantered side-by-side, passing a dry riverbed that opened into the green valley through which they rode. 'Go and join Captain Eaton, Jack. I will catch up in a minute.'

'Watch the hounds.' Jack sat up in the saddle, observing Hemmings's return, feeling his own importance: he was a free man, riding a horse and advising the king's representative. An African American, who did not identify with Jamaica, he was very much an outsider. 'Maroons in the hills.' By now, the bloodhounds were barking and howling, looking up into the hills. 'Maroon scent. They're full of it. Maroons on our tail, Colonel!'

'Corporal Birch, take up your position as rear guard.' On high alert, Hemmings took up his former position and sandwiched himself between Eaton and Lydia, with Jack shielding his back from missiles. 'The hounds have caught their scent, Jason.' The Colonel lifted his eyes to the green hills. 'We cannot give chase without endangering the ladies.' The sight of vultures circling above caused him to draw up his horse, holding up his spyglass as if it were an extension of his right hand. 'You shall lead us into battle, Lydia dearest,' he jested, 'rather like Joan of Arc.'

'More like the Morrigan, Celtic goddess of battle,' Eaton said. 'Something is afoot.' Along the road, heaps of gravel triggered alarm bells. Two decomposing corpses, dead bodies, caused a stink to drift up the valley from where buzzards hovered. 'Awful stench.' Clusters of yellow primroses bloomed in the hedgerows by the roadside where butterflies fluttered like colourful chiffon scarves flying in the breeze.

'I can smell those Maroons.' Known first as a strategist, Hemmings slowed his pace and studied the landscape. 'We are being watched.' Dismounting, he turned Lydia's horse, Sultan, loose and seated her on his horse, Munda. 'I wager there are at least fifty pairs of eyes up there.' Aside from the obvious and critical issue of the Maroons, he needed Eaton by his side; he needed his lover to protect his flank. 'I am thinking about St Clement's Churchyard and Moorfields. The South Side of St James's Park, Blackfriars Bridge.'

'Can't say I recall.' Eaton looked about him. 'This is no time for small talk.' Picturing an old queen flashing himself on Blackfriars Bridge, he galloped off to join the troops. 'Jack!' He sensed imminent danger and put aside their quarrel. 'Keep them covered.'

Hemmings sniffed. 'Jack, they are close.' Minutes later, a horn – the abeng – sounded above the treetops. Events took an unexpected turn when a soaring boulder crashed into the valley floor, though not before a valiant cotton tree broke its fall, snapping when a second boulder hurtled down the hill along the same path. This was followed by a landslide, which sent loose gravel and rocks raining down the slopes.

'Look out, Corporal Birch!' Staring death in the face, Jack let out a cry, 'Aaarrrrgh!' All at once, he was aware of a warm, wet feeling on the seat of his suede trousers before a soaring boulder crashed into him square-on and smashed his body.

'What the hell!' In the distance, Eaton stared in horror when Hemmings fell off his bucking horse and smashed his spyglass. As fast as it had started, the landslide was over. Turning in his saddle, Eaton galloped at speed, dismounted and flung himself down at his lover's side. 'Open your eyes, Orla.' First on the scene, he cradled him in his arms and held him close to his chest. 'Breathe, damn it.' The scattered rocks and broken bodies were ignored. 'Don't die on me.' He rocked him gently, slipping into the habit of play-acting. This time it was John Vanbrugh's *The Relapse*. They had often incorporated this drama into their lovemaking, and now he sought refuge in the old queen, Coupler, saying, '*Ha! You young lascivious rogue, you: let me put my hand in your bosom, sirrah.*'

Upon opening his eyes, Hemmings's first thought was of Lydia. 'Jason, cut out the tomfoolery.' A look of fear crossed his face when he saw her lying on the ground with her eyes closed. 'I shall deal with those *yahoos*, belligerent blacks!' He managed to stand up and staggered over to her. 'Retreat! I want that rebel's head on a platter later. Retreat!'

'One hundred guineas for the man who brings me that audacious Maroon leader alive.' Eaton gazed into the hills where tiny figures were silhouetted against the hilltop. 'Dead, he's a martyr.' He disregarded Hemmings's order to retreat and released three of the fiercest hounds. They were soon crushed by the tumbling rocks that were being rolled down by the rebels, who had a good view of the valley. He mounted his horse, and ordered the troops to form a defensive square around Hemmings and Lydia. 'If we do not pursue,' he argued, blinking because a flying object had hit him in his right eye, 'they will be emboldened by this daring act. We are in a perilous position in this valley, Orlando.'

'It would be foolhardy to give chase.' Having survived the ambush, the relief in Hemmings's eyes was clear. Much of the confusion that followed resulted from the rest of the hounds being crushed by falling rocks as they raced up the valley floor. The noise was deafening. Amongst the jumbled pile of rocks lay the remains of two soldiers and a horse. The rocks that had fallen on them were weak and collapsed during the landslide. 'I shall burn them out of those hills.'

* * *

'Vengeance!' Captain Kalu balled his right hand into a fist. 'Dis is not over.' Flanked by four bodyguards, he gazed down into the valley of death, across a panorama of woods. The firing continued. 'Dem kill mi son.' Dressed for warfare, he was disguised in a cloak made of green leaves. 'Let's tek 'is body back to Wild Pine Mount.' The abeng sounded the retreat and the son of Chief Jumoke II of Osun recalled his capture by Major Fitzroy-Campbell in 1771: tied with a length of rope, he was made to trot behind the horses. An ambush in this same valley had saved his life. 'Com', breddas.' He looked on.

* * *

'Retreat!' Hemmings, the landslide still ringing in his ears, ordered a humiliating fallback while the rest of the troops bunched up around Lydia. 'We will pursue them, but not today.' He was a man of action and, naturally felt sensitive to Eaton wrestling command away from him and insinuating that he was not in his right mind, not fit to command men of a lower ranking. When he heard the bugle, he turned to Eaton who was sitting astride his own horse. 'We shall hunt them until there is no mountain left to run and hide.'

'*Au feu.*' Lydia looked deathly pale. She could still hear the rumbling of rocks. '*Comment t'appelles-tu? Tu es très beau.*'

'Oh no! She has forgotten how to speak English.' Pierre arrived on the scene and dismounted from his horse. 'She is concussed, Colonel.' They were surrounded by the troops. He was loath to disclose to Hemmings that she had sustained a serious fall in St Domingue during the first wave of the revolution and had been unconscious for two days afterwards. 'Try to keep her awake, Colonel; talk to her. She is concussed.'

'We can't leave Jack to the vultures,' the bugler interjected. He played while Corporal Birch's corpse was interred in an unmarked grave. 'Jack was one of us.' There was no time to dig a separate grave for the scout, whose corpse was left by the roadside for the carrion birds. The bugler continued playing.

'Stop that infernal noise,' Hemmings said with a furrowed brow, knowing that Eaton blamed him for his grave error. 'Captain Eaton, ride with me, by my side.' Although he was unsteady on his feet, he mounted his horse and slipped an arm around Lydia's tiny waist. Impatient to leave, Hemmings sat in the saddle waiting for the troops to move off, but the ambush rankled deeply. 'Forward march!' All around, the road verges were ablaze with tropical flowers ranging from purple to orange and golden yellow. 'To Lafayette.'

'*Lundi, mardi, mercredi.*' Lydia began to recite the days of the week in a childlike voice, adding, 'Come out of the sun.' She soon regained her command of English. 'You naughty little girl. No, *Maman*. I won't move, not if I have to see Tante Edessa today.'

'Is Mademoiselle Fontane okay, Colonel?' Duncan had been waiting beneath a fig tree with Christopher. 'Good-oh. We're off to Canongate. We'll drop by tomorrow morning.'

'Do be quiet, Lydia.' With her nostrils flaring, Edessa's eyes were glitteringly hard but she consoled herself that the engagement was official. 'No one would blame you if you walked away, Colonel.'

'When I want advice,' said Hemmings, alarmed at her callousness, 'I shall ask for it.' He was annoyed with himself because there were two routes to reach Lafayette: the scenic pass through the hills or the main road that accommodated horse and carriage. The valley was the ideal place for an ambush, but also the best route to Lafayette. While Edessa seemed pleased to see him comforting Lydia, he questioned Pierre's position as her ward: '*Bonus pater familias? Good family father*, eh?'

* * *

Less than twenty-four hours had passed and the sombre mood at Lafayette was a far cry from the Redcoats' previous jubilant arrival. Hemmings had had a shock, but he tried to suppress the ambush and the way Eaton had gazed into his eyes as he lay by the roadside. A few hours ago, Pierre had consented to the marriage and, in truth, it was about damage control now. Lydia was just getting used to the idea of being a military fiancée, and Hemmings had also silenced Edessa, who feared that her niece would not recover.

Slowly, the minutes ticked away. Silence descended on the hallway where Hemmings paced the floor, listening to the clock until he could no longer bear the sound of the cuckoo on the hour. It was 6pm. There was a bruise on the side of his head, which throbbed under Eaton's pressure to put down his horse, Munda, who had limped back to Lafayette. It had not been possible to bury Lydia's horse. Feeling both physically and emotionally bruised, Hemmings now sat down at the foot of the stairs, studying a chameleon with a broken back on the floor, knowing that Eaton was still seething.

'You ought to send some blacks to fetch Jack's body.' Eaton imagined conspiring vultures swooping down on the corpse. Jack had striven to make camp life bearable, telling riddles and singing songs in his baritone voice. 'He slogged his guts out as your scout and our lookout, too. In return, you give him a kick in the teeth.' The Black Loyalist had taken their secret to the grave. *'Agreements must be kept; pacta sunt.'*

* * *

'So, you are finally awake.' Four hours after their return to Lafayette, Miss Bidwell stood at the foot of Lydia's poster bed with Flavia and Portia. 'Ho! I hear Colonel Hemmings is to resign from the Army. How dreadful.' It did not take long for the mask to slip. 'Count yourself lucky,' she spoke crisply, 'you're not following the drumroll to Bengal. We must protect our memsahibs from the frightful morals of the brown ladies, the cobras slithering through the streets, the smell of dung and spices and the awful monsoon season.'

'Well, Miss Lydia, yuh leavin' Lafayette at dawn.' Snivelling, Mammy Scribbles had earned her nickname after her nursling had tried in vain to teach her how to write when the young Lydia was a child. 'Yuh leavin' me behind, Pu-tus.' Her birth name was Modupe, later changed to Adele, but neither were of much use to her since everyone called her Mammy Scribbles. She had taken to the Jamaican creole, explaining to Lydia that Monifa had set her fractured legs and used folk medicine to dress the wounds. 'I sorry fi yuh, Pu-tus.'

Unlike Mammy Scribbles, who was a visible presence in the great house, Monifa remained on the periphery and trusted no one, not even her fellow Africans. Jack had spotted her long before Hemmings did. She was loath to meet with the Colonel, who would have recovered from his 'head knock' sooner had she treated him, but bandaging Lydia's crushed legs was an opportunity to seal her reputation. Confidently, she gave instructions in her own handwriting, explaining to the Colonel how to care for Lydia's legs until she could be transferred to Kingston to be examined by a physician.

'Don't cry,' said Lydia, pleased to have her nursemaid fussing over her. Miss Hastings and Miss Freeman, meantime, sat on either side of her bed, taking it in turns to read James Thomson's *Seasons* – a fitting choice: '*When first the soul of love is sent abroad/Warm through the vital air, and on the heart/Harmonious seizes, the gay troops begin...*' Her one advantage over her rivals was that there was an inexplicable bond between her and Hemmings, which she did not understand. She pulled at the sheet and spoke with a quiet intensity, causing her nursemaid to burst into tears. 'Mammy Scribbles, please fetch my fiancé. Miss Bidwell, have you come here to gloat?'

'You are undone, missy,' said the Englishwoman, hinting that some men were more easily inflamed than others. 'You lay there looking pale and pure, but you weren't so prim and proper when you accompanied Colonel Hemmings into the grotto this afternoon for your clandestine meeting. I hope for your sake that your virgin flower is still intact, or you'll have nothing virtuous to give another suitor, if he changes his mind. You set that old Scotsman's pulse racing last night with your trembling and panting. I pray for your sake that no one has cropped the rose that is blooming. I am still mistress of that darling treasure.

Come, girls. You must not lose your jewels until you are married. As for her, she should have told the Colonel to go trifle with a naga, if he felt the need.'

'You insult my intelligence, Miss Bidwell, to say nothing of Miss Freeman and Miss Hastings,' Lydia spoke and the two young women murmured. 'You are blackening my character.' She tried not to focus on her injuries but, despite her placid nature, she could not suffer in silence. 'Leave me. I'll thank you to stop sticking your nose into my business.'

'Lotus-eater,' said Miss Bidwell, implying that French creoles had forgotten their origins. Then, more directly, she offered a parting shot: 'Trollop.' Upon reaching the door with her girls in tow, she inclined her head towards Lydia, unsmiling. 'Here is what I think. Last night, you had your cap set for Colonel Hemmings.' As if that wasn't insulting enough, she continued, 'You have been trifling with Squire Foulkes's emotions, too.' There was a gasp. 'Forgive my outspokenness, Colonel Hemmings.'

'Oh, how humbly you speak now, Britannia's daughter.' Hemmings stood outside the door, face resembling a pillar of salt. 'You walk on padded claws like a cat. Vanish! Get out before I put you to the sword!'

* * *

'She made me feel wretched and utterly worthless for taking a stroll with you, Orlando.' Lydia waited until they were alone before looking down at the outline of her feet, hidden beneath the sheets, and afraid to think about her long-term prognosis. 'Mammy Scribbles, please inform my uncle that I'd like my fiancé to keep my company tonight. I don't want to be alone, not tonight. Oh, don't forget to pack all my books.' She mused, 'Orlando, Miss Bidwell says you've brought the wedding forward. Is this true? I'd rather wait until I'm up and walking.'

Hemmings, standing protectively by the side of her bed, said with concern in his voice, 'I am taking you to see the military physician.' As a senior officer, he spent much of his time teaching men not to fear and was not used to nursing young women. 'You'll be fine, dearest.' Born in an age of turmoil, he had not known a time of peace and, despite the excruciating headache, he remained optimistic. 'You there.' His gaze settled on a stout woman, believing that Africans were brute beasts. 'Give me a hand with these boots, girl.'

'Yes, sir.' Mammy Scribbles sank to her knees, grumbling that she only had two hands. 'Time to tek out yuh earrings, Pu-tus.' She was laughing, inside her head, having heard through idle gossip that Squire Foulkes was in love with Lydia. 'Oh, let dem stay.'

'Yes, Monifa said it is best to keep them in,' remarked Lydia. 'Don't forget to polish Orlando's boots and tell Monifa she's a saint. I should like to see her before I go.' Lydia dismissed Mammy Scribbles.

'There are no saints among us, dearest, only good people,' corrected Hemmings, closing her travelling box. 'Negroes are not people.' Clothes lay folded on the bed. He sat on the edge of it, lifted the sheets and examined the calico bandages which bound her legs tightly onto strips of board. 'You feel no pain, my love, and I feel a story coming on. *One day, Heracles, son of Zeus, and a mortal mother, Alcmene, was found prattling away in his crib, holding a strangled snake in each hand. He had defeated his father's jealous wife, Hera...'*

'Don't treat me like a child, Orlando.' Lydia lay back on her pillow, listening while he explained that the time had come to cut ties with the house servants, including Monifa who had given her a sedative for the pain in her legs. The herbal brew had caused a temporary paralysis from the groin downwards. 'Please don't call Monifa and Mammy Scribbles mean names, Orlando; they're used to bandaging me.'

'We must make you well.' Hemmings could not rid his thoughts of a boulder rolling down a hill towards them. Lydia had made the sign of the cross. 'You break easily, dearest.' The mysteries of faith held no fascination for him, but he thanked the gods anyway: a gigantic tree had stalled the boulder for a few seconds before it flattened Jack and killed his horse. 'I have heard rumours you are the real owner of Lafayette.'

'My father and grandfather invested in stocks in England.' Whatever resentment Lydia felt against her guardians was never expressed. 'My uncle used my inheritance to purchase Lafayette.' With a wan smile, she remembered that he had taken her into the gunroom after breakfast and had said that they would spend their married life in Bengal. 'Do you recall how we met?' Lying flat on her back on the four-poster bed beneath the mosquito netting, she observed him resting his sabre on the green *chaise longue* by the window. 'I was on my knees in the chapel. You and Captain Eaton came up from the unused crypt.'

'Aha! Didn't your aunt tell you men in uniform are dangerous?' Hemmings turned red, wondering if she suspected. The question and the mention of Eaton were soon forgotten when she began to gasp for breath, audibly: 'There now, there; breathe slowly.'

With those words, Lydia took a breath and exhaled, remembering a black scout and a Redcoat riding behind them. 'Oh, my poor Sultan.' The dead horse was soon forgotten, and she craved sundried tomatoes, cheese and a wedge of bread. 'When I opened my eyes, I thought I was back in St Domingue with my family. I thought we were going to die.'

'*Nil desperandum*,' Hemmings chided, stripping to his white knee-length linen drawers and climbing carefully into her bed. '*Never say die.*' Gently, he placed a hand on her forehead until she was becalmed. Then he removed her earrings and placed them on the bedside table alongside a string of rosary beads and a Bible. 'We are alive.' In this feminine space, he was aware of the rise and fall of her breasts beneath the white sheet. 'You've barely had a chance to get to know me and, here I am, half-naked in your bed.'

'I have visitations,' blurted Lydia, who sometimes felt quite sure that God was calling her to say 'Yes' and to live a celibate life. At last, she felt able to share her visions with someone who often made intuitive decisions. 'I had a vision on the day we met in the chapel. I saw a nun cultivating a vegetable patch with the wind whipping up her veil.'

'A little convent in Languedoc, perhaps?' jested Hemmings, stressing that it was a mistake to see her visions as anything but the workings of a troubled mind. 'Vowed celibacy, no. Your cross is me. You don't know what life has in store for you.' With his contempt for institutionalized religion threatening to break out, he quickly rose, took a flask from his breast-pocket, slipped back into bed and took a swig of brandy. 'I am your path to salvation. I shall do everything in my power to give you the life of a lady of quality, Lydia dearest.'

'Get out of my bed, Orlando.' Scoffing at him, Lydia peered through the mosquito net when his sabre fell off the *chaise longue* with a clatter.

He was still grinning at the idea of her becoming a nun. 'What if Miss Bidwell walked in? What if I never walk again?'

'You will,' assured Hemmings, keeping optimism afloat. 'Where is your faith?'

'I am not suited for marriage, Orlando, and to a military man like you.' Lydia lapsed into an introspective state of mind. 'I had my heart set on becoming a nun. I don't know how to explain it to you.'

Unconvinced, Hemmings drained the flask and dropped it on the floor with a hint of brandy on his breath. 'You've been cooped up in this old house for too long.' He picked up an ivory-handled hairbrush. 'Which is it to be, dearest, the cloister or the hearth?'

'Get out of my bed, I beg you.' Lydia kept her eyes riveted on a moth fluttering on the ceiling while he brushed her hair vigorously. 'My hair is all in a tangle from the fall.'

'Queen Mab has tied it in knots,' Hemmings said uneasily, sighing in irritation when he heard a knock and saw Eaton holding the door ajar. 'Enter.' With no time for strategies, he placed the hairbrush on the bedside table. 'What do you mean by this intrusion, Captain Eaton?'

'And so to bed.' Eaton borrowed a phrase from Samuel Pepys's diary. His eyes never left Hemmings as he thought of Henry Mackenzie's book, *The Man of Feeling* (1771). 'Aha, *Mars Sleeping in Venus's Lap.*' Jealous, he glanced around the room, recalling that in the novel an innocent girl is seduced by a rake, then abandoned and forced into prostitution. 'There I was thinking she was a vestal virgin of the goddess, Vesta, of the hearth. Alas, she is worth not a shilling of value to any man of means.'

'You have a funny sense of fun, Captain Eaton,' growled Hemmings, feeling torn because he had deserted the man whom he had loved for two decades. 'What's on your mind?' He matched his lover's stare. 'As you can see, I am otherwise engaged within.'

'Brave decision you made today.' Eaton gave Lydia a pitying look. 'The men would like a eulogy for Corporal Birch. As for Jack, he showed courage and daring in the line of duty. I think you should slip his name into the eulogy. You can't acknowledge him as an equal, but you are alive because of his courage. Nice place for a rough and tumble.'

'You dirty everything with your filthy mind.' Hemmings slapped him down. 'You could make life easier for me if you were to assume command.' Weary of the privations of camp life, he ran his fingers through Lydia's long black hair. 'Take command, Jason.'

'It's rather sudden, but the offer deserves thanking.' Eaton gave him a side-eye. 'It's been a confusing day, what with the ambush, losing Jack and Corporal Birch, and now you're nursing a cripple. If I say so myself, pain and pleasure are grim bedfellows.'

'Why are you still here, Major Eaton?' Hemmings said warily, rising to his feet and preventing him from speaking further. 'You are loitering in a lady's boudoir.' Up until then, he had ignored his lover's weeping right eye until Eaton began to dab it with a lace handkerchief. 'Lead by example.' Half-undressed, he slipped between the sheets again. 'If Hindustan does not agree with you, Jason, I can offer you a warm bed at The Warren.'

'*Exit, pursued by a bear.*' Eaton filched a line from Shakespeare's *The Winter's Tale*. He walked out and said coldly, 'Dismissed.'

'He dismissed you, Orlando?' Lydia was stung by the sarcasm between the two men, but something in her fiancé's voice confused her. 'Tell me about your family.'

'Let us look to the future.' Hemmings yawned, 'I am so tired.' It was a decade since he had lost his mother and his brother. 'Kent is beautiful in spring. We shall ride out together and go hawking. I shall get you your very own hawk. You will love England.'

'I hope so.' Lydia tried to look forward with optimism, saying she was concerned about his fractured relationship with Eaton. 'Tell me about your mother and brother.'

In the winter of 1785, Baroness Allegra Hemmings, her husband and son Octavian, had embarked on an Alps tour, marvelling at the stunning views of gargantuan peaks and snow-topped massifs on their alpine walks. One day, a sudden snowstorm reared up and a swirling mist encircled the mountains. Caught walking in an avalanche, Hemmings's mother and her other son were buried, and their bodies were never recovered. Although Baron Hemmings himself had lost three fingers and two toes to frostbite, Orlando never got over losing his mother and still blamed his father for taking her on the Grand Tour.

'Tell me about Major Eaton.' Lydia asked, 'Why does he resent me and why do you allow him to disrespect you?' The unstable climate brought thunder without warning.

'You are a rare bird, dearest; three men warring over you.' Hemmings had no desire to share his and Eaton's hidden history with anyone, let alone his fiancée. 'Well, perhaps two.'

'But why is Major Eaton so disagreeable?' Lying on a sheet of board to straighten her fractured legs and support her bruised back, Lydia reached out to him, remembering vaguely that he had sustained a blow to his head, though he never mentioned his discomfort. It was one of the most emotional moments of her life, trapped on her back in a state of passivity while two enslaved Africans ululated in the thunder and lightning, spending another night in the stocks for wanting freedom. 'Why is he so angry, Orlando?'

'Jason is my boyhood friend.' Hemmings began to snooze. 'We were all taught to be forceful and brutal, not soft and lily-livered.' He nodded off and his dream turned to injured men in military hospitals and old soldiers with disabilities and disfigurement. Breathing heavily, he had seen numerous wounds sealed and cauterized with tar and heard the groans of dying men. He opened his eyes. 'Given half a chance, I'd punish every Negro except that wench who saved you from the butcher's knife.'

Lydia turned to look at the flickering oil lamp. 'Monifa is no ordinary slave, and neither is she a wench. She has saved many lives, using her skills as a herbwoman. She has been in the family ever since she was a girl, so my uncle says. She is invaluable.' Although she experienced no pain, Lydia felt trapped when he flung his arm across her chest and dozed off. 'When I am back on my feet, I shall join the anti-slavery movement.'

'Send the hounds after those *yahoos*, Jason,' murmured Hemmings in a doze, dreaming of hummingbirds in the bush. 'Those blasted Maroons got the better of us today, *yahoos*.' With rapid eye movements, he saw the dazzling tips of the hummingbirds' green plumage and was mesmerized by them. 'I have made up my mind, Jason.' The doctor birds captivated him with their skill and vitality, cutting away at the sides of the angel trumpet flowers to get at the juice. 'Leave me be, stop pestering me about Jack.'

'Something happened between you and Major Eaton today, didn't it?' Lydia considered, gazing at the lamp's wick burning low with the smoke darkening the shade. 'You talk in your sleep.' She watched the immolation of a moth in the fluted lampshade and listened to the howling wind and the two wailing freshwater Africans outside. When she was a child, she was told a story which stayed with her about a tribe in Guiana with heads beneath their shoulders and eyes in the middle of their breasts. 'Wake up, Orlando.' Accustomed to seeing him in his military garb, she now saw Samson stripped of his power, head shaved. 'Why do people tell children scary stories when the wind howls?'

'*Alvina weeps*,' mumbled Hemmings, wanting desperately to get a good night's rest. '*The winds of change*.' Although it had been a quick nap, he had slept more peacefully than he had done in weeks. 'Forgive me for compromising your virtue. I am bone tired.'

'I am not paralysed.' Eyes wide open, Lydia moaned softly when a surge of pain spread through her legs. 'I can feel pain.' She dug her nails into his arm while he described the manor house where she would live. Countering the pain, she tried to visualise the rustics and the shepherds carrying their crooks. 'I fear this is God's punishment.'

'I have no belief and I do not subscribe to a God who punishes the guiltless.' A sleepy Hemmings repudiated the idea of an omniscient God in heaven, living in a palace and sitting on a throne. 'Shhh!' He removed her hand from his arm, got up and said the scratches could help to cast doubts on her virtue. Reaching for the decorative chamber pot beneath the bed, he urinated at length and stopped in mid-flow when lightning lit up the sky. After he had finished, he crossed the room when a roll of thunder caused the shutters to rattle. Reluctantly, he went and stood on the balcony, shouting in the semi-darkness, 'Monsieur Fontane, I told you earlier to release those wenches. I am the King's Hand in these parts. If my orders are not obeyed, I shall have you shot at dawn, sir!'

'You wouldn't,' Lydia said anxiously, groaning when the pain reliever began to subside and wishing Monifa had stayed with her as she had done in St Domingue when she fell ill there. 'Tell me about the blue-stockings – take my mind off this dreadful pain.'

'I'm not used to taking orders from women *per se*.' Hemmings returned to the room from the balcony and said, 'You poor thing.' He rubbed his eyes and told her that his mother was a bluestocking. 'She ran a monthly book club.' He pulled a cord by the bedside and his autocratic tone echoed throughout the house, summoning Monifa to prepare a stronger draught. 'Fontane, send that Negro doctress to me at once. Your niece needs a draught to deaden her pain!' Hemmings slipped back into her bed and barked further orders. 'No, on second thoughts, send that Negro boy who served us by the river.'

* * *

'Come in.' Fifteen minutes had passed. 'Come!' Lydia was embarrassed to see Juno, a tall, yellow-skinned servant, loitering outside the open door. 'I'd prefer to see Monifa, Orlando.' She looked at her fiancé and was reminded of the time a house boy had made a flirty comment. Her father had swiftly had the African garrotted. 'What is that on the tray?'

'Major Eaton sen' dis tray an' a message fi yuh, Colonel,' answered Juno, entering the room and not daring to look Lydia in the eye. 'Him say yuh mus' answa back, Colonel.'

'Audacious,' Hemmings's voice was terse, glaring at a pig's bladder bleeding on a solid silver platter in Juno's trembling hands. 'Take that abomination back to Major Eaton with my reply: "This is not honour-able." But first, pour two cups of tea and drink one.'

'Me not suppose fi use di good cup.' The teacups rattled on the tray in Juno's hand. He poured the lukewarm tea and hesitated.

'Do as you are told and don't speak unless I ask you a question.' Infuriated because his lover would not let him go, Hemmings stood up and accepted the other cup of tea. The impact of Eaton's bloody gift, languishing on an old monogrammed (OH) handkerchief left him wondering whether he would ever be free of his past. Instinctively, he put out his left foot and tripped up Juno. 'Creep out softly, on your knees. Send Major Eaton a bottle of red wine.'

'He saved my life in St Domingue,' protested Lydia, brightening when Juno crawled out with his tail between his legs. 'His arms were badly burnt, too.' Accustomed to social distinctions always being observed, she was still shaking at the idea of a house boy entering a lady's bedroom. 'Juno, Joy, Mammy Scribbles and Monifa are the most loyal slaves I have ever known. What turned the other slaves in St Domingue so wicked?'

'Freedom.' The storm abated and Hemmings spoke disdainfully, 'Africans are a conquered race and should be treated with contempt, like the Irish. They too are savages who eat raw meat and raw fish. On the one hand, the Irish are at least humans but, of course, are different from us. On the other hand, Negroes are a species of sub-humans.' He spoke about a new way of life, advising her to forget about her old life in St Domingue and promising her a lifetime of commitment and love in England. 'Try to get some sleep. I must go down and speak with Major Eaton. I had hoped to pursue that bellicose Maroon chief to the death but, alas, that is no longer possible. I shall delegate the task to Major Eaton, perhaps.'

'Those drums are driving me to distraction.' Lydia was unaware that the Africans had banded together and buried the scout earlier. The drumming, a dirge, was brought to a frenzy when the workers began to praise their many gods and the Christian saints for saving the young mistress' life. But, in general, the coming together of different cultures exasperated Lydia, whose reading included the lives of the saints. 'I shan't see them, Orlando; they are too noisy.' Always she saw God as a Frenchman with blue eyes and long black hair, in a white robe, sitting on a golden throne surrounded by angels blowing trumpets. 'I cannot bear that unholy noise, vile music of the heathens. How dare they corrupt the sacred rites of the Church with their jamboree. Send them away Orlando.'

'You will soon forget them.' Bemused, Hemmings rose stiffly in his linen drawers, ignoring the anvils beating in his head. Having crossed the room, he opened the French doors and stood on the balcony in the dark. 'Go and bed down, people.' His raised voice sounded strained and tired, 'I am happy that you are happy for my intended, but she has a long journey ahead of her tomorrow and needs her beauty sleep! Er, is that you, Major?'

'It is I. You promised the men a eulogy for Corporal Birch.' Out of the darkness came an accusing and familiar voice, faltering on the words, 'T-they are expecting you to give a fitting tribute to Corporal Birch and I would personally like you to say a few words in honour of Black-Jack.' Although the Major had denigrated everything African when he was growing up in England, he had come to regard Jack as a trusted pair of hands and knew that he could be relied on to keep his nerve under extreme pressure in battle. 'We lost one of our best scouts today, Orlando. He was selfless and reliable.'

'As your superior, I hate to lose a man,' Hemmings replied. 'Corporal Birch exemplified the best of the Redcoats: conscientious, confident and reliable. He was a fine soldier.' This was also the cue for the roundup of the hill Maroons to begin: 'Major Eaton, we are delivering the Negro, Kuki, to Fort Dundas for questioning. That runaway is an ally of the Maroons.' Raising his voice in the night air, he rubbed the index finger against the thumb, adding, 'Today we also lost a reliable scout, Jack to all of us. I once ordered him to wear a green uniform like a Frenchie on April Fool's Day. He said, *No, Mr Land-o, not over my dead body. I am a Loyalist.*'

'Is that all you have to say about Jack, our loyal scout and mascot?' Eaton stepped out of the shadows and stood in full view in the dim light cast by the first-floor balcony. 'He has kept us out of many tangles, especially in London and America. Let us not forget the services performed for King and country. He fought for the British, risking his life against his own countrymen. Just what exactly are you going to do about his body? We cannot leave it by the roadside to rot like those two corpses stinking up the valley.'

'Black-Jack was an asset to us!' Others had already mentioned the scout's attire and his habit of telling riddles and stories, even when he was offended by an unacceptable remark aimed at his colour. 'We shall find a way to honour him.' Hemmings issued more orders, wondering if Eaton would ever release him and whether Lydia would be able to respond to the challenges of being his wife, bearing his children and forgiving him unconditionally if she were to discover his secret. 'Major, send a messenger to Squire Foulkes to fetch two powder-monkeys and six horses.' He smiled in the dark. 'I'll be down at midnight to turn out the guard. I also want to discuss our next move against those damn Maroons. I want them cornered and caged like animals. I shall delegate that task.'

'Very well.' Smiling triumphantly, Eaton looked around when Juno appeared with a bottle of wine and two glasses. The foot shuffling continued until he added, 'Midnight it is.' The sight of Hemmings standing on the balcony semi-nude reinforced what he believed was a betrayal of everything they stood for. 'Jack would have been proud of that speech, Colonel.' The Major decided that he would send no more obscene messages to his lover.

'He was a good man but, alas, the world does not recognise his sort, certainly not his worth.' By contrast, Hemmings had always enjoyed a privileged life as the son of a baron and a member of the nobility; hence he was educated at an elite boarding school and university before taking up the call of military life. 'I'll be down as soon as I have settled my fiancée, Major. Be sure to turn out the guard before I come down.' His tongue hesitated on the tip of saying something, but he turned his back. 'Major, send an urgent message to General George Walpole: tell him we were ambushed today by a splintered group of the Trelawny Maroons. We were outnumbered and need more chasseurs and Cuban hounds.'

* * *

Wild Pine Mount was the name chosen by Captain Kalu for his stronghold in the hills far beyond Mountain, the name given to the provision grounds belonging to Canongate. To reach this stronghold, a journey through the hills and valleys was necessary before climbing a steep, precipitous mountainside that was several hundred feet high. When the Maroons had built the village, they saw that in their isolation from the black population, the enslaved Africans on the many plantations scattered throughout the parish were powerless and needed a figurehead to unite them.

Wild Pine Mount was difficult to reach, for there were numerous sinkholes and narrow passes en route, which could only be traversed in single file. Intrepid climbers were obliged to strap whatever they carried onto their backs. Their hands had to remain free to cling to the slippery rock faces. Pragmatically, and to sustain the Maroons, the settlement had been built near a freshwater spring. Mullets and jangas swam in the many streams and hundreds of wild pines grew from the bark of indigenous trees. Clutches of plump grey birds – ringdoves – made a soothing 'coo-cooing' sound. In this terrain, ground doves stalked the woods; wild pine sergeants perched on branches and wild hogs rooted in the thickets. The hogs' flesh was seasoned with pimento leaves and pepper elder. The meat was then salted, smoked and preserved by the Maroons. This delicacy was known as jerk pork, which they ate washed down with coconut water.

For two decades, Captain Kalu and his men had lived a nomadic life until they came to Wild Pine Mount, where they built a compound with a long hall and decorated it with animal skins on the walls. Here, they lived a fairly peaceful life, hunting, farming and cultivating vegetables and plants: fever grass, leaf of life; wild sage and search-mi-heart. Outside one of the huts, a middle-aged woman sat on a stool, using the bark from the lace bark tree (Jamaica *Lagetta lagetto* tree) to make a delicate, soft fabric for clothing. In preparation, she had peeled away the tree bark and removed "the inner netting of the white veins." Several days ago, she had "soaked and beat the bark strips until they were smooth and supple."

'Mi one son dead.' Captain Kalu sat under a cotton tree, surrounded by his closest advisers. 'A man mus' not bury 'im son.' Without Akin by his side, he struggled to shake off the bouts of depression. He could not rid his mind of images of dead children being thrown over-board the *African Empress*, victims of dysentery and hunger. 'If only Faddah could see yuh, 'onorary brodda.' His voice echoed comments their father would have made. 'Yuh 'ave di body of a ooman, mi sista, but di 'ead of a wise man.'

'Yuh is widout equal, mi brodda,' Monifa said graciously, accepting the compliment and a broom made of palm fronds. 'T'ank yuh, dawta.' The broom was given to her by a teenager whose Gold Coast-born mother had made dukanoo for supper. This pudding was also referred to as tie-a-leaf, dukunu or blue drawers. It consisted of grated bananas, sweet potatoes, coconut, sugar and spices, and was tied up in banana leaves and steamed in boiling water. Monifa had earlier washed down a slice of dukanoo with coconut water. 'Yuh 'ave a price on yer 'ead, a 'undred guinea.'

'Is dat all mi wut?' Reflecting on the long hard road that they had travelled, Captain Kalu did his best to rally himself. 'An' yuh, 'onorary brodda, yuh is di custodian o' we culture. We com' to dis lan' naked, carryin' nutten 'xcept we stories an' wi memories in we 'ead.'

'Yemaya, Mother of Mercy, guide mi steps to yuh.' Monifa peered at the adolescent girl in the dark, who was being groomed to become a priestess. 'Man seh dere is no justice in dis worl'. I seh dere's no justice fi di African. We a warrior, Brodda. Dis is we fite.'

Since 1765, when the young Kalu and his bodyguards had been freed for their bravery by a superstitious Mengis Hunter, they had walked free in Jamaica. They had secured their liberty on the road to New Hall (Lafayette), but freedom for an African in a slave colony was a fragile thing. They had joined the Trelawny Maroons, even though they had reservations about doing so. The main problems Captain Kalu saw were that the Maroons could not conceal their fugitives and were legally bound to have a white man living amongst them. He understood why the Maroons sued for peace and adhered to the treaties agreed, but he did not believe in returning runaways unless they were ill or pregnant or needed the kind of care impossible to give on the run from blood-hounds and the Redcoats.

'Me *naah* go lie dung an' die like di *Arawak* dem, dead race,' spat Captain Kalu, whose forehead showed a receding hairline and specks of grey hair. 'I say we season pork wid poison an' scatter pieces o' di meat in di valley below fi poison dose killer dwags.'

'No poison,' argued Olokun, the eldest of his three bodyguards, who used his cutlass to slice off a piece of jerk pork. He began to chomp on the tough meat. 'If we poison dose killer 'ounds, di Redcoat will bu'n us outa dese 'ills; we a wood 'awks.'

'Di chile yeye sick,' interrupted Monifa, who was visiting her brother's village a few days after the ambush that sent shockwaves through the hill villages. 'Wat gwine 'appen to 'im?' She had made the perilous journey through a series of labyrinths in Brecon's Cave (where she had spied on Hemmings and Eaton), which veered off in one direction towards the hamlet of Flamborough and then continued through thick foliage to the hamlet of Quashie Grass, climbing steep hills and a series of ravines. 'Redcoat sen' Akin to di ancestors an' di news sen' Ulalee inna labour, breach birth. Yuh could sign peace treaty.'

'Dis a nuh Cudjoe time.' Captain Kalu sat under the tree with his back against the trunk, sharpening the blade of his cutlass. 'Me naah sign peace treaty wid nuh white man an' walk free while mi breddas inna bondage.' He had not expected such a disaster, losing his son and daughter-in-law in the space of two days, and grieved for all that had been lost since he was taken. 'Di government import killer dwags fram Cuba an' Mosquito Indian. Dem track us by di scent of wi wood smoke.' He continued, '*Bakra* use we own *peeple* fi scout an' track us dung, Black Shot.'

'I 'ear a voice. It seh, *Tek yer warriors an' go weh fram 'ere.*' Monifa could also hear a white man's voice in her head, knowing that the English accent belonged to Colonel Hemmings, shouting, *Scout!* And ordering Jack to, *Cut out the buffoonery.* That morning, having seen the hounds in the yard at Lafayette before the picnic by the river, as she was getting dressed to go and forage for medicinal herbs, she had smothered herself in dog repellent, a precautionary measure. 'Everybaddy tell Nancy 'tory. I like riddle bes'. Listen. *Wat run but 'ave no legs?*'

'A river.' Captain Kalu raised a half-smile, saying that he was made of tougher stuff than wood. An owl hooted in a nearby tree whose burnt trunk was blackened. 'Some of us fightin' fi we very life, odders season wid di whip an' plenty of us grievin' fi Mama Africa.'

With the wind starting to rustle, Monifa returned the broom to the adolescent girl and dipped the hem of a clean cloth into a gourd of water, wiping the baby's sticky eyes. Gently, she cradled the child while praising her brother for creating a sense of community and a shared purpose. She told him that their father had appeared in a dream: he had held a man-child aloft, bringing him to rest on his own head like a crown.

'Aiee!' Captain Amri cried. 'Aiee!' He was a tall man with flared nostrils, hooded eyes and worry lines on his forehead. 'A son is a man crownin' glory.' A former Trelawny Maroon, he was the son of a rebel who had told him stories of Lord Balcarres marching on Trelawny Town in the 1730s, to subdue the Maroons under the leadership of Cudjoe. On that occasion, the Englishman was forced to retreat after his regiment had suffered many casualties. Captain Amri did not agree with the treaties signed by the Maroons, for a white man in a Maroon camp could only be a spy. 'Blood fi blood, mi 'onorary brodda...'

'Den is in oonu interest fi mek sure dem nuh catch oonu unaware,' Monifa snatched away his sentence before cooing at the child in her arms.

'Yuh wut more dead dan alive to di whites.' Bristling with umbrage, it goaded her that enslavers such as Pierre Fontane and Duncan Foulkes had the power to grant life or death. She and her brother had been stolen a long time ago and still there was a sense of dislocation, but pride of race too. 'Dat Colonel Hemmings sen' fi reinforcement 'cause 'im married di French girl, Lydia Fontane, an' gone 'ome to Englan' wid 'er. Di ambush, rollin' stones, bruk 'er legs an' di Redcoat dem 'untin' yuh dung.'

'Yuh mus' be careful 'bout yer tracks, 'onorary brodda,' advised Captain Cuffy, Jr. A serial absconder, he had lost three of his toes on a plantation in Falmouth and was nicknamed Tumpa-foot. 'Yuh sure nobaddy nuh follow yuh?' He joined the Trelawny Maroons in 1780 but was subsequently returned to his master as a fugitive. 'Di ambush was a bold act an' now di troop scourin' di 'ills lookin' fi us.' His son had spotted a handful of freed Africans (Black Shot), wearing cotton shirts and white breeches, scouting in the bush with sniffer dogs. 'Dere's a price on wi 'ead, wanted man, an' no loyalty among naga.'

Anxious for their safety, Monifa held the baby-boy, Babatunde, protectively. 'I tekkin' dis man-chile to di *pickney* nursery at Lafayette. He must stay alive. We chilvren mus' preserve we story fi generations yet unborn.' A guerrilla at heart, she had pursued her goal with a single-minded energy, knowing that the only comfort she could offer her brother was a promise to raise his grandson in order to ensure their late father's immortality. 'Massa t'ink I gone to Canongate fi deliver slave baby overnite.'

Prior to the landslide, the bloodhounds had filled the hills around Edinburgh Castle with their barking. The Maroons had already sighted their target and moved to a more advantageous location high above the trees. After the ambush, Captain Kalu's men had signalled the retreat with the abeng at strategic points in the hills where wild pine leaves also acted as camouflage. Akin's death had shaken his father to the core. It was noticed by others that he moped around all day, looking crestfallen, and was reluctant to give simple orders. This behaviour was not in line with their ways. His bodyguards, in their late fifties, were waiting to see what would happen next. There was nowhere to run to. 'Mi son conceive on a slave ship an' now 'im dead,' lammented Captain Kalu.

'Yuh too own-way.' Monifa admonished him when he vowed to raise his grandson as a proper Maroon. 'He will live to see freedom.' She was afraid that there was no time to pass their sacred traditions on to the children. 'Dis is fi yuh.' One hundred stolen guineas were counted, one at a time. 'We faddah dream to me dis marnin'. Yuh was on a ship goin' to a cold climate. Dem seh General Walpole in charge of di Redcoats. Rite now soldiers 'untin' di Trelawny Maroons wid som' bad dwags.'

'Why mus' we liv' like animals, gruntin' an' sweatin' unda di white man law?' It was an emotional moment for Captain Kalu. 'Dem mek brute of us all.' He longed to see his beloved homeland again, nursing images of hunting big cats and sharpening spears, and the grey beards in conversation. 'Dis misery an' oppression cahn continue forever. Mi a free man in a white man worl'.' He took his grandson, reliving the horror etched on the young Monifa's face when she learned he was disembarking from the ship in Kingston, rattling her chains and kneeling dramatically. 'We com' a long way, 'onorary brodda. W'enever yuh visit us, yuh giv' me 'ope.'

'Di Englishman seh yuh mus' be punished fi 'im ooman's bruk foot an' di soldier weh dead, mi brodda,' Monifa said calmly, though she felt anxious for him. 'To di white plaanta dem di ambush is a good subject at di dinner table, but is life or deat' to yuh.' Under a spreading canopy of branches, a lone breadfruit was cushioned between the broad leaves in the dark. As if lost in the mists of time, some tall indigenous trees stood in the shadows darkening up the hills. 'We cast adrift, brodda-man, no longer African an' not class as 'umans – we is fugitives.'

'Me not animal.' Captain Amri sat beneath the cotton tree, chewing tobacco and spitting the dark saliva into the air. 'Kuki gwine betray us. I dohn trus' dat man, snake crawlin' on its belly in di grass.'

'Wi tek blood oath, breddas, even dat dwag,' grunted the vexed Captain Cuffy, distrusting Kuki who was nicknamed Frighten Friday. His upbringing in West Africa had profoundly shaped his thinking about life and death. 'Wi fite 'til wi die, mi breddas. Wi on di battle-field.' He had repeatedly warned Captain Kalu about harbouring the runaway Kuki. 'No surrender fi us.'

'Walk wid me, mi 'onorary brodda.' Digesting the news of Kuki's capture, Captain Kalu removed himself from the group of warriors and strolled towards a forested mound nearby, where twisted vines and tree roots ran along the path. Tough characters walking side-by-side, he smiled when Monifa explained that the bundle she carried contained a goat's horn filled with fresh grave dirt, a deceased Black man's toenail clippings, a clump of the dead soldier's black hair, white rum and a concoction of herbs. 'Kuki will tell dem eberyt'ing unda torture.'

'T'ings nuh go ascordin' to plan but, lucky fi us, survival in wi blood.' Monifa, carrying a calico sack in one hand, sucked her teeth. 'Poh!' Looking back, she saw the smashed body of a Black man and told her brother that she had had the gruesome task of laying Jack out for burial. Immediately, she knelt to scoop up a handful of earth, throwing it to the wind meaningfully. 'Healin' in di balmyard,' she paused, hearing a low whistle that caused her to look over her shoulder. 'Di Redcoat comin' afta yuh wid di weight of di law, mi brodda.'

Captain Kalu spat, 'Bush nuh 'ave no law.' Ominously, a bongo drum sounded, faintly, across Wild Pine Mount, calling the Maroons to form a circle. An adolescent, meantime, balanced a kerosine lamp on her head, doing the *Kumina* dance. 'I fret 'bout forgettin' mi ole life.'

'Wi carry di pas' in wi 'ead.' Monifa withdrew a rooster from the sack. Its head was tucked under its wings. 'Som' peeple 'ead bad, cahn 'member nutten.' The frightened girl-child on the *African Empress* had grown into a *rebel woman*, mentored by a *voodoo* priestess in St Domingue. After a quiet word with her brother, who gave his grand-child to a young woman, she watched him slit the rooster's throat and drink some of the warm blood, which she had mixed with a secret cocktail. 'Yuh gotto 'ave a guide.'

The air was redolent of ripe jackfruit, night jasmine and also *jerk pork*. Captain Kalu had been aware of his sister's skills as a *Kumina* priestess, but this was the first time he had actually seen her in action. She had buried the rooster's feet and the head with the comb attached, and effigies of two white men stuck with pins. There was also a white lace handkerchief and a black three-cornered hat, which had flown off Hemmings's head and into a thicket, moments before the rockslide.

'Ah who deh? Black-Jack-o! A yuh deh?' Monifa invoked the deceased scout by *calling out* his name, so as not to attract passing spirits, while the devotees danced in a circular pattern. 'A who deh? Black-Jack-o!'

'I sense 'im, 'onory brodda.' Captain Kalu began to rotate his head on his wide shoulders. 'Black-Jack-o! A yuh deh?' For most of his Jamaican sojourn, he had heard his father's voice in his dreams. A strong lad who had enjoyed his childhood, he recalled that he could throw a spear as fast as his father. When his half-sister, Bayo, committed suicide and his friend, Bami, was slaughtered on the *African Empress*, the ties of blood, friendship and honour had been tossed away like confetti in the wind. Rotating his head in a trance-like state, his mind drifted to his mother, Olafemi, and Bayo's mother, Aduke; those two co-wives had clashed. He called out, 'Black-Jack-o! Me wahn a guide.'

'*Ekabo!*' Monifa made hand gestures, contorting her body like a python. 'Welcome!' Summoned thus, the spirit guide began to manifest itself. '*Ekabo!*' Dancing in a circular motion, anti-clockwise, Monifa, the *Kumina* Queen, welcomed the deceased scout and bade him good evening, '*Ek'ale!*' She had called him up and would instruct him to lead her brother, Captain Kalu, as he had guided Colonel Hemmings in life. She knew in her heart that where her brother was going, he would need all his resilience to survive the rigours of this second sea voyage and the cold Canadian climate in Nova Scotia. '*Ek'ale! Ekabo!*'

'*Fire on di mountain! Run, bwoy, run!*' Captain Kalu began to sway, arms wide open and flapping, as if he were taking the shape of a prehistoric bird. He began to sing when the spirit, *Black-Jack*, manifested himself by possessing Monifa. '*Yuh wid di redcoat, fire wid di gun. Di gun shall lose an' yuh shall win. Fire on di mountain! Run, bwoy, run.*'

* * *

In October 1795, Duncan and Fiona marked their twenty-fifth wedding anniversary two months after the big day. This was to be a quiet affair, for he was conscious of the second Maroon War and the ambush of the Redcoats by Captain Kalu, who was on the run. In solidarity with the Maroons, the Africans on Canongate and Lafayette had become sullen and un-cooperative in the fields and the sugar mill. They had been on a 'go slow' since it was discovered that a handful of supposedly 'look-out' workers from Canongate had been sold to a plantation in Cuba, which was owned by a planter named Mark Anthony DeWolf. He was said to be the second richest slave owner in America, with plantations in Cuba and a family mansion in Bristol, England, where his sugar was sent to be made into rum.

'I am beginning to think I ought to expand my sugar gardens.' Duncan placed a napkin on his lap. 'I hear the DeWolf dynasty owns forty-seven ships and plantations in Havana and Charleston. Oh, to have my own rum distillery in Glasgow. Allegedly, the DeWolfs sail their ships from Bristol to West Africa with rum to trade for Africans…'

'What irks me is that those big American slave owners are investing in estates across the West Indies,' complained Pierre Fontane, accepting a glass of rum and lime cordial from Seraphima. 'Whenever there is a revolt on their plantations out here, they can simply ship the trouble-some leaders over to one of their plantations in the South.'

'The sooner that Maroon renegade is captured, the sooner I can get a good night's sleep,' Duncan sighed deeply, looking down at the ginger cake that the cook had made for his and Fiona's belated wedding anniversary. 'When I got married, I was naive to think we planters and those bellicose Maroons could co-exist together, as long as they kept away from our land and our slaves.' Reflecting on his wedding day, he remembered being criticised by his fellow whites for his handling of 'peace talks' with Captain Kalu on the lawn. 'Och!'

'As for Major Fitzroy-Campbell, he was letting us know he was in charge.' Fiona sipped red wine, saying she had an unwavering belief in the superiority of whiteness but doubted the Redcoats were up to the task. 'He did nothing to quell my fears then.'

'I can remember my father taking me and my brother, Dougal, and our cousin, Iain, to Edinburgh that last time before he installed us in boarding school.' Looking out the dining room window, Duncan put down his napkin. 'Ah, those halcyon days of childhood. Today I look back on my idyllic childhood in the Highlands with envy. Who could have imagined that I would be sitting here in limbo today, waiting for the dreaded Redcoats of my childhood to rid us of those blasted Maroons?' An ardent supporter of the British Army, he admitted that time was a great healer, for he no longer despised the Redcoats. 'You know, if dogs are treated properly, they will respond to you and they will want to please you.' There was a desperate desire for reassurance that the island would soon be rid of not just Captain Kalu, but all the Maroons in Jamaica. 'I say again, if dogs are treated properly, Fontane, they are a man's best friend. Come, let us inspect the merchandise.'

'My main worry is how long before the trade in horse flesh comes to an end,' said Pierre, following Duncan into the hallway and out onto the lawn. There stood a half a dozen Africans, recently purchased in Kingston. 'I presume they are your anniversary gift to your wife, Foulkes?' Like his host, Pierre was not in a celebratory mood, for with the sporadic slave rebellions across the Caribbean and the loss of livelihoods, nobody could guarantee that slavery would continue into the nineteenth century. 'How many can you part with?'

'Let's draw aside to a quiet place,' Duncan suggested. 'Away from the ladies.' He did not want to involve Fiona in the business of buying and selling black bodies, certainly not at their belated anniversary dinner. 'I can let you have the lot of them, with a runaway thrown in.'

'I feel like Elijah at the brook Cherit, sent there by God, only to see the water dry up during the three and a half years of famine.' Pierre had left a dispassionate Edessa in the dining room, complaining that it was not safe to travel to Kingston to buy slaves. He sniffed loudly: the unwashed captives gave off a rancid odour, rather like stale coconut oil. Kuki, who had escaped from the Redcoats, had wanted to turn and flee but his ankles were chained. 'That runaway with rotten teeth, I've seen him before.' Pierre's forehead shone with perspiration. 'How much?'

'He's yours.' Somehow, Kuki had miraculously escaped from the Redcoats. 'Don't you recognise him?' His bottom lip hung like a piece of liver, which was a trick he had perfected in his youth to gain sympathy from his previous master's children. Duncan lowered his voice, 'I found him hiding in the stables where he used to steal forty winks during the rainy season. My wife put a stop to that caper. You know, a dog always returns to its own vomit.'

Fiona and I have celebrated 25 years of marriage. The war between the Trelawny Maroons and the 83rd Regiment continues. Christopher and I were on our way to Trelawny to collect some abandoned horses when the war broke out. My man, Cassian, was with us. He being a man-mountain and familiar with the freed nagas and the locals on the North Coast, we did not feel in the least bit threatened. I am proud to say we Scots now own nearly 30% of the estates out here; hence the shadow of St Domingue hangs over us, too.

You may recall my writing to you about a shipmate, Evan Brown, back in '65. He turned up a few days after the war started, bringing three children with him and claiming that they were orphans for whom he was caring. He was until recently an overseer and it seems that his common-law wife ran off with an Irish overseer, leaving the bairns with him. I managed to get the lads enlisted as drummer boys with the Redcoats – good riddance.

To my dismay, I was in my study when Brown rudely interrupted, complaining that his 13-year-old daughter had fallen into the snare of one of my semi-retired white men, McTaff. I called him out, though he insisted that someone else had been 'working the Maidenhead Mine' first. Well, the damage is done. McTaff is a good employee and still in demand. He is a skilled carpenter and he brings Canongate an extra income.

My library includes a copy of Hugh Kelly's Memoirs of a Magdalen, or the History of Louisa Mildmay (1767), which Brown said he'd read. He is an unscrupulous man. He complained about 'the ruin of his child,' saying she was no longer 'mistress of that hidden mine that most men seek.' He demanded £500 for 'the value of her innocence.' I felt bad for the child's defloration and so I gave him £20; even that was sheer weakness on my part. With great difficulty (swearing, scratching and spitting by the child), Fiona cropped her hair and dressed her in boy's clothes. Disguised as a boy and carrying a knapsack filled with Christopher's old clothes, I sent her and Brown packing. I told him in no uncertain terms to stay away from Canongate in future.

As for the Redcoats, there was a picnic at Little River the other day. This Englishman, Colonel Hemmings, is effeminate and ruthless, but he represents the Crown, so we must obey him. Though no longer a young blade, he is devilishly handsome and the women fawn over him. When he proposed to Mademoiselle Fontane (whom I have mentioned), he went down on one knee and presented her with an ancient ring, a fortune. I may be wrong, but I am sure I noticed that his lips said one thing to her and his eyes said something else to his right-hand man. A very affable Redcoat perished in the valley during an ambush after the picnic, along with the Negro scout, a Loyalist, who seemed to spend his time capering around like a buffoon.

To return to that good-for-nothing Evan Brown, what really incensed me, Dougal, is that Hemmings ordered me to fetch Brown's two lads as if I were a plebeian. That popinjay, a mere dandy fop, seems to be living in another century, possibly the Roman world. Can you imagine it, Dougal? I was awoken at 4am in the morning by four Redcoats and Cuban dog handlers, trying desperately to control six bloodhounds. They had come to fetch my most valuable horses and the lads. I sent the British Army a bill for the horses and am still awaiting a reply. Your usual remittances should have reached you by now. I also enclose a letter for Fiona's family.

Frankly, we Scots are living in limbo. Thank God for our man, Henry Dundas. Apparently, he continues to argue in Parliament for 'gradual' abolition of the slave trade. The word 'gradual' means that we can purchase tens of thousands more Africans before those do-gooders (the Clapham Saints – hypocrites!) change it to 'immediate' abolition of the trade. I have instructed my attorneys in Kingston to make the usual funds available to you promptly.

Your same,
Duncan.

5

Lafayette

Canongate was a tribal community in which all the Africans – be they Yoruba, Igbo, Fanti, Ashanti or Bantu – were categorized as chattel by Duncan, who had been known to say aloud, 'fodder provided.' The enslaved Africans, meanwhile, saw themselves as individuals, separate and different from many of the people whom they were forced to work with for twelve hours a day. This cultural and ethnic blindness created tension on the estate, where small slights heightened distrust and divided loyalties in this febrile atmosphere.

To say that the end of 1795, four years ago, was a trying time for Canongate and elsewhere was an understatement. While Duncan had been sleeping, the bongo drums and the abeng conversed across the hills, informing the Africans that Captain Kalu had been captured by the Redcoats. He was betrayed by Kuki, a snitch whom Duncan had sold to Pierre Fontane because he seemed to create tension wherever he went. Pierre had delivered him up to the Redcoats.

Canongate was by now averaging an income of eighteen thousand pounds per annum but, faced as he was with the unpredictable climate, Duncan felt that he had two antagonists with whom he had to do battle: the Maroons and the uncertain weather. He feared the drought as much as he dreaded the seasonal winds, for both extremes affected his labour force as well as the estate's sugar production. It did not occur to him that the capture of Captain Kalu could affect Canongate's fortunes. Less than seven hours after the Maroons were taken, he rode towards the canefields at 9am with a mixture of feelings running through him. He had heard the news through Cassian and was full of joy and cele-bration, planning an early Jonkunnu which nobody wanted to miss.

'Blood fi blood!' It did not matter to this field worker that he was unarmed and likely to lose his life at any moment. 'Kill!' Swiftly, he executed his movement, rushing forward. 'Blood fi blood!'

'I'll cut your throat if I hear another word out of you.' Darnley, his horse circling the dissenter, was not in the mood to play the diplomat. 'That is rebellion talk. I'm going to string him up.'

Under the morning sun's rays, trickles of water ran down Kumasi's face. A freshwater African who was not yet broken down, he wittingly ran into the path of the horses. Aiming his hoe, as if it were a javelin, he then flung it with great force at Christopher. The horse reared up in fright and the boy instinctively ducked the missile, crouched, dug his knees into Peppa's sides and clung on for dear life. It had not escaped his notice that Kumasi had murder in his dark eyes. A line repeated in his head: *Negroes are not human beings.*

'Who is that?' Steadying Diamond, Duncan looked round for his white men, who were almost genetically driven to tread on African minds like ancient grape stompers.

'Wata!' ranted Kumasi, whose temper had been made worse by thirst and lack of sanitation in the fields. 'Wata!' He had entered an informal marriage with one of his shipmates and hated leaving their bed at 5am, so his temper was often tried. They had cut a *cotta* into two halves, both keeping half of the circular head-cushion that was made of dried plantain leaves and placed on a person's head beneath the bundles of sugarcane, usually the women's heads. After weeks of watching from the side-lines while the drivers quenched their thirst with sugar-water, Kumasi was tired of the forced labour and near starvation. He refused to wait for a break. 'Me wahn wata.'

'Most people would have you on the rack for that, boy,' Duncan blasted, watching while Darnley and two drivers grabbed the rebel and pinned him down. 'It is death to strike a white man, naga.' The hoe was deftly aimed at Christopher but it barely touched his shoulder. 'I am not a vengeful man. Given your complaint is about water, I shall spare your life, this once. Let me think of a fitting punishment: thirty-nine lashes. No, don't kill him.'

'I'll roast his brains over a fire, filthy naga,' Darnley said, recalling a conversation with Thomas Thistlewood back in '81. 'You there, Ocean, drop your trousers and shit in his mouth, boy.'

'He's a troublemaker.' Christopher felt himself trembling and was annoyed with his father for showing weakness in front of the workers. 'That really hurts.' His heart had leapt when the African jumped out in front of the horses and flung the hoe directly at him with all his strength. 'That is disgusting.' Becoming nauseous, Christopher turned his face aside. 'That is vile, Father. He's really shitting in his mouth. Oh no! I'm going to vomit.'

Kumasi had also become disgruntled because Ocean had told him of Captain Kalu's exploits, and this hero of the people had given him hope, that one day he too might gain freedom. He and Clotilda, his common-law-wife, had planned to pull foot during the New Year festivities so this blow, the news of Kalu's betrayal, had come as a huge shock and dashed his hopes of joining an established community of free men. He did not care to think of his woman standing at a 'cauldron stirring sugar for twelve hours,' ingesting the strong smell of rum. She had had six weeks off before the birth of their child. Two weeks later, as a nursing mother, she was back in the sugar mill, breathing in the fumes.

'Mercy!' The air was full of disgruntled voices coming from the strong gang, railing against the pitiful sight of Kumasi. He was in the act of choking on Ocean's dump, which the enslaved Africans referred to as *the devil's bulla-cake*. 'Sufferation!' One onlooker was almost trampled by a nearby driver, whose horse broke free and galloped into the midst of the crowd. 'Mercy.' An enslaved woman crawled through the animal's legs to get away. 'White devils!'

'Enough of that.' Loved and vilified in equal measures by his people, Duncan felt sick to his stomach at the sight. 'Put him in the stocks for the time being, man.' He was tempted to reprimand Darnley there and then but, as a rule, he did not like to undermine his overseer in front of the Africans and his visitors. 'You there, boy, go and get him some water.' By 7am the Africans had been hard at work for two hours already, but it seemed that none of them was willing to take up a pickaxe or a hoe that morning. 'All new mothers will be given 9s.6d as a reward for their hard work.' He tried to appease the women, but the gesture was met with a torrent of abuse from nursing mothers, who were primarily complaining about the long working days and their lack of sleep, which prevented them from spending quality time with their younger children. 'Nine and six.'

'There is nothing but hatred in their eyes.' Christopher spurred Peppa and the horse trotted alongside Diamond, circling the labourers. 'That hoe could have struck me in the face.' For the first time since he was a child, he cut a nervous figure in the saddle.

'I'll see yuh dead, massa.' Kumasi felt totally violated and the loss of dignity was incalculable. 'I gwine dance on yer grave.' He gagged and was sick over his feet, looking down at the shit, resembling brown stew, on his feet where flies had gathered. 'Me nuh 'fraid of yuh!' Since the birth of his son, he had generally resisted all attempts to return to work, for he wanted to spend time with his family. Kicking at the flies, his anger exploded into wrath and he rushed at Ocean, who had cleaned himself with leaves, aiming wild blows at his face and head. These two were usually the greatest of friends, working side by side. This cruel act of forced degradation had severed their relationship for good. 'Me gwine chop up yuh *warra-warra*.'

'Nuh blame 'im, bredda-man,' grunted a troublesome African named Nimbus. 'Yuh lucky it wasn't buck brukin'.'

'Slavery is livin' deat'.' Old Brer Tacoma was on his way to join the weeding gang. 'Whai! Me jus' wahn fi be free like bird in di trees.'

Looking at Duncan, a surge of emotion swept over Kumasi, causing him to call out, 'Who gwine free us fram a lifetime of sufferin'?' He had lately received a fracture to the left eye socket and his cheek bone for insolence. 'Yuh t'ink me 'fraid o' deat', Massa Foulkes?'

'Give them water,' ordered Duncan. 'If we kill him, it will inflame the situation.' The assumption that Africans could be ruled by violence was being tested, too. 'I shan't make a martyr of him by killing him.' As the clamour of voices rose, he looked at Christopher. 'I have just the job for him. The way to silence dissenters is to give them a meaningless title: Ranger.'

'He's dangerous as a leader, Father,' insisted Christopher, pushing fear behind him. 'You should make an example of him. He scares me.'

'White people are never afraid. We fear no one.' Duncan knew that the rebel's action took courage, that the African was prepared to meet death. 'You there! What's his name, Darnley? Oh, yes, Kumasi. I want to see you tomorrow when you have calmed down.' The African did not reply, for he simply wanted his freedom. 'Remember, son, violence is not the only way to control nagas. I'll make him a ranger, responsible for patrolling the boundaries of Canongate and for disciplining his fellow slaves. I shall permit him to travel to Lafayette and Ginger Hall. Mind you, I shall get one of my white men to watch him closely.'

'Brilliant idea,' Christopher agreed, becoming aware of a commotion. 'What about the women?' Two of the females had begun to quarrel because they abhorred the sight of each other. Duncan, intending to make them suffer for wasting time bickering on the job, had recently swapped their men and matched them with the other's partner. 'Och!'

'Ocean has always got a load of shit ready to dump in the field,' quipped Darnley. 'That Kumasi is dangerous. We must break him: take away his name, dignity; culture and his honour. I shall call him Uriah.'

'You need a bodyguard, son,' mused Duncan. 'No, don't change his name.' Last night, he dreamed of black figures surrounding Canongate and he begged them not to burn the house down. There was fierce resistance from the field workers but after a hiatus he and Fiona were allowed to leave without Christopher or their personal belongings. Today, Canongate was producing 600 hogshead of sugar and his main concern was not to fall below that target. 'If dogs are treated well, they are a man's best friend. Darnley, no more buck breaking. I forbid it.'

* * *

With the recent destruction of Trelawny Town, 1799, the Maroons were no longer a threat to security and the guardians of the empire had now turned their attention to war with France. Although Fort George was still in use, the new Colonel was vehemently anti-French and keen to see off Napoleon Bonaparte, who had allowed the insurgents in St Domingue to wreak havoc among the white population. Colonel Hoffmann cared not a jot for the French people in St Domingue, which would become known as Haiti. His right-hand man, Major Benbow, had called on the Fontanes on 31 December 1799. This was his last visit before returning home. He carried orders to empty their gunroom and convey all weapons and ammunition to Fort Dundas. Unsurprisingly, he had risen through the ranks because the skeleton of a seventeenth century admiral rattled in his ancestral cupboard.

'Redcoats!' hollered Joy, standing in the yard. It was 11.30am. 'Redcoats!' Born in West Africa, she carried vivid memories of being pinned down by an elderly aunt, after running from her mother, and pleading with her father to, *Save me, Baba*. At the time, she had hidden behind their hut in terror at home. She had undergone a severe form of genital cutting, including the removal of the clitoris and her outer vaginal lips were sutured. Seeing the troops, she gathered up her calico skirt in her hands. Her period had instantly arrived and, to calm her fears as she hid at the back of the great house, she began to sing a slave song about the infamous Three-Fingered Jack: *'Beat big drum, wave fine flag, Bring good news to Kingston town, O…no fear Jack's obi bag, Quashee's knock him down…'*

'Send them away, Pierre,' Edessa's voice came from within the great house. 'Send them away!' She was in labour and would give birth the next day. 'We are under-staffed.'

'Welcome, Major.' Striding forward and clasping a proffered right hand heartily, Pierre spoke warmly, 'Welcome.' At fifty years of age, the main worry keeping him awake at night was the abolition of the slave trade, though he had no desire to open his heart to the Major. Desperate for information from the outside world, he said, 'Might I offer you some meagre food and drink, Major? And how is your lovely wife?'

'We are expecting our second child,' Benbow replied proudly, heading towards the great house while the small detachment of troops made for the stables in an orderly fashion. 'A plate of something cold will suffice.' At thirty years old, the quiet, sensitive Major was not suited to the rough and tumble of active service and was keen to secure a desk job in England. He stood on the veranda watching a chameleon crawling up the front door; it flicked its long tongue out and caught a fly. 'I miss the old days when we tracked the Maroons, before they were deported to Nova Scotia with that rebel, Captain Kalu…'

'That's right – they were deported to Canada. Peace at last,' Pierre spoke with relief, standing on the veranda trying to erase the memory of his last meeting with Colonel Hemmings. On the morning of Lydia's departure, the Colonel had demanded one hundred guineas for her dowry. Upon receipt, he counted the gold coins and dropped them into a box in the chapel at Lydia's insistence. The tranquil existence at Lafayette had been shattered by the Maroons. 'Is Major Eaton still in Bengal and is Colonel Hemmings well?'

'Aha.' Benbow, lacking the aggressive attitude that most of the men who served under his mentor displayed, said with a note of indifference, 'Colonel Hemmings is a baron, lucky hog; his old boy dropped dead at a most convenient time. Baroness Hemmings is on her third pregnancy, two boys so far. The baron is writing his memoir.' Smiling slyly, he accepted a glass of ginger beer but failed to recognise the yellow-skinned house boy in the plaid headtie. 'As for Major Eaton, I'm afraid he left India under a cloud. There was a shooting incident in which he lost his right arm and was forced to retire; his health has deteriorated since, I hear. Your niece insisted on him living in a cottage on the estate. There are rumours he drank himself into a wreck. Bengal is not exactly *Shangri-La*.'

'Poor fellow.' Not having had any visitors for a while, Pierre was glad of the company. The news of Lydia's new role was particularly galling since she had not communicated with her aunt. Pierre felt isolated, for Duncan and Fiona were seeing out the old year with a Hogmanay party. He could not attend as he was expecting his son and heir. 'My wife has written several letters to our niece, but she has not responded.'

Benbow, acting as if he were sharing privileged information, said coolly, 'I hear the baron deals with all her correspondence.' He had recently passed an unmarked grave in a valley where lush vegetation and wild flowers covered a mound of earth, containing Corporal Birch's bleached bones. 'The baroness is happily ensconced at The Warren, Monsieur. They say the baron cuts a dashing figure in society. He has also taken up his seat in the House of Lords.' The Major tried to picture a military wedding in Kingston: white feathers were fired from a cannon when Hemmings carried his lame bride from the chapel. 'The Warren is a haven for soldiers returning from the West Indies: *ex gratia*.'

'Overblown generosity,' said a vexed Pierre, watching Juno serving tongue sandwiches. 'That boy developed a nervous condition after you all left.' It transpired that Major Eaton had ordered him to slaughter a sow and deliver the bladder to Colonel Hemmings. 'He's not been the same since.' Pierre stepped onto the crunchy gravel drive and looked toward the chapel-cum-gunroom. It had not been in use since 1795: the one hundred guineas that he had paid for Lydia's dowry had disappeared the following day. Even now, he was convinced that it was stolen before the Redcoats had left Lafayette with his niece.

'Oh, to be born a woman.' Benbow sighed, 'My wife is lying in at Beckenham. It seems the goal of every woman is to find a mate, build a nest and produce a male heir.' He gazed at the drive nostalgically, recalling the crunching gravel as the carriage sped away from Lafayette with the ladies and their trembling chaperone, who had developed an intense fear of Hemmings after he had placed the tip of his sword on her lips before the horses sped off. 'I say, Miss Bidwell is *persona non grata* at The Warren, something to do with a pig's bladder bleeding on a platter. Apparently, she produced the thought and Major Eaton acted upon it. Incredibly, Miss Freeman took her vows three years ago and joined *the Poor Clares*. She was never quite the same after that dreadful ambush, frightened out of her mind.'

'A man-hater.' Instead of pressing the Major to go, Pierre lit another cigar and tried unsuccessfully to imagine a community of praying women living in celibacy. 'I once read that to kiss a nun is to prepare yourself for hellfire and damnation.' Whatever uneasiness the master of Lafayette had felt about his niece's filial piety, for she knelt on the stone floor in the chapel for hours, these thoughts vanished with the news that she had embraced motherhood as her calling. A lone buzzard swooped over the chapel and he observed the Major's raised head studying a patterned flight of birds, as if searching for a bird of prey. 'Please excuse me. My wife is in labour and I am needed. Women! *Men must work and women must weep*. We all have a role to play. Stay alive, Major.'

'I too shall be a father before the day ends, Monsieur Fontane.' Not for the first time, Benbow's mind strayed to England, thinking of The Warren: cowslips and purple orchids, larks singing; a little stream with a summery pool, deer stirring in a frost-covered field; cherries ripening in summer, green fields; the rustics and wood pigeons cooing. 'I can't think of anything more gratifying than holding a new baby.' Benbow imagined himself standing on the deck of a ship sailing up the English Channel: Sir Francis Drake on his *Golden Hinde*. Puffing out his cheeks, he dusted his perfume-scented gloves against his right thigh. 'If I can remember my way to the latrine. I take it there's a stack of old newspapers there, Monsieur? We're given gut rot food at Fort George.'

* * *

Shortly after the Redcoats left Lafayette, with a pock-marked young soldier holding the Union Flag high, Pierre sat on the veranda mulling over the past eight years: he had fled St Domingue with his wife and niece to escape the slave uprising but his brother, Chevalier, and his wife, Luella, had been burned alive in their home. Juno had rescued Lydia from the conflagration and carried her to her uncle's home. The servant sustained burns to his feet and arms while carrying out this heroic act but showed no signs of his traumatic experience until they left St Domingue where Pierre had been a failure. In fact, it had been a battle for survival. His plantation had operated at a loss while Chevalier, the older son, who had been told by their father that he could succeed at anything, became a prosperous planter. After the dramatic escape from St Domingue, Pierre had been too busy trying to make a new life as a planter to worry about Lydia. If he were honest, he would have admitted that he was glad when the troops arrived at Lafayette a month after he took over the reins of a plantation that had been in existence since the 1750s. Mengis Hunter, the previous owner, had milked the place dry and when the price of sugar soared, he sold the plantation for a profit and returned to Glasgow as a wealthy sugar baron.

* * *

Back in the spring of 1791, which seemed so long ago, the aristocratic Colonel Hemmings was not interested in an introverted adolescent with no conversation. At the time, she hid in the chapel-cum-gunroom when the soldiers and horses arrived. That evening, he had humoured her guardians and listened while she played the piano and later recited Christopher Marlowe's poem, "The Passionate Shepherd to His Love." Then in 1793, before he went overseas, the Redcoats called at Lafayette to take stock and he was surprised to see an attractive nineteen-year-old on her knees, praying in the chapel-cum-gunroom. Pierre had been preoccupied with his overseer, FitzGerald, when Eaton had wagered that Hemmings could not bed Lydia for ten guineas. Even now, on New Year's Eve 1799, at 9.00pm, Pierre could still see Colonel Hemmings putting a scented handkerchief to his nose.

'We have a suicide, boss,' declared FitzGerald, picking his large red nose. From an early age, the Irish overseer had loathed the English and was particularly patriotic when he was drunk, heaping insults on his betters. There was a story circulating on Lafayette that his father had suffocated in his own excrement after the floorboards in his privy, in Ireland, became so rotten that he dropped into the outhouse. FitzGerald often sat outside his own latrine with his five brown children, telling stories of Olde Ireland with a large dose of Irish pride, solemnly repeating, *At the Creek of Baginbun, Ireland was lost and won.*

'Who's dead? Why, that worthless shithouse,' huffed Pierre, walking towards a half-naked corpse hanging from a tamarind tree behind the outhouse. 'How dare him!' Getting closer, he unfolded his whip and a vein stood out in his temple. His anger arose from the simple fact that the death of one African meant buying another one, and in times like this when the birth rate was declining. Showing his pink tongue, Pierre lashed out until the skin on the deceased house boy's back was crisscrossed with welts. 'How dare him defy me by taking his own life, my property.'

'*Kooyah!*' Monifa exclaimed, spotting semen on the back of Juno's soiled breeches, corpse swaying in the breeze. 'Dem rape a girl-chile, too, massa.' Blazing with rage, her eyes bulged as she revealed that a girl of eleven was haemorrhaging in the sick-room, having been ravished by a soldier whom she described as *a pock-marked Redcoat*. At the mention of the child, Monifa noticed a group of women looking on. They were angry because Juno had often given them tamarind sweets for their children. In St Domingue, the priestess who trained Monifa had once left her in a newly dug grave for ten minutes, refusing to lower the rope-ladder. When Abi, a wiry Yoruba priestess, had finally rescued Monifa, anxious and nervous, she had learnt a valuable lesson about self-reliance. She now pictured a freshly dug grave. 'Why flog a dead 'orse, massa? Wat use is dat?'

'I use my whip to ensure my slaves continue to fear me,' Pierre said readily, looking at the corpse's soiled breeches. Conscious of the scars on Juno's arms in the moonlight, he turned from the dangling corpse, whom the Africans had nicknamed Miss Nancy, and remembered a mild-mannered Redcoat in chimney-pipe breeches. A pair of scented military gloves had been carelessly dropped outside the outhouse. 'Chameleons are masters of disguise.'

'Yet anodda *dinki mini*,' Monifa said furiously, planning 'a set up' for Juno whom the male servants referred to as 'Lettuse.' Even though she was a tough, determined woman, she never felt safe at night and often woke up with a start, as if she heard wailing. Two of her children had been sold in St Domingue. 'Unforgivable.' When an African died on Lafayette, Monifa organised 'a nine-nite' rite for the deceased, which included singing, ring games, Anancy stories and telling riddles. 'Wind blowin', spirit around in di air.'

'What use is a spirit to me?' Pierre shrugged, strolling away from the mopping up operation, when he saw the chameleon crawling across the veranda. 'My door is closed.' Footsteps behind him grew louder and louder on the gravel, until he turned around, trying to look relaxed. Presently, the moon's reflection fell on the path. 'Where is your horse, Christopher? You missed the Redcoats; they were here this morning. I trust all is well at Canongate?'

'A corpse dangling in the night air on New Year's Eve?' remarked a tanned, clean-shaven Christopher. 'It's Hogmanay and my friends haven't turned up. I got fed up of dancing with father and old man Grandison, so I thought you could use the company.'

'Foulkes is lucky to have a son like you,' smiled Pierre, heading for the stables. He was keen to show off his latest buy, a handsome brown steed. 'A naga hanged himself.'

'Sad story.' Monifa looked under her eyes at Christopher, thinking of his demands on her niece, Seraphima: *White man an' bwoy always wahn fi possess black ooman.* With a concerted effort, she pushed all thoughts of revenge from her mind and watched the Irish overseer, FitzGerald, cutting down Juno's corpse. *'Free at last.'*

In the background, a group of enslaved children, who had been up since dawn, clapped their hands over their mouths while the adults looked on in silent fury. A stench of powerlessness pervaded the air. When Captain Kalu was betrayed, his capture had aroused a visceral passion in most of the Lafayette workers. So far, none of them dared to voice their discontent publicly. Fighting back tears, the children tried desperately to rid their minds of the image of a boy-child on the end of a rope. He, Heron, had been hanged for falling asleep while the cattle strayed into the canefields.

'Come, Christopher.' Pierre walked towards the sugar mill, where the day's activity had ceased, noticing the big African shadowing his guest. 'So, this is the big buck I've been hearing about, Trivia, a eunuch.'

'I better go an' see to di mistress first.' Unusually, Monifa asked after Duncan's health before heading for the back door, accidentally stepping on a black furry centipede, known as a *stone bruise*. Lately, these insects seemed to be everywhere; this troubled her because it was unusual and unsettling to see so many *stone bruises* in the canefields, the yard and even inside the *pickney* nursery. 'Josette, I soon com'. I gotto see to di mistress first, Pu-tus.' Her sixteen-year-old daughter was six months pregnant by Pierre. She heard four-year-old Babatunde crying. It troubled her that her great-nephew had not had his own mother's milk. Often, she watched the babies and toddlers snoozing on their enslaved mothers' breasts, sucking gently, some dreaming and smiling as they did so mechanically.

'I thought we could have a look at the horses,' Christopher suggested, gazing back at Monifa who knew that he had come to Lafayette to meet Seraphima in the usual place. 'There seems to be a mouse infestation in the chapel, Monsieur. I sheltered in there out of the rain last week and they were running around as if they ruled the place.'

* * *

A month into the New Year, the wind became even stronger across Lafayette. Inside the house, Pierre and Edessa lunched alone, served by a heavily pregnant Josette who fretted about a rival named Emilé. Josette learned early that she could rely on no one except her mother, Monifa, and especially not her master, Pierre. Before the pregnancy, she wore a cord around her waist with notches an inch apart. Pierre had stressed that, after the pregnancy, he would leave her if her waistline did not return to the twenty-four inches he had marked out on the cord. Eavesdropping on her master and mistress' intimate moments, Josette (big of belly and bloated) realised that she was completely shut out of their world. She craved bread and cheese, too, but Monifa had insisted she eat vegetables and take long walks to Little River where she liked to swim in the sparkling water.

About a week after the pregnancy was disclosed, Edessa had placed Josette in the stocks. She and Pierre had exchanged words, for she had blamed Josette for sleeping with him. The house girls did not comment on her fat lips and two Panda eyes, but gossip wafted across Lafayette like bush fire. Emilé, the mother of Pierre's first mixed-race child, put it about that the master's bed, bought from Mengis Hunter, was so elderly that he and the mistress could not avoid rolling into the middle where they fought like cat and dog. Josette had been thirteen when she became Edessa's personal maid. Mistress and servant took long walks with the adolescent holding the parasol, walking on tiptoes to reach Edessa's height: five feet six. The first time that Edessa saw Pierre slipping his hand down the thirteen-year-old girl's blouse, she was speechless with offence and indignation. After two years of grooming, he had pulled the teenager's bloomers down and had penetrated her doggystyle in his dressing room. Edessa had walked in on them, but again kept her counsel.

'I long to eat sun-dried tomatoes, olives and freshly-baked bread with walnuts,' Edessa said languidly while waiting for Josette to serve her. 'I hope this is not bone broth; it makes me nauseous.'

'Yuh ring di bell, ma'am?' Emilé appeared, standing outside the half-closed door. 'I was eatin' mi dinna: dukanoo an' roas' sal'fish, ma'am.'

'When I call, you run,' replied Edessa. 'Imbecile.' A fidgety brown girl put her head round the door, smelling of patchouli, which caused Edessa to cough and choke on the hot soup. 'Come here. I told you never to enter this dining room.' She seized her chance to assert her rank and threw the soup at Emilé. 'Your place is in the kitchen, fool.' Pierre coughed and looked away. Edessa snarled, 'Get out!' For the mistress of Lafayette, insults were regularly used as a weapon of humiliation. There was no need to use a horsewhip. 'What are you waiting for, idiot?'

'I gone, ma'am.' Emilé volunteered, 'Mi haffe go 'elp out inna di kitchen at Canongate an' me gotto walk dere in di dark.'

'I hear Squire Foulkes is celebrating his eightieth birthday this year.' Pierre sneezed, trying to lighten the mood and appease his jealous wife, whose anger could not be contained. 'I was thinking we could give Foulkes a book on nature, or a nice watch. What do you think, *chérie?*'

'That old Scotsman is more dangerous than you think,' Edessa replied snappily. 'He had his eye on Lydia. He would have made her his mistress, ogling her constantly.' Although the birth of their daughter, Odette, had initially plastered the cracks in the marriage, the incessant crying did not endear the child to her mother. 'It seems as if he'll live forever, old goat. Most men of his age are either bedridden or six feet under. He'll soon be eighty and is still riding with his son – daily. They'll have to carry him out of Canongate; he'll be kicking and screaming into the next world.'

Pierre was not amused. 'Foulkes swears by steamed spinach and bone broth – the minerals.' He disregarded Josette, who was serving up rounds of beef. 'And he believes that riding keeps him fit and active.' The past few years had been difficult for his wife, but no European ventured into the sugar business without being changed forever by the experience. 'I have a lot of respect for Foulkes. You know he had a soft spot for Captain Kalu? I think that Maroon respected him, too, because he was the only white man willing to smoke a peace pipe and barter with him. He once met him and his followers on the road to Fort George and turned them back, you know. They were armed and determined to attack the fort.'

'Brave decision,' tushed Edessa, turning her nose up at the rounds of beef, sweet potatoes, carrots and string beans on her plate. 'Anyone would think he's Pope Saint Leo, turning back Attila the Hun and his men on their way to sack Italy. There is talk that Mengis Hunter set that Maroon free for saving his life. That is why he's never raided Lafayette (old New Hall to us). They say he had a sixth finger, like Monifa's. Are they related?'

'Hunter and Father were in Africa in 1765, and kept in touch; that is how I heard of this place.' Pierre paused, fretting about the remaining French planters and British soldiers in St Domingue. 'I want to go to Kingston, but there are rumours that some British planters are pointing the finger at us for bringing our French creole slaves into Jamaica.' It was reported that some soldiers sent from Jamaica to St Domingue by warship were either massacred or succumbed to yellow fever. 'They believe their slaves might catch the rebellion infection.' Pierre's words concluded with a snort of derision. 'What about the Trelawny War and the many slave revolts they have already had?'

'Protocol,' cautioned Edessa, gesturing in Josette's direction. 'She is a slave, and not a European servant. They say that in some houses, the serving slaves listen to gossip about the abolition of the slave trade and hardly ever change the plates while their masters are dining.'

'Me can go now, massa?' Josette winced when the child kicked in her stomach. 'Me on mi foot all day an' me tired.' Becoming tearful, her most painful memories were of being placed in the stocks, rainwater soaking her clothes, when she was in early pregnancy. She detested Edessa's child, Odette, and had stood over the crib telling the whining white child to, *Hush up. I cahn be yer maddah. I 'ave a baby on di way.*

'*Point de Convention.*' Edessa had been gifted a reproduction of Louis-Leopold Boilly's painting of a French woman refusing money from a gentleman. 'Count yourself lucky you are not on your knees in the weeding gang, whore. I shall sell that child when its born.'

'Be quiet.' Pierre admired the reproduction he had purchased in Kingston, hoping to have a collection to rival Canongate's lot.

* * *

'Oh Gawd, no. Yuh gwine see mi *punny*.' Two days before the birth of her child, in March 1800, Josette had sounded nervous when Monifa told her to hop onto the bed, in the room adjacent to the *pickney* nursery at Lafayette, so that she could perform an internal examination on her. She lay back, feeling her mother's probing hand. 'Dat rough, Mama.'

'Dis expected chile is mi faddah bloodline,' Monifa had said to soothe the anxious Josette. A sudden chill draft crept into the delivery room, named the Hut, causing her to look up. 'A who deh?' She was on the alert, sniffing the scent of asafoetida, which she had used to treat a female with a stubborn sore foot. 'A yuh deh, Ulalee? Go back, go back to Akin!' She had examined her late nephew's woman days before the breach birth of Babatunde, knowing that no amount of coaxing could turn the expected child. 'Open yer legs.'

'Yuh t'ink Ulalee spirit still 'ere?' Josette gave an involuntary fart and closed her eyes tightly. 'Dat painful, Mama.' There was a spot of blood on the sheet where she lay, occupying a dingy but comfortable room. 'Sometimes, I know yuh sad 'bout dem sellin' mi sistas, Maryse and Aimée, wonderin' wah 'appen to dem, if dem still alive. Yuh miss dem?'

'Yes,' Monifa's voice was terse. 'Not a day go by w'en I dohn t'ink of mi poor *girl-pickney* dem.' An honorary son, she carried her father's banner – Chief Jumoke II of Osun – proudly and was glad that her nephew, Akin, had had a son before he was killed. The children were her father's bloodline, his immortality. 'Di baby due in two days.'

* * *

The abolition of the slave trade was seven years away. Meticulous, Pierre and Duncan kept a record of all their slaves, including births and mortality. Monifa was given the task of ensuring that the females on both plantations were productive, keeping a record of each woman's monthly cycle. During their fertile period, they had to mate with hand-picked men who had already fathered more than six healthy children. After three months of mating, if a female did not conceive with one of the chosen studs, another woman took her place. This practice of 'covering' caused much friction in the slave quarters where the young women competed against each other for the men who had fathered their children. Fortunately for Joy, having been genitally mutilated in West Africa and now sickly, she was spared the emotional roller-coaster upon which her sisters in bondage were trapped.

Thirty-five years had passed since Monifa had been trafficked to the West Indies. What really incensed her was that white men such as Pierre Fontane and Duncan Foulkes pocketed the profits from slavery while Africa's children had been reduced to brute beasts. When she thought of Duncan, and then Seraphima being forced to abort Christopher's babies, worry lines appeared around her eyes. Moving quietly in their domestic world, Fiona had suggested that Edessa sell Josette, saying it was improper to have a naga wench with child in the plantation house.

In the midst of chaos and restlessness, Monifa remained a calm figure as she stared out at the great house. She had instructed Josette, from an early age, on how to avoid conception by resorting to certain sexual practices that Pierre's father, Monsieur Alain Fontane, had taught her when she was eleven. How well she recalled being given to his eldest son, Chevalier, a week after her twelfth birthday, and hearing his father tell him to 'stay firm in the saddle.' Cunningly, the lone wolf, who preferred her own company, had instructed Josette how to keep her body smooth with a pat of butter flavoured with cocoa.

Monifa, looking up from the registration book on the cedarwood desk, squinted at two pairs of dark eyes trailing her from the other side of the room (the Hut): a first-time mother and a woman on her tenth pregnancy. Both women had pleaded with her to smother their unwanted babies at birth to save them from a life of suffering in *the house of bondage*. She was not an abortion-doctor, though she had assisted several vulnerable victims who had been raped by white men. Tormented, the enslaved women had no desire to fulfil their maternal obligations, but Monifa had played deaf. Perched on the edge of the stool, her eyes caught sight of her grand-nephew's name in the registra-tion book, dated 1795. The record showed: *Babatunde (b.1795), male slave; mother, Ulalee; father, Akin.*

Monifa had earlier returned from Canongate in the afternoon but did not go to Josette in the big house. Instead, she had stopped at the barrack-style *pickney* nursery and adjoining delivery room where she had washed her hands in a bucket of water. There were two women waiting to give birth. She had examined them and had informed them that their cervixes were not fully dilated. In the centre of the delivery room, there was a roughly hewn birthing table. Having looked in on Seraphima at Canongate, Monifa had also delivered a man-child whilst there. The mother had been in labour for seventy-two hours; the child had not lived to see her tired face. He came into the world, took a breath and expired. Monifa had tried to revive him. No time to linger, she now reassured the two expectant mothers that she would return before they could say, *Kooyah*. She had picked up a calico bundle and disappeared like a shadow.

'Me only 'ave two 'ands, Pu-tus.' Monifa had slipped into the great house via the back door. 'Me needed in di delivery room, Pu-tus, but me will be back before yuh can seh, *Whoop bam.*'

'I need yuh, too,' whined Josette, seeing her mother's eyes shut as she paused to regroup. She was unaware of the fact that a baby-boy had conveniently died at Canongate that day. 'Get it out!' After nine hours' labour, watched over by Joy, she was exhausted and wanted the pain to stop. 'Di mistress wahn me fi feed 'er chile an' massa nuh seh nutten, Mama. Go an' talk to 'im, Mama. Yuh know 'im listen to yuh, well, w'en 'im in a good mood.'

'Yuh too 'ard ears, girl,' replied Monifa, reassuring Josette that Pierre wanted her. 'Stop worryin' nuh.' She patiently explained that Pierre could not leave her. 'Stop bawlin' an' concentrate on di pain, Pu-tus.' Monifa looked up when Joy entered the room with a basin of hot water and a clean piece of calico folded into a thick napkin.

'Is wash day an' dem need me to 'elp wash di clothes, Miss Monifa.' Joy, not entirely a half-wit, kept smiling and her black eyes seemed to dance each time she looked at Monifa's poker face. 'Yuh gotto call Emilé if yuh need any 'elp, ma'am.' Seemingly unconscious of the two women staring at her, she continued to smile, as if she had caught sight of her own reflection looking back at her in a mirror. 'Me gone, ma'am.' Being a house servant made her feel a cut above the rest, so she looked down on the field workers and kept away from the *pickney* nursery, which she saw as dirty work. 'I gotto go, ma'am.'

'I got a job fi yuh later,' Monifa said, feeling more relaxed now that she was back at Lafayette and eager to deliver her grandchild. 'Yuh think yuh can get away at dusk? Yer job is to keep up di scream.'

'Keep up di scream, Miss Monifa?' Suspicious, Joy blinked at the unusual instruction and said in a whisper, 'Mistress dohn like me mekkin' noise inna di 'ouse. Me cahn scream 'cause it will wake di baby. Mistress will *kunk* mi inna mi 'ead an' box me up.' Dressed in black and wearing a white apron, Joy was hypersensitive to every worry and immediately burst into tears. 'Me nuh sure, ma'am. Me nuh wahn fi get lashes from massa like poor Miss Juno. Anyway, why yuh wahn me fi scream?'

'Go away, fool-fool,' Josette scoffed, squatting over a chamber pot. 'Lawd! Mi back a 'urt me, Mama. Whai! Mi belly bottom a drop out. Me cahn lie dung an' me cahn siddung, Mama.'

'I gone,' said a cringing Joy. 'Me gotto go.' Once, when she had not had a period for four months, she had gone to Monifa saying she did not want to tell anyone that she was expecting a child, for she did not know who the father was. 'I dohn wahn do nutten bad, ma'am.'

'Yuh too frighten-frighten.' Monifa blew a breath of exhaustion and silenced the house girl. 'Jus' stay 'ere an' wait 'til I com' back.'

* * *

Three months after Monifa had delivered the heir to Lafayette, Odette Fontane, she sat at her desk in the *pickney* nursery. There were no more expectant mothers that day. Presently, she looked down at the list of names written in the book lying open before her. She was perched on a stool, swallowing a tear, for this was not the role she had imagined for herself. Sniffing, she wrote her granddaughter's details in the book: *Nana Fontane, 17 March 1800; Mother, Josette; slave.*

Monifa now left her desk and made her way to the big house. She was blessed with her mother's calm disposition and her father's height. She and Josette resembled each other: tall and dark-skinned, they stood shoulder-to-shoulder, walked with silent tread and wore headwraps. Like their sisters in bondage, they had been sexually abused before they came of age. Monifa had by now reached the luxurious nursery where Josette was preparing to feed the master's child. Pierre strode into the room. Monifa stood up but continued staring at the white child in her daughter's arms.

With her head bowed, Josette guided a teat into the ravenous child's mouth while her own new-born child, Nana Fontane, was kept waiting to be fed. There was a loud sucking noise then a small explosion when the white child passed wind on the breast. Monifa regarded this as a bad omen, stressing that it could cause Josette's nipples to become sore and tender. Shaking her head at the situation, she immediately left the room.

'Self-expression doesn't seem to be one of your problems.' Pierre watched Monifa disappearing before placing an arm on Josette's shoulder briefly. He was anxious to leave the nursery, for he had his eye set on a banana-yellow house girl, Hildy, of whom Josette was already jealous. Edessa had engaged Hildy as her personal maid to replace

Emilé. 'You are expected to breastfeed Odette for six months. Let us see how you go.'

'Me nuh 'ave nuh milk.' Josette, on the edge of tears in the nursery with the rocking horse and the mosquito net over a pink cradle, suckled the child. 'I cahn mek milk.'

Monifa returned to the nursery. 'Quiet, Pu-tus, or di spirits will bex.' The sun fell on the window and cast a shadow on the crib in which her grandchild slept, and the grandmother's intuitive eyes glanced down at her milky coffee cheeks. 'Di chile content to wait.' After a moment's pause, she drew a clockwise circle around the cradle, creating a protective area. 'Dohn mind me, sah; me keepin' yer outside chile safe from bad spirits.'

'You talk about the dark arts as if I were not here,' Pierre baulked, clearing his throat and stepping to one side instinctively. 'I will not tolerate black magic in my house. There is no parallel world inhabited by spirits.' Touched by his illegitimate child's innocent face, he walked over to Josette and looked down at his legitimate heir before agreeing that his mixed-race child should remain in the nursery so that Josette could keep an eye on both babies during the night. 'I will not have black magic practised in my house. Clear!'

'Um.' Josette, nervous and sulking as she breastfed the child, knew that he was bedding her rival, Hildy. 'Six months o' ches' feedin'?' Her mind pictured a glistening river and the place where he took the curvaceous Hildy, saying boldly, 'Yuh 'ave anodda girl, massa?'

'That is a pointless question,' scoffed Pierre, standing beside her, noting that one breast was much larger than the other. 'I will not be questioned by a slave.' He was an enigma to his people. 'You may sleep in the nursery, but the babies must not disturb your mistress.'

'Gwane, massa. Everyt'ing unda control. Me deh yah, sah.' All this time, Monifa watched over her granddaughter's crib. 'Gwane, sah.' She glanced at the door. 'Yuh nuh wahn yer wife fi com' in an' find yuh neglectin' oonu *pickney*.' Taking the child from Josette and placing her in the richly decorated cot, she waited until Pierre had left. 'Yuh not a girl anymore, Pu-tus. Yuh's baby-maddah now.' Musing, she crossed the room and stood by the window, thinking of the African women who had furtively sought abortions. 'Hush up.'

'Di mistress should be nursin' 'er own chile, Mama.' Josette had no emotional attachment to the white child. 'Move from di window, Mama. Com' an' pick up Nana.'

'Who's a good girl?' Monifa peered between her fingers. This child, gurgling, was not free, but her grandmother was working on that. Now standing over the cot, Monifa smiled at a hesitant Joy, who had come in to coo over the master's mixed-race child.

'She nearly white,' Joy gasped, incredulously. 'Eh, all brown babies look white w'en dem born?' She glanced around, astonished to see so many toys. 'Is like puttin' nuff-nuff milk inna coffee-tea.' Going gooey over the cot, she burst out laughing when the child sneezed. 'Pretty-pretty baby, t'ank God yuh nuh black an' ugly-ugly like tar-baby.'

'Eh!' Monifa raised her eyebrows, walked over to Joy and took both hands. 'Yuh callin' yerself black an' ugly, baby.' Her silver earrings, shaped like teapots, had been gifted to her by Pierre after she had delivered the tenth baby boy in January 1800: hands for the canefields. She also wore a set of silver bangles, which were a gift from Edessa. In St Domingue, she got on well with the mistress, who still missed her sister-in-law, Julia. If anyone could keep Pierre away from wenching, it was Julia Fontane, who patrolled the plantation on horseback almost every night. 'Dis is mi gran-baby, Miss Nana Fontane.'

'She got a extra finga like yuh, Mama,' Josette's voice was high-pitched. 'Special.' Standing and removing her headwrap, she ran her fingers through her uncombed hair with difficulty. 'I know she'd be pretty like money.' The child's eyes moved magnetically and she leaned forward as if she had won a prize. 'Mammy's baby got curly 'air an' straight nose like 'er white daddy.' To Josette, and to most of the house girls on Lafayette, *all white women were beautiful because of their silky hair, thin lips, button noses and lily-white skin*. At least, that was what Edessa had said over and over. 'Nana Fontane, yuh pretty-pretty.' Eyes brimming with tears, Josette sighed happily, 'Mi 'air need washin', Mama.'

'Di baby 'ave six fingas.' Joy, staring at Josette's unkempt hair and then back at the milky coffee-coloured child, often tried to envisage what her own life would be like if she were a smugly privileged white lady cocooned in a plantation great house with servants doing the chores. 'Di bangles yuh giv' me, Miss Monifa, I cahn keep dem. Di mistress will beat me, ma'am. I dohn go anywhere to wear such shiney-shiney trinkets.'

'Dat's a strange t'ing to say.' Baffled, Monifa had forgotten that she had given Joy two of her bangles last Christmas. 'Yuh 'ave soft, black skin an' big brown eyes, Pu-tus. Yuh pretty, too.' She got to her feet and her older girls, Maryse and Aimée, who had been sold in St Domingue, appeared in her mind. 'Josette, dohn spoil 'er or yuh'll feel it 'ard w'en is time fi 'er to leave 'ere. Fi sure, she gotto go out in di worl', Josette.'

'Pretty-pretty dolly.' Characteristically effusive, Joy edged forward, smiling at the child in Monifa's protective arms. 'She barpin', ma'am. Yuh got to burp colic baby to bring up di wind – barp!' She lifted her black dress, preparing to leave. 'Me gone, ma'am.'

'Mama, please wash mi 'air before yuh go back to di *pickney* nursery. I dohn 'ave time fi look afta myself.' Josette clasped her fingers around a tiny hand while Joy crept out. 'Yuh gotto 'elp me to wean Miss Odette, too.' She was getting increasingly desperate, for one of her breasts had swelled so much that she felt like a milking nanny goat. The master's child was fed on demand and the breasts had become her soother, even while asleep. 'Whai, me tired.'

'Dry yer yeye, Pu-tus.' Monifa stood by Josette's side.

* * *

'Me nuh in di mood fi quarrel.' Having washed Josette's hair with aloe vera, Monifa's next stop was Canongate. While heading for the great house, she veered off the path and strode across the green lawn, walking towards the back door. She had hoped to avoid meeting anyone as she was needed back at Lafayette where two of the children from the *pickney* gang had swollen necks and a fever. 'Howdy-do,' she said, giving a quick nod and brushing past Kush, the gardener on Canongate. 'Yuh skin up yer face.'

'Yer dawta white-minded like yuh.' Put to pasture due to his asthma, Kush was no longer part of the weeding gang. 'She tu'n 'er face fram naga-man. She t'ink she white like di mistress.' For the next minute, he leaned on his broom and vented his anger on Monifa as she passed

274

by, trying not to listen to him. Even though it was only 11.45am, his breath reeked of rum, which was his favourite vice. 'She sellin' 'er front to di massa fi a cool bed in di big 'ouse. Mi ooman 'ave pain an' swellin' round 'er finga joints from weedin'. Mi son baby-maddah 'ave pain eena 'er fingas an' di joint dem swell from usin' cutlass widout any 'andle.'

'Time too short fi teeth an' tongue to meet tidday, massa-man,' Monifa replied. 'Yuh too even-up, mu-mu.' Dressed in a white starched apron and matching headtie, she was used to Kush hurling insults at her. 'Wat 'appen to yer fork? Why not tek out yer anger on di lawn instead o' mi dawta? Gweh, yard-bwoy.' She was on a mercy errand to assist the twenty-three-year-old Seraphima, who was pregnant again. 'Kirrout, yard-bwoy.'

'*Awa di raas*!' Spitting phlegm towards her, Kush's response was swift. 'Yuh put yer 'and in ooman's parts like a man's 'ood.' The fuzzy-haired, dark-skinned African with grey eyebrows was itching for another one of their arguments about female genitalia and its mutilation. 'Pouf! Di man wid di clitoris.' He hawked and aimed in her direction, spitting and accusing her of discouraging women from submitting to 'the cut.' His body shook and his voice rose to a shriek, 'Yuh forget weh yuh com' from, Yourba ooman? Yer dawta is a *slut-dwag*.'

'Kirrout!' A horse whinnied loudly in the canefields some distance away and Monifa's face hardened. 'Me is an old memory bank,' she replied, not willing to engage in a shouting match with an informant. 'Yuh t'ink of yerself as a man wronged. I t'ink o' myself as a ooman on a mission.' Eager to see Seraphima, she knew the argument was pointless. 'Get off mi back, Kush.' She halted. 'Wat yuh doin' out 'ere, Baba?' A boy of five caught hold of her hand. 'Serafima suppose fi keep yuh inna di kitchen, Baba-Son.'

'I gwine tell massa yuh 'idin' Maroon bwoy in di kitchen,' said Kush, whose kinsman, Kuki, had betrayed Captain Kalu to the Redcoats under torture. 'Who yuh t'ink yuh is?' He turned the broom upside down and shook it. 'Who is yuh to look dung on me?'

'I am Monifa, daughter of Chief Jumoke II of Osun. Who yuh is?' A long time ago, he had brought his daughter, Eniola, to Monifa for 'the cut,' to make her, allegedly, compliant. Monifa kept walking, thinking of some of the women whom she had de-infibulated over the years.

'Kirrout!' In St Domingue, her surrogate mother, Abi, had taught her how to perform the delicate operation on infibulated women to save their lives during childbirth. She reflected on how Kush's second wife, Gifty, had haemorrhaged in the bridal bed after he had de-infibulated her himself with a knife on their wedding night. The following day, he paraded around Lafayette with the weapon on his right shoulder, seeking approval from his male peers. Running into Fiona, Monifa was troubled. 'Marnin', Mistress Fiona.'

'Get on with your work, perishing idiot.' Fiona, wrinkle-faced and wearing a straw hat to cover her white hair, had enough power to silence Kush. 'Lazy dog.' In a testament to the strawberries grown in her green house, she carried a basket in the crook of her left arm, containing sweet peppers and strawberries. Glaring at Kush, who had been leaning on the broom until he saw her and realised that he had been spotted in an idle pose, she snapped, 'We need a grass-slasher, boy. There are plenty of brambles in the kitchen garden to keep you busy. Get to it.' He played deaf, causing her to lift her liver-spotted left hand and point. 'If you weren't so old, I'd send you back to the weeding gang.'

'Is he back-chatting you, Mother?' Christopher stood outside the privy nearby. He had stuck his left foot in the door, obstructing the yellow-skinned Hildy who had disposed of Edessa Fontane's none too fragrant day-soil, which had been left in the guest room for quite some time. The mistress of Lafayette had had enough of babies and was lunching at Canongate. Christopher and his mother pretended not to notice Monifa. 'I'll take the hide off you, boy.'

'Good marnin', massa,' Kush said swiftly, lowering his eyes. 'I jus' finish sweepin' di yawd. I gwine wuk solidly, weedin' up all di bindweed. Good marnin', massa, good...'

'What's good about it?' Christopher was in a foul mood and had just finished leering at Hildy, whom Edessa was hoping to sell to Fiona since Pierre had his eye on her. She had been seeing Christopher behind Seraphima's back. The mixed-race girl's freckles stood out against her yellow complexion. If he got the chance, Christopher would have set her up in a little cottage elsewhere. 'Don't stand there, woman.' He felt the need to acknowledge Monifa. 'I'm sure you haven't come here for a picnic on the lawn.'

'Dat bwoy gwine shame 'im daddy one day.' Monifa watched Hildy heading for the great house via the back entrance. The girl's hair was tightly plaited into intricate, seductive patterns. Monifa knew that if she did not act fast, Seraphima would take second place behind Hildy, whom Pierre was also bedding. 'Poh!' Before she could think of anything further, Babatunde tugged at her sleeve. 'A'right.' She took his hand and they began to march, reciting: 'Left, rite; left, rite! Hear di trumpet soun'.'

'Stop that commotion.' Peering out, Duncan had been listening to Kush's voice from the open window in his study. Although he pretended not to know why Monifa had come, his fears were realised when he saw the calico bundle in her hand and was horrified that she would, that day, perform an abortion under his roof. Seen from the study, the look Fiona had given Christopher reminded him of when Seraphima had miscarried their first grandchild. Even the song of a nightingale in the tree nearby seemed to be mocking them as Christopher and Fiona walked towards the front door. 'Have I not told you not to cause a disturbance and not to interfere with that midwife?'

'Marnin', massa,' Kush repeated, bowing when Duncan came out onto the lawn wearing his spectacles and leaning on his walking stick. 'Marnin', sah. I was mindin' mi own business w'en dat man-ooman tek a set 'pon me.' He remembered how he had staged a play for Duncan's wedding way back in '70, how he had fancied himself as a king sitting on a throne surrounded by women and living in the lap of luxury. 'Howdy-do, massa.'

'I am not deaf, boy, and you're a nincompoop.' Duncan peered over his spectacles, looking warily at Monifa, who acknowledged him with a nod before making a U-turn towards the back door. 'The front door is for my guests.' He had been reading about the national census. There were roughly 300,000 Africans, 20,000 whites and around 11,000 people of mixed-race on the island. 'Fiona, why have you left Madame Fontane alone in the drawing room?' He had formed a good rapport with Pierre and expected Fiona to be hospitable to their French creole neighbours. 'Christopher, a word, please. I am thinking of ordering a carriage from Edinburgh.'

'Madame Fontane, please excuse my manners; I'll be there in a minute!' Rolling her eyes again, Fiona moved off slowly. 'You're having bone broth for dinner, husband.' She had gained weight and looked plump. 'Not so fast.' She handed the basket to Christopher and headed towards the open front door. 'I suggest you entertain Madame Fontane while I freshen up.' She had an obsession with "freshening up" after a spot of gardening and would not go into the drawing room until she had changed her clothes. She dined with Edessa earlier on but abandoned her, bored of hearing about Pierre's antics at Lafayette, especially with Josette and Emilé. '*Yes, massa; good...*' muttered Fiona, mimicking Kush, who seemed to have shrunk to a pea in her presence. Most of the Africians dreaded crossing her path, for she had grown harder and more uncompromising with age. 'Och!' She watched Monifa striding towards the back door, recalling that the midwife had performed the *Kumina* dance when one of the female field labourers had died unexpectedly and they had sent for her, causing goose bumps to form on Fiona's skin. 'Madame Fontane ought to sell that midwife. She's a witch, always skulking about.'

'Be quiet.' Duncan followed her into the hallway without realising that he was standing on the spot where she had aborted their first brown grandchild. 'You have a guest.' Although he believed the Fontanes were similar but different, white but French creoles born in St Domingue, he was an ardent supporter of hospitality and would not dream of insulting Edessa, who had come seeking relaxation and respite from the humdrum at Lafayette. 'That cunning midwife has become a willing collaborator in Christopher's sordid love life in an attempt to save her own skin. She has made herself indispensable to us whites.'

'You'd think a man with your experience of women would know me better,' Fiona climbed the stairs and hurled the words down at him. 'Amina is giving Madame Fontane a foot massage.'

* * *

The Warren, a large mansion house, was nestled in fifteen hundred acres of land in the Kent countryside of England. It was said that the Duke of Wellington had passed by en route to London and the former Baron Hemmings had held a function in the great hall in honour of his esteemed guest. He was highly respectful of the then Baroness

Hemmings and fond of his sons, Orlando and Octavian. A sociable man who enjoyed hunting, shooting and fishing, the late baron had organised a fair on the estate in 1783, celebrating his soldier son's safe return from the American Revolutionary War. He had told his guests that he wanted the townsfolk to mingle with the country crowd, seeing the estate in all its glory with workers transporting corn through the fields, and smelling pigsties stinking up the place. Baroness Hemmings, a bluestocking, had been a talented needlewoman. Now that the old baron and his lady wife (who had perished on the Continent with their son, Octavian) were deceased, those occasions would never happen again.

The mansion had a formal entrance with marble columns and was surrounded by an estate so vast it seemed unmanageable to anyone with a city garden the size of an allotment. With its rustic surroundings, the interior boasted a huge drawing room with exposed wood beams, a low leather mahogany coffee table and a pair of antlers on either side of the red brick fireplace. The centrepiece was a painting of Claude Lorrain's *Landscape with David at the Cave of Adullam* and there were murals up the four walls. Burgundy silk damasks dressed the windows, not so much to keep prying eyes out but to keep light from reflecting on the glass. Oil lamps sat on gold embossed tables in cosy corners, giving off an air of intimacy, while a large Persian rug graced the floor.

A far cry from Lafayette with its wooden verandas (top and bottom), The Warren housed a traditional library with leather-bound books dating back to the sixteenth century. In the grounds, the late Baron Hemmings had had a Pope's Seat built, which was naturally named after Alexander Pope, the English poet. This was where he relaxed, reading Pope and Ben Jonson.

The new Baron Hemmings's decision to marry an innocent creole girl from the West Indies was the best decision of his military life as a Redcoat. He counted himself lucky, for, while he had become a responsible husband and father of five boys, she had transformed into a doting mother who had done everything possible to ensure that their children grew up with happy childhood memories. Of course, this was very different from her own upbringing in revolutionary St Domingue and at boarding school in England. She had also removed most of the heavy, dark velvet curtains throughout the house and had replaced them with silk to create a cheerful homely atmosphere, which was perfect for entertaining.

News of Admiral Lord Nelson's death reached the Hemmingses in October of 1805. At the same time, Lydia was delivering a girl-child. The proud father of five boys, Baron Hemmings was delighted with this new addition to his growing family. He had just finished declaring that Admiral Nelson allowed the French fleet to escape to the West Indies and that, although Nelson had secured a victory at the Battle of Trafalgar, his ill-judgment had clearly cost him his life. Having read the obituaries in The *London Gazette*, the baron scaled the stairs when he heard a newborn baby yelling. He rapped on the door.

'Is that you, Pater?' Being part-French creole and part-English, Lydia had often felt that she had been made an object of curiosity, especially at social gatherings in the country, but now she sat up in bed smiling. 'I'm so happy, Pater; it's a girl – at last.'

'She smells divine, Mater.' The baron's eyes opened wide, taking his daughter from the midwife and at once declaring that she had a noble brow. 'I was planning to name her Isult Hemmings, but Mycenae Athena Hemmings is more in keeping with our tradition of classical names.' After a difficult birth, Lydia's only concern in her exhaustion was that the child was healthy. Her happiness seemed complete. The baron reflected that when he held his firstborn, Romulus, he had felt a great sense of responsibility as a father. 'I daresay she will be wanting a little sister soon. The family unit is incomplete, Mater.'

'Are you suggesting we try again, Pater? The family is complete.' Lydia had no wish for a stable of rumbustious boys. 'Mycenae Athena Hemmings,' she repeated, sitting up in bed, looking understandably bedraggled. 'That was thoughtful of you, Pater. After all, why bother to consult me about naming our long-awaited daughter?'

In the early hours of that morning, the baron had had what felt like a prophetic dream and awoken bolt upright in bed. In his dream, he rode a white horse at breakneck speed until the animal collapsed with its legs splayed, blowing and sweating. He suppressed the dream and returned the newborn to the midwife while Lydia unbuttoned her nightgown. Despite having six children, she had managed to retain her weight.

The child refused to be suckled, which caused Lydia to give a look of unfeigned relief, though she instantly put on a face of disappointment for her husband's benefit.

'The boys went straight to the breast at birth, Mater.' The baron's brow furrowed.

'They say boys are more contented and easier to raise than girls.' The quick-thinking midwife had struggled to deliver the difficult breach birth. 'Boys tend to be less demanding.' She lowered her eyes, for the baron's response was less than welcoming.

'Don't let the three Rs near her. Romulus, Remus and Rodney have a cold.' The light from the window threw a yellow shadow across Lydia's face, making her look pale and jaundiced. 'Nurse, please introduce her to Mark and Antony.' She ran a slender hand across her damp forehead and her voice was replete with maternal anxiety. 'They may see her for five minutes. After you've introduced her to them, I'd like a word.'

'You don't say.' The baron felt as though he had imposed himself upon his wife by suggesting another a child – half an hour after she had given birth. 'Leave us, nurse.'

'I simply want to discuss feeding arrangements, Pater,' Lydia said flatly, objecting to the midwife-cum-nurse being dismissed. 'Leave us, nurse. Come back in ten minutes.'

* * *

During his time as a dashing ponytailed Redcoat, the then Colonel Hemmings had enjoyed Jason Eaton's filial devotion. The years in Bengal had made Eaton promiscuous. He had spent considerable time amusing himself with libertines until he had eventually caught a dose of syphilis. Discharged from the Army, he spent hours in front of the mirror at The Warren, looking at his reflection and feeling disgusted with himself for not shaving and for losing his right arm. He loathed Hemmings's sons and referred to Lydia as a 'super breeder,' producing a hatchery of boy-children. Four days ago, the gamekeeper had hauled his dead body out of the lake after he had drunk a bottle of brandy. The following day, the baron had dressed him for burial in the cottage where he sat in a chair day-after-day writing letters, and where a suicide note in French had been found: *Elle baise comme elle respire – she fucks like she breathes.*

'About Jason,' Lydia flinched, glaring at him, 'the great passion of your life…' Her face contorted with pain. 'It was good of you to offer him a warm bed, Pater.'

'Why bring it up?' In an otherwise serene English village, the suicide had driven the baron to great lengths to cover up his past passion. 'Once I loved a man, like a brother and a friend,' he bristled at the suggestion of an improper relationship, 'and now you want to put my head in the pillory for it.' Unmasked, he stood with a whistle on a velvet string. 'Duty calls, Mater; it is time to line up those skittish chaps and check their nails.'

'I think perhaps we'd better have that talk,' Lydia said firmly, stressing the last two words to emphasize a change of subject. 'You are thin-skinned and intolerant of being criticized.' She sat on a doughnut ring cushion, nursing the haemorrhoids that appeared towards the end of each pregnancy. 'Well, I shan't play the good wife anymore, Pater. There'll be no more babies, do you hear me? It is my body, after all.' She turned her eyes towards the window, to where a grey squirrel sat outside, trying to crack open a walnut. It had been visiting her for a fortnight. 'Oh dear, I must look a fright to that dear little squirrel.'

'You were never more beautiful.' The baron cocked an ear and placed the whistle in his pocket. 'Imagine the boys' faces when you produce another girl.' He could hear their squeals and laughter in the nursery above. 'Two girls would be nice, Mater. We'll wait a year and try again.' Gazing beyond the quivering squirrel, which he regarded as vermin, still sitting on the windowsill struggling to crack the tough walnut shell, he looked out the window at a giant oak tree in the sculpted garden. 'We have just welcomed another Hemmings into the family, yet there's a feeling of the day after the funeral in this room.'

'Major Eaton and I had a *tête-à-tête* in the library last week.' For Lydia, gazing at the precocious grey squirrel, the day was less celebratory. She had been left distraught by Eaton's confession and had fled to Pope's Seat with her copy of Ann Radcilffe's novel, *The Mysteries of Udolpho.* 'He gave me a bundle of love letters you supposedly sent him in Hindustan. They're in my trunk. I daresay the loaded cannon was his last hurrah.'

'In India, he knew no peace, Mater.' Rather than hold back, the baron sought to play down the storm. 'This inquietude caused him to pour out his heart on paper.' The thought of Eaton's suicide brought tears to his eyes once again. As he approached the four-poster bed, he pulled out a battered trunk and made a show of flinging items of unused clothing onto the floor before retrieving the incriminating evidence. 'Jason was my oldest friend, Mater. He was my right-hand man and my trusted confidante.'

'I can't tell you what it was like reading your letters to him,' Lydia said coldly, looking at the squirrel intently. 'I felt embarrassed and humiliated.' At ease in her role as wife and mother, the baroness had grown tired of his preoccupation with his thumb and index fingers. 'That is a dirty habit, Orlando. Stop it!' Her distaste for homosexuality became evident when she grimaced. 'I have been forced to see you in a new light.'

'Unsee me.' Shredding the letters, the baron halted. 'In this family, women know their place. I'll have you know the Fontanes were at Court in the reign of Henry VIII.'

'Poor Queen Catherine.' Lydia winced at the pain, listening to the children's voices in the nursery. 'She was banished to make way for Anne Boleyn's bastard, Elizabeth; an ugly affair.' There was an emotional disconnect and she felt her temper beginning to fray; her throat tightened as she deliberately took out the pearl earrings which she always wore in labour. 'If you're innocent, swear it on the Bible.'

'This is absurd.' The baron reacted defensively. 'You have no idea how privileged you are, wallowing in the smug satisfaction of being holier than thou.' It took him some time to dispose of the shredded letters in the fireplace, working at them with the poker while reminding her of the night Eaton had sent him a pig's bladder on a platter. 'All right, Jason was my right-hand man.' Despite a mounting crisis, he tried to bluff his way out of a tricky situation. 'My only regret in life is not capturing that blasted Maroon chief, Captain Kalu.'

'In her note, Monifa referred to you and Jason as having a kind of man-to-man love, Orlando,' revealed Lydia, aiming with her right hand

and flinging the pearl earrings towards the fireplace. 'You don't know what a low opinion I have of you.' There was a cold silence between them. 'Frankly, you are immoral. I no longer respect you, Orlando.'

'When did you start calling me Orlando again?' The past and present seemed to be packed in the baron's head. 'I am not ashamed of my life with Jason.' He had recognised her potential as wife-mother material on his second visit to Lafayette and set out to woo her. 'If I hadn't turned up when I did, old man Foulkes would have turned you into his *paramour*.' With Eaton dead, he yearned for contentment. 'Count yourself lucky you weren't cast adrift in the Saragossa Sea like so many creole girls your age back then.'

'You walled me in.' Lydia rebuffed the idea of being Duncan Foulkes's mistress. 'I will say this, at least Jason had the decency to go to his grave free of guilt.' She no longer respected the middle-aged man standing before her, specks of grey in his short black hair, trying to justify himself. 'Are you not ashamed of living a double life?'

'In life, we are all attached to a particular person or place.' The baron had moved on from Eaton and felt that she should focus on their boys, whom he loved taking for long walks. 'My conscience is clear, Mater. By fathering a stable of boys, I did what was best for The Warren.' He rifled through her writing desk, barking: 'Left, right; left... Attention!'

'This is not Woolwich Barracks.' Reluctantly, Lydia accepted the piece of *Taino gold* that he held out and then threw the fertility symbol at his cheek. 'Hah! I saw you and Jason the moment I sat down in the chapel at Lafayette. Mammy Scribbles slipped a note into my hat box before I left; it was from Monifa. I knew your secret.'

'A naga's word is not noted for its veracity.' The baron, staring from the inter-connecting door to a tapestry on the wall, rubbed his cheek where the gift had struck him. The tapestry depicted a maiden with knee-length hair in a vineyard with a fox reaching up to devour a bunch of grapes. 'You are affecting a phobia. What is it you fear?'

'It's as if someone has just uncorked a bottle,' said Lydia. 'I will not be churching after the lying-in.' The grey squirrel had disappeared. 'Our marriage is a sham.'

'You shall do as I say.' The baron was a pillar of the rural landscape and his wife had to be 'churched' after each birth. 'Jason will always be a special chapter in my life, but my sons are my life.' He sat on the edge of the bed in a silk robe, holding it together. 'That's the thing about the West Indies, you never know who you are talking to, do you?'

'I am half-French and half-English,' Lydia countered, in a bid to defend her racial purity. 'Jason was a broken man, destroyed by you. He left you his copy of *Sodom, or The Gentleman Instructed. A Comedy.*'

'Attributed to Lord Rochester.' Behind the mockery was the fear that she no longer esteemed him, even after he'd fathered five boys. 'Get some sleep.' No sooner had she dozed off than there was a peremptory rap on the door. 'Enter.' He flagged the midwife, indicating that she should put the baby to Lydia's breast. 'My wife is fast asleep.'

'Please hold the child while I fetch the birth tray.' With a bland look, the middle-aged midwife returned and placed a tray, covered with an embroidered white cloth, on a chair beside the bed. It contained a plate with a boiled egg, bread, cheese and a glass of milk. There was also a trinket box with an opal ring. Lydia jerked into a sitting position. 'Lie back, ma'am.' With her knee on the edge of the bed, the midwife latched the child on to Lydia's left breast. 'Baron, after the last birth, I advised your wife to consider the rhythm method, a sponge dipped in vinegar or prolonged breastfeeding.' She suggested, 'You could wear a sheath made of a pig's intestines, try coitus interruption or abstinence.'

'The question is, how hungry are you, nurse?' The baron frowned, telling her that he had dismissed a 'Touching Gentry' for taking liberties with his wife's privates. As he pondered male midwives pretending to dilate pregnant women while digitating, he turned. 'I am travelling to London tomorrow to attend a debate in the House. Henry Dundas, First Lord of the Admiralty, is debating the abolition of the slave trade.'

'Perhaps if your wife falls pregnant again, she should terminate.'

Unlike the former dashing Redcoat, the baron looked the picture of an older military man at this suggestion. 'I no longer enjoy taking life.' The air was fraught with tension. 'If you'll excuse me, nurse, I have an obituary to write and a birth to announce in The *Daily Courant.*'

'It is a huge task to be a husband, father, landowner and Member of the House of Lords.' The flushed-faced Miss Cressy Royse guarded her reputation as a sought-after nurse-cum-midwife in the homes of the gentry. Unmarried and past the age of finding a wealthy suitor, her only recourse was to make the best of the situation. 'Will you be churching your wife when the lying-in ends? Another girl would be good.'

'Yes indeed!' the baron said. 'Soranus recommended introducing solids to babies at six months: bread soaked in wine. Poor little sods, drunk in the cradle.'

* * *

The days when Mademoiselle Fontane played piano at Lafayette were spoken of with fond memories, but the house servants were forbidden to speak of the Maroons, whose names they whispered behind their hands in moments of frustration, saying, *Do we not share di same desire fi freedom?* Slowly, life had picked up its rhythm in the big house where the clock was cleaned, once again annoying cat-nappers and late sleepers. In the fields, the days revolved around the position of the sun and the crack of the whip or the *cat o' nine's sting.*

In the *pickney* nursery, Monifa had not forgotten that devastating day, in 1795, when her nephew, Akin, had been killed by the Redcoats. For the time being, she was torn in all directions, fretting over Josette's attachment to the cruel Pierre Fontane. As if she did not have enough on her plate, being the midwife at Lafayette and on Canongate, too, she had a full-time job protecting what was most precious to her: her granddaughter, Nana.

'Guess who I am, Granny?' Five-year-old Nana put her head round the door in the *pickney* nursery-delivery room, waiting for her grandmother to abandon the deskwork and tell her to enter. 'Go on, guess who I am, Granny!' Having come straight from the breakfast table in the kitchen up at the big house, she was full after wolfing down a bowl of porridge and a boiled egg. She ate in the kitchen because if she wanted a biscuit, she could ask for it there, and Edessa did not like to see her gracing the dining room table. 'Guess!'

'Yuh talk too much.' Monifa put down the inventory and placed her hands over the child's hands. 'I didn't tell yuh fi com' in. Yuh mus' learn fi wait an' den nobaddy can call yuh rude.' She had only yesterday told her granddaughter about how tadpoles turned into frogs, preparing her for the facts of life because Josette was finding it difficult to approach the subject. 'Yuh is Jewel.' The midwife looked over at a row of beds in the far corner, which was partitioned off when there were sick babies in the *pickney* nursery, and winked at the inquisitive dark eyes watching the child. 'Yer name is Jewel.'

'No, no, no! I am Nana Fontane.' The child coughed up a bubble and burped without apologising, then added self-importantly, 'I am Nana Fontane and I am five.'

'Yuh forgettin' yerself, Jewel. Wat did I seh yessiday? No tantrums.' Contentment washed over Monifa when she heard the defiance in the child's voice. 'I say yuh is Jewel.' Since Odette's fifth birthday party, when Christopher Foulkes gave her a pony, Nana had been telling all the Africans on Lafayette her name and age as well as pleading with her mother for a pony. 'Yuh is Jewel an' yuh is six. Dohn answa back.'

'I am Nana Fontane and I am five,' cried the child, stamping her feet and completely forgetting the expectant mothers in the far corner of the room. 'Granny, can I have a goat for my birthday?' Her frizzy hair had been oiled and teased into ringlets by Josette. 'Yes?'

'Yuh must learn to satisfy wid di likkle yuh 'ave, Jewel.' Monifa stood up, pulled the child towards her and hugged her before holding her by the shoulders and looking into her eyes. 'No goat.' She remembered how she had tiptoed up the stairs in the great house and placed a doll beside the sleeping child for her birthday. 'Yuh is Jewel, nuh suh?'

'It isn't true.' Over the next few minutes, Nana calmed down when her grandmother swept her off her feet and placed her on the desk, disregarding the women waiting to give birth. 'Look!' She pointed up at the ceiling, showing her grandmother a butterfly trapped in a spider's web. 'Why do you speak so funny, Granny?' She noticed, as if for the first time, that her grandmother's arms, neck and forearms were black against her own beige skin.

'Ah, Baba-Son, yuh's a good bwoy.' A smile spread across Monifa's face when she saw her ten-year-old grand-nephew. 'Me soon com'.' She put down her grandchild. 'Wat yer name, Jewel?'

'I'm Nana Fontane!' The child followed her grandmother into the yard and her eyes brightened. 'Aww!' Curled up in a basket outside the *pickney* nursery was a grey cat named Jewel, busily licking the faces of her two newborn kittens. 'Here, kitty-kitty.'

'She 'ad dem in di nite, w'en yuh sleepin'. Di brown one is yours an' di grey one is fi Baba,' said Monifa, recalling that the night sky was bright with stars when she heard Jewel meowing outside the *pickney* nursery and realised that she was in labour. 'Yuh can keep yours in a box in di nursery, Baba. If yuh was back 'ome, yuh'd be 'untin' big cat.'

'I dohn like pus-kitten,' Baba said, poking out his tongue at Nana and then staring at his feet. The two children did not see eye-to-eye. 'Me nuh wahn it, Gran-Aunt.'

Monifa put her hand in his. 'Yuh haffe understand, Baba; mi gran-baby special. She carryin' wat it takes to free mi 'hole generation an' fi 'elp even yer *picknies* w'en di time com'.' She let his hand go abruptly and, cautiously, expressed support for the Maroons when her voice lowered, 'Wat was I t'inkin', givin' yer gran-faddah bloodline kitten fi play wid? Bwoy, go an' see if yuh can 'unt a rabbit in di bush. Gwane.'

'Go away, boy.' Nana squatted by the side of the box, stroking the purring kittens and her eyes twinkled. It was important that this child of the future had a secure childhood among the whips, leg irons and chains on Lafayette. 'I am going to get them some milk.' She looked up and cried out at once, 'Monkey-man,' pointing towards the path where a dark shadow had appeared, tugging a goat on a lead behind him. The shaggy-coated spectre was none other than a Canongate labourer named Nimbus, who was also known as Pra. 'Monkey-man, Granny.' The child inhaled audibly and immediately forgot the much-admired kittens. 'He scares me, Granny. He's a duppy-man.'

'Monkey-man!' Babatunde laughed, scarpering in the direction of the slave village from where he would go into the bushes with his slingshot to catch a rabbit. 'Me gone.'

'Poh!' There was a resounding thud, as if something had fallen off a shelf in the *pickney* nursery. 'Nuh bring yer *Myal* spirits com' war wid me tidday, Nimbus.' Lurking in the background, undetected, was a Black man who had been observing the scene. 'Yuh spyin' on me?' She found herself laughing when he scrunched up his face and bared his teeth, startling Nana: *Teeth like dese, longer dan dese.* An idea had sprung into Monifa's mind. 'We need fi talk.'

'*Awa di raas*!' Quite suddenly, a rockstone came soaring down beside the box with the kittens. 'Ah who deh?' asked Nimbus, recognisable by the basket on his back and the bundle of firewood on his head. He made some extra income for Canongate by selling much needed firewood and chickens to the hill planters' wives. 'Is stone talk – bit like drum talk.' He was not, however, someone whom the workers trusted. 'Spirits abroad.'

'Duppy know who fi frighten.' Monifa's memories came flooding back. In her mind's eye, she saw Seraphima and Christopher Foulkes sneaking off to the chapel-cum-gunroom on the estate. 'Ah-o! Secret message.' She remembered how her niece – who was in fact Captain Kalu's daughter by a house girl on Canongate – had groaned and wept during the planned abortion. 'A yuh deh, Sera?' And then it dawned on her that the stone-thrower was, in fact, no other than her grandnephew, Babatunde. 'Poh!'

'He scares me, Granny.' Curious, Nana peeped out from behind her grandmother's skirt and stared at the goat on a lead, chewing its cud. 'What's in the basket on his back?'

'*Curiosity kill di cat.*' Nimbus, with his long teeth, began to grin. A tentative smile appeared on Nana's face and he said coaxingly, 'Wat yuh name, likkle gal?'

'I am Nana Fontane and I am five.' The child looked up into his face while still clutching the hem of her grandmother's skirt. 'He frightens me, Granny.' The thing she found oddest about him was the missing big toe on his left foot. She looked at her sixth finger and said, 'Would you like my extra finger to replace your missing toe?'

'Aye, sah!' Monifa laughed so hard she almost fell over the box with the kittens. 'Yuh too brite, Jewel.' She observed Nimbus closely, noting the way he clenched his long white teeth together. 'Tek yuh yeyes off mi grandawta, sah.' Monifa's eyes were slitted in defensiveness. 'If yuh so much as sneeze near 'er, yuh dead. Tell 'im who yuh is, Jewel.'

'How do you do?' The child smiled sweetly, taking the hand that was proffered to her. 'I am Nana Fontane. Did they chop off your toe because you ran away?'

'Mi foot 'urt too much to walk any furdah today.' Nimbus gave an embarrassed grin, looking down at his toes. 'Dis chile is a gift from di ancestors, a bridge between two worlds.' She smiled and, noticing this, he tentatively continued, 'Yuh trainin' 'er, ma'am. I like di way she repeat 'er name ober an' ober. She jus' five an' talk like big *pickney*.'

* * *

Odette Fontane turned seven years old on 1 January 1807. Even on such a happy day, the talk focused on the abolition of the British slave trade. Edessa had been forty when she became a mother. Educated at home by a French tutor, who had fallen several rungs down the social ladder during the Haitian Revolution, Odette was a slow developer and was generally indifferent to her surroundings. When her half-sister, Nana, got her first tooth, Edessa had sleepless nights of quiet anger. She could not understand why her husband's illegitimate mixed-race child was developing at such a rapid rate while her own child's growth seemed stunted in comparison. Disgruntled, she complained bitterly that Josette had been stingy with breast milk for Odette, but Pierre knew better. The children were, after all, fed simultaneously by Monifa and Josette, usually in Edessa's presence.

Practically raised by her grandmother in the *pickney* nursery, Nana was already crawling at nine months and had cut four teeth; she laughed readily and was always greeting visitors, saying, *Nice to meet you*. Once, when she tugged at Edessa's hem, she had pinched the child until she hollered. Edessa was desperate for Odette to do something, anything, even if it meant pulling the ornaments off her dressing table. She seethed when Nana recognised herself in the mirror, at twenty-two-months-old, after Josette had combed her hair and decorated her thick dark curls with pink bows. On Nana's second birthday, Monifa chortled when her grandchild licked her salty black arm and called her *O-ma*.

Odette was thirteen months old before she began to walk unaided; even then, she did not seem to be particularly curious about the world around her. Edessa had reflected bitterly that, after a labour lasting twelve hours, her daughter's first word was *Da-Da*. One evening when Pierre had decided to retire to bed early, the child sat on her mother's knee in the sitting room playing with a rope of pearls around her neck. Before leaving the room to join Josette in his dressing room, Pierre had casually remarked that they should have more cosy evenings as a family. Edessa then tensed when she heard her husband chatting in the hallway with Josette, removing Odette's hand from her pearls; she found the child irritating and grumbled to herself that she was too slow and sluggish.

For Odette's seventh birthday, Pierre had ordered a rocking-horse from Paris and had invited Edessa's old friend, residing in Martinique, and her large family to spend a month at Lafayette. Astrid and her husband, Jules Paquet, had fled to Martinique with their children during the Terror in France between 1793 and 1794. Theirs was a troubled marriage: on a trip to Paris, in 1788, the young Astrid had fallen head over heels in love with a pious young man who had been living a life of celibacy. During the Revolution, the husband and wife fled to Martinique where Jules's uncle had left him a sugar plantation. Inevitably, children started to arrive. By the time Astrid was forty, she had produced twelve children. What had happened since the marriage was hardly a happy ever after story.

'Yuh go meet an' greet dem, ma'am,' suggested Josette, standing on the veranda with a cord around her slender waist and wearing her usual white headwrap. 'Is a long, long time since we 'ave any white visitors fram overseas, not since Major Benbow...'

'Astrid is honest and open about everything, Josette,' Edessa said with delight when the horses and carriages came to a halt on the gravel drive. 'At last, at last; they're here,' she cried, rushing to the carriage to greet her girlhood friend. There were tearful hugs and kisses of welcome. 'This is Josette, Pierre's full-time occupation; she is less of a servant and more of a helpmate. Ahem! You and I have no secrets, my darling Astrid.'

'You are the model of restraint.' Astrid, hoping to settle the children before catching up on old time stories, looked around her as the heavy silk of her burgundy and cream dress rustled. 'We white women have a lot to put up with in the West Indies, dearest Edessa, not least our men behaving disgracefully.' She was a full six feet tall with blonde hair and blue eyes, which all her children seemed to have inherited. 'Where are your white people?' asked Astrid, speaking rapidly in French and noting a group of brown boys out walking, exercising at least a dozen horses. 'Do you plan to have another child, *chérie*?'

'We can but try.' The sight of her oldest and dearest friend, sweet, intelligent and loyal, was good for Edessa's soul. 'We have a chapel,' she smiled. 'I hope you are bringing up your brood as good Christian children.' Reluctantly, the older children returned her embrace before running off to see Odette's room. Almost immediately upon meeting her, the Paquet children adored her and treated her like a long-lost sibling.

'The children are exhausted and at least two of the younger ones seem to be down with a fever,' sighed Astrid, requesting dampened cloths to cool the children's brows. 'You have a lovely home, but the British West Indies is very disagreeable.' Scores of workers had alighted from a single carriage and rushed forward at the command of their mistress, ready to change the children into fresh cool clothing. 'I am so glad we are in the French West Indies.' Astrid turned to look over her shoulder at the sound of a gong, glad that there was no talk of abolishing the slave trade in Martinique. 'You ought to sell up and repatriate to France.'

'I do miss St Domingue, to be honest with you.' Enviously, Edessa looked down at twin girls; they were not yet four years old. 'Children grow up so fast in the West Indies. Given the bloodletting in St Domingue and the dreaded Jamaican Maroons, I don't believe plantations are safe for children. We all know the blacks have long memories.'

'You ought to spend some time by the sea, *chérie*, eating oysters and admiring the spectacular sunsets.' Notwithstanding a few factual errors about the Jamaican Maroons eating their children after bashing their skulls against boulders, Astrid put the subject of slave revolts and long suppressed grievances to bed with a cheerful smile. 'What a lovely view.'

'Yuh ready for a cool drink of lemonade, ma'am?' asked Hildy, who had been loaned to Lafayette at Pierre's request. 'I goin' back to di kitchen 'til yuh ready, ma'am.'

'I shall take you to Canongate, a much better prospect.' Edessa led the way into the great house. 'This isn't Martinique, Astrid dearest. There is no time for a change of scenery, I'm afraid. Pierre and I have a full-time job keeping our creditors at bay.' She dismissed the lingering Hildy with a cut-eye and continued, 'How was the sea voyage?'

Although Europe had had an industrial revolution from the 1760s onwards, planters such as Pierre Fontane frowned at the idea of steam. Stingy, they still required their workers to use picks, shovels, wheelbarrows, horses and carts on plantations like Lafayette, where slave labour involved hard physical graft from dawn till dusk.

'Boss is on his way, ma'am.' While they were admiring the cuckoo clock in the hallway, the overseer, FitzGerald, appeared with his mixed-race children, who had been craning their necks by the open door to peek at the French visitors. The Paquet children, meantime, were still spooked from last night's storytelling session with their father, who had told them tales from Celtic folklore about *kelpies*: spirits that took the form of fearsome, powerful horses with dripping manes. These white and sky-blue horses often changed into beautiful women, luring men into their traps. The children had barely slept. FitzGerald, feeling slighted in a way that piqued his curiosity, said casually, 'The boys have groomed the horses so the children can go riding tomorrow, ma'am, and get some proper exercise.'

'That will be all.' Edessa dismissed the Irishman, who sauntered off with a calico sack over his shoulder. 'He picks breadfruit to feed his seven mixed-blood children,' she explained to Astrid, purring at the very sight of her girlhood friend and shooing the house girls upstairs with the trunks and hat boxes. 'Let us go into the drawing room.'

'The last time I discovered Jules with a house slave,' Astrid lowered her voice to a whisper, looking around the wood panelled hallway past the huge mahogany clock, 'I raged and fought with him until I grew sick and lost our thirteenth child. As we get older, I've noticed, we women are not so naive. We tend to be more vocal than our mothers.'

'You have always behaved like a wild cat,' Edessa remarked casually, entering the drawing room and kneeling in front of a quiet child with pink cheeks. 'I am planning a birthday party for Odette. We shall have a wonderful time with the children in fancy dress costume.'

'*Maman, Maman*, there's a tiny servant in the nursery,' cried one of the children, clutching a doll. 'She's Odette's sister. *Elle est une négoro, Maman*. She is a *Negro*.'

'*Oh cher*.' Odessa, the heat rising in her cheeks, looked on longingly as they sat down in the drawing room surrounded by a mob of screaming little children, pure blood, some tugging at their affectionate mother's sleeves, competing for her attention. 'How delightful.'

Astrid smiled apologetically, turning when her husband entered the room. 'We are Martinicans,' she said, as if that explained everything about their views and their behaviour. 'We like the children to roam free, have a healthy childhood, free from restraint of any kind. We want them to get to know us; to express themselves without fear.'

'Jules!' Pierre came rushing into the drawing room, tripping over a child's foot before he managed to embrace his old friend, clapping him on the back. 'Jules, Jules! It's good to see you again. I wanted to change out of my workday clothes, but I had to see you first. I'll be back in a tick.'

'Pierre!' Jules Paquet, elegant and looking like a typical Surinam planter, arrived at Lafayette sporting a broad-brimmed hat, with an army of nursemaids behind him. Uninhibited because of their upbringing, the children rushed at Pierre, jostling and laughing until their indulgent father told them to behave or they would be sent to bed immediately. The threat seemed to work, for they pressed their faces to the windows, quietly staring out at FitzGerald's brown children looking in at them. Summoned, Jules was relieved to see one of his children tugging at Pierre's sleeves in the hallway, pleading with their host to release the wooden bird from the cuckoo clock. 'What a nice clock.' He swept the now weeping child, who was trying to reach the bird, up into his arms.

'How lovely to find myself in the company of children smelling like spring flowers.' There was a prolonged laughter from Pierre, thinking that only a child would weep over an annoying wooden bird trapped in a clock. There was even more laughter when one of the little girls asked if bread grew on trees, having heard mention of breadfruit. 'No.'

'Miss Josette seh dinna ready, massa.' Joy stood behind Pierre, frozen to the spot. Her bottom lip trembled. 'Din-dinna re-ready, massa.' The sun was starting to dip over Lafayette where the children crowded the hallway. 'Di slave chir-ren waitin' fi sing 'appy birthday to Miss O-Odette, sah. Mistress tell dem to wait 'til yuh come 'ome, massa.'

Boldly, at first, a Black child named Irma called from the back door, but then lost her nerve. 'Miss Odette, ma'am, we com' fi wish yuh 'appy birthnite,' said the child, aged nine, holding out a rag doll. 'We wish yuh a vary…ah cahn 'member di wuds.' She stood shaking, reduced to tears, when the chubby seven-year-old turned her nose up at the gift.

'*Sacre idiot!*' Astrid had come from the drawing room to investigate the noise and had explained to her children that laugher was a knee-jerk reaction to black humour.

'We are having a watermelon contest tomorrow.' Edessa came into view. 'I hope you've got the melons, Joy? Honestly, slave children are slow and lazy, always forgetting or garbling their words. Look at the insides of their lips, Odette, pink like watermelons.'

'It's happy birthday,' said Nana, standing inside the doorway. 'Give it here.' She snatched the doll from the nervous child, offering it to Odette. 'Her birthday is tomorrow.' Two of the three Black children stood at the back door gawping at the white children who were milling around Odette. 'I'll keep it.' Seeing that Odette had rejected the black-faced doll, Nana took it and walked off, heading for the *pickney* nursery, repeating over and over, 'I'm Nana Fontane. I'm almost seven.'

* * *

A week later, on a Sunday, Lafayette played host to another French couple, opening the stone chapel to prayers. 'We are hoping to retire to René's father's vineyard in Languedoc, in a pretty village named Marseillan,' lied Giselle Dupont. Walking towards the chapel with Edessa and Astrid, the French creole woman was small and unassuming beside Astrid. Although Giselle and René were by no means wealthy, they would have been considered middle-class in France where she had developed a taste for fine wines and Oriental silks. 'When I was first married, I begged René to go into banking, away from these animals in the West Indies.' She battled against memories of her daughter, Amity, being pinned down by a gang of Black men who had sacked their home in St Dominque and killed her only child.

'I wasn't going to tell you this, but we hardly ever go to church.' Edessa stood at the chapel door, glancing over her shoulder at Pierre. 'What is the point when our lower-class white workers are Protestants? Even the Irishman, FitzGerald, says he's Church of England.' She had been reading the Bible in preparation for today's service, which would be given by Jules who had styled himself as a lay preacher. Conversation had been stilted since Giselle Dupont arrived. She seldom visited the

Fontanes at Lafayette, and now Edessa felt that a genuine friendship was growing between Giselle and Astrid. 'Follow me, please.'

'We often drive to Clarendon on Sundays. The act of worship is simply a habit Christians observe.' Giselle was the first to sit down. 'If you had a resident priest, we'd make this our place of worship.' She took care to let Edessa know that she was not a threat to the already established bond between her and Astrid. 'Glory of glories,' she proclaimed, looking up at sunlight streaming through a hole in the thatched roof. *'Oh cher.'*

Edessa, already tiring of Giselle and the boisterous Paquet brood, refreshed her smile when a dozen white children fell silent upon entry to the stone building, ushered into the chapel by an array of nursemaids. In the space of barely ten minutes, the holy place was back in use with the pews filling up.

René Dupont, stretching out the stiffness in his knee, sat down beside his wife and paused to catch his breath. 'Fontane needs a resident priest.' He had been born in France but had settled in St Domingue upon his marriage to Giselle, a French creole heiress. Having fled to the island during the first wave of the Revolution, he took frequent trips to Kingston, visiting the waterfront to recruit sailors as estate workers and the auction houses to purchase African labourers. The Duponts adored the cultural life in Paris but would not risk a return until after the emperor was dead and the Napoleonic Wars had ended.

'I hope my dog's barking didn't disturb anyone at dawn,' apologised René, opening the conversation while looking towards the pulpit. 'He likes his morning walk, especially on Sundays.'

'Sundays have a different rhythm.' Pierre, who was yet to give Odette the rocking horse for her birthday, was brimming. Except for the Foulkeses, the white families were all sitting together, filling the front rows in the recently whitewashed chapel adorned with images of Catholic saints. The benches had been scrubbed-clean and polished too. 'I am so glad we arranged this thanksgiving service and the party.' He had forgotten to have the leaky thatched roof repaired. 'It means everything to Odette, having playmates of her own age.'

'This is wonderful,' gushed Edessa, 'wonderful,' noting that the rest of the congregation was filing into the chapel, including FitzGerald and his brown children. They sat morosely in the middle section of the chapel while the Africans gathered at the back. 'Astrid, *chérie*,' she said gently, 'it is a pleasure to have you here. Odette is having a wonderful time.'

'The children and I would have been sad to miss Odette's birthday.' Astrid unfolded her long legs and pictured her brood running around at dawn, jumping up and down on the beds and screaming until their father told them to go back to bed. 'Children, coffee was introduced to Jamaica from our island by Governor Lawes in 1712.' Lafayette was not the sort of place to unleash a dozen unbridled children, who seemed to be using up all the energy and space in the great house. 'Oh, your very own chapel.'

'Good morning.' Pierre stood up, noting the solemn faces staring back at him. 'Today, we commemorate the lives of our friends and the families who perished during the Reign of Terror. Before we begin, I invite our visitors to introduce themselves.'

There was a couple of minutes left, but it was not every day that the chapel was the focal point for an hour. Jules took off his broad-brimmed hat and laid it on the bully-pulpit, finding the right expression. As a young man, he had abandoned his seminary to marry Astrid but did not like to bring up his youthful change of heart in conversation.

'Please open your Bibles to 1 Corinthians 13–1.' Jules, seeking respite in a spiritual sanctuary, felt as if he were standing in the light: *'Though I speak with the tongues of men and of angels and have not charity, I am become as sounding brass, or a tinkling cymbal.'*

Before Jules had time to swallow saliva, Duncan, Fiona, Christopher and his new bride, Jane Tremayne-Foulkes, were halfway down the aisle. She was already six months pregnant and not feeling at her best, knowing that everyone would want to meet her. Astrid had been to Canongate two days prior and told her that she had craved oysters when she was pregnant with all the boy-children. After settling herself, Jane smiled, listening to Jules Paquet's accent and imagining the slithery, slimy texture of the oysters slipping down her throat, which reminded her of eating crushed snails. Jane noted the hole in the roof.

'Hallo there.' Christopher, who was always aware of what was going on around him, hailed Edessa and a chubby girl-child who waved at him. 'My little wife,' he said as he patted Jane's hand, noting the Paquet children giggling and their mammies shushing them out of habit. 'You don't look so good.' He felt his wife's brow, risking a look at the young woman with the sixth finger, sitting at the back of the chapel. Seraphima stared intently. He followed her gaze to the gunroom while listening to Jules reading Psalm 121: *I will lift up mine eyes unto the hills, from whence cometh my help.* Burping quietly, as he had eaten a breakfast of fried breadfruit and fried fish, he rolled his eyes at Jules's French accent and leaned towards Jane, whispering, 'Working among slaves for so long has dulled my senses to what women want, dearest. I'm sorry I was a flop last night.'

'You are too energetic, Christopher; think of the child,' whispered Jane, sitting in the pew behind the fidgety Paquet children. 'Now, will you please let me enjoy the service.' She was not in a talkative mood and had avoided being seated beside Giselle Dupont, whom she did not entirely warm to. 'Oh cripes, there's a thing called order of service.'

'Indeed.' Duncan rested his walking stick between his legs. 'Psalms, hymns and prayers.'

'Are they bothering you, Jane?' Fiona looked bored, watching a girl of fourteen nudge her younger sister. At the side of the chapel there was a door leading to the gunroom, where Hemmings and Major Eaton had had their trysts back in the day. It was empty, except for two used metal mugs and two tall glasses. Unaware of this, Fiona had imagined bottles of expensive wines and yards of Oriental silk stashed away in there.

'Good-oh.' Life at Canongate had been far from harmonious, but today Duncan felt at peace with the world. He opened the family Bible at Psalm 23: '*The Lord is my shepherd...*'

'How long is this charade going to last?' Agnostic, Fiona sat back and admired the blonde girls, passing time during the service. 'Their father, Jules, is getting on my nerves.' She was trying to forget Seraphima's forced abortion but was conscious of her presence at the back of the chapel. 'I suppose it's cheaper by the dozen – the Paquet children.'

'The more the merrier.' Jaunty and optimistic, Duncan patted a five-year-old blonde boy on the head. Jules was talking about *The Parable of the Talents*. 'We ought to christen the expected child here, Jane.' Duncan smiled, gazing at his pregnant daughter-in-law with warmth and real contentment. 'Stand up, wife.' He rose to his feet with the congregation: '*I believe in God the Father, Almighty, Maker of heaven and earth…*'

'French Catholics,' Fiona muttered something under her breath when the service ended, looking around the chapel and taking in the three-tiered system in the house of God: whites at the front, browns in the middle and blacks at the back. 'Aha.' She instinctively glanced at the door leading to the gunroom, for her mind was turning over with worry about Christopher and Seraphima. 'I wonder,' she said, suspiciously. There were rumours that they met at Lafayette in secret.

'Well, that was edifying.' Christopher was deep in thought as they were leaving the chapel, which was his and Seraphima's love nest. There were no secrets on Canongate and he was conscious of the house girls in the back pew, Joy and Emilé, whispering among themselves and nudging Seraphima. 'My little wife.' He clutched his hat in his hand and smiled when Edessa brought Odette over to say good morning to the Foulkeses. 'You get to be a princess today, dressed up for a fun-filled afternoon.' His face lit up as he handed his hat to Jane and scooped up the child in his arms, carrying her outside the chapel and chatting to Edessa. Giselle trailed off with Jane, whose white maternity dress skimmed the ground. 'My wife is not having a good time of it – pregnancy.' A grin spread across his face when he saw the boy-children rushing towards a clump of trees. 'You don't have to apologise for them, Madame Paquet. It is a pleasure to see boys climbing trees and running wild. Come to Canongate for lunch tomorrow. Bring the boys.'

'My dream was to have a solitary life in a monastery,' said Jules, putting on his broad-brimmed hat and catching up with the Foulkeses. 'Odette seems to have taken to you, Squire Foulkes. I have seen the way her eyes follow you, almost as if you were her father.' He watched his boys rushing towards the newly built swings which Pierre had ordered the overseer, FitzGerald, to erect. Ironically, they stood on the spot where the servant Juno had committed suicide, in 1799, after he had been raped by Major Benbow.

'That's a bit of a stretch,' chortled Christopher, looking back to see if Seraphima had left the chapel. 'Admittedly, she does seem to like me.' A smile plastered his face. 'Children are intuitive.'

'The moment she set eyes on him, at two days old, she smiled as if she recognised him.' Edessa, her face lighting up, watched Odette traipsing after the little blonde girls towards the swings. She turned to Jules. 'Squire Foulkes is her second father.' She observed another child sprinting across the grass and a third throwing stones at the brown children, shouting something about organizing a game of *nigger knocking*. Frown lines creased Edessa's brow and she reminded herself to push a note under Astrid's door to ask her to tell the children to say 'naga' instead. She did not care to upset her friend but would not see the brown children stoned; after all, their father was a white man.

'This is a good way to spend time with the family,' Duncan said, regretting not giving Christopher the memories he had shared with rumbustious boys at boarding school. 'Oh, for a Sunday carriage ride.' Much to Duncan and Fiona's relief, the crested carriage had arrived from Scotland in time for their son's wedding, in April 1806. To add to Duncan's contentment, Jane fell pregnant within a few months. He longed for some lusty grandsons to carry on the old bloodline and fill Canongate with activity and laughter. A building in the style of the English country house, the great house with its mahogany staircase and hard-wood floor was built over a vaulted cellar with a flight of stone steps. Christopher smoked cigars in his father's study, for Jane disliked the smell of tobacco in the bedroom. On the marriage certificate, her name was given as Jane Tremayne. Christopher had playfully renamed her Pinky because of her habitual blushing. Duncan had approved and wished them a long and happy married life.

'I envy you, Foulkes.' Pierre approached Duncan on the lawn. 'I've always wanted a son like yours, a companion.' He noted Christopher's manservant, Trivia, walking in the young man's shadow. 'Watch out for that sambo; he's as big as a horse,' he said jokingly. 'I hope the day never comes when he's called on to lay down his life for his master, a fine specimen.' Away from the gravel drive, Pierre had organised a series of games on the lawn, declaring that after being bullied from the pulpit it was time to enjoy some simple pleasures such as eating Sunday lunch outdoors and watching a small army of boisterous, healthy boy-children at play. Without the slightest pang of guilt, he declared, 'I'm off to tame a colt, Squire Foulkes.' He winked salaciously. 'Old habits die hard.'

* * *

Back on the lawn, the sun was blazing down from a deep blue sky. Joy brought out the gingham tablecloths. Duncan sat in a chair with a dish of fish on his lap, wondering what Fiona and Jane were up to in the house. That horrible clock in the hallway was making a din again, getting on his nerves. *What,* he thought, *only 1pm?* Quickly, he checked himself. Joy and half a dozen Africans served the assembled guests on the lawn, pouring tea into bone china cups and returning to the great house to prepare pudding. Duncan exhaled, saying it was stifling at Canongate and the fresh air was welcoming.

Smiling, Edessa reached out and touched Astrid's arm. 'Thank you for bringing the children. I can't tell you enough how nice it is to see Odette making friends her own age, happily playing with her own kind.' As well as the children, Astrid had also brought Edessa two silk scarves, a bottle of *eau de cologne* and an exquisite pair of Oriental slippers that were too dainty to be worn on a plantation. 'I was thinking, my black dress won't look drab with those silk scarves. Perhaps I'll wear one to Canongate tomorrow. Squire Foulkes has kindly invited us over there to lunch. We don't socialize much, more's the pity.'

'*Maman, Maman,* Jacques is stuck in that tree,' whined a boy-child. 'Look! He and Gaston climbed right up that cotton tree over there. Send a slave to rescue them, *Maman.*' He leaned his golden head against her shoulder and added in the most pathetic tone that he could muster, 'Jacques pushed me and I fell out of the tree.' The lawn was now equipped with children's wooden toys on wheels, swings and even a hobby horse. 'My head hurts.'

'For goodness' sake, child,' Astrid said with a puff of impatience, 'you are the most untruthful of the bunch.' She felt a heaviness on her shoulder, piling cheese and sundried tomatoes onto a slice of cassava bread. 'Go away, Jacques. Go and play.'

'*Bonjour.*' Jules, now dressed down in a black beret and red necktie, had been discussing shellfish harvesting with Duncan when his attention was drawn to a small child. '*Comment tu t'appelles?*' He put out his hand to be shaken. 'What is your name?'

'*Je m'appelle Nana Fontane,* I am almost seven; *ma mère est Josette.*'

'She is bilingual.' Hiding her annoyance behind a mask, Edessa stared at the child who looked pretty in pink, sniffing the smells of fried onions, peppers and garlic, which Seraphima had brought over from the kitchen garden at Canongate. 'Where is Pierre? We are supposed to be entertaining guests.' The child crept under her skin and she waved Nana away with a quiet rebellion brewing inside her. 'I had no idea Jules was such an eloquent speaker, Astrid. I am mulling over today's lesson: that men who dally with naga wenches are in danger of bringing the mothers' sins upon the future generations. It doesn't help that our lower-class white workers are the sons of unmarried mothers, too.'

'*Maman!*' While Astrid was engaging in polite conversation with Edessa, a strapping girl-child scurried over to loudly whisper in her mother's ear. Astrid's face softened. 'Ask her.' The child grabbed Nana's hand and led her away, squealing. 'Mariel is my eighth child. She knows that playing with naga children is forbidden, but she has an impulsive spirit. Sometimes I shout at her until my voice fails.'

'Steady, boys,' FitzGerald called out, pleased that his children were included in the games. 'Steady, easy!' The brown children were at one end of the rope, with the white children at the opposite end, tugging on the rope and wincing from the heat of the friction. 'Steady, boys!'

Duncan sipped a glass of Fiona's strawberry wine, muttering, 'Baked Irishman.'

'When René first came out to the French West Indies, he had thought he would find simple rustics leaning over gates; instead, he got a rude awakening: blacks swinging cutlases in canefields.' Laughing at his naivety, Giselle shooed a fly away. 'Ah, the melon contest.'

The grinning Lad, a superannuated African, stood on a rickety chair balancing on one foot. 'Arrrr!' He fell off the chair while two Africans stood not far off, roasting a pig on a spit.

'Clownin' again.' Cutting her eyes on Lad, Monifa watched six Igbos chomping on huge slices of watermelon, the juice escaping their pink lips. The white children began to chuckle. 'Nimbus a *kin-puppa-lick* like fool.' Monifa turned and walked away without looking back.

'*Maman, Maman!*' The younger children ran towards their mother, screaming when they saw a wiry Black man somersaulting on the lawn. This man, Nimbus, had a permit to travel freely and had come to entertain the guests by somersaulting or *kin-puppa-lickin'*. 'Krampus, Krampus!' Barefoot and dressed in rags, his hair standing up like horns at the front, the entertainer carried a basket on his back. 'Krampus!' wailed the children, frightened by the fixed, menacing expression on Nimbus's face. 'He's black and ugly like Krampus, *Maman*.' In the confusion and sobbing that followed, one of the children was heard to exclaim, 'Krampus is going to take us to hell in his basket, *Maman*!' The cries grew louder when the watchdogs started to bark, and Nimbus began to roar like a bear.

'Enough.' Duncan found it difficult to concentrate, trying to attack a giant crayfish on his plate. 'What trick is this, imbecile? Who gave you permission to leave Canongate, boy?'

'Mistress, massa.' Coming to a standstill, Nimbus's head was bowed in defiance, for he was under strict instructions from Monifa. 'Me a play,' he said when Fiona came out of the house with Jane, who was looking for Christopher. Nimbus looked at his mistress, expecting her to back up his explanation for why he was there; she, however, had other things on her mind. He looked directly at Duncan. 'Mistress okay it, massa; she did so.'

'Beasts will roar in the dense wood.' With her face turned toward a small child, Astrid untangled herself from the children's sticky grasps and, while dusting herself down and patting her hair into place, she glanced at the basket on Nimbus's back. 'A-ha, Santa's evil helper?' Before she could say another word, he set down the basket on the grass and half a dozen disoriented yellow chicks appeared, fluttering and falling about. The children began to coo over them and their mother laughed anxiously, remembering the Alpine folklore of Santa's evil helper, Krampus. The demonlike creature of legend wore a stinking goat fur and carried chains and bells, punishing naughty children at Christmas. While the kind and caring Santa gave good children gifts, the black, evil Krampus whipped unruly children and carried them down to hell in the basket on his back. Shuddering, Astrid imagined Nimbus as a demon, flying at full speed, snatching up her children and whisking them off to a fathomless depth, devouring what flesh was left on their bones.

'Quite the clown.' Duncan gazed at his lobster, relaxing when Monifa returned with a goat. 'A court jester.' He watched with a placid air while she placed a stool alongside the nanny goat and showed the children how to milk it, pulling down on the teats until milk gushed out. Before long, the goat bucked wildly. 'Cool down, children.'

'We ought to pay you a visit tomorrow, Squire Foulkes.' Astrid's senses were alerted a split second after she had said these words and she began sniffing the air. 'I can smell fire, Jules.' Perspiring, she pushed the blonde curls back off her face. 'There's a fire!'

'What!' Duncan stood up anxiously, shielding his eyes from the sun. 'That smoke looks quite thick. It's probably a grass fire, but one can never be certain in these hills.'

'Don't let me spoil your fun.' Everybody sat down again when Pierre rode onto the lawn and reassured them that the slaves were burning two cotton trees that had been colonized by wasps. '*Bon appétit!*' Perhaps the explanation was credible, but this did not stop Edessa from giving him a black look. 'I'm off. We're burning a two-foot wasps' nest.'

'Why don't you bring your lively boys over to Canongate,' Duncan said invitingly, looking around habitually for Cassian, forgetting momentarily that he had buried him a week ago. He was glad that his manservant had died before him because everywhere they went people remarked that the man-mountain would have been bereft with nothing to occupy him once his master had died. As he grew older, he had begun to lean more on Cassian and asked his giant companion if he wanted his freedom. He could hardly believe it when Cassian had looked him in the eye and said, *No, massa; me nuh wahn freedom at mi age. Weh me gwine liv'? Me cahn wuk an' me nuh 'ave nuh wife or fambily.*

'Papa!' With the endless supply of entertainment laid on, a girl-child abandoned the ferny bank where she had been catching butterflies and came rushing over to her father. 'There's a cat (one of Nana's kittens now fully grown) eating a toad over there. Shall I get one of the nagas to catch it?' Even at the tender age of five, the child instinctively knew from her interaction with their retinue of Black mammies that they were superior and that Black people were much lower in the racial ranking. 'Shall I, Papa?'

'Wait,' trying to speak calmly, Astrid sniffed the air, for there was something rotten in a clump of bushes nearby, a dead bullfrog. 'Go and ask your nursling to rescue it.' She paused in matronly contentment.

'I am sure I saw red spots on two of the boys' legs this morning. I hope it's not chickenpox. No, perhaps not; the red ants and ticks are feasting on their lily-white flesh, the poor little darlings.'

'It's more likely to be flea bites.' Duncan, who had almost lost hope in Christopher marrying an eligible bride and fathering legitimate white children, caught sight of his son discreetly slipping into the chapel and, as he had anticipated, Seraphima soon followed. 'Och!' Fortunately, Fiona and Jane had returned to the big house to snatch forty winks. 'My legs are going to sleep.' He turned to René Dupont, who had drunk a great deal of rum punch and was snoozing in the sun. 'I don't know about you, but I'm going to get a quick shut eye.'

* * *

At 5am the next morning, the swish of a lash slashed through the air at Lafayette, followed by the usual sound of a *conch* blowing across the plantation. Pierre was worried and tired, for he had been kept awake by the Black mammies going up and down the stairs and Edessa was already complaining about the children's lack of proper supervision. The hyperactive Paquet boys seemed to need little sleep and had been sliding up and down the bannisters in the early hours of the morning. Pierre, roused from his slumber by a disgruntled and equally tired Edessa, had stood at the top of the stairs, motionless and disappointed because the boys reminded him that he did not have a male heir.

Jules, on the other hand, had slept and was raring to go when he was awakened from a dreamless sleep by the sound of a *conch*. If anything, he was excited about accompanying Pierre on an early morning tour of Lafayette. The pink shell was blown by Lad, an elderly African who was nursing bitter memories of the night before. Leaning on his broomstick, he stood on the lawn watching the Martinican planter and four boys, between the ages of nine and fourteen, riding through the morning dew.

Pierre was waiting by the outhouse to give his guests the grand tour, sitting upright in the saddle. The atmosphere in the plantation house was celebratory but heavy with anxiety. On days like these, riding with Jules, blessed with a stable of boys, he felt less of a man. He would have given anything to trade places with Jules whose well-behaved sons were experiencing the kind of jolly West Indian childhood that the enslaved child labourers could not dream of.

'This is quite a place, unique really.' Jules slowed his pace, praying that his host would not expect them to cover four fields of cane in one day. 'I hope the boys didn't disturb you. I caught two of them hanging over the balcony railings. I've brought them along for the exercise.'

'*Bonjour*.' Pierre, more morose than usual, listened to the second call of the *conch* shell, which was part of the daily rhythm of life on Lafayette, marking 6am. Eventually, after a long pause, he replied, 'Don't worry. Chevalier, my brother, and I were the same when we were small.' The boys looked coy, keeping pace with their father and minding their manners. 'I suppose you boys think girls are pests. I daresay you pull their pigtails. I used to pull my sister's hair.'

'Girls can't climb trees,' the four boys said at once, between gusts of laughter.

'Get to it,' FitzGerald said sharply, riding up and down the field, with his whip cracking in the morning mist. 'Feckin' lazy dogs.' At this ungodly hour, when the white elite were snuggled up in their beds, a group of newly purchased Africans gathered in front of FitzGerald, who wore an old straw hat and a soiled white shirt with the sleeves rolled up to his elbows. While he was instructing the sleep-robbed field hands, most of whom had recently arrived in Jamaica, five brown boys sat on a flat stone eating their breakfast porridge without looking up. The boys' attention was attracted when the white men rode past, including Duncan, who was there to show solidarity with his fellow white planters.

'Morning, FitzGerald.' Pierre nodded and rode on, explaining to the Paquet boys that the brown boys belonged to the Irish overseer and were exempted from field labour; hence they were eating their breakfast porridge like masters of their own destiny. 'I'm off to visit the strong gang, the backbone of Lafayette. Join us when you're done here, Fitz.'

'Wise move.' Duncan smiled inwardly, knowing the importance of having a good working relationship with loyal overseers, especially one who showed solidarity with his betters, irrespective of class position, to maintain their own dominance over the enslaved Africans and to uphold the *status quo*. 'Don't slow down on my account.'

'Nice morning for riding.' Pierre started to whistle. 'Pity the ladies aren't up. I daresay they must be getting their beauty sleep.' He kept up a conversation with the Paquet boys, telling them that the strong gang consisted of the fittest Africans, rock-hard biceps and horse teeth, whose early socialization with the whip and other forms of coercion had taught them to cooperate; hence the handful of white drivers had no need to fear the man-mountains digging with their heads bent in obedience to their overlords. 'Look and learn, boys.'

'I am on your flank, Fontane.' Duncan did his best to keep up with the riders. 'This tour is a lesson in slave labour and control, boys. You will learn how to get the nagas to behave in our own interest, to improve productivity and enrich a plantation like Lafayette.'

'Where is that Mercy?' Pierre spurred his horse and rode past clumps of ferns and wild pines growing on the indigenous trees in an old field that had been reclaimed. 'How goes it, Mercy?' Here, women with babies strapped to their backs pulled up weeds while a group of meagre-looking boy-children tied dried sticks into bundles in another section of the field. At one point the girl-children, resembling blobs on a canvas, looked up coyly, kneeling and clearing the rows of decaying cane stems. 'I have told you before, Mercy, no snacking until break.'

'Sorry, massa.' An elderly woman with yellowish-grey hair took the cane snacks away from the sleep-starved children, who had been up since sunrise and had chased the cane rats out of the field. 'Me really sarry fi di lapse, sah. It wohn 'appen again, massa.' Years ago, she was owned by the DeWolf family who had plantations in Cuba and the United States as well as rum distilleries in Bristol, England. 'I gwine giv' dem sugarloaf an' banana at 10am.' In her youth, she participated in a small-scale revolt on one of the DeWolf's plantations in Cuba and had been deported to America. But she had absconded in Kingston where she was caught and sold to Pierre. 'Dem can play batos later.'

'*Piccaninnies* are miniature adults, boys.' Pierre, who had dubbed Jules the great master of brevity after the Sunday service, noticed that the Paquets had caught up with him, having lingered to watch the child labourers like tourists visiting an art gallery in Europe. 'Watch out, Foulkes.' There was a moment's panic when a yellow snake spooked the horses. 'We introduced the reptiles to keep the rat population down.'

'Good morning.' The yellow snake slithered into the bushes. 'I've brought bananas for the boys.' Christopher, shadowed by his bodyguard, Trivia, reined in his horse. 'It's wonderful to see what can be done with a few stems of cane.' Pausing to look back at his father, who was riding at a comfortable trot with René Dupont, he gazed at the overseer, FitzGerald, who had delegated his work to one of his sons and was determined to show his worth as Pierre's righthand man on Lafayette. 'It's too early for a flogging.' He had spent an energetic night in the chapel, sleeping with Seraphima. 'Give the whip a rest for one day.'

'It goes against all my principles to spare the whip, son,' said Pierre, who had earlier on given Joy a backhander for dropping a mug whilst serving his black coffee.

'If us whites are to prosper, we must keep the nagas weak, keep 'em subdued so they will become compliant and work.' FitzGerald unfurled his whip, observing four boys dressed in frill-fronted white shirts and morning jackets and straw hats. Silent and sullen, the strong gang was hatless and hard at work in the morning sun. 'They work twelve hours a day,' he grunted, checking his fob watch and glaring at the strong gang, one of whom pumped his arms and yelled (*Freedom*!) at an ear-shaking volume.

'What the feck!' Pierre exclaimed while the men in the gang bristled. 'I ought to string him up and flay him alive. That is rebellion talking!'

FitzGerald, in the meantime, responded by cracking the whip across the enslaved African's back. 'Get to it, you effin' naga!' He had told his brown skin boys that the darker a person's skin the more difficult it was to control them, for they were likely to have been socialized in Africa and usually refused to act in an inferior manner. 'Two lashes, boss.'

It was a tense few minutes and then the spokesman for the strong gang appealed directly to Duncan, 'We jus' tryin' to get oonu fi treat us better, Massa Foulkes.'

'Come here, boy.' Duncan, who had assumed that his enslaved Africans had learned to accept their fate at the bottom of the racial hierarchy on Canongate, had stressed to Christopher and Fiona often enough how important it was for the African children to learn their inferior status in the cradle. 'How do you know my name?'

'Just two lashes!' barked Pierre, spurring his horse. 'It's too early in the day for a revolt.' He steadied the animal. 'You boys would be safer playing in a tree house, but you do need to experience the rough and tumble of life, to prepare you for the world which you will inherit from your father. It's a mistake to mollycoddle boy-children, Jules.'

'A plantation is not only a business: it's a way of life,' Christopher informed the boys, turning in the saddle to check that Trivia was shielding him. 'FitzGerald, that's enough – two lashes only.' There was something odd about the scene: the young master of Canongate placating a whipped African, who calmly picked up his hoe and resumed working. Like most white creole children born in a slave colony, Christopher understood from an early age the significance of racial hierarchy; he knew the value placed on whiteness, especially for boys who would become leaders and girls who would grow up to become plantation mistresses or the wives of bureaucratic men. 'What are you doing out here?'

'Early morning burial, massa.' Monifa, approaching the riders, was returning from the burial ground, having helped to inter a Congolese woman named Hero. This had been necessary because the plantation's bookkeeper had tied her hands behind her back and flogged her to death for feeding salt to her newborn child. There was also a third grave. Hero's man, a freshwater Fanti, had not been taught how to use the cutlass properly, swinging so hard that it took a slice of flesh out of his left leg, a wound which had soon turned gangrenous. Monifa had been taking a short-cut back to the house, having spent the night in the slave village. Purposefully, she tried to perplex Pierre and Christopher (the men bedding Josette and her niece, Seraphima) by inserting herself into the tapestry of plantation toil. 'I searchin' fi cerasee, massa. Nana catch a fever. Me mindin' mi own business.'

'Everything you do is my business.' Gritting his teeth, Pierre pulled up his horse and addressed Monifa. 'Feeble excuse.' Everything about her had become legendary, from Lafayette to Canongate. He also knew that she was associated with many of the incidents in his life, from the revolt in St Dominique to the birth of his mixed-race child, Nana. 'I know what you are capable of, woman. I hope you're not inspiring the strong gang with your leadership. Get going before I lose my temper.'

He watched her heading towards a mammee apple tree. 'She is like a millstone around my neck but, regrettably, she is also indispensable.'

'I could kill that effin' *cunt* now,' FitzGerald said, watching Monifa climbing the tree and picking cerasee vines whose bitter fruit hung from the branches. She would use the cerasee to treat period pains and the mammee apple leaves for a laxative. 'All the slaves look up to her, effin' monkey in a tree. She's more dangerous than a snake.'

'She is an economic necessity.' René Dupont dismounted on the edge of the field, relieving his bladder. 'That's better.' He himself was a seducer of women and made no secret of his endless exploits with society women in France. Back in the saddle, he yawned. 'If you kill her, you'll provide your slaves with stories of martyrdom. I would have sold her years ago, midwife or no midwife. She is not indispensable.'

'The reason for her praise remains elusive to me,' responded Jules, checking to make sure that his sons were still enjoying the tour of the various fields. 'You want to bring her down from the stars before she leads a petticoat rebellion, Pierre, my old friend.'

'My woman says she employs *punny power* and *obi* to get her way,' remarked FitzGerald, dismounting to take a pee, too. 'She's one of the ugliest *cunts* I've ever seen.' In his eyes, Monifa was the ultimate racial Other, whose movements on Lafayette he tried to monitor, using spies such as the superannuated yard boy, Lad. 'Feckin' *cunt*!'

'Mind your manners, man. There are boys of an impressionable age present.' With a smile, Duncan rode in silence for a time, thinking of his daughter-in-law, Jane, who would soon gift him a legitimate grand-child, preferably a boy. 'I will say, naga wenches are not attractive, not unless they are of mixed-blood. Of course, the more refined gentlemen among us are influenced by our Northern European standards of beauty.'

'What the hell is going on?' FitzGerald mounted his horse again. There was another commotion and he felt Pierre was undermining his authority in front of guests. 'Boss, I've got to use the whip or the nagas will think we've gone soft.'

'We is man, not animal,' cried a muscular African, Kwaku, turning his back on the driver of the strong gang. 'Di end mite be tomorrow, it will com' before freedom, so I mite as well bring it on.' Exhausted from the daily grind and feeling at that moment that he could not go on, he threw down his hoe and refused to work any longer. 'Kill me, massa; kill me!' His earliest memories were of his mother holding him close to her bosom and singing a lullaby in the Ga language. 'Kill me!' He rushed forward and seized a driver by the throat before he could cock his rifle, grappling in the canefield with the white man while the other labourers looked on. 'Me nuh fear deat', massa; di ankcestors waitin' fi greet me.'

'I 'ear yuh, *braah*,' grunted Quashie, who was quite a character. This Gold Coast man, who felt sharp pains in his knees when he bent or twisted them, moved from his place in the strong gang and he, too, refused to work. He thought, *I wahn mi sons to be like di white bwoys lookin' dung on me from dose 'orses.* The muscle-flexing monologue earlier on (*Freedom!*) had earned him two lashes. 'Freedom!' he felt emboldened, speaking loudly in his thick accent and ripping off his short-sleeved shirt to expose his torso and his bare chest. 'Freedom!' The smile vanished and he sank to his knees when the butt of a rifle caught the back of his head. 'Blood fi blood, breddas!'

'Freedom!' Kwaku took up the call and response, even though there was a nervousness in the air. 'Blood fi blood, breddas. Blood!'

'Dem dead.' Bilal, a Fulani with whip-scarred back, heard the *conch* blowing. 'Say nutten, Adina,' he cautioned with a blank stare. 'Yuh keep yer mout', yuh keep yer life.'

On the edge of the strong gang, a cat attempted to breakfast on a 'bufo-bufo' toad with speckled brown skin, which instantly turned red when the feral animal bit into its skin. It was open revolt now: fists flying, clubs swinging and rifles sounding. The visitors galloped off to a safe distance from where they observed the retaliation: three white men had pinned down two Africans, who accepted their fate, declaring that death was preferable. They were trying to counter the overwhelming force imposed upon them, and openly rejected the idea of being enslaved for life.

'Cut off their testicles!' With the shadow of St Dominque hanging over him, Pierre held an unshakeable belief in Frenchness and liberty, but only for the white creoles and expatriates. 'Those slaves threatened our safety. If we don't make an example of them, they will influence the other blacks and stir up dissent on Lafayette. No, shoot them!'

It was, by the standards of a rebellion, perhaps a storm in a teacup, considering that no white lives had been endangered, albeit the Paquet boys looked as if they had wet their breeches. Forming a human shield, Christopher, Jules and René Dupont rode on in front of the boys. Of course, Pierre, who often twirled a cane or a whip whilst dealing with complaints, made the most of the incident, guiding the small party of riders out of harm's way. Quite bizarrely, a rabbit crossed the horses' path and disappeared into a thicket, which caused Pierre to turn his horse around to face home, dismissing FitzGerald and the white workers.

'That's sorted.' Christopher looked round for Trivia. 'Let's get out of here, boys.' Their faces, white, turned grey when two gunshots rang out. 'I want to show you boys my secret hideaway, Brecon's Cave.' They headed off in the direction of the weeding gang, a more sedate setting than the half-naked torsos in the strong gang. 'I enjoyed growing up in that cave. It has some interesting *Arawak* rock carvings and prehistoric drawings.'

* * *

'Whai-o!' The skirmish, supposedly put down, was not quite over. 'Me dead!' Tirzah, a pregnant African, was pulling up weeds when she heard the gunshots and got an instant whiff of her man's sweat. 'Lawd, a macy!' Big with child, she was allowed to leave the field at 5pm in the afternoons and used the opportunity of leaving early to walk past Quashie and to see him wielding a pickaxe with monotonous regularity. He would look up and stop for a few seconds, pretending not to notice her, with a foolish grin spreading across his face. 'Quashie-o!' Her eyes were full of tears. 'Mi belly drop dung, Quashie!'

'Quashie-o!' Adina, known as Patoo because of her big eyes, bent beside her, breathing the warm smell of molasses on Tirzah's breath. She, too, craved the black, syrupy substance and carried a small amount, which was hidden in a pocket in the folds of her Osnaburg frock, for both of them. 'Aye, mi sista.' Also pregnant, she could not understand how the manly Tirzah had gotten big strong Quashie to fall at her feet. 'Whai! Mi belly drop dung.' She took some risks in stealing and hiding the molasses in her pocket, but they both needed the sugary treat to stave off their cravings. She was often tempted to tell the two outspoken, now-deceased, men to be still and to wait for the right moment.

'Kwaku-o!' Abla had travelled on the same ship as her man and both were sold to the same master. 'Di blood of Africa cry fram di grung!' This was their third child. He would snap the heads off dandelions, bring them home and blow them with the children. 'Kwaku-o!' Abla boiled the herb, as instructed by Monifa, and drank the tea for shortness of breath. The plant was also given to the children to ward off colds and the leaves were used to treat ringworm and rashes. This tonic, known as piss-a-bed, was also drunk by elderly men and women to cure their bladder problems. 'Kwaku-o! Me wahn dandelion tea.' Picturing the small yellow flowers with thin seeded pods, she wet herself. 'Miss Monifa-o! Di baby comin', ma'am!' Two days ago, the midwife had parched and grounded dandelion seeds, giving Abla a mild laxative for constipation. 'Lawd, mi wata bruk! Di baby early. Mi belly drop dung, Miss Monifa. Whai-o! Mi cahn tek di pain, ma'am!'

'Get back to work or I'll skin you alive.' Merciless, one of the drivers, a thickset man, noticed that Abla was standing in a puddle of water. 'You there, old Mungo, go and fetch the midwife. She was skulking about; she can't have got far. Fetch! Time is money.'

'We is 'uman weeds to yuh,' wailed the full-eyed Patoo, retching at the sight of Abla's amniotic fluid and imagining her own unborn child swimming in her fluid like a fish against a fisherman's dragnet in the sea. 'Oonu shoot me man, Quashie.'

'I'll cut yer throat, whore.' The rough-talking driver, who had heard somewhere that the juice of watercress was a cure for his baldness, steadied his horse, whinnying to add to the confusion. 'Slaves are used to play-acting, Squire Foulkes.' He was the head of the weeding gang. 'Shut yer effin' mouth 'fore I put my cock in it, whore!' He dismounted and kicked her in the rear. 'Don't be fooled by her, lads. She's a she-devil.'

'Kwaku-o!' Abla, who sometimes picked blood-sucking ticks off her man's *buddy*, groaned. Kwaku had been whipped twice for standing up for others. 'Mi belly drop dung!'

'Whai!' Retching, Patoo stood up and tried to move out of the way of a flying kick, hindered by her swollen ankles and wobbling stomach, railing about her children's stolen childhood. 'Ah, mi *picknies*...' The shapeless woman had borne four children, all of whom were small in stature like stunted trees on a windswept hillside. She wanted to take advantage of Abla's situation so that she, too, would be taken to the sick room. Although she risked a whipping by taking such a gamble, she refused to bend her back to weed, for she was experiencing what became known as Braxton Hicks. She knew her body and the regular contractions confused her as she was not due to give birth for two more weeks. Cursing, she fought back when the driver, whose sunburnt face featured large purple bags under his eyes, put the tip of his boot against her stomach and gave her a big push. 'Miss Monifa, me wahn pee-pee! Mi belly drop dung. Sen' fi Miss Monifa, I beg.' A moment of relief was followed by a flicker of fear when her amniotic fluid began to flow. Hawking, she rocked on her heels and spat in the driver's face when he uncurled his whip and lashed out. 'If yuh kill me, is one less 'and fi weed.' She squatted. 'Miss Monifa, di baby comin', ma'am.'

'Mi belly drop dung-o!' Wailing, Tirzah joined in the call and response, too. 'Miss Monifa, mi belly painin'. A beg, com' ban' mi belly, Miss Monifa. Di baby comin', ma'am.'

'Shurrup!' Glaring at three squatting women, the driver had heard stories that some pregnant women pretended to be in labour to get time off. 'Get up before I wallop you!'

'Send for the midwife.' Realising that the drama had much larger implications for Lafayette and Canongate, too, Christopher spurred his horse. 'They are carrying the next generation of workers.' The females were breeding and increasing the *pickney* gang exponentially. 'Anything that threatens sugar production, threatens your livelihood.'

'I feel like a toad waking from hibernation, ready to mate,' Pierre said miserably, watching Monifa's return. She, it must be said, was no stranger to strife and had been loitering in the bushes, expecting trouble. The workers had been angered by the Sunday afternoon picnic on the lawn at Lafayette where Odette, a princess for the day, and her friends enjoyed no amount of distractions. Pierre snarled, 'I'll take over. Don't let me keep you from your duties.' The white driver rode off. 'Get a move on.'

'Mi was at *dinki mini* las' nite,' Monifa said flatly. 'Me tired, sah.' The Africans had conducted a funeral in their quarters where they plotted in secret to stage a rebellion. 'Get two o' di strong gang fi tek dem to di *pickney* nursery.' Last night, the older folk had gathered around the fire and told stories about Nanny of the Maroons and folktales. They had spent most of the night in contemplation and spoken in hushed tones about murdering the Fontanes, stressing that the time had come for a leader to emerge among them. They needed Monifa to be their voice, for she was African to the core. She had told them that the white man was killing them with his religion, stating, *We nuh 'ave nuh image of nuh ole white man wid beard in Africa, pointin' a finga to 'eaven.*

'God grant us peace.' Jules, whose wife and children had been held up as models of the colonial family in the West Indies, saw from his brief stay at Lafayette that Monifa did not respect religion and neither did she hold Edessa Fontane in high esteem. 'I'm not sure I agree with the treatment of your slaves, Fontane.' As a religious man, he felt that, although he was not an ordained priest, he had a good relationship with God and had long since stopped searching for spiritual succor. 'Of course, I am not here to judge your morals. Come, boys. Let us return to the house. I am in need of sustenance.'

'Perfect timing.' Serious, yet playful when in Seraphima's company, Christopher waited until the Paquets left before turning his attention to Monifa from the lofty vantage point of his saddle. 'Don't provoke that firebrand, Fontane. She'll only resort to spitting premonitions. I'm not in the mood for a song and dance, not after all the communion wine I drank last night. Trivia, you have my permission to fuck her.' He winked at his bodyguard. 'Put your wood in her mouth.'

Monifa observed Pierre's shoulders shaking and Christopher's wide-spread grin. 'Is no use settin' yer eunuch 'pon me, Massa Chris. Di man widout a *tickle tail*.' She stopped to check the position of the sun, noting a young mother snoozing under a tree with a tiny baby desperately trying to latch on to a leakin' breast through her Osnaburg shift. 'Ah sah! Di poor soul tired an' worn out. Tirzah, Abla and Patoo will haffe squat an' deliver di baby dem inna di canefield rite 'ere.'

'Marnin', *peeple*.' In a neglected area, Polybius, a superannuated African, had come down to forget his painful sciatica. He sat under a flame tree making a stringed gourd from the shell of a granadilla fruit, which he was trying to transform into a banjo. 'Whai-o! Ooman birthin' in public like *slut-dwag* a 'ave puppy? No! Tek dem back to di Hut, Miss Monifa.'

'A festival of pumpkins.' Christopher lingered while his father, Pierre and René Dupont rode towards the great house. 'It looks like there's a thunderstorm on the horizon.' Pumpkins grew adjacent to the flame tree. 'There goes the breakfast gong. I'm ravenous; time to grab a little *pussy* before I get too full up on breadfruit and fried eggs.'

'Yuh look better tidday, Massa Foulkes.' Monifa shook her head, gauging how long it would take for the three women to deliver their babies. 'Perhaps dere's time to tek dem back to di Hut.'

'Look better for who?' asked Christopher. 'Out of the way, fool.' He galloped off, passing a tall Ashanti carrying plantains on a pole slung across his broad shoulders. 'Monsieur Fontane wants those three babies delivered alive! More hands for the canefields.'

6
Riverhead

Enjoying a period of relative calm and prosperity, life was much slower now for The Much-Honoured Duncan Foulkes who had purchased Inverkin House, his childhood home, in the Highlands of Scotland. The English owner had mortgaged the property and invested in shipping but, with the abolition of the slave trade, he had gone bankrupt. How Miss Euphemia Booth would have applauded Duncan. Although not a lord in accordance with English heraldry, Fiona was entitled to be addressed as Lady Foulkes under Scottish law. The winds of change blew too late! Duncan was too old to travel but hoped that one of his future grandsons would return home. In the interim, Dougal had been made caretaker of Inverkin House, which would be turned over to the nation if no legitimate grandson arrived before Christopher's demise. Duncan felt down, though not completely out.

'I want a grandson with good Scotch blood.' Entering the drawing room on the morning of his ninetieth birthday, Duncan greeted his daughter-in-law with a smile and the irritating question, 'How is my grandson coming along?' The first two grandchildren were healthy girl-children and he remained anxious, even in his dotage, for a male heir to succeed Christopher and continue the family line. 'I hope you are eating properly. I don't want you wearing those restricting gowns that the fashionable young ladies wear when they come out from England and the rest of Europe.' Amina entered, carrying a tray with a crystal water jug and four matching glasses. 'I expect you to drink water and scalded milk every morning and to eat liver, spinach and okra. You must not restrict my grandson's growth. I want a grandson before I close my eyes.'

'I am not a baby-maker like those blackies, Father.' Jane, now on her third pregnancy, smirked, 'They are happy to show off the latest man-child to Christopher: '*Look, massa, I brung yuh new naga fi di pickney gang.*' Her patience wearing thin, the fair-haired beauty lolled on a champagne-coloured *chaise longue* by the window in a gauzy, flowing gown. She changed the subject; she was most relaxed when reading English literature, preferably alone. 'Would you believe it, Father,' she sought refuge in humour, 'Adolphus, the son of a West African prince, marries an English girl and has a half-caste child, awful.' Dropping Anna Maria Mackenzie's novel, *Slavery: Or, The Times* (1792), on the floor, with a languid movement, she gazed at the windowsill, where a black cat was trying to put its paw into a bowl containing six goldfish. 'No, Sukey, no!'

'That reminds me, my dirk, powder horn and my musket need cleaning.' Duncan raised his eyes to the obsolete objects on the wall. 'When I'm gone, Christopher will dump them.' He was busy fretting about a male heir to succeed Christopher and this had, on several occasions over the dinner table, escalated into an argument. 'You must find out what the naga wenches at Pimento Walk eat to produce so many boy-children, Jane.'

'It won't work,' Jane reacted instantly, looking disinterested with Duncan's suggestion. 'I hear some of those naga wenches neglect their *niglets*; they are heartless mothers.'

'I don't like that inflammatory pap.' Fiona, sitting in a comfortable armchair after breakfasting on porridge oats, frowned. 'That book is an abolitionist tract. Whoever heard of a white woman marrying a naga?' In the early days, she had felt like a country bumpkin in the company of her upper-class English daughter-in-law, who spent hours completing her 'toilet' in the mornings. '*Slavery: Or, The Times?* This is outrageous.'

'If you ask me, female authors should be censored to prevent them from writing about taboo subjects: white women equally yoked with naga men!' Jane scrunched up her face in disgust. 'Mother, shall we invite the Fontanes and the Duponts to lunch tomorrow?'

'I am not feeling sociable.' Fiona's face hardened at the mention of playing host while she and Duncan were waiting for a grandson. 'I have no desire to see that domineering Edessa Fontane and I have no wish to dine with that dull French woman, Giselle Dupont.' Looking at Jane's pale complexion, which had been maintained in the hot sun, and her rosy cheeks and red lips, the Scotswoman with working-class roots often wondered what it would have been like to have had a daughter. 'I've decided to bring three of the quadroon girls from Flamborough to train as seamstresses, Duncan.' She was secretly glad that mother-hood had curbed Jane's irritating habit of idling with her toilet chest, smoothing her forehead and eyelids with castor oil and applying a white paste to her face until the freckles disappeared. 'I'm glad you've stopped drawing black lines round your eyes and rouging your cheeks, Jane.' She lifted her right hand, inspecting the calcium spots and the wrinkles, trying to come to terms with the ageing process. 'Painted women are so unladylike.'

'I am not a courtesan, Mother.' Jane continued to watch the goldfish trapped in the bowl, swimming around to escape the shadow of the cat's paw. 'My own *ma-mah* adored the *Kitty Fisher look* when she was young. Sir Joshua Reynolds painted Kitty, you know, a bit of a seduc-tress.' She pictured the dark-haired beauty swathed in gold and cream silk and posing with a parrot perched on her right index finger. 'Sukey, do leave my goldfish alone. Mother, could you place the bowl on a table somewhere else.' She looked up when a three-year-old, with wheat-coloured hair and rosy cheeks, entered the room accompanied by Seraphima. 'I don't approve of half-caste people, Father. I don't think I told you at the time, but Christopher and I met the Darnley boys while we were out for a drive last week; they addressed him as Lachlan. How rude! They have ideas above their station.'

'God's stepchildren.' Fiona accepted a glass of water from Amina. She was anxious for the expected child to arrive, for she knew that women's properties would legally pass to their husbands at marriage. 'Marian and Virginia are growing fast. I don't want them associating with children of mixed-blood.' She recalled that when she had first arrived at Canongate, she was cautioned not to associate with the coloured ladies on moral grounds. 'Take the younger Darnleys, their mothers are half-caste but they're quadroons, almost white but not quite. They are slaves, albeit your father, Laird Foulkes,' she looked at Duncan, 'has allowed them a great deal of freedom in Flamborough.'

'Father is too generous.' Jane disregarded Marian. 'I have noticed that the red-haired brown girls tend to blush when you approach them.

Why are they always combing their hair in public? They have no shame. Get out, Amina. You stink.' She waited for her to pour water and leave. 'I cannot understand her unintelligible gobbledygook.'

'Grandpa, may I play with the little *niglets* on the lawn?' asked Marian, holding out her hands for Duncan to pick her up. 'I taught them to sing *London Bridge is Falling Down* and to recite *Jack and Jill*. I'll tease you by calling you *Lord Foulkes* until you say yes.' At the age of three, she was already learning how to use her feminine wiles on her grandfather, who held her for a short while until she began to snivel. 'I promise to be good. I won't take your hat out to the gate and try to sell it to the darkies again, *Lord Foulkes*.'

'You should have whipped them for stealing your hat,' Fiona interjected, inspecting the lead crystal glass in her hand for any scratches or smudges. 'No matter how you whip nagas, they're always laughing, jumping and dancing. There is nothing they like more than a *Pickney* Christmas, or a John Canoe. Slaves have no shame.' She paused. 'Oh do stop fidgeting, child. I cannot abide wiggly worms and mewling infants.'

Marian snivelled and fidgeted in Duncan's arms. 'Where's my *History of Jack the Giant Killer*?'

'Your man, Boggis, says flogging inflicts no wounds on their minds.' Jane allowed a sluggish Sukey to cosy up on her lap, stroking the purring cat. 'A few days ago, Gabriel and I saw a group of wenches idling in the weeding gang. Guthrie, or Boggis, told them to feed their *niglets*, who were yelping on their laps. There was a group of thirty-somethings with long breasts, resembling udders, being milked by dairymaids on a farm in the English countryside. Boggis says they're always spitting snakes at him and have no mothering instincts. They don't understand the needs of children. What has happened to the nagas' maternal instincts, Mother? Oh, Marian, do stop fidgeting. Your poor grandpa.'

'Maternal instincts?' Fiona looked surprised, like an impoverished milkmaid who had been given a sixpence instead of a farthing. 'Nagas are not capable of showing maternal love. They are not humans.'

'Those slaves are our livelihood,' Duncan said tetchily, putting Marian down. 'That is why their *niglets* fail to attach properly.' He gazed at Seraphima, who was sitting on a footstool by Jane's chair as

Marian climbed into her lap. The child was reciting, *Lucy Locket lost her pocket. Kitty Fisher found it...* He did not like this image. 'I think we ought to hire out the quadroon girls as seamstresses in St Elizabeth. The adolescent boys can be hired out as jobbers, perhaps in St Mary.' Seeing Marian on Seraphima's knee, he felt a flicker of conscience. 'Och.' Since Christopher had got married, he had advised, cautioned and threatened to disown his son, all to no avail. 'No drinking tonight, Jane. I'm off to my study. Marian, what have I told you about playing with the *niglets*? Jane, it is Guthrie, not Boggis. I don't think you'd appreciate being called Apple.'

'I do like the scent of apple blossoms in spring.' Fiona, conscious of her ongoing back problems, chipped in, 'No wine or sherry for you, Jane. If you're not careful, you'll end up birthing a tipsy boy-child. Marian, I forbid you to play with those *piccaninnies*, do you hear?' She gave Seraphima a fleeting glance. 'You'll end up speaking like those *walk-foot buckras* – white nagas.'

'Mother, please could you tell Simple to prepare a plate of steamed spinach and a slice of braised liver for me – I am ravenous.' Jane longed for freshly-baked bread, poached eggs and devilled kidneys. 'Oh, for an English breakfast.'

'Oats porridge will do me nicely.' Fiona felt a frisson of disquiet run through her. 'We must recruit an English governess for the girls, or they'll end up speaking with that ugly creole drawl, *Yees, ma'am, 'im railly too fresh.*' It made her uneasy to see Seraphima at Jane's feet, urging Marian to recite an English nursery rhyme about an infamous courtesan. Jane had told her how Kitty courted publicity and that she was famous for her affairs with wealthy men; that she was the rival of Lady Coventry, a celebrated beauty in her day, whose husband, the 6th Earl of Coventry, had had an affair with Kitty.

'Mother, while you're at it, tell Simple to crush the spices properly.' Jane slapped a delicate ankle where a mosquito feasted. 'Oh gosh! This is not how I pictured Jamaica.'

'I keep telling you to wrap your legs and arms with brown paper when there's no company.' Fiona looked down at her daughter-in-law, who was petting a docile bundle of fur. 'Mosquitoes tend to like dark rooms and black skin. That is why our slaves kindle a fire in their huts while they sleep.' Yesterday, she had whipped the house girl, Amina, for forgetting to shut the wrought-iron gate, allowing a superannuated old African to regain entry. Guthrie, the Scottish overseer, had sent the vagrant packing and told him not to return. Having nowhere to go, he then sat outside the gate, cutting the flesh from a dead cat and eating it. 'Christopher says he doesn't want you to breastfeed, Jane.' Some years ago, she had planted a pawpaw tree close to the house; it was said to render the air healthy and was a good weaning food. 'He is just concerned about your figure.'

'Ouch.' Jane roused herself, shooing the snarling cat away. 'You scratched me.' That morning, she had watched Christopher kill a 'red-tailed' scorpion on the lawn. It was glassy and jet black in its appearance and had stung a white cockerel on the side of its head without effect. It later bit old Minah, Ezekiel Darnley's 'sable' widow, who succumbed to hysterics. Monifa was now treating her with fitweed. Looking miffed, Jane ranted, 'I am having no monkey babies in the nursery playing with my children while their ape mother feeds my child.' She looked towards the door when Christopher walked in, and Fiona left the room.

'I am so hungry I could eat the bark off the trees.' Christopher, who had been outside giving his brother-in-law, Gabriel, a guided tour of the sugar mill, strolled into the room and planted a kiss on Jane's forehead, resisting the urge to look at Seraphima. 'At last, I have brought Canongate into the modern age. We have now got a steam engine to power the mill. This means that we can look forward to increased sugar production.'

'I've always said windmills are useless when there's no wind.' Jane's immediate reaction was to sniff, thinking he needed to douse himself in perfume, which she repeated like a mantra daily. It did not occur to her that he had just toured four fields and the sugar mill and had worked up quite a sweat, which she could not abide due to her sensitivity to unpleasant odours during her pregnancies. 'How does it work?'

'It crushes the cane waste, *bagasse*, which is dried and used as fuel,' Christopher explained, bending and reaching out to take Marian from Seraphima. 'The fuel is used to heat the cane juice, which turns to sugar. The sugar ends up in your cakes and tea, too.'

'Blood-sweetened beverage.' A young thirty-something bounded into the room dressed in white breeches, a blue morning coat, black top hat and black boots with brown cuffs. 'Have you seen Gillray's cartoon of a black boy in a vat of boiling sugar being stirred by an overseer using a whip? I wouldn't say no to a dish of tea, sweetened.' He had sailed from Liverpool six months ago and was doing a tour of the island, having come straight from Worthy Park in St Catherine where the medical doctor was a kinsman. 'If I were you, Foulkes, I'd do something about those impertinent Darnley boys. I was simply asking the half-caste wenches how to get to Edinburgh Castle when this great ox came up and told me to clear off.' The Englishman stood in the centre of the room with his hands on his hips and his legs wide open, owning the space. 'I told him to go bugger himself or he'd feel the sting of my whip. Foulkes, he looked me in the eye and said his father was a Scotchman. No white man can whip him. He was eating corn on the cob, too.'

'It's absolutely hideous.' Jane was surrounded by an aroma of French perfume: a heady mix of sandalwood, orange blossom; tuberose and jasmine. 'They're like pigs gobbling acorns.' She grimaced and turned her face away from her brother's gentleman's walking stick, topped off with an ivory monkey with green eyes and a red tongue sticking out. 'How monstrous.' The walking stick was standing by the fireplace. 'Oh drat.' Her eyebrows raised when Christopher approached, bent and kissed her forehead again. 'Oh, do stop slobbering over me like a wet puppy, Christopher. Do try to moderate your enthusiasm.'

'Lachlan, I goin' dung to Pimento Walk to see poor ole Minah.' Seraphima got up and took the child from Christopher. 'Ole Minah is really poorly, Lachlan. Can I go?'

'Why on earth did you bring Father that awful walking stick, dolt?' Jane stared at her brother, who had settled himself down and reclined in an armchair with his feet on a side table. 'It looks like an excavated object. The ivory is ancient. Where did you get it? I am sure I've seen it before. Erm, did I tell you I'll be Lady Foulkes when Mother dies?'

'Did I tell you I have an heirloom in my possession?' Gabriel took a deep breath before adding, 'It's splendid, representing two lives drawn together.' He now presented Christopher with a twisted gold band laid with an intense blue sapphire, explaining that it was made of pure gold and came from a world where magic was important. 'What! Lady

Foulkes?' He coughed behind his hand, saying, 'Is there a deal to be done, Foulkes?'

'This belonged to a distant relative, ninny,' Jane said reproachfully. 'It's extremely valuable and belongs to me, given that Mother is dead. It's not yours to sell, Gabby. You cannot sell off the family silver without my permission. You are a thieving magpie.'

'It could be yours for two hundred guineas.' Grinning, the brown-eyed Gabriel had fled to Jamaica to escape a spell in Newgate jail for debt. 'Father left it to me, Janey, he did so.' Keen to gain a West India fortune before returning home, he was disappointed to discover that the Foulkeses were far from being a soft touch. 'I could just as easily be back in my bedroom in Fitzrovia.' He stared after Seraphima, using a prickly pole as an elegant toothpick. 'I say, that girl is rather brazen, Foulkes, referring to you as Lachlan. Jamaica seems to be more equal than equal – white men and their sable mistresses. Hardly a picture of beauty, is she? Ahem! Lady Foulkes? You've landed on your feet, Janey. It's a pity we can't travel to Spanish Town to see the Rodney Memorial, carved by John Bacon. Good old Admiral Rodney saved Jamaica from the French at the Battle of the Saintes.'

'Two hundred pounds is a lot of money.' Christopher examined the crude blue sapphire. His mind was running over the Rodney Memorial, wondering why Gabriel had pulled this subject out of the bag. 'It was a combined French and Spanish invasion.'

'Men and wars.' Jane sniffed when Gabriel broke wind discreetly. 'We ought to build an orchid house. The smell is divine.'

'It must be tough being you, living in luxury with all these exotic bed-wenches and affected manners around you,' Gabriel hit back. 'Take that girl, Seraphima, a nice little buy for your wife, Foulkes. I don't know how you sleep at night with her around. There is a certain (how should I put it?) firmness of body and mind about her. I bet she's got a tongue on her. Janey, ring that bell and tell your girl to draw my bath. Perhaps we could pop over to Greenwood Plantation, owned by the Barretts, or Tharp House in Falmouth. It's built on the wharf.'

'Whatever for?' Christopher raised an eyebrow. 'Perhaps. Let's make your stay a good one. Choose a brown wench. Seraphima is off limits to guests. That is final.'

'Do stop meddling, Gabby.' Jane opened a fan. 'It's suddenly got hot in here, or is it me?'

'Well, who wouldn't?' Gabriel hit back in a cynical tone, turning over a series of prints which he possessed in his head. 'I think I'll have one of the brown girls tonight.' He had come to Jamaica with a copy of Lt Abraham James's prints, a caricature of *Johnny Newcome* (1800). In this print, the transient falls for a Black woman (*Mimbo Wampo*), declaring his love for her while she rids his toes of chigger. In the third sketch, he visits an *obeah-man*, a wizard, to secure her hand. Using his charm, he makes *Mimbo* queen of his harem of brown and black concubines. In the fifth sketch, he fathers nine mixed-race children and, then, leaves the Frying Pan Islands, having had nine children with names such as *Hannibal Pompey Wampo Newcome*. Gabriel winked. 'So, Seraphima is spoken for.'

'It's absolutely scandalous, the brown people are multiplying like salmon spawning across the island.' Jane had quickly become angry with her brother. 'I find it hard to believe that a white man would make love to…I daresay if they came up for auction, they'd fetch about two hundred pounds each.' She felt sick at the thought of racial intermixing and planned to sell Seraphima as soon as her father-in-law closed his eyes. 'This must feel rather stifling, Gabby, not being able to do the social rounds in the bush.' Three shadows stood outside the window, lingering for a split second. 'Well, my day has got better: Lady Jane Foulkes has a nice ring to it, don't you think? Oh cripes! It's almost time to dress for second breakfast. I also need to decide what I'm wearing tonight.'

'*The Female Art of Getting Rich in Jamaica,* according to Sir Nicholas Lawes, *is predicated on two short rules – marry and bury*!' Gabriel removed his feet from the table. 'From what I hear, life is brutal and short-lived out here: *marry and bury*! Janey, when old man Foulkes snuffs it, we ought to return home with the girls. We shall make fine gentlewomen of them. Think on! We shall go to the races, too: *Newmarket and Glorious Goodwood* – a bit of excitement.'

'My wife gets enough excitement from me,' Christopher snapped, directly facing down his cocky brother-in-law. 'She follows my advice.' He paused for a breath, then continued in a measured voice through his scowl, 'I am not the sort of man you can push around, Tremayne. I decide where my wife goes, whom she sees and how she spends my money.'

'*Balderdash*! Your father was an impoverished Highlander turned *Lord Paramount*.' Gabriel pictured the house with wood panelled walls, marble fireplace, antique vases, paintings, sofas with multi-coloured cushions, armchairs, nest of tables, cabinet of curiosities and over-sized Persian rug. 'No wonder Bryan Edwards said Jamaica's survival as a sugar colony depended on the successful defense of the slave trade.'

'The mother country (banks, insurers, stockbrokers and aristocrats) is drawing profits from her sugar gardens.' Losing his patience with Gabriel, Christopher returned the heirloom to Jane. 'What are you qualified to do, apart from pushing a pen at Lloyds of London? There's an advertisement in a back copy of The *Daily Courant* you brought over from London: *Fabric merchants in Quaker Street, Spitalfields, seeking two salesmen to sell English-made woollens across North America. No experience necessary.*'

'Oh Gabby.' Jane, watching the goldfish swim around in confusion, had no idea where her cat had gotten to. 'You know, if you are short of cash, you only have to ask Christopher nicely.' She observed her brother sizing up the room. 'Here, take it back.'

'It's my lucky mascot.' Gabriel accepted the ring. 'I have letters of introduction, Foulkes. I was actually hoping for a position as a private secretary at Government House.' A quick glance around the estate had told him that the Foulkeses were sitting on a fortune. 'If it's all right with your husband, Janey, I'd like to take a turn in the grounds with you. We need the exercise.' The day before, he had awoken stiff and had forced Amina to perform a sex act when she came in to give him a pitcher of warm water and a face basin. 'Where is your harp? We'll sit under a shady tree while you charm the nymphs.'

'No harp.' Christopher pulled a thinnish grin, imagining golden-haired nymphs and Pan stalking the woodlands. 'I am off to the slave village for a quick visit: Pimento Walk.'

* * *

'Where did you meet that blockhead, Janey?' At mid-morning, Gabriel rounded on his sister behind the stables, with his beak nose raised in a questioning manner. 'How much is the estate worth?' He was in his shirt sleeves and white breeches. He had tiny veins crisscrossing the whites of his eyes and his complexion was slowly succumbing to white rum and wine. *'A hot place belonging to us,'* he repeated the worn mantra. 'It's all right for those poxy Scots. Life has become worse, rather than better, for us English who left home to follow our dreams to the horizon and beyond. What! Are you accusing me of stealing my inheritance, Janey? After Father died, Mother said I could have it, she did so.'

'You've always been good at lying.' Stopping to rest on a chair in the fresh air, Jane feigned deaf, pretending not to hear the muffled sounds coming from the stables. 'I'll talk to Christopher – I promise. He is more amenable when I perform my wifely duties.'

'He's got shitloads of *filthy lucre*. He's got everything! I never get what I want, Janey.' Gabriel tore into his sister, half aggressively and half pleading, urging her to be more generous. 'I can't understand why you're not doing more to support the family.' He reminded her, once again, of her obligations. 'You promised Mother you'd take care of us. It's positively beastly living in poverty. You, meanwhile, are living the high life…' There was a younger sister, Leticia, who needed a dowry to enter society. The three younger siblings had been born to their father's second wife. An admiral's pension did not go far, especially when two expensive homes in London and Hertfordshire were factored in. 'Leticia begs you to write to her. She's literally destitute. Is that what you want, Janey? She'll soon be an old maid.'

'You and Leticia are an expensive encumbrance,' Jane said, feeling mean while thinking that her brother was being unreasonable. 'You have come here to cause trouble, to make a nuisance of yourself.' The row earlier had caused tension between her brother and her husband, which she resented having to cope with and resolve. 'I'll do my best.'

'Consider the interest of the children, Janey.' Gabriel pretended to be concerned about his nieces, inviting her to peep through a hole into the stables. 'It cannot be right to condemn them to live in this hell-hole, being looked after by that hideous girl or, let's face it, whore. They will spend their lives locked in a world where the only half-humans they see are brown nagas and have no morals at all. I won't have my father's grandchildren sleepwalking their way into brownness.' He cocked his ear, smiling because she had taken the bait. 'Shush.' He held up the palm of his right hand. 'Don't say a word.'

'What are they doing?' Until she saw them together, Jane did not dare to believe it, that her husband was intimate with a dark-skinned house girl whose job it was to look after their children. 'I ought to walk right in there and horsewhip her.' She understood that white women competed against each other to marry important men, such as wealthy West Indian planters and English aristocrats with vast estates in the shires, but this relationship made no sense to her because Seraphima had nothing of value to offer a man, let alone the heir to a vast estate. 'I ought to leave him and take the children back to England with me. There is nothing disgraceful in doing so. Yes, the safest thing is to go back home.'

'Don't look away.' Gabriel, hiding a secret smile, saw immediately that his sister's marriage was a sham and one that had come to an end, at least the love story, if there was such a thing as love. Her tears started to flow and he smiled secretly. 'You never think, Janey. What would you do without me? Honestly, you have no grey matter.'

'Don't patronize me.' Jane could not tear herself away. 'I am certain my eyes are deceiving me.' The mystery surrounding her husband's long-standing affair with an enslaved young woman was finally out in the open. Curious, yet furious with him for being unfaithful with an enslaved African whom he often referred to as 'illiterate and infantile,' she felt even more betrayed because there was no animal passion, which could at least explain the attraction between black and white. He was now seated on his horse; Seraphima was standing beside him, head leaning on his right thigh. 'I can't take it in, Gabby.' When her husband spoke, there was a tenderness in his voice that Jane had never heard addressed to her. 'But she is an insignificant looking naga.' Seen through the peephole, Christopher dismounted from the horse, walked away from Seraphima and expertly made a bed of straw. 'He came to her like a gentle, embracing lover,' Jane said, transfixed. She did not move from her spying position. 'I am in utter despair, Gabby. I am absolutely speechless.'

'That is perfectly understandable, Janey,' Gabriel put in, urging her to keep up the voyeurism. 'You have been in denial for too long.' He placed an encouraging hand on her shoulder. 'You ought to leave him. He wants you for possession; his sort always does.'

'Yuh cahn go in dere, mistress.' Trivia, snoozing under a tree, jumped to his feet and approached Jane. 'Dohn go in dere.' He lowered his eyes, speaking with alert caution, though not loud enough for Christopher to hear him. He wanted to 'shock up' the snooty Englishwoman. 'Massa wohn like it if yuh walk in on 'im an' Miss Sera.'

'What nonsense.' Fresh tears broke loose as Jane continued to watch her husband and Seraphima. 'You knew they were there, didn't you? You had this all planned. I will not leave Canongate for that thing in there.' The prospect of putting up with her husband's concubine for the foreseeable future filled her with dread. Only that morning, whilst completing her toilet, she had told Christopher that she hoped to get her figure back as quickly as possible after the birth by eating plenty of vegetables and fresh fruit, rising early, exercising and taking a little wine. 'You are trying to break up my marriage, Gabby.'

'I'm so sorry, Janey.' Gabriel kept his fingers crossed, musing, *The trap is sprung.* He sent Trivia into the house to fetch his pipe. 'You ought to demand a settlement and go.'

'Go where?' Jane heard a nightingale singing in the pimento tree nearby. 'It's her fault. She has bewitched him.' She gasped and, with a startled look, said, 'Mother!'

'Are you out of your mind?' Fiona said disapprovingly, creeping up on Jane. 'Here you are, the mistress of Canongate, behaving like a peeping tom.' Even though she instinctively felt that Seraphima was not entirely to blame for her son's infidelity, she took her daughter-in-law's hand and tried to lead her away, unsuccessfully, at first. 'Come away from here. Whatever is going on in there is none of your business, Jane.' She did not acknowledge Gabriel, standing behind his sister with his shoulders hunched. 'If you make a scene about this, the house girls will mock you mercilessly and see you as weak. Think on: Christopher will not thank you for interfering in his affairs. He has given you a family.'

'I am going to sell her!' Overcome with emotion, a teardrop trickled down Jane's face. 'I am surprised he hasn't made her pregnant.' She looked mortified, seeing the undignified spectacle of her husband and Seraphima. 'He was saying to her, *You've got to try the milk before you milk the cow.*' Bewildered, she calculated that they had had no intimacy for seven months. 'If she were white, I'd say theirs was a case of forbidden love, but she's a barefoot naga, a nobody.'

'When you have a son,' Fiona said unconvincingly, 'he will be faithful.' They walked away from the stables, stopping under the annatto tree. 'In the meantime, the way to punish that strumpet is to hold your nose whenever she comes near you. Naga wenches are always washing themselves, trying to wash away their blackness.'

Jane, who succumbed to blushing, resisted the urge to turn and look at Gabriel's face as they walked back to the house. Although she did not love her mother-in-law, Fiona had undoubtedly created a mood of calm and she respected he for that. Exchanging a fleeting smile with her, Jane allowed herself to be led up to the familiar oak front door where she was greeted by a purring Sukey. Though infrequent, there had been occasions when Christopher had gone missing before the second breakfast, which provided a talking point at the dining table.

'I know you'll do your best to fill my shoes when I'm gone,' said Fiona, presenting the same unshakeable exterior she always did. 'Lady Foulkes.' She had ordered Trivia to shadow Gabriel ever since his arrival. He reported overhearing the Englishman stirring up tension and creating division by repeating gossip, which had caused the overseer, Guthrie, to fall out with the bookkeeper, Dyer. She had, therefore, told Duncan that Johnny Newcome's constant trickery would be his undoing. 'Christopher is expecting you to play your harp later on, dear. You wouldn't want to disappoint him, would you?'

'He likes the intimate sensuality of the harp at bedtime.' Jane paused, then retched and spewed her rage all over the polished floor in the hallway. The fire glowed red in her eyes at the thought of her husband mounting Seraphima. She, Mrs Jane Tremayne-Foulkes, the object of admiring glances in English country homes, at social events in London and at Government House in Kingston, could not understand how a man of her husband's standing could behave like a lower-class white estate worker. 'Slaves, are they people?'

'When Christopher was a boy, I told him often enough that we whites are the only human beings.' Fiona watched Sukey sniffing the vomit. 'Slaves are non-persons.' She had been standing on the spot where she aborted Christopher and Seraphima's first child, which sent a chill through her body. 'They are subhuman, but I admire their resilience.'

* * *

'I am going to make use of you for what you're worth. Oh, don't give me that look, Sera. You're not a shrinking violet and neither are you a victim.' Seemingly oblivious to the drama going on in the great house, Christopher knelt naked on a bed of straw in the stables and tried to coax Seraphima into performing a lewd act. 'I am faced with *a Hamlet dilemma*: *To be or not to be*? Must I do the right thing and send you away, Sera, or continue to hold you prisoner?' He had been enjoying himself so much that he had not stopped for a moment to consider the impact of his actions. 'I know Pinky heard us. I can smell her perfume.'

'She tek me fi yer 'hore.' With one eye on the door (the lock was broken), Seraphima complained that he treated her like a woman in a brothel. In reality, as an enslaved woman, she had no control over what happened to her body. 'Me only doin' dis 'cause me 'ave nuh choice,' she added. 'Ocean pesterin' me again, Lachlan.'

'You may consider him dead.' Christopher scoffed at the thought that Ocean, an enslaved man, had his eye set on his posession. 'I want you to stay clear of Johnny Newcome. He has been warned that you are off limits to male visitors.' Three steeds and two knackered mares munched hay in the brick-built stables where bales of hay were stored in a loft space to deter Charles Price rats. 'This morning, when I gave him the grand tour, he looked at Canongate as if it already belonged to him.' In his mind, he pictured his wife's gown falling to the floor and her rounded pregnant stomach. 'I'll have to change Father's will if the expected child is a girl. That chancer is banking on me snuffing it. I have a feeling he encouraged Jane to spy on us. I know she'd sell Canongate and he'd squander the proceeds, living the high life in some gentleman's club in Mayfair.'

'Yuh 'ear di drums?' Seraphima asked. 'Scorpion sting ole Minah. Auntie Monifa use pindal nut an' 'erbs as poultice, but she on 'er deat'-bed, confessin' all 'er bad deeds. Wat di slave dem gwine do? Minah used to spin wicks fi lamps in crop time w'en dem haffe wuk late, an' she mek 'ammocks fi di white workers. I ask yuh to meet me 'cause di *peeple* wahn permission to praise Minah's life, even if she did liv' wid Maas Darnley an' neber object w'en 'im beat di oomen in di weedin' gang. Is all rite if som' of di slaves from Lafayette an' Ginger Hall com' to di nine-nite?' Minah was a *Myal* woman and she could already see a ring of people around a male and female dancer, singing and dancing to the drumbeats. 'Yes?' She knew that he grew sensitive to perceived slights and if he did not get what he wanted, she would return to the slave village without his blessing. 'We need bickle fi Minah funeral. Auntie Monifa bringin' food from Lafayette an' Comfort bringin' *bickle* from Ginger Hall.'

'We say victual.' Christopher, whose senses had been alerted to Jane's presence, could hear a pin drop a mile away. 'Slave funerals are riotous. Mother hates those grand Negro dances. Some of our slaves are only waiting for an excuse to rebel. No, Sera.'

'Kumasi and Auntie Monifa will be dere fi keep dem in line,' assured Seraphima. 'Eberyt'ing unda control.'

'If there's any trouble, Sera, I'll hold you responsible.' Christopher mounted her. 'Very well, but if there is any trouble...' One of the steeds neighed, causing him to crack a smile. 'Quiet, you.'

'Dere'll be no trouble.' Seraphima hated the system of slavery that had swallowed up so many lives and ripped apart so many dreams. 'I'm not a 'hore.' Meantime, a two-penny chick had got into the stables and was flying around noisily, trying to find the exit. 'Unlike yuh, I see miself in a way dat yuh dohn an' cahn see me. I 'ave big dreams, too.'

'Humour me.' Christopher acted surprised, telling her that he hated it when she made him feel guilty for her enslaved status. 'You know, Sera, you're as much woman as any other woman.'

'If dat's true, 'ow comes Jane call me monkey?' Naked, Seraphima lay on her back while he eased himself into her. 'In private, yuh admit me is 'uman but...' They had been attached for nearly two decades and she understood that their relationship was based on power and control over her body. 'Yuh mumma kill we first chile an' I kill two babies fi yuh; dat's tree *picknies*, an' yuh expect me fi accept mi situation 'cause dem seh me not 'uman. Well, I goin' frig Kumasi: big, tall; dark an' *yeye* pleasin'. I 'ave a choice.'

Christopher bent his head and bit her ear, picturing the insides of Jane's soft, white thighs and the pink guava surrounded by bush. 'If you mention Ocean or Kumasi again, I'll fuck your tripe out, do you hear?' In the enclosure, a brown steed with white markings on its face raised its ears. 'Down, Oban.' Gyrating, he removed her headtie and got hold of a handful of hair, then he pulled back her head. 'I could break you by letting Kumasi or Ocean fuck you senseless.' He knew that rape was a way of shaming enslaved women. 'Tonight is important.' The closer he got to her, the more he wondered if his desire for her was an obsession. 'Don't fool around with Gabriel, Sera, or I'll break your neck.'

'You white man all di same, always rapin' or t'reatenin' fi kill us.' Seraphima gazed at a steed, swishing its tail. 'Cho!' She was ready to explode, for he had threatened her with rape on numerous occasions. 'I gotto wash mi *pussy* again or yer mumma will 'old 'er nose an' say I smell fishy. I got to look after yer chilvren, Lachlan. I gotto tek care of miself. Everytime I go to Ginger Hall, poor Comfort smell fishy. Monsieur Dupont always rapin' 'er.' She wanted him to feel guilty for threatening to set two Black men (leading members of the strong gang) on her. Angry, she reached out and picked up his knife. 'I overhear yer daddy tellin' Miss Fiona yuh gotto tek yer pleasure w'en di need arises.' She sat up on the bed of straw and levelled her eyes to his hairy chest. 'All white man in Jamaica 'ave dem brown or black mistress. Me is jus' *pussy on legs.*'

'Give me that knife, Sera, and don't use that derogatory term again.' Christopher, placing her head on his bare chest, toyed with her uncombed hair while she refused to part with the glinting blade. 'I've got a nose full of you, *pussy on legs.*' He did not understand why he could not leave her and would not let any man near her. 'You know I care for you in my own way, but white men cannot love naga wenches. There's nothing I wouldn't do for you, Sera, but things have changed. I am a husband. Promise me you'll give Pinky no reason to get upset, not with a son on the way.'

'I gotto stand behind 'er chair tonite.' Seraphima put down the knife and handed him her bloomers, which he used to wipe his *man juice* off her back. 'She put 'er 'ands in 'er ears w'en I say I cahn wash 'er dutty draaz: *Lah, lah; lah, lah...*' Seraphima, expressing the person she most deeply was, said, 'Me lose t'ree babies an' yuh never ask 'ow me feel. No wonder dem seh slavery is livin' deat'.'

'Why must you make me feel so wretched and guilty?' Christopher cautioned her to remember to control her tongue indoors or she would anger Jane and his mother. 'I know it must be hell for you but, like it or loathe it, you women will have to get along. You know I feel bad for you, but I must have legitimate white children to carry on Father's legacy. I'm a son, father and a husband. For God's sake, accept your situation and stop complaining about Jane and my parents, too. You are more of a servant than a slave.'

'Servant is jus' anodda polite wud fi slave.' Seraphima accepted the bloomers and took a swipe at him. 'If yuh seh jump, Sera, I ask 'ow 'igh, Lachlan?' Then she took a second swipe at him. 'Me cahn leave yuh, for yuh'd 'unt me dung.' Her whole life was bound up with the domestic life at Canongate where visitors were often lecherous white men with violent tempers or sexual incontinence, some almost without exception. 'Johnny Newcome keep feelin' mi ches'. Wat 'appen if 'im rape me? Yer mumma an' Miss Jane would blame me. Cha! I gotto go an' clean up, Lachlan. I goin' to Ginger Hall to do Mistress Dupont 'air fi tonite.'

'Why lock the stable door when the horse has already bolted?' In came Duncan, walking slowly, without a shred of surprise on his face. 'Christopher, last night you left your wife to sob the night away and today, my birthday, you upset your mother by cavorting with that thing. I do not understand you. I have never understood you. What do you see in this promiscuous naga that you cannot see in your wife, a beautiful English Rose?' Pointing with his walking stick, he said, 'I don't like to shatter the peace, not today; however, it is second breakfast time and Jane and your mother are waiting for you. Please indulge me, Lachlan.'

'I am utterly selfish.' Christopher provoked Duncan, pretending to hold his knife to Seraphima's throat. 'I am the master of Canongate, yet

I am forced to take my pleasures in a stable.' The knife pressed against her flesh. 'If you want her dead, say the word: kill.'

'Oh, stop humouring me.' Squirming, Duncan felt that his son was being disrespectful whereas he was constantly policing himself against offending this self-indulgent man-child whom he had created and who was Canongate's future. 'You have a responsibility to your legal wife and children.' Although he did not have the ability to stand outside himself and to view life from a different perspective, he said with stoic resignation, 'I know she fulfils a carnal need, but you can't bed her in the stables. In doing so, you devalue your whiteness. For the sake of Canongate, you and your wife must maintain the appearance of respectability. You should be discreet.'

'Sera, it's time to squat and piss; I know you're bursting.' Christopher slapped her bottom with the knife, echoing a comment she had made about jumping. 'Father, I refuse to be the only white planter who hasn't got a brown or naga mistress. I'm a reprobate.'

'*We are what we repeatedly do.*' Duncan quoted Aristotle, turning away while Seraphima urinated. 'Och!' Observing his son's erect manhood, he lowered his eyes. 'Acht!' He blamed himself, for it was he who had shown Christopher a 1799 print which depicted a large fleshy woman spilling out of a green dress, exposing a nipple. She had hoisted the dress to show her soiled white knee-high socks whilst peeing on a London pavement in Broad St Giles with a cat looking on: "Indecency." That was the title. The caption read: *B – t you. What are you staring at?*

* * *

Sitting in a carver chair at the extended dining table, with Christopher at the opposite end, Duncan was momentarily lost in thought. Fiona had persuaded him to throw a lavish dinner party, even though he had not wanted a party for his birthday; he feared it would be a long and uncomfortable affair. Fiona had earlier fastened her freshwater pearls in the hallway and reminded him that they were living in an age when hospitality reigned in Jamaica, bringing the white community together in an important show of unity. They therefore had to show a confident face. While at the beginning of the century the worry had been about the abolition of the slave trade and the need to get slave labour via Cuba and Hispaniola, the talk now focused on the latest means of controlling slave behaviour.

Except for his second wedding in 1770, Duncan did not hold with the excessive consumption of food and had shuddered back in 1801 when the then Governor George Nugent and his American-born wife, Maria, had toured the island. They had stopped off in Clarendon to see the Vere militia and then went on to St Ann. Wherever Governor Nugent stayed, the table was loaded with food and drink. Needless to say, gossip naturally flittered across the land where the prosperous planters were notorious for hosting sumptuous banquets to mark any occasion: Victory Day, special birthdays; homecomings or the King's Birthday. Although the Crown's representative did not stop at Canongate, Duncan and Fiona had had the satisfaction of standing at the gate to see the carriage drive past with the governor and his dark-haired wife, Lady Maria Nugent, who waved at them in her white bonnet.

Gabriel Tremayne was *persona non grata* at Canongate, having lured his sister to the peephole at the back of the stables. After the defining incident, he found himself in a tangle at the dinner party, for he had failed to address Duncan in a respectful manner: either as Squire Foulkes or Laird Foulkes. Seething from the fall out with his sister, he had not wanted to attend the birthday dinner and had drunk a large amount of wine before he took his seat, deliberately defying Duncan by suggesting that the abolition of slavery was imminent.

'You forget yourself, young man.' At ninety, Duncan had the vitality of a man of seventy at most, though he had lost his hair and his teeth were yellow from years of drinking black coffee at 5am. Desperate for something to occupy his daughter-in-law's overwrought mind, he had kindly asked Jane to arrange the table. She had placed the men and women in alternate seats and the children were relegated to a small table nearby. 'I am not averse to criticism – constructive criticism.' Despite initial reservations about hosting the dinner, Duncan relished muscular conversations and Fiona had provided their guests with a family dinner fit for a Lord Mayor's banquet. 'Would you mind saying a few words over the table, Rev'd Ellis? It is good to see you again, *a pillar of rectitude*.'

'Bless this table, Lord.' The Rev'd Robson Ellis bowed his head. 'Providence has given you a bountiful harvest, Laird Foulkes.' He had arrived but an hour ago, riding atop a mule and wearing a dog-collar, setting the tone for the rest of the evening. 'Dig in, people. By the time you decide to make the most of what's on offer, most of it will be gone.' He had joined the American Black Baptist, George Leisle, back in 1783 and had since travelled across the island as instructed, baptising the Africans in holy water and offering them the hope of salvation. 'I picked the right day to call, Lady Foulkes. I go wherever the Lord leads me.'

'*Volte-face*,' René Dupont muttered beneath his white whiskers and full grey beard. 'You've done a U-turn. Rumour has it you've lost your faith and are no longer a Christian?' He picked up a turkey leg and proceeded to devour the flesh. 'You're not going to be a problem for us planters, are you?' He had forgotten to clean his dirty nails. 'Since the abolition of the slave trade, you missionaries are regarded as friends of the slaves and we planters are their enemies.' He was resistant to change. 'I for one don't want another John the Baptist in these hills. Remember what happened to him?'

'What are you implying?' Duncan spooned the bone broth with okras into his mouth and admired his latest acquisition on the wall opposite. 'We must welcome the harbingers of light.' A Caravaggio replica of *Salome with the Head of John the Baptist* had recently arrived via a dealer in London. 'I have come to the realisation that it is a good idea to Christianize our slaves. Doing so will drive the *Myal* cult underground. I have lost track of the amount of times Cassian used to report them: digging up buried *obi* and charms and catching shadows.' Chewing the slimy okra and listening to the drums in Pimento Walk, his eyes moved across the wall to a reproduction of Rubens's painting of *Daniel in the Lion's Den* in which a semi-nude Daniel posed in a prayerful scene, surrounded by lions. 'Acht! All this dancing, drumming and possession can't be good for them.'

'You've got the *Myal* lot to deal with and I've got the *Kumina* cult on Lafayette.' Pierre eyed up a leg of lamb while gorging on a slice of beef. 'I tell you, *Myalism* is a threat to authority – all that dancing until they fall into a trance.' He swallowed, looking down the table to where Edessa was seated next to Josiah Grandison, Sr. 'I have it on good authority that *Kumina* is all about healing, whereas *Myalism* is about working the spirit to harm your enemies. Who do they see as their enemies, I ask you? We white people, I hazard a guess.' His gaze fell on the Baptist minister, who was gnawing a leg of mutton with fat dribbling onto his dog collar. 'If we free the slaves, as you missionaries want, they'll run riot and it will all end in a bloodbath like we saw on St Domingue.'

'Righteous anger.' Rev'd Ellis put down the leg of mutton and sipped wine before responding, 'I have lived among the freed people and they've not gone on the rampage. I've been learning about their religions. Belief systems like *Myalism* and *Kumina* are intended to protect devotees. It seems there is no central biblical text behind the act of worship, but they do involve spirit possession, animal sacrifice and knowledge of bush medicine. Alas, we missionaries must rescue the perishing.'

'So, you are here to deliver them from evil?' Jane, drinking wine against Duncan's wishes, looked across to ensure that the children were not listening to the grown-ups' discussion. 'When I am mistress of Canongate, Lady Foulkes, I shall stamp out the dreaded *obi*, that I will.' She was pleased to see that ten-year-old Odette Fontane was supervising the children, cutting up their food and teaching them polite French words. 'I will not have our slaves imposing harm on one another, using their charms. I was warned about this before I got married – it is absolute poison. They are pagans, heathens.'

'The dark side of slavery.' René Dupont dipped his hands into the nearby mahogany hand-wash stand and dried them with his napkin before selecting a pink lobster. 'I've worked up an appetite today.' He continued, 'The *négres* are shadow chasers, as we used to say in St Domingue, always catching a man's shadow. Perhaps I was a bit too hasty, Rev'd Ellis. Come to Ginger Hall. I'd like my slaves baptised in Little River.'

'A great reformation is required.' Rev'd Ellis sprinkled salt over his food. 'The slaves have infused their creole religions (*Myalism, Kumina, Santeria and Vodun*) with Christianity. Consequently, the heathens will plead with you to baptize their children in the river; they believe it is the house of the dead.' Listening to a gabbling bird outside, he raised an eyebrow when the black bird flew onto the window-sill. 'Sadly, they don't like the Church of England – the white man's religion – but they embrace the Baptist faith. I daresay it is the idea of immersing in water that attracts them. They like the Methodist habit of falling into trances too. Take the Catholic saints, they are linked to a panoply of African gods in the Spanish islands, like Cuba. There are many rituals surrounding death, marking the deceased person's life and transition to the other place. Slaves are easy to control, if you know how: split them into mind and body…'

'And you want their tiny minds?' Jane focused on a reproduction of Gainsborough's landscape painting, *The Watering Place,* in which a group of goats and cattle drank from a pond, surrounded by green foliage. 'Do you flog yourself with a scurge, Reverend?' She glared at the serving Seraphima. 'I've heard it said that the way to control nagas is to strip them of their beliefs, language and culture.'

Gabriel put in, 'They say Dundas's 'gradual abolition' of the slave trade led to thousands of Africans being transported to Jamaica before the trade was abolished in '07. I gather this form of amelioration has stirred up hopes that the abolition of slavery is just around the corner.'

'This is quite a congregation, Laird Foulkes.' Raising his voice to silence Gabriel, Rev'd Ellis caused Duncan to lift a worn smile before adding, 'Slaves tend to be more docile, pliant, once they're baptised and brought into the brotherhood of man.' The minister was forward-looking, but he was not content with what he had achieved in the first decade of this new century. 'We are in an extraordinary situation, tasked with correcting past wrongs and bringing light to the Negroes.' He pictured a chained, cowering female being whipped by a sweaty overseer. 'We cannot legislate for human cruelty; it is within us.'

'*The elixir of youth* in a glass,' mocked Gabriel, looking into his wine goblet. 'Based on my travels, the Scots have scoffed the turkey and we plebs (impoverished whites) have to make do with the wish bone. I hear the Ewings of Glasgow are the richest sugar producers in Jamaica.' He admired a solid silver fork, referring to Canongate as a prosperous outpost of the British Empire. 'I daresay you'll be hosting a Burns Night Supper on 25 January: piping, haggis; singing *Auld Lang Syne.*'

'Don't forget the *neeps and tatties* and good Scotch whiskey to toast the haggis.' Duncan reflected that Robert Burns had not soiled his hands with the blood of Africa, for a publishing contract had saved the Scottish poet from sailing to Jamaica in search of a West India fortune. 'Gentlemen.' Raising his wine glass to be filled by Seraphima, Duncan watched Christopher carve a plump duck and momentarily felt like the carcass to be picked over by his guests. 'We must rescue our slaves from superstition and barbarism. I shall set an example by allowing Rev'd Ellis to baptise them in Little River.'

'Don't be so righteous.' Gabriel suggested that there was no heaven nor hell. 'You simply put the fear of God in them with the whip. Have you not read Edward Long's *History of Jamaica* (1774)? He stated that Negroes have the same bestial manners, stupidity and vices which debase their brethren in Africa.' Having downed four helpings of wine, he held up his goblet for a refill. 'Laird Foulkes, you ought to read Bryan Edwards's poem, "Voyage of the Sable Venus from Angola to the West Indies."' The penniless Englishman examined his goblet. 'This wine is definitely from the vines of Olympus.'

'Negroes have inherited the curse Noah put on Ham's son, Canaan.' Rev'd Ellis stuffed his mouth like a chipmunk cramming acorns into his cheeks and then held out his plate for more duck. 'The *Myal* men conduct their own law court in secret, you know.' Due to the generous food and wine, his fat neck chafed against his collar. 'They make decisions on disputes.' Fit to burst, he made a show of ripping off the dog-collar and added, 'I have always wanted to do this. I will not wear it again until the Emancipation Bill is passed.'

'Wilberforce is doing his damnedest to destroy us planters.' Réne struggled with his own plate of beef, pork and lamb, unable to imagine a world without cheap labour. 'Not to mention that we recently found a mass grave on Ginger Hall, crammed with baby skeletons – odd.' Flinching, he grimaced and said, 'How can mothers kill their babies?'

'We must tackle this appalling mortality,' remarked Duncan, side-eyeing Gabriel who grated on his nerves. 'And destroy *Myalism*.'

'I say, Rev'd Ellis, let's all ride over to Bryan Castle Great House in Trelawny tomorrow.' Gabriel, muttering about Edwards being a wealthy planter historian, began to play a childish game of I-spy: 'Shoulder of wild boar, beef; turkey, chicken; fish, barbecued hog; turtle, mutton; black crab pepperpot and whatnot.' Too drunk to care about his table manners, he refused to meet Jane's icy blue eyes across the table. 'I've come to Jamaica with my cap in hand.' He waved his fork in the air and, turning to the Senior Josiah Cameron's wife, Mirabelle, said rather crassly, 'I should have been born a woman. I could spend all my time on my back, produce a male heir and then wait for grandsons to come!'

'Well, this is a rare day.' All eyes turned to Rev'd Ellis, who was by now holding his chin in contemplation, admiring the paintings on the wall. 'If you don't mind me saying so, you slaveholders are conspicuous consumers: antiques, books; paintings, fine wine and the best silverware.' As part of his stipend, he lived in a sparsely furnished house, covering a circuit consisting of four districts. 'Oh, the Lord has yet to free me from envy.' Alluding to self-flagellation, he said swiftly, '*Thou shalt not covet*…Exodus 20 – 17.' With a fleeting smile, he requested a dash of rum in water. 'Shame on me, the devil's brew.'

'They say that the Maroons drank grave dirt and blood from each person to make them invincible.' Gabriel's fork fell at his feet and he looked at a serving Seraphima, who was within groping distance. 'You don't mind me sizing her up in company, do you, Brother?'

'*Ferme la bouche*.' Wrestling with an impulse to whip Gabriel, Pierre lapsed into French instantly, expelled a delicate fish bone, flicked it away and turned to eye Trivia, who stood behind Christopher's chair watching like *the Sphinx of Giza*. 'The good thing about having a eunuch around is that you don't have to lock up your daughters.'

'Ah, my little wife.' Christopher again overheard Odette teaching his girls French, raising her voice: *S'il vous plait*. The child's effortless charm endeared her to everyone. 'Encore, encore!' Perspiring openly, Christopher half-unbuttoned his white dress shirt. 'Encore!'

'You should mate her with an orangutan.' Gabriel's hand hovered over his goblet, eyeing Seraphima. 'So, this is your palate cleanser, Foulkes? Any red-blooded male would be tempted with her around, wild jungle cat. I bet you don't grind your teeth sleeping with her. I'd wager you are a cuckold. Have you seen the tongue on that eunuch?'

'I dislike the sound of that din outside.' Jane spooned okra soup into her mouth. 'Why do nagas play banjos?'

'I don't consider that worthy of an answer.' In the noisy atmosphere, Duncan found himself struggling to be heard. He set down his spoon and pushed his soup bowl aside. 'I am not going to let a boy make derogatory remarks about my son's private life. Stop poking your nose around here, boy. Have you considered the consequences of your sister having another girl-child, dunderhead? Has she the wherewithal to live in London, let alone according to the lifestyle to which she has become accustomed?'

'Your son married a lady of quality.' Gabriel's gaze travelled across the walls. 'Why all the counterfeit paintings, Foulkes?' He looked perturbed, thinking of the intimacy between Christopher and his black mistress. 'Titian's *Venus and Adonis* is missing.' He ogled Seraphima, who was pouring wine into Jane's glass. 'I say, Foulkes, she has a certain *je ne sais quoi*. And you are like a lost Scottish sheepdog who has to learn to adapt to life in a pack of black sheep. You there, wench, I feel as stiff as a board.'

'This is ungentlemanly.' Mumbling like a drunken monk in an alehouse, Rev'd Ellis pictured Titian's fleshy nudes and regretted having to leave his overstocked plate to do the walk of shame with Gabriel. 'I think you need some fresh air. Let us go outside. Come along.'

'I'll be damned if I apologise.' Gabriel left the table reluctantly. 'I am simply poking gentle fun at our sugar barons.' He had come to Jamaica with a collection of sketches ridiculing the plantocracy. He turned back to look at the men gathered at the table. 'Has anyone seen Abraham James's print of *Segar Smoking Society in Jamaica*?' While he was being led towards the front door, he thorough-coughed and vomited in the hallway. 'I've got a copy of Adam Smith's *The Wealth of Nations* for sale. Do I have a deal, parson?'

'Free labour!' The irony was not lost on René, who informed everyone that Gabriel had made attempts to sell him a pair of silver cufflinks and a copy of Maria Edgeworth's anti-slavery short stories, *Popular Tales*, urging him to read the story of "The Grateful Negro," which had been widely circulated. 'He pays lip service to misguided abolitionists, those virtuous white women writers who have never done a day's work. Indeed, he fancies himself another William Beckford: make a fortune in Jamaica, and become the Lord Mayor of London.'

'He is not anti-slavery.' Jane was numbed by the mental picture of her husband and his mistress in the stables. 'Seraphima, fetch my harp and tell Amina to clean up that vomit.' She wanted to clear her head of Christopher's infidelity by playing the harp – her comfort blanket. Tipsy and downing her fifth glass of wine, the thought of another daughter flashed across her mind. 'I am thinking of taking the girls back to London with Gabriel to see Leticia.'

'You'll do no such thing. I forbid it.' Not a flicker of emotion crossed Christopher's face. 'Empty threat.' In their own way, every planter sitting at the table would fight tooth and nail to preserve what they had worked for. 'What nonsense. Keep that Gabriel out of my way, Pinky, or I swear I'll shoot him.' He chewed beef. 'You can go, but the children are mine.'

'Let us leave the gentlemen to their cigars, dear,' Fiona chirped. It was not the first time that Jane had threatened to take the children away and return home. 'Seraphima, go and fetch Amina. I don't want the ladies' dresses trailing in that mess in the hallway. Don't just stand there!'

'It would be nice if you could take the ladies into the drawing room, Jane.' Patient and calculating, Duncan put down his cutlery on his plate. 'Go and play something lively on your harp. Gentlemen, my son will entertain you while I nip out. I'll see you all at second breakfast. Good night.' Pausing, he stood up and excused himself, saying, 'Seraphima, Fiona, follow me.' Hunched, he walked slowly across the dining room with the two women trailing behind him in complete silence. 'Come into the study, please.'

* * *

'Christopher is a fool.' Fiona, sauntered into the study, looking at Seraphima in her white headtie and blue dress, with its fitted bodice and white sleeves. 'I don't know what has come over that English boy, Gabriel. He'll have to go, Duncan.' She picked up a telescope off his desk while he put his signature to a piece of paper. 'What is that?'

'We cannot pretend nothing is going on, that she doesn't exist.' Duncan took matters into his own hands, for Gabriel had shone a spotlight on the darker side of the landscape. 'Put that down, wife.' Gazing at the telescope, back on his desk, he handed Seraphima a piece of paper. 'Take it and go. You've been babysitting Christopher since you were seven and he was four. You've filled his nostrils with your womanly scent. That will be all.'

'But, where would I go, massa?' Seraphima held the sheet of paper, turned it over in her hand and watched the ink drying. 'I born 'ere. Wat good is freedom to me if is me alone free and no family? Auntie Monifa is a slave. She cahn tek me in at Lafayette an' Madame Fontane 'ave Josette on 'er 'ands, massa. Where me gwine liv'? Wat good is freedom to me if I cahn feed miself, cahn own lan' an' buil' a likkle 'ouse o' mi own?'

'What nonsense! You, like all my nagas, are emotionally immature and ill-equipped for life outside Canongate.' Fiona, having policed the boundaries of whiteness thus far, turned tail and said over her shoulder, 'Pack your things and go, strumpet; you're getting above yourself.'

'Wat Lachlan gwine say w'en 'im find out yuh sen' me weh, massa?' Seraphima, watching her mistress leaving before studying the inky words on the paper, sniffed. 'Is t'ree babies me lose fi Lachlan. I neber wahn baby; 'im gimme dem. Is yuh giv' me to 'im w'en 'im was a likkle bwoy. Yuh see fi yerself in di stable. Yuh know Lachlan *lov' me gaan to bed*, massa.' She listened to the sound of the drumming outside, which was calling the *Myal* devotees to honour Minah, who would have nine nights of celebrations before the burial. 'I cahn tek dis paper, not until Lachlan see it. Di odder day Maas Guthrie tu'n out ole slave an' 'im sit at di gate eatin' one o' Mistress Jane black puss. Lachlan wohn let me go, massa.'

'Stop butchering the King's English.' Deflecting the blame away from Christopher, Duncan tore up the paper and chewed his gums. 'You think you know my son, don't you? You should be ashamed of your conduct in the stables. You know Christopher loves you and that gives you a certain amount of power. To me, you are an indulgent pet and an enchantress.'

'Me, massa?' Seraphima caught him looking at the sixth finger on her right hand. 'I once 'ad a dream dat I saw a t'ousand stars fallin' fram di sky. Yuh scatter dem, massa. Ocean wahn fi marry me, massa.'

'I will decide who you mate with. You'd better apologise to your mistress and my daughter-in-law for your lack of judgment today. Your adopted passivity does not match the image of the she-devil I saw in the stables.' Duncan, sitting back and gazing at the box of Cuban cigars lying on the desk, which belonged to his son, saw in his head a campfire blazing before a hut. 'What do you know about your past, about Africa?'

'Africa?' Furrowing, Seraphima admitted that beyond Jamaica lay a world about which she knew little. She remembered her aunt Monifa's shrewd warning not to sentimentalize Africa in company. She knew he made most of the enslaved women quake; that one word had been enough to end a life. 'Look, massa, a big black spider on di floor. Kill it nuh, massa!'

'Strip.' Spurred on by the scene in the stables, witnessed through the man-made peephole, Duncan gazed at her through the telescope; Thomas Thistlewood had planted an idea in his head in 1781. With his eye-brows tightly arched, he felt ashamed when she covered her bush with her left hand and pressed her right arm across her breasts, as if she were one of Rembrandt's female nudes. 'Spread your legs, bend over, cough and spread your buttocks...'

Seraphima turned her back. 'Yuh wahn touch me *pussy*, massa?' With her legs wide apart and her vagina resembling a fig's interior, she was naked, except for her white headwrap. 'Me nuh keep secret from Lachlan. Las' time Miss Jane tell me fi wash 'er dutty draaz, 'im box 'er. Amina wash dem. When Mistress Fiona mek Auntie Monifa kill di second baby fi Lachlan, 'im tell 'er she coulda mek a pet of it. Why yuh 'ate me, massa? Me is nutten but wat yuh see, wat white man call *pussy on legs*.'

'You've got a lot of lip.' Duncan, turning his back while she picked up her clothes, regretted that he had forced her into a sexual relationship with his adolescent son, which turned into an emotional bond. 'You have a sixth finger like your aunt. Captain Kalu had a sixth finger. He kidnapped one of my slaves – your mother – and impregnated her. You reek of patchouli. You are wearing it to ward off my male guests. Come in, son.'

'Lachlan!' Seraphima, tongue twisting like a river of many branches, dressed hurriedly. 'Yer daddy wahn to see wat yuh see w'en mi stark naked; di same way Maas Gabriel ask me fi undress an' size me up. Yuh know Ocean wahn me, but yuh wohn let 'im near me. Look, Lachlan, a big black spider crawlin' 'on di floor. Kill it nuh, kill it.'

'Leave us, Sera; your tongue is as sharp as a blade. Go!' After the long day, Christopher was more than happy to bring down a heavy foot on the spider. 'If you're planning to lecture me, Father, save it.' He had come to the study smoking a cigar and carrying two glasses. 'Please don't do that again, Father, ordering Sera to strip.' He pulled up a chair and made himself comfortable, placing his feet on the wall and turning his back to his father, imagining a room full of planters and their wives and a parson, all inebriated and sitting with their feet up against the wall. '*Segar Smoking Society in Jamaica*,' he scoffed out loud, pitying Gabriel Tremayne. 'I doubt we'll have a day like this again, Father.'

'I'll take a brandy.' Duncan smiled, turning his chair to face the wall and struggling to lift his skinny legs, for the muscles had shrunk with age. 'But no cigar, son.'

'When I was a boy, you built a ladder for me.' Christopher puffed on his cigar. 'You got one of the slaves to carve three wooden toys, shaped like boy-children.' Around him, even while facing the wall, he could see a library of old European books. 'There was an image of a white boy at the top of the ladder (me), a brown boy balanced on the middle rung (the Darnley boys) and a naga with one foot on the bottom rung.' Unlike his father, who grew up in Scotland during the age of enlightenment, he was not a David Hume devotee. If he were honest, his relationship with Seraphima had caused him to look at Africans as human beings. 'Father, don't ever ask Sera to strip naked again. Did you get a lift, lecher?'

'If I've said it once, I'll say it again: with power comes responsibility.' Duncan was resolved to keep the peace, but added cautiously, 'This house used to be a happy home, the girls laughing and Jane painting her face. Don't forget you're the master of Canongate. That wench has a disruptive effect on the household. How can one barefoot naga make fools of so many of us? She has put you under a spell, Christopher.'

'Going without her, Father, is like subjecting oneself to the merciless withdrawals of Lent.' Christopher crossed his legs and closed his eyes, picturing the over-sized glasses, bottles and decanters on a green tablecloth. 'Johnny Newcome has a book of sketches: *A West India Sportsman*. I'll get him to show it to you tomorrow.' In the foreground of one sketch, an old planter is seen sitting with his feet up on a stool. Sporting a blue jacket and white breeches, he is being served by a small child holding an oversized glass on a tray, while a slave in a blue jacket and loincloth stands behind him holding an umbrella. At the same time, a third slave stands beneath a coconut tree where there is a table laden with meat and fish. Christopher snorted. *'Make haste with the sangree, Quashie, and tell Quaco to drive the birds up to me – I'm ready...'* In the background, an obedient Quaco runs around with his arms wide open, driving the birds away, while a second planter languishes in bed with an enslaved woman holding a parasol to shade him from the sun. 'When you first came out, you saw what you wanted and you got it. I have caused you much grief...'

'Forgiven and forgotten.' Duncan inhaled his son's cigar. 'When you were fourteen, I ordered her to strip. The plan was for you to get an idea of how to examine the female slaves at the auction houses in Kingston.' He continued to inhale the scent of tobacco. 'You were supposed to examine her breasts, teeth and her *punt* to make sure she had no unhealthy discharge. I am a patient man, but my patience grows thin. You must put that girl aside for your wife's sake. I don't want Jane catching a disease. Is she clean?'

'Steady on! That's an unpleasant thing to say.' Christopher drew on his cigar with vague feelings of guilt and remorse threatening to puncture the truce as he sat with his father. 'Forget domestic woes. I came here for a serious discussion. Now that the slave trade has ended, the West India Lobby has lost most of its friends in Parliament. Why must our rules and regulations be dictated by Westminster?' He exhaled with an image of Jane, naked and pregnant, sitting on their bed surrounded by mosquito netting and an aroma of French perfume. 'Our friends in the House of Commons can no longer bend the ear of politicians and statesmen. We must now focus on the changing dynamics of slavery.' He flicked the ash onto the floor and downed more brandy with a heaviness on his chest, having overindulged in the black crab pepperpot soup. 'What we do affects people in a serious way, from our slaves to the hangers-on, relatives in Scotland and England, too.'

'Running a plantation and making a profit, while maintaining the extended family, is a very arduous road.' Duncan rose to sit over at his desk. 'That naga wench, would you be proud of walking into a room with her? I never expected you to make her your bedmate.'

'They say Thomas Jefferson had a fourteen-year-old concubine, Sally Hemings. Allegedly, she bore him six children and lived under his roof with his legitimate family.' Sucking on the cigar, Christopher held it between his fingers and exhaled. 'Well, I got it from an American chancer in Kingston, perhaps it's hearsay. I know I'm your Achilles heel. I realise that and I think you do too. Without me, your name will die; Canongate will fall. Not a day goes by without sloth and unrest in the fields. I am under pressure to recruit more white workers.'

'I'm no use to man or beast, an old and obsolete object, and you're like Narcissus looking at his reflection in the pond.' Haunted by the past, Duncan gazed out the window as darkness covered the land. 'When I first saw Jamaican blackberries, I was frightened that any flavour stronger than pickled onions would cause my taste buds to rupture. I grew tired of eating blackberries. What is wrong with eating English strawberries?'

'The land of lost content,' Christopher said reflectively. 'My wife has not given me a son to carry on your name. She is in this marriage for economic gain. It is always the same: *You reek of perspiration. You smell of cigars. You grind your teeth in your sleep. Leticia has to marry. She wants a house in Berkeley Square. Oh, the gardens at the centre.* Father, please will you be the one person who doesn't attempt to judge me.'

'That brother of hers is an adventurer.' Duncan opened the desk drawer and took out a pair of scissors. Annoyed by the recollection of the scene in the dining room, he sat at his desk trimming his beard. 'What does that she-devil do for you, apart from opening her legs?' There was a planters' Almanac on the desk. 'Still, she is pleasing to the eye.'

'You think that's what I want from her?' Untroubled by norms, Christopher halted when he heard the call of drums in the slave village and the sensual sound of Jane's harp coming from the drawing room. 'About Sera, why must she put up with those bloated old gropers? God knows, she's my eyes and ears on Canongate. We gel like glue.'

'*Inflagrante delicto.*' Duncan, with a feeling of destiny, gave up on trimming his beard. 'I want a grandson with old Scotch blood. We must put reason first or we run the risk of dismantling fences. The day the nagas begin to see themselves as humans, that is the day Canongate falls. I hope it never comes to that. Nagas feel powerless because of the badge of their shame: blackness.' He had been internalising his thoughts and, smiling at the memory of a naked Seraphima, tried to conjure an image of Rembrandt's dignified old man: *Aristotle with a Bust of Homer.* 'We must let them think they're inferior, put a bit and bridle in their mouths and lead them, or production will fall.' Looking at his son's open white dress shirt, he said, 'Don't let me keep you from getting your jollies.' He then picked up the Almanac. 'Lachlan, I will not have you contaminating my bloodline – put a glove on it.' The scene in the stables had left him feeling powerless.

'Oh, it's Lachlan now.' Outing the cigar, Christopher stood up and brought his foot down on a second black spider. 'Are you done with the sermonizing? Draw up fresh papers for Sera.' After a hiatus, he signed them. 'When we are dead and gone, and they've cut off the head of slavery, the world will undoubtedly wag a finger at us Scots.'

'Before I came out, I took a boat from Aberdeen to Lerwick and on to Unst.' Duncan picked up his walking stick. 'When I'm dead, please send my body home, Lachlan. I have given Rev'd Ellis instructions…'

* * *

Running his fingers through his wheat-coloured hair, a dishevelled Christopher sat on the edge of a single bed in the loft after midnight. Now in his thirties, he had grown to six foot two and kept in shape, eating well, riding out to the four fields daily and never touching a drop of raw white rum, unlike his white workers. A hot surge of air came into the loft through the open window, causing perspiration to trickle down his back, soaking his white cotton shirt. He was used to saying one thing in front of a crowd and another thing to Seraphima. The battle had been hard won and yet it seemed to him that the victory was hollow, for his wife would be alone in bed, possibly sobbing her heart out.

'Somehow, you've managed to raise the temperatures of a group of lecherous old goats, Sera.' Christopher felt jealous, even though she had been self-effacing and made no effort to attract any of the ageing white men who had visited Canongate since she came of age. 'I could have killed Dupont, rubbing himself up against you before supper. I don't know, you act as a sort of magnet for the elderly.'

'Me gwine sugar yer armpit.' Seraphima sniffed his perspiration, holding a bowl of paste made with sugar, lemon juice and water. 'Yuh look like yuh wanted to thump 'im.' She was satisfied with the way he had handled the situation in the dining room, which was something he should have done years ago, but she could not forget that she had been forced to abort two children; his mother had aborted the third. 'Tek off yer shirt.' Watching him undress, she stood by the side of the bed and proceeded to apply the paste to his armpits with a fish knife. 'W'en me finish dis, me gwine apply a nice smellin' ointment, a sort of sweat remedy.'

'Oh good, you've washed off the patchouli scent.' Christopher sniffed. 'That tickles.' He laughed with his arms held high, pretending not to notice that she was wearing a loose gown which Jane had given her. 'So, you threw the dogs off your scent.' He did not care to see her in his wife's cast-off either. 'You smell nice. What is it?'

'Jane seh yuh smell like onion.' Seraphima placed the bowl of paste on the floor and used a blade to shave his excess underarm hair. 'Auntie Monifa mek a phial of scent fi me: frankincense, jasmine; rosewater, vanilla an' myrrh. I wahn to smell nice fi yuh, too.'

'I can't always protect you from those leeches.' Christopher watched her gathering up the hair in a white handkerchief, noticing the way the gown fell open to reveal glances of her nakedness, a topography he often explored. 'Father offered to free you and you refused. I'll give you the papers tomorrow. What if something were to happen to me?'

'Where would I go to? Yuh wahn me fi becom' *walk-foot ooman*?' Gazing at her square-jawed lover, it was as if Seraphima had been waiting to exhale. 'We been togedda too long, Lachlan, too long to play dolly 'ouse inna di attic.' Thoughtful, she sniffed his armpits and when she was satisfied that the strong smell of perspiration had gone, she picked up the bowl and applied a thin paste of corn flour and herbs to them. 'W'en yuh seh jump, I ask 'ow 'igh?'

'I'm not letting you near my groin,' Christopher said with a wicked twinkle, taking the bowl and placing it on the floor. 'Oh hell.' He trapped her between his thighs. 'What's that infernal noise?' They both turned and looked towards the window, for loud drumbeats had interrupted their conversation. 'It doesn't seem right to be here with you, not with so many guests in the house. I hope Pinky manages to keep her temper at breakfast.'

'Why must I always see miself di way a bunch of ole white man see me, a 'hore?' At the word *whore*, Seraphima slapped his face before gathering up his hair off the floor, placing it in the oil lamp. Sniffing the burning hair and listening to the drums, she added with her back to him, 'If I was born in a white skin, yer daddy would never order me fi strip naked. Dat old goat shame me.' She slapped his face again. 'I kill two babies fi yuh an' yer mumma kill one an' all yuh talk 'bout is yer white chilvren. Yuh tek me fi butcher.'

'You forget yourself, Sera. If a wench had done what you did, I'd have had her broken on the rack.' Christopher blocked her hand, knowing that his father would have had an apoplectic fit had he witnessed the incident. 'Don't cry. It will be okay. I'm making you housekeeper.'

'Anodda bribe.' The gown fell off Seraphima's shoulders, but she did not feel any elation because she knew that he would never let her go, not in this life. 'Dohn touch me.'

'Oh, stop trifling with me. I've got to be up early to inspect the fields and the mill.' Christopher, looking down at his horn, said with a sigh, 'You ought to be more submissive, Sera.'

'We gotto talk.' Seraphima called to mind Ekuwa, a sneaky girl with hooded eyes, who came to Canongate after her master had gone bankrupt upon the abolition of the slave trade back in 1807. A devotee of *Myalism*, she was initiating the other female labourers. 'Ekuwa seh di Darnley bwoys been skulkin' around on Lafayette. Now Minah on 'er deat' bed, dem in di slave quarters.' Their presence was an affront to the field workers whom they had whipped and disparaged. 'Dose drum not talkin' 'bout Minah. Storm cloud gatherin' ober Pimento Walk rite now.'

'What are you trying to say?' Christopher asked, taking the piece of brown paper from her and holding it close to the lamplight. 'It doesn't tell me much. It says, *Blood fi blood.*' They were only a couple of feet away from the storage room next door and René Dupont could be heard entering it with a new house girl, Lupin. She had been helping

Miss Simple in the kitchen and had gone straight to his room after he sent for her the moment his wife, Giselle, fell asleep. The iron bed began to squeak. Christopher pretended not to notice, even though he had vowed to stamp out the practice. 'Are you trying to tell me those Darnleys are dangerous, Sera, that they're plotting a rebellion on Canongate?'

'Di Darnleys 'ell-bent on revenge.' Occasionally, Seraphima shared intelligence with him on a need-to-know basis. She had witnessed the punishment of many rebels and did her best to ensure there were no unnecessary outbursts that would lead to the fatal demise of dissenters: lynching. 'I wouldn't normally tell yuh, but dose bwoys use naga ooman an' wipe dem foot on dem.' Often, as he slumbered, she would lay awake thinking of Kumasi and Ocean. They fought over her whenever the opportunity arose but, by ignoring their advances, she was actually saving their lives. 'Dohn seh me didn't warn yuh: forewarn is forearm'd. Ekuwa is a gossip, so it mite jus' be a puff o' wind.'

'I'll string those bastards up.' Catching a whiff of her perfume, a concoction made up by Monifa, Christopher banished the thought of a rampaging mob of blacks brandishing billing blades. 'This is a matter of urgency. I have to send a clear signal to anyone thinking of joining those rebels that I am not a pushover.' After some consideration, he gave her a wondering glance and adopted the missionary position, blotting out the squeaking bed in the storeroom. 'We belong together.' The talking drums had been beating in the slave village since dusk: *Chick-a-bow, chick-a-bow, chick-a-bow, wow-wow.* Catching the rhythm, he moved with the drums. 'I know you want Kumasi; he has a woman and children.'

'Kumasi is di only man I'd stray wid. If yuh kill 'im, yuh mite as well kill me.' Wriggling out from beneath him, she sat up and, burnt too often, felt frustrated and fearful for the future. 'Wat if I fall?' How many days had she spent fretting, waiting to see her monthly blood? Looking around the sparsely furnished loft with the small window, an old trunk and a clothesline hanging across the iron bed with its lumpy coir mattress, she lay back and stared into the ceiling where cobwebs were visible during the daytime. 'Yuh should go frig yer white wife.'

* * *

'Out of sight, out of mind.' The slave village of Pimento Walk was constructed on the fringes of Canongate, with its leaf-roofed huts, far removed from the plantation house and the fields, with the suggestion given that sugarcane was planted and harvested by nature's own hands. 'Once you see inside one hut, you've seen them all.' Old Minah was the last survivor of the bankrupt plantation known as Riverhead, which Duncan had bought a year after his arrival and changed the name on the deeds to Canongate. Slavery had dominated Minah's life and now, on her deathbed, she raved in her delirium, quoting her original owner, Nathan Taylor, a grouchy Englishman whose Riverhead estate had been mismanaged by two greedy attorneys in his absence, living the high life with his wife and children in the English shires. *'Jamaica is the most deadly place on earth.'* She had been stung by a scorpion and there was no hope of a recovery. *'Oh, for a glass of raspberry ice! – I am melting away,'* she parroted Robert Charles Dallas, who wrote *The History of the Maroons.* Born on the island, Dallas had been sent away to school and later returned as an adult. This quotation was repeated often by Darnley, who had made fun of the white elite in their private conversations. *'The sun is exhaling all my juices.'* She laughed until she cried, raising a trembling hand to point at a passing spirit. *'Crakka Juba – crazy somebody.'*

'It soon ober.' Monifa had bled the swollen area where the poison had entered Minah's foot and bandaged it with a poultice made with *pindal* nuts and herbs. She had, over the years, urged Minah on several occasions to teach the younger women how to make wicks for the lamps that were used in the dark huts in Pimento Walk. She had also begged her to share her hammock-making skills with the girl-children, but to no avail. Nevertheless, Minah was a *Myal* woman and a crowd had gathered outside her hut, which was furnished with Darnley's mahogany bed, a washstand and a small wooden bench.

'Poor girl, she is *In Miserable Slavery.*' Minah remembered Thomas Thistlewood, who had come down to Darnley's hut to smoke a cigar, in 1781, after the dinner party celebrating Christopher's christening. Minah and Darnley had a mutual relationship, which the white elite privately accepted, but she was not entertained at Canongate. It was her job to prepare the young full-breasted women for Duncan's male visitors, ensuring that they bathed after returning from a hard day's work in the fields and oiled their black bodies, even innocent girls as young as ten years old. After Thistlewood had left the white men's quarters, Minah had quarrelled with Darnley, who punched her in the face, for he had forced two girl-children (Ithaca and Molinera) to sleep with the male guests, a practice that Fiona either knew nothing about or chose not to know. '*William Dorril, of Westmorland, lives openly with his wife and coloured mistress.* Dat's wat Thistlewood tell Zeke.'

'Long-memory *Myal* ooman.' Monifa, a *Kumina* priestess, regarded *Myalism* as bad *obeah*. 'Dem seh yuh punish a slave 'cause she com' back 'ome two 'ours late. Imagine, yuh strip 'er, beat 'er an' put 'er 'ead in a yoke an' den rub molasses all ober 'er body. Mosquitoes an' stingin' insects feast on 'er all nite long. Dem seh Darnley burn a runaway alive, fram di foot up, afta puttin' 'im in di stocks.' As the common-law-wife of a white man, Minah had been given shoes, clothes, soap, sugar and a small provision ground. 'Dem seh Darnley mek Argos piss inna 'im ooman, Cubbah, mout'. White devil.'

'Sen' fi Pollux.' Old Minah was distraught and begged forgiveness as she lay back, looking at a black beetle crawling up the wall in the daub and wattle hut. She remembered the time when half a dozen young women had been called from their cooking pots, ordered to wash, change their clothes and make their way to the white workers' quarters where they were required to dance for Duncan's male guests and accommodate their sexual advances. While this was going on, their men had been left in charge of the cooking pots, rage building up in their huts, stoked by jealousy and the desire for revenge. 'Call Pollux.'

'Poh!' Monifa climbed into the soft bed, with Darnley's old horse-hair mattress sagging. As she held Minah and listened to the *Myal* drums beating, it occurred to her that Minah had gained notoriety. 'Go.' Once, when she was ill, she received two handkerchiefs, nutmegs, Scottish herrings and a plant from several plantation women. 'Gwane.'

* * *

The night had started with a dark moon and now Seraphima lay asleep in Christopher's arms. Jane, meantime, lay in an uncomfortable poster bed reading Oliver Goldsmith's novel, *She Stoops to Conquer,* which Gabriel had gifted her with a copy of Aphra Behn's book, *Oronooko.* An expatriate white woman, Jane did not understand the family that she had married into: the affair between her husband and an African woman, dark secrets, and the stalking around after hours. She had left England thinking that Christopher was not good enough for her, being the son of a Scotsman who had made his fortune from slavery. When he proposed, her family had made enquiries about his background; no record could be found of the Foulkeses of Jamaica. The theory was, therefore, that they had risen from nothing. That was held to be the truth until her brother, Gabriel, had discovered that Duncan had changed his surname from Hutchinson and was also entitled to style himself 'Laird,' which meant that he was a part of the landed gentry in the Highlands of Scotland.

In time, I shall be mistress of Canongate, thought Jane, looking down and smiling at Marian's innocent face as she slept. She inclined her ear towards the bedside lamp, reaching over to turn up the wick. 'Oh, it is the second *conch*: 6am already.' Abandoning her book to the side-table, she arose, pulled on her dressing gown and watched the sun come through the window and fall onto a chair like a huge pearl drop. 'I shall go down to the kitchen and order breakfast: liver, spinach and milky sweet coffee.'

'Marnin', ma'am.' On the landing, Trivia had slept on a mattress outside his master's bedroom. 'Marnin', mistress.' The big Black eunuch had tribal scarification on his face but, despite this, he was regarded as a safe pair of hands. There was a stiffness in his muscles and his joints ached. Wide-eyed, he watched Jane walking past and down the stairs. His master's safety was his main concern, but he knew Christopher was with Seraphima and had simply overslept. His features burst out into a wry smile, for he enjoyed unswerving trust and Christopher demanded absolute loyalty from him. At dinner, last night, his master had been bad-tempered and curt with him, for he had failed to warn him that Gabriel and Jane were approaching the stables. He stood up, sounding slightly smug, 'I better wake Massa Christopher and Miss Seraphima.'

He looked over the banister as she walked down the stairs. 'Watch yer step, mistress.'

'Why don't you bugger orf back up your tree?' Jane, jittery and sleep-thirsty, crossed the hallway and approached the study. There was a light under the door. Duncan, indomitable as ever, was sleeping soundly at his desk. She found him slumped over, but there was no movement and his face was sallow. She had taken her marriage for granted; that as expectations changed, she would become the matriarch of the family and be respected like her mother-in-law, Fiona. 'Good morning, Father,' she said brightly. 'Are you awake, Father?' His chin rested on his desk. 'Wake up, Father.'

'How is my grandson this morning?' Duncan stirred and sat up, ramrod straight in his chair, all earnest and happy to acknowledge his legitimate daughter-in-law. 'What are you doing up at this ungodly hour?' He and Christopher had had an extensive discussion about the future of Canongate. Seraphima's new status had prompted him to write a codicil and her 'free papers.' He had written to his lawyers, naming Dougal's son, Fergal, as the heir to Canongate if Christopher died without fathering a legitimate male heir. Inverkin House was to be gifted to the Scottish nation. 'Let me get to the point, Jane. Plantation wives are expected to keep everything hidden behind closed doors. You must learn to adapt or, mark my words, you'll be consumed by jealousy and destroy yourself.'

'I've not come here to get an earful of self-righteous lecturing from you,' Jane said, through choking sobs. 'Something ought to be done about that strumpet. Last night was the most hypocritical moment of my life.' She noticed an empty glass on the floor and a cigar butt. 'One question, if I may. How on earth did a naga whore manage to get a handsome man like my husband in her clutches? She is a worthless piece of trash.'

'Don't interfere in my son's business again, Jane,' answered Duncan, rising to the indelicate question. 'In the West Indies, a white man of means is master of all he surveys. Sometimes the line between master and slave blurs and this often leads to them forming an emotional bond. In Christopher's case, Seraphima is a childhood attachment, rather like an old rag he can't part with. It's perfectly understandable and, I am afraid, predictable. Christopher was a wilful child. His mother gave in to him and the more we objected to his attachment to that naga, the more we unwittingly pushed them together. He is my son and I know his faults and his personality better than anyone. Like it or not, he will not let her go. You should try to get on with her, in the meantime.'

'She put a spell on Christopher.' Jane, feeling sleep-deprived, stared at the wine glass on the floor. 'This marriage has turned me into a prisoner. If Christopher prefers to sleep with his naga whore under your roof, I must assume you've accepted her. Is this not a justification for saying she's human?' There was a look of mild panic on her face and she knew that she had overstepped the mark. 'Christopher spent the night with that filthy slut. I daresay she prepared the first supper of liberty. Is there nothing you can do, Father? Why not sell her!'

'She's a free woman, Jane.' If Duncan had expected her to play the compliant wife, he was mistaken. 'Life consists primarily of give-and-take situations. If you are not giving by providing Canongate with a male heir, you are taking.' Spurred on by her outburst, he felt that he was coaxing a reluctant animal into a pen. 'When you accepted my son's proposal of marriage, you did so with the knowledge that your acceptance would mark your entry into this family as the mother of a stable of boys. Frankly, the future of Canongate is more important than my son's sexual probity. I hope this conversation has helped you to gain clarity about your role as the wife of a sugar planter. Och! By my calculation, you have brought nothing to this marriage. What use are girl-children to Canongate?'

'But you dote on the girls.' Jane stared at him in astonishment, feeling that she and her girl-children were becoming a liability. 'This is not what I want.' She glanced at the chessboard on his desk and said resentfully, 'I don't choose to share my husband with a naga.' Musing, she prowled the room with leaden feet. 'If this child is a girl, I shan't try again. I am not sleeping with Christopher any longer. He has gone native.' She looked towards the door with a defiant stare. 'Why can't he get that whore off his mind and out of his head?' Her eyes watered when Fiona walked in. 'I cannot bear to think of him sleeping with that *nigger*.'

'Fine talk for the next mistress of Canongate.' Granny Fiona held Virginia. She stood at the door, eavesdropping. 'Ginny needs you.'

Time had sucked the flesh from her cheekbones. She added in a calm tone, 'Your brother tried to sell our bookkeeper the *Narrative of the Enslavement of Ottobah Cugoano...*' Her rope-veined, mottled hands were visible as she held out her second granddaughter to Jane. 'Why would anyone bring an anti-slavery book into a plantation house of all places, Jane?'

'There are three of us in this marriage and you are using Gabriel to deflect attention away from Christopher's appalling behaviour.' Jane ignored the child in Fiona's arms. 'For the love of God, please sell that whore, Father,' she implored. With an unfading frown on her brow, she accused Christopher of humiliating her by installing his concubine under the same roof as her and his legitimate white children. Everyone knew that Seraphima occupied a special position in the great house and across Canongate. Jane accepted that Duncan and Fiona wanted a dutiful daughter-in-law, but she could not make them understand that she felt tainted by association in this *ménage à trois*. Her admiration for her in-laws had sowered. She and Christopher now slept in the same bed without touching. 'Send her away, Father. Slut!'

'Hold your tongue,' Duncan said wearily when Amina arrived with a tray containing steaming hot coffee and a chunk of bread. 'Your brother has come here to stir up trouble.' He noticed that his daughter-in-law's cheeks had flushed and that her face was already tear-stained. She took Virginia from Fiona and practically seated the child on her high stomach. 'Jane, why don't you take Ginny into the nursery and get Lupin to look after her and Marian. Go and put your head down for an hour. Go with your mistress, Amina.' He dipped a small piece of bread into the hot liquid and waited for Jane and the child to leave with Amina, trying to achieve a delicate balance. 'Fiona, Christopher is more concerned about the future of Canongate than you think. I have given Seraphima her own room so she and my son may have some privacy. Apparently, most slaves tend to trust a master who has a constant companion of their own race. A good example was the late Thomas Thistlewood and his naga, Phibbah.'

'Och!' smirked Fiona, wearing a white linen dressing gown over a cotton nightdress. 'Thanks to your burst of generosity, she is a free person with all the rights of a human being.' Gazing at her husband with a blank expression, she turned when Christopher entered the study, looking decidedly hungover. 'Don't mind me.' It seemed to her that elite white men in plantation society were driven by ambition, lust and envy of the more successful planters. 'I am off to supervise breakfast for our guests.'

'I have invited Jane to join me for a walk after second breakfast.' Christopher gave his mother a fleeting nod. 'This attitude of yours does nothing to endear you to me, not when I was an adolescent and certainly not now. Despite what you think, Mother, I am not evading my responsibilities. You knew before I got married that Sera came with the marriage. This decision has not come out of the blue. You consented to it, otherwise I would not have married. I think it is worth reminding you of this. I know it is a hammer blow to Pinky, but she has to adjust to my domestic choices.'

'You cannot expect your wife to befriend your concubine,' Fiona replied, refusing to think about how to make the situation bearable. 'What will you tell your children when they ask why you are sleeping with a naga wench in the loft instead of sleeping in your marital bed? That is the concern I have, son. You are self-indulgent.'

'Mother, do something useful and help us to make life easier for everyone. If you can't manage that, then for goodness' sake please stay out of my way.' An average day in his life usually began at 5.30am and now he was late for work. 'Father, go to bed. You look like death warmed up. Please tell Gabriel not to put his feet on the table in the drawing room.' He then called out, 'Trivia, saddle my horse. I am running late!'

'Not so fast.' Fiona, shutting the door behind her, looked at her son and lowered her voice, 'You are telling us that you're living in a polygamous marriage under our roof? I remember when Thomas Thistlewood attended your christening in 1781; he spoke unashamedly of living openly with his naga companion, Phibbah. You are asking too much of your father, an old man. I told you long ago: *Nagas are brainless, even if some are more like us than we'd like to admit.* You cannot live with her under my roof.'

'I think you'll find this is my house.' Christopher prided himself on being a hands-on planter. 'Enough said! I have four fields to inspect.'

* * *

The new arrangements infuriated Fiona. Her eyes followed Seraphima who walked up the stairs. 'Oh, it's you. Don't think I don't know what you're up to.' Christopher had given her the morning off to clear Amina's belongings and place them in the storeroom, for the house girl was helping Miss Simple to prepare breakfast. 'I see your game, you little slut.' Despite father and son having freed Seraphima, Fiona questioned their motivations and did not agree with them. 'It's a new experience for you, isn't it? No more, *Yes, ma'am; no, ma'am.* I expect it will take a few days for it all to sink in.' The delicate balancing act that Duncan was attempting wasn't for her. He wanted to take his son's private life and feelings into consideration, while also protecting Canongate's future. 'If you answer back, I'll beat you to within an inch of your miserable life. I can easily revoke your freedom. Watch me.'

'Tek it up wid Lachlan.' Seraphima continued walking up the stairs, carrying a tray with a mug of hot chocolate and a plate of callaloo and boiled green bananas. She had promised Christopher she would keep out of his mother's way and resist the urge to talk back. 'Lachlan tell me to tek di marnin' off an' clean mi room. Lupin is lookin' afta di *chilvren* dem an' Cousin Josette com' las' nite. She 'elpin' Madame Fontane an' di ladies, ma'am. Ekuwa is 'ere, too. Madame Dupont bring 'er yessiday. She is 'er new personal maid an' she also 'elpin' di ladies. Me is di new 'ousekeeper. I'll be dung at second breakfus.'

'You're a shameless hussy, that's what you are,' Fiona said harshly, stomping up the stairs all the way to the loft, behind her. 'You may be able to fool men like that bloated René Dupont and my son, but you don't fool me. I'm disgusted with Christopher for setting you up under my roof, in my home. So, you're not saying anything, trying to hide behind that cynical smile of yours. I told you years ago that I would not have a brown grandchild. I'll never acknowledge you. Mind you,' she stopped, not wanting to go too far, 'my son keeps you for the exercise.' Unbending, she looked out the window towards the canefields where Christopher was already riding around his daily inspection course in the morning sun. 'You're an informer. You tell Christopher everything and he pays you for services rendered. Don't expect me to welcome his *niglets* by you, not over my dead body. If I were you, I'd be ashamed of myself, sleeping with a married man, and a white man, too. Have you no shame?'

'Lachlan is a white naga,' Seraphima tished. 'Marnin', Miss Jane.' She and her rival stared at each other. 'Marnin'.' The most disturbing thing about her promotion was that she walked with a new-found air of authority, emboldened by the fact that they all knew she had Duncan's blessing. 'Yuh nuh know seh *peeple* call 'im white naga?'

'Let's not be naive,' Jane pouted from the doorway, looking on. 'Apparently, this girl is the glue holding Canongate together.' While Seraphima was down in the kitchen making her breakfast, Jane had crept up to the loft and was astonished to find a plain but serviceable room with a single bed, a clothesline and some of Christopher's clothes strewn over a chair. She had never climbed the stairs to the loft before and it was nothing like the gloomy space that she had imagined, which led her to believe once again that she was not woman enough for her husband.

'I am absolutely shattered. Last night I had to sit and listen to a bunch of drunken ruffians, gorging themselves around the dining table.' Jane crossed the floor and stood shoulder-to-shoulder with Fiona, looking down at the flourishing sugarcane plants and the Africans toiling far in the distance. 'This is not your fight, Mother. I owe it to Father to be civil to that wretch, if only for Canongate's sake. And I'm sure everyone downstairs is listening, waiting for snippets of gossip. They'll be pleased with your conduct.'

'As yuh can see, I 'ave a room of mi own, t'anks to Massa Foulkes.' Grim-faced and ready for confrontation, Seraphima had expected a reaction from Fiona, but she had not counted on Jane showing up. 'Why dohn yuh com' back w'en Lachlan is 'ere? Massa Duncan giv' me 'is blessin', too. Why yuh nuh ask 'im yerself? Me is a free ooman. I dohn haffe say mistress, 'cause I free, but I'll say ma'am to please Lachlan. I couldn't get rid of 'im w'en 'e was a bwoy, wantin' me to frig 'im. I used to carry 'im on mi back w'en I was a girl.' It would take a while to sink in that she was free and could, at least theoretically, go anywhere in the world. Averting her eyes from Jane's stomach, she felt a hollow pang, thinking of her three aborted children. 'I'll tek dat to mean yuh not sure whether to see Massa Foulkes, ma'am. Wat's di worse yuh can do, kill me?' She brushed a speck of dust off her right shoulder, as if brushing off her rival. 'Me born dead. Slavery is livin' deat' an' me is just a ghost.'

'When I got married, your Maroon father, Captain Kalu, arrived like the proverbial uninvited guest,' said Fiona, whose dry body skin was crying out to be oiled. 'Under the Barbados Slave Code of 1661, I could have you killed for hitting a white lady. There's an idea.'

'And what would Christopher say?' Jane said warily, leaving Fiona's side and picking up the mug of hot chocolate. 'I don't suppose you ate anything. May I call you Sera? What a beautiful name. It is a derivative of seraphim, you know, meaning powerful angels.' She felt it wise to at least try to be civil, for appearances' sake. 'Oh please, eat your breakfast, Sera; it's getting cold.' She proffered the mug of chocolate. 'Do take.'

'Me not 'ungry,' Seraphima said quietly, taking her bloomers off the clothesline and folding them up into a neat pile before placing them under her pillow. 'Yuh got a really pretty face an' di bluest *yeyes* I ever see. Why dem call yuh Jane? I know Lachlan call yuh Pinky sometimes, but Jane nuh suit yuh. It mek yuh seem too plain.'

'I have no idea, but my second name is Diana – the huntress.' Jane's eyes flashed into Seraphima's gaze. She surveyed her rival close-up, looking at her for inspiration, calculating how best to break her down with kindness. 'Christopher is having second breakfast with the family and our guests. Will you be serving us? You don't have to stand behind my chair. You are the housekeeper. Your job is to delegate. Oh, there is a bottle of my scent missing. You stole it. My husband will soon tire of you, missy.'

'So why 'im an' so many ole white men always unda brown an' black ooman skirt?' Seraphima, seating the enamel plate on her lap, looked into Jane's blue eyes as they sat side-by-side, as if they were exchanging pleasantries. 'Lachlan like 'im food on di plate in a certain way. I gotto mek 'im coffee wid scald milk jus' right.' She paused and raised her eyes to see Fiona quietly leaving the room. 'Massa Foulkes like 'im egg boil soft, not runny, jus' so. If yuh like, I can teach yuh to satisfy Lachlan in bed. Me seh too much?'

'Clever monkey, hardly a picture of dignity in the stables.' Jane, still searching Seraphima's brown eyes, brought her gaze down to the sixth finger, noting her clipped fingernails. 'Given that white men in the West Indies have their brown and black whores, neither one of us has a choice in this *ménage à trois*. Put simply, what Christopher wants, Christopher gets, isn't it? I am surprised you have no children.' She spoke with an air of condescension, 'What I find so amusing about nagas like you is that you haven't even got the sense to lie when you are caught in the act of thieving. Stupid. You are welcome to Christopher. He reeks of raw onions.'

'Not anymore.' Seraphima placed the breakfast tray on the floor. 'I shave 'im armpit an' mek up an anti-sweat potion fi 'im to use.' She was stony-faced. 'Next time 'im frig yuh, 'im gwine smell nice but yuh haffe wash yer fishy first. Yuh smell like a fish on di turn.'

'Praying mantis.' Frustration boiled over and Jane got up heavily. 'It does make one wonder what he sees in you, witch. Why else would he want to sleep in a hovel with underwear hanging above his head?' She lifted her eyes to the line strung across the bed and then lowered them. 'After all those intellectual types at Government House who show up his scant knowledge of philosophy, Latin and Greek myths, you must make him feel superior with your broken English and your woolly hair. Is it difficult to brush? Oh, there are too many *tittles* in his letters, dotting his *i's*. I don't suppose you know what that is?' Changing her tone, she now stood by the door. 'Marian sat on a wasp earlier on and Virginia has the runs. You are their bottom-wiper. Nay, you are their black arse-licker.'

'*Kaka!*' With anger churning in her stomach, Seraphima swallowed a mouthful of cocoa-tea. 'Go ask Mistress Fiona wat 'appen to mi t'ree aborted babies fi Lachan. She should know. She kill di fus one. Gweh!'

'And there I was thinking your body was defective.' Jane stood with the door ajar. 'I am sorry if I've made you feel less of a person,' she made a mocking apology. 'It is in our interest to get along; you're the children's nursemaid and my husband's erotic fantasy.' She refused to acknowledge that enslaved women had no choice about what they did with their bodies. 'We are crammed cheek by jowl in this old house, rather like the slaves at Pimento Walk. Christopher and I once toured the village at twilight. I was appalled to see two families sharing one daub hut. The *niglets* were curled up on the dirt floor, sleeping amidst the smell of body odour and wood smoke.' There was a deep-rooted fear of Africans, especially the field workers. 'The women at Pimento Walk use scraps of rags to make patch-work sheets, too. I daresay you and I have something in common, cooped up like concubines in King Solomon's harem. You're a slut.'

'All married ooman a *slut-dwag* to man.' Seraphima pushed back, feeling as if they were locked in a box. 'Yuh enjoyin' di fruits of we labour. Wat would Canongate do widout dose slaves at Pimento Walk? Me talkin' about free labour.'

* * *

Two years later, Duncan folded a note into two halves and tore it into strips before placing it in his pocket. That was the third anonymous message he had received. The notes were addressed to Christopher but had been intercepted by old Kush, who had found them pinned to the iron-gate leading up to the great house. The notes claimed Christopher had fathered a poor white boy whose grandfather was Evan Brown, the *walk-foot buckra*. Doubting the veracity of the three notes, Duncan wondered once again how to deal with the situation: at what point should he inform his son of the alleged presence of the child and what action might be taken? He did not want to hurt his family by making enquiries about this illegitimate boy. There was the possibility that the child's mother had fallen on hard times and was trying to benefit from a web of lies.

With the exception of Duncan, there was no one else in the great house. Everyone was seated on the lawn, waiting for the festivities to begin, and the new generation of Camerons, Grandisons and Murrays sat together and chatted. The Fontanes and the Duponts were there, too. At ninety-two, disillusioned by the arrival of his third grand-daughter in five years, Duncan had allowed the field workers time off at Easter to stage a Jonkunnu festival, which was also called John Canoe, by the white elite. This long-awaited event usually occurred on Boxing Day, though Duncan and a few planters allowed their slaves to hold a similar celebration during the Easter festivities. This was known as the '*Pickney* Christmas' and was held in May, this year.

Bespectacled, slow-footed and bushily grey-bearded, for he had stopped shaving, Duncan stood by the window in his study looking out towards the lawn where his seventy-seven-year-old wife, Fiona, sat with a grandchild on her lap. Jane, on her fourth pregnancy, fanned herself vigorously. She had gone into labour six weeks early with the third child. With no doctors in the hills to call, Duncan had summoned Monifa to deliver the child. Looking around, he felt that he had finally accomplished his life's work: Canongate was prosperous and full of life. He remembered visibly the first time he hosted a John Canoe.

'Stable my horse, Trivia.' Christopher shut the front door behind him. 'Father, are you there?'

'Christopher, a word,' Duncan's voice sounded strained. In fact, he himself had wanted to have several words with his son – to discuss the Jonkunnu celebrations, to caution him not to make a scene over Seraphima and Ocean and, finally, to disclose and discuss the blackmail notes that he had received. 'I want us to clear up a few things.' He slowly crossed the room on his walking stick. 'I understand that Ocean is to play the John Canoe King and Seraphima is playing the Queen. Jane has given her one of her dresses and a glass bead necklace. I gave Ocean one of my old suits.' Standing by his desk, he decided not to sit down. The seat was sagging and Jane had promised to upholster it after the birth of the expected grandchild. 'You made a fool of yourself over Seraphima once. Take care that you don't do it again. I don't want Jane getting upset in her condition. A word to the wise, never underestimate a jealous woman. Are you listening? You must learn to make sacrifices.'

'Pinky and Sera understand each other, Father,' Christopher said unconvincingly. 'The more I learn about the women in my life, the less I understand. There are days when I repeat in my head: *She loves me; she loves me not.* I am teasing you, Father. Anything else?'

'Suddenly, I'm old and my knees crack when I bend.' Duncan smiled half-heartedly, sitting on the edge of the desk for support. 'You are the master of Canongate. You don't need another distraction. Our livelihood depends on breeding more slaves and treating them humanely now that the abolition of slavery is looming on the horizon. We had the Tacky Revolt back in 1760, the Maroon Wars and the Haitian Revolution.' At around 6am, he dreamed that there was a mountain of dead men's bones piled high in the canefields and now he feared that something was about to go wrong. 'Gone are the days when I could join in the Jigs and the Polkas at John Canoe time, for the sake of social cohesion.'

'Let us look ahead to the John Canoe.' Already Christopher could picture the masqueraders: King and Queen, Horse Head, Cow Head, Devil, *Belly Woman* and even a Red Indian. The festivities had begun and everyone was eagerly awaiting Duncan. 'We have guests and they are impatient to see you, Father. The musicians and dancers won't start without you.' Christopher cocked his ear, hearing footsteps outside. 'Who's there?'

'We're being stalked.' A dark shadow fell across the window. Duncan spoke again, 'You are being blackmailed. I have intercepted three notes about an illegitimate white boy of seventeen. When you were fifteen, I entertained my old shipmate, Evan Brown, and his three mangy children. The girl, Gayle, later accused McTaff of deflowering her. She is claiming that the boy is my grandson and that you sired him. Is this true?'

'No idea what she's talking about,' Christopher said hesitantly, gazing at the chess board and suggesting that they flip a coin to decide who would go first. 'Heads or tails?' There was a pause while his father glared at him. 'Oh, all right! I slept with her once, but someone else beat me to it; the hog's bladder was already burst. She reeked of stale sex and I withdrew. I gave her 2s.6d, which she duly handed over to her father behind the sugar mill. I swear to you I did not force her. He put her up to it. I am not the boy's father.'

'Some men will lie about anything, son.' Duncan stood up straight, clutching his walking stick and heading for the door. 'There is nothing more I can teach you, except to remind you to purge once a month; get rid of the worms. You are a grown man, son, and I am obsolete, old and bone weary. I can only hope that I'll live long enough to hold my grandson, though this longing is tiring.' He closed the subject and moved to leave the study, clinging to life with a tenacity that was matched only by the enslaved Africans' desire for freedom. 'I want you to make Jane happy today. Remember, we have rules in public.'

'I barely have time to knock boots with Sera,' Christopher said, half-joking, as they crossed the hallway and headed for the front door. 'I've been trying to sire your grandson.'

'Don't remind me. When I am gone, you must treat our slaves humanely.' Duncan stood outside the door. 'Some of them have been with us for decades. They know the slave trade has been abolished. They also see the quantity of sugar they produce and they know it's valuable. If you maltreat them, production will fall and they will not cooperate.' Waving his walking stick in acknowledgement, he caught a glimpse of the masquerade: drummers, elderly Africans lining the path; two floats, enslaved children and their parents in Jonkunnu costumes. The mood was both celebratory and expectant, yet Duncan felt a sense of unease. 'They fear our laws. That is why they tolerate slavery.'

'Get off my land!' snarled Christopher, stepping onto the green lawn behind his father. He came face to face with one of Ezekiel Darnley's boys, Pollux, whose brother, Perseus, was prone to sleepwalking as a boy. 'You were lying in wait for my father, weren't you?'

'Och!' Duncan had sent them away in March when the Darnley gang came begging for paid work during the Aponte Rebellion in Cuba. 'I see you brought your women and children.' The brothers had returned when the uprising ended in April, pleading for work. It turned out that the Cuban revolt had been led by Black José Antonio Aponte, who was an activist who strove to free people of colour from Spanish colonial rule. 'I want no trouble today, boys.'

'Dere's plenty of us beggin' fi work,' Pollux said bitterly, 'but yuh wahn free labour.'

'After a lifetime of grudge-bearing, you dare to challenge me.' Waving his stick, Duncan stood behind Christopher, whose bodyguard was now stabling his horse. 'I gave you and yours leave of absence from Canongate, but I did not set you free, not legally.'

'You are my property,' Christopher said assuredly, cocking his gun and addressing the group. 'If you challenge my authority, I will clap you in iron-coffles and sell you.'

'Pappa put eberyt'ing into dis wretched place, all 'is labour.' Pollux was surrounded by a group of brown people, a gaunt-looking white woman and her adolescent son, who looked unwell and uncared-for. 'Yer daddy promised to free us, liar an' a t'ief. Massa Lachlan, Gayle 'ere seh yuh is 'er son's faddah. Yuh rape 'er w'en she young. Yuh is a rapist, like mos' white man.'

'Yuh's di daddy.' Castor had grown stout through inactivity, living off the proceeds of his father's land in Flamborough. 'See yer daddy dere, white naga.' He ignored the sounds of beating drums, *shakas* rattling and a number of fifes playing in the background. Everyone was waiting to see the King and Queen on their float. 'We nat 'ere fi mek trouble.'

'Yuh keep dis up an' yuh is a dead man.' Monifa sauntered up to the group with her twelve-year-old granddaughter, Nana. 'Dis young lady do di same t'ing to a shopman in Clarendon. 'Har puppah dead an' gone, so she lookin' fowl roost to *kotch*.' The Jonkunnu was an important event and Monifa did not want her granddaughter to miss it because three disgruntled brown men had an axe to grind with Duncan for not giving them paid work. 'It looks like she fool yuh up, Pollux. She dung on 'er luck.' She noticed that the undernourished white boy had two black eyes and his mother's eyes were hollowed. 'She been turnin' tricks, Massa Foulkes.' Monifa decided that it seemed a most appropriate time for the Darnleys to air their grievances, knowing that they would not hesitate to start an uprising. 'Dem saltin' di tail of a Brer Anancy story, massa.'

'I daresay you know more than most what it's like to lie your way through life.' Duncan stepped out from behind Christopher, planting his stick firmly on the ground when his granddaughter, Marian, came to tell him that everyone was waiting. 'Where is that Trivia? If you make any trouble, motley bunch of warmongers, he will deal with you.' He watched the terrified young white woman and her son being ushered away by the three brown men. 'Perhaps we could find her something to do in the house.' He gave her a brief sympathetic look. 'After all, she's a poor white and her father was a shipmate.'

'Di gal tellin' tales, massa,' Monifa cut in, clutching Nana's hand, noticing that Duncan's hands were shaking. 'I 'ope dose bwoys nuh spoil di *Pickney* Christmas.' Her grand-nephew, Babatunde, walked behind, pockets full of stones, ready to throw them at children. 'Keep up, Baba.'

'Who asked your opinion?' Duncan said testily, looking down at Monifa's mixed-race grandchild. 'That is a white girl you're talking about. They are taking advantage of her vulnerability.' In order not to lose his temper, for he knew the midwife would be overseeing the birth of his next grandchild, he added, 'Evan Brown was my shipmate. He's proof that you need luck and tenacity to succeed in this society. Jamaica is an unforgiving place.'

'Hurry up, Grandpa,' five-year-old Marian said impatiently, tugging at his sleeve and leading him to his seat on the lawn. 'Papa, Mother has saved you a seat next to her.' This was the first year that she had been allowed to watch the Jonkunnu outdoors and she was excited, but scared of the masqueraders. They were known to speak in coarse whispers, disguising their voices, and scaring the onlookers.

'They are breeding like rabbits,' muttered Duncan, observing the Darnley men congregating with over twenty brown people who did not associate with the Africans. 'I stopped you from playing with those boys for a reason. I told you that when they grew up, they'd be dangerous, angry about their dual heritage and about not being treated as equals.'

'The *niglets* are all dressed up.' Four-year-old Virginia spotted a throng of Black children, the *pickney* gang, wearing masks. 'Look, Grandma,' she said, pointing across the lawn and getting carried away by the moment. 'It's a scary horse-man, Grandma.'

'The Queen.' Fanning herself, Jane remarked that the unborn child felt like it was playing ball in her stomach. 'This is the highlight of the John Canoe. Seraphima looks nice in my dress and necklace. Ouch! It's kicking!'

'My son.' Christopher rested his hand on Jane's stomach while the donkey-drawn float glided past to goat-skin drumming, fiddle music and dancing. 'Is that a real Red Indian with arrows on his back?' He placed his two-year-old daughter, Jane, on his lap, pointing out a man with a cow's head. 'That must be the King.' So far, the focal point of the *Pickney* Christmas had been the main float and he felt uncomfortable watching his mistress dressed in his wife's clothes and shoes. 'Oh look, Marian, that's the Queen.'

'Kiss me, Ocean.' Seraphima, wearing a crown on her head and an old gold shawl around her shoulders, turned her face away when she saw Christopher's hand on Jane's stomach. She was clad in Jane's cast-off blue silk dress to play the part of Abena, the infamous Black Queen of

Kingston, who was banished to Cuba in 1766. Although she was exiled, Abena returned to the island, was captured and then she vanished from history. 'Kiss me.'

'Yuh tryin' to mek Massa Chris jealous.' Ocean watched his peers going wild with excitement, ringing bells and beating old kettles and drums. 'Remember di centaur?' For years, he had wanted Seraphima to want him. This was a significant milestone in his hopes. The kiss left him purring, but he resented being told that he should be grateful she had consented to play his queen, for she was not interested in him. He gave a grudging wave. Resplendent in a black suit and an elaborate African headdress, he held a wooden sword with a red feather attached to the handle. 'Howdy-do, massa; howdy, massa!'

'Just like old times.' Beaming, Duncan waved at his people, who were blowing cow horns, strumming banjos, rattling their shakers and beating tom-toms. 'This must be the John Canoe.' Riding a huge black horse, the hero of the day wore a fussy headdress with a pair of ox-horns. He carried a large wooden sword. '*The King of Nubia.*'

'Appearances can be deceptive.' Already the sun was blazing down and Christopher, seeing Seraphima flirting with Ocean, could not understand why, after all these years, he was still possessive and would kill any man who touched her. 'Do we really need to have an annual float with a carnival queen, Mother? I daresay this John Canoe malarkey allows the slaves to assimilate into our culture and come tomorrow they will not be so morose and easily cajoled in the fields. Clever old you, Father. I've not thought of it like that before.' He too waved at the revellers and the float inching its way along. 'Hm. John Canoe is another way of getting the field workers to behave in our own interests, showing more solidarity together: master and slaves.' Then he turned to Odette and smiled at the twelve-year-old. 'Look, Miss Fontane, it is Nimbus.'

'Remember Krampus, Jewel?' Monifa stood on the side-lines with Nana sitting on her shoulders. 'Him frighten di Martinican *picknies* at Miss Odette birthday picnic: Nimbus.' Feeling the strain of Nana's weight, she looked at the Black children behind the float, waving at the spectators. 'I wonder if dat *bakra* gal is Pollux's ooman? If Massa Foulkes nuh careful, dose bwoys gwine use 'er as pawn in dem war 'gainst Canongate.'

'Something is not right.' The look on Duncan's face said it all. 'I tell you something is wrong, son.' He stared in disbelief at the barefoot white boy. Like his younger brother, Dougal, the boy was short with thick brows, though he had hazy green eyes. Tapping Christopher's shin with his walking stick, he snapped, 'Get that filthy-looking boy away from those beasts. This is Ezekiel Darnley's revenge on me!'

'*Carpe dium.*' Christopher took no notice of him. 'What's Sera up to?' he muttered under his breath but was distracted by the Fontanes, who looked in his direction. 'Ah, my little wife.' Waving at Odette Fontane again, he was livid with Seraphima for flirting with Ocean. 'Happy?' He smiled at Jane while the fiddler fiddled furiously and the banjo player plucked violently. 'Girls, look at that masked dancer, a goat-head man.'

'There seems to be a lot of brown people around.' Tight-lipped so far, Jane cradled her baby bump. 'Are they really like us, humans, or are they a breed apart?'

'They, like their mothers, are as near beasts as may be.' Fiona smiled and said fleetingly, as if she had her fingers crossed behind her back, 'Don't think too much, dear, or your waters will break and you'll have to deliver my grandson right here on the lawn.'

'Why are those two white people dressed in rags and sitting in the Darnley pen?' Jane, waving an exotic fan along with the other elite white women, watched one of the brown men insert a makeshift toothpick between his front teeth where a tiny gap was developing. 'Christopher, we ought to invite those poor whites to sit on this side.'

'You're a damn fool, Christopher.' Duncan, seeing the white boy who reminded him so much of Dougal from afar, wished that he could put shoes on the boy's dirty feet and give him the happy childhood his own granddaughters were enjoying. It was the most significant, perhaps the most dangerous, moment in the history of Canongate. Darnley's sons were sending a message to him: *My enemy's enemy is my friend.* Somewhere in the hills, Duncan heard drums beating and his first thoughts were of Captain Kalu and the Maroons but when he tried to speak, only a trickle of saliva escaped from his mouth. For a few seconds, he was seized with muscle spasms down his left leg.

'Roaches.' Pierre turned to René Dupont in the white enclosure. 'I have a bad feeling.' Scanning the lawn, he felt that something was not right about a white woman drowning in a sea of brown men but when he saw her barefoot son surrounded by a bevy of brown beauties, he laughed and said derisively, '*Porc chanceux;* lucky hog.'

'They look like brown bees clustering around a white queen in her hive, only this queen lives in a hovel,' René Dupont said unkindly. 'What is going on!' he exclaimed when a flight of green parakeets was let loose by the Darnleys. 'Aha! A distraction, Foulkes.'

'Isn't she sweet, Mother?' Elegant and aloof, Jane was appalled to see a mixed-race child, Nana, who resembled Pierre's daughter, Odette. Both girls were wearing frilly pink frocks and white shoes. In the habit of always using a cold voice when dealing with poor whites, she stared icily at the *walk-foot buckra* woman. The disparity between what she was brought up to believe a white woman should be, and what she saw in front of her, led to more questions. 'Mother Foulkes, why is that *buckra* girl sitting with those obnoxious half-breeds? It's obscene, a white woman living with a brown man. Who is the boy's father? Why have they come here, Mother? I don't like it. I don't like it at all.'

'She is a white Negro,' replied Christopher, who wanted a snooze. The majority of his free time was spent with his three children, whom Jane had been deliberately using to keep him and Seraphima apart. 'Sadly, her father was a *walk-foot buckra*: a poor white.' The drums sounded across Canongate and the screeching parakeets circled above their heads while the ululating old women sang long forgotten songs of home, heightening the drama. 'She has placed herself beyond the pale, more's the pity.'

'Even a vagrant on the streets of London values his whiteness above all else,' said Jane in a tone of dismay and revulsion. 'Vile person.' Looking regal and maternal in a loose gown made of gold, her English accent fell on the ground like acid rain. 'She is a disgrace to white womanhood. She's drinking from a gourd. I cannot bear it.'

'Ditto.' Duncan watched two enslaved children throwing a saucer-shaped fig leaf into the air. 'Good God!' He wanted to put a bullet between Pollux's eyes and to ensure that the barefoot white boy's basic needs were met. The adolescent sat with his head bowed and his eyes lowered. This image sapped his vitality and a wave of sadness came over him. He could not turn his face away from the barefoot boy who was overshadowed by three big, brawny brown men. 'For God's sake, he is a pawn in their game, Christopher.'

Rebuffing his father, Christopher leaned close and whispered, 'I would do anything to give you some grandsons with scraped knees and muddy faces.' He paused for effect and then added, 'Any fool can see the boy is not one of us. He is a *walk-foot buckra*.'

'This would not happen if I were still a young man,' sighed Duncan, wearing a black top hat with sweat beading on his forehead. 'He's mucked it up, that damn Evan Brown.' The enslaved children began to assemble, ready to portray an interesting array of characters after which their master would acknowledge their hard work with the gift of a red *Otaheite* apple each. Duncan thought, *I must look to the past to find what caused this injustice.* He had to make an effort to shake off his thoughts before he could stand up and make his annual speech, putting the children's contribution to Canongate into perspective. Cheers of goodwill rang out on the lawn. 'Red apples, please!'

'See dem 'ere, massa.' Flirting with Ocean, Seraphima plumped her breasts on the float and waved before passing down the basket of apples to Nana. Meantime, six horse-headed men sauntered up to the children, speaking in hoarse whispers and spooking them until they covered their faces in fear and excitement. *Lachlan better not com' near me tonite 'cause 'im wife bex wid 'im,* she thought. 'Nana, giv' Massa Foulkes dis basket of apples, Cousin.' She was determined to flirt and to make Christopher jealous. 'Lawd, di sun 'ot.'

'*Otaheite* apples?' An unimpressed-looking Jane stared hard at Seraphima. 'They are not a patch on our English apples.' Her forehead gleamed with the heat while she studied her rival, who was the most demonstrative of all the revellers, flamboyantly calling out and waving to friends and field workers. 'Vulgar! She has no sense of etiquette: a carnival queen should sit like a lady and wave in a regal manner, too.'

'What on earth was that?' A green saucer-shaped fig leaf sailed past Duncan, who ducked his head. 'Christopher, someone else can distribute the apples.' He felt the energy radiating from the people gathered. 'This noise is too much for me – intolerable. I have done my bit and recognised the contribution of the *pickney* gang.'

'You'll have to grin and bear it a while longer.' There was a sense of dislocation, pride of race and fear as they sat watching the procession on the slightly tatty old estate chairs and benches set out on the lawn. A frosty Fiona looked across at Seraphima's low-cut, hand-me-down silk dress, and beckoned Monifa to approach the white elite's space. 'Get rid of these apples. Oh look, there's Little Red Riding Hood's grandmother!'

'Really, Mother, this John Canoe isn't quite what I had expected,' Jane sighed, hearing strummed chords in the air and grumbling that she did not care for such cross-cultural fusion: European masks and stories, animal heads, goat skin drums, dancing and singing. 'There she goes, Seraphima, screeching and waving like a demented *harpy*. I mean, really! I should not have given her my nice old frock.'

In handing out the apples, Monifa had inserted herself into the Jonkunnu. The female team behind the costumes had also included characters from nursery rhymes, which Christopher's children often recited within earshot of the enslaved children. Along came a girl-child wearing a white mask, tugging a goat-kid behind her: this was, of course, *Little Bo Peep* and her lost sheep. So immersed was Monifa in the characters that she did not notice the disturbance until it had turned into a fracas.

'I beg yuh, Pollux, fram di bottom of mi 'eart, giv' 'im a chance!' What happened next took everyone by surprise when Gayle Brown, the *walk-foot buckra* woman with the sunken eyes and bad skin, dropped to her knees, pleading with Pollux not to throw her son out. 'I beg yuh, in di name of Gawd, let 'im stay a while longer.' Worn down by the hostility she had encountered at Flamborough, she cried out in anguish, 'I beg yuh, mek 'im stay.'

'Get that girl away from that devil,' Duncan shouted crossly, eyes settling on a dead mouse whose skin was swarming with flies. 'He has come here to make mischief.'

'In all my days, I have never seen anything like this.' Horrified by the sight of a white woman on her knees before a brown man, Fiona could not bear to look. 'You must do something, Christopher.' She was so preoccupied with Seraphima that she had not given the *walk-foot buckra* woman any attention until that moment. 'Do something.'

'Oh dear! She is yowling.' Jane, recalling lively evenings playing her harpsichord in London society, could not find any empathy. 'This is one of the most unpleasant days I have ever had.'

'She has been living a life of depravity among those half-breeds, René.' Confused, Giselle Dupont fanned her face and turned to Edessa on her left. 'She is not socially acceptable; she sounds like a *nègre*. What on earth is she doing living with that brute?'

'He's a cruel, abusive person.' Duncan, embarrassed by the scene, said not unkindly, 'She has placed herself outside of her community. She is mistress of her virtue.'

'Di bwoy got small foot, Lachlan.' Perseus, the least vocal of the Darnley gang, challenged his childhood playmate. 'Big shoes to fill.' He laughed at the memory of Evan Brown trading his daughter for cash in Flamborough. 'She frigs like a *burr-head* slut.'

'That young lady is not of your kind.' Publicly humiliated by what was going on, Duncan was shocked as he took it in and did not want to give the Darnleys the attention they craved. 'Leave the boy alone.' He stood up. 'Miss Brown, rest assured that you are not to blame for this outrage. You were in need and did what you thought was the right thing. Please join us.' He waved his stick. 'You and your son are under my protection.'

'No way!' There was a new hierarchy of white, brown and black emerging, and Pollux was not to be dismissed so easily. He bristled, 'I bury 'er daddy an' pay 'im bills.' He felt that his family had been wronged, all the way back to his father's post as overseer. 'She's mine – mine alone!' The broad-chested mixed-race man thumped his chest, picked up the distraught young woman's limp body and plonked her on a chair. 'I pay fi 'er.' He felt empowered, knowing that her white skin was leverage with which to beat the Foulkeses. 'I pay 'er daddy twenty guineas fi di bwoy, too, w'en 'im seh 'e was a Foulkes.'

Dismayed, Duncan rued the day that he had given Evan Brown and his children a cool bed. 'Son, if you had any gumption, you'd take your gun and shoot him.' Over the course of his long life, he had been key to every decision made on Canongate. 'Guthrie,' he summoned the overseer.

'This is grossly offensive, Foulkes.' Josiah Grandison, a well-dressed young man, was home from England for good. 'This is not on.' He had inherited his father's estate. 'You cannot have the nagas behaving as if they were the masters and us the slaves. String him up.'

'In Gaad's name, help me, Massa Foulkes.' The focal point of the Jonkunnu was meant to be the masquerade and the floats, but instead Gayle Brown had seized the chance to draw attention to her plight; all eyes were on her now. 'Pollux gwine kill me wid licks if me go back to Flamborough. Mi son is 'im whippin' bwoy, Massa Foulkes.'

'That is awful – vengeful,' Jane said with disbelief when the woman received a slap which sent her reeling. 'Good grief! He struck a white woman. Christopher, do something!'

'Say the word and he is dead, boss.' Guthrie, the expatriate overseer, stared at Duncan's hunched shoulders. 'This could have an impact on our slaves. Me an' the boys will string him up, boss.'

'We have to take action, son.' It was a body blow for Duncan, who felt his flesh pulsating. 'Now!' He gesticulated with his stick. 'Shoot the brute!' That was where the verbal sparring had ended and the war began. 'That boy over there is your son, my grandson, a Foulkes.' He had spent most of the morning holed up in his study and now a sense of imminent disaster overwhelmed him. 'He resembles Dougal, the spitting image – I swear.'

'I've had about enough of this.' Christopher, who had earlier been caught up in the excitement, watching Seraphima's hips gyrate on the float, tried to recall a roll in the hay with the unhygienic Gayle Brown. 'We can't be sure he's mine.' At this point, Gayle put on a squeaking voice, pleading for her son to stay at Canongate until he could fend for himself. Her voice heightened and Christopher's thoughts turned to the past, to the one moment of indiscretion which had caught up with him so publicly. 'You there, Pollux, step away from that boy. First, you are chattel, covered by our property rights; second, you struck a white woman; third, you raised your hand at a white boy – unpardonable.'

'Uh-uh.' Monifa called out, 'Com' away, Jewel.' She strode into the midst of the frightened children and lifted Nana, placing her onto the float where she sat beside Seraphima. The euphoria of the Jonkunnu had evaporated. 'Stay wid yer big cousin an' don't move.'

Within the great house, a clock struck. Outside, Gayle Brown threw herself face down on the lawn while the white estate workers formed a ring around the pregnant Jane and the children. Things turned unpleasant when the Jonkunnu crowd came to a standstill. Pollux, defying calls to leave Canongate before he lost his life, was hell-bent on a show-down and was confronted by a determined group of armed white men, including Christopher, Guthrie and ten white drivers, who were all militiamen and used to mustering.

'He struck two white people, Christopher.' Duncan felt weary, gazing at a group of warriors in loincloths who had been distorting their faces and speaking in hoarse voices to frighten the *pickney* gang. It seemed they believed the drama was part of the entertainment. 'I gave you land and hoped you'd become farmers and live independently.' One Red Indian stood out amongst the revellers in his feathered headdress. Duncan said, 'You've tied a noose around your own neck.'

'You there, Pollux.' Christopher aimed his gun and turned to ensure that Trivia was shielding him. 'One false move, boy, and you'll have a massacre on your hands.'

'We jus' want yer 'elp to tu'n we life 'round, massa, not jus' fi us but fi generation to com'.' Castor, having taken on the role of spokesman for the mixed-race offspring of Darnley, Smith, McPhee and McTaff, aired their grievances. 'We not 'ere fi cause nuh trouble. We wahn di security of a regular wage. We 'ave lan' but no money to bring about di prosperity our faddahs used to dream of. Di ole fox walk into a trap, Massa Foulkes.'

'A champion has emerged, Julian Fedon.' Duncan was disinclined to negotiate, saying to those close by him that the flare up was more an issue of the rise of the brown man than a clash about past injustice. 'Or is it Vincent Ogé, the *mulatto* leader of that brief rebellion in St Domingue, 1790? What became of him? Ah, he didn't include the blacks in his fight.' In Pollux, Castor and Perseus, he envisioned the rising players of the future and knew that they had to be cut down or Canongate would be doomed. 'Ogé's limbs were broken and he was tied to a wheel, beheaded and his head was speared on a pole. Your fate, I fear.'

Between the three Darnley brothers and their peers, they had agreed in advance that the Jonkunnu festivities presented the perfect opportunity to embarrass the Foulkeses. It was an intimidating move, designed to catch their fathers' enemy off guard in front of his social circle of friends. Drawing strength from one another, they prepared to engage in a full-frontal assault by addressing the most disaffected Africans, planting the idea that Duncan was the antagonist and that they themselves would overturn the oppressive slave system by seizing Canongate. Pausing for effect, Perseus provoked widespread concern among the field labourers by arguing that although the slave trade had been abolished, they remained trapped in a state of dependency on the sugar planters and their women were still allotted to studs, breeding with them like sows.

'Is true, sistas,' cried Calysta, an aggrieved female who was given to Jules Paquet for the night when he had visited Canongate in 1807. She had borne him a son. 'Is true!'

'Who's on our side, breddas?' Loud and belligerent, Pollux, who had drawn the colour line, grasped the initiative in the confusion and consternation of those gathered. 'Yer enemy is our enemy!' In a move that shocked everyone, he whipped out a large Bowie knife with a wooden handle and pressed it against the barefoot boy's throat. 'Who will join us?' The tall redhead knew that the Africans looked forward to the annual Jonkunnu, even those who despised Duncan. '*Kooh* pon dem, twenty-odd *bakras* 'gainst t'ree 'undred black an' brown *peeple*.' A hoe flew into the white section, just missing Christopher. 'Mistress Fiona, God's likkle stepchildren tu'n into big beasts!'

'Cover me, Trivia,' ordered Christopher, who was taken aback by the revolt. He was determined to rid Canongate of the troublemakers, too. 'I want Pollux strung up.' What he did not want was for the white children to bear witness and yet, at that crucial moment, they could not be moved without endangering their lives.

'Fer dose of yuh who wahn fi leave dis place, dere's plenty of lan' ober at Flamborough to share,' assured Castor. 'Dere'll be no jumpin' off di *pussy* at 5am.' His ego was bolstered by the sight of Duncan, who looked old and wizened in the white enclosure. 'Blacks own an' control nutten; oonu 'ave no rights.'

With the barefoot white boy in Pollux's grip, Monifa noticed Kush sneaking off. 'Massa 'ave lan' an' free labour, but we nat fightin' fi yuh!' She knew Kush, the grass-slasher, was thick with the brothers. 'W'en was di las' time any of yuh wuk in di canefield or inna di sugar mill, dwags?'

'Go back to Africa, Guinea gal!' Egged on by his brother, Perseus, Castor unfurled his horsewhip and his tongue, 'Yuh touch naga ooman mud 'ole, tommy. Get lost or I'll bash yer *burr-head* in like coconut, porch monkey. Yuh is a dutty *obeah-ooman, cunt.*'

'Watch yer dutty mout', bwoy,' Trivia barked at him. 'Is who yuh callin' *obeah-ooman* an' Guinea gal?'

'Bruk-up 'im *warra-warra*, Trivia!' Over the last few years Luana, who was one of the hardest working females in the strong gang, had grown to know Monifa, for the African midwife was always on call at Canongate. 'Is who 'im callin' *burr-head*!' She would have flown at Castor's throat but was held back by Trivia, whose muscular arms were scarred from the whippings he had received for insolence. 'Oonu 'ear weh dat 'alf-blood bwoy call Mama? *Cunt*! Puddung oonu cutlass an' mek di dutty bwoy an' 'im breddas fite dem own battle.' She had spent her adolescent years marred by fear and insults. '*Kirrout*, dutty bwoy!'

'That's enough.' Christopher and the other white men had formed a protective circle around the women and children, for the route back to the great house had been blocked by the donkey-carts, floats and the evergreen branches that had quickly appeared, further fuelling whispers of *inside help*. 'Trivia, I cannot risk my wife going into labour. This was a well-organised plan. The thing to do is to talk them down.'

'Dem not in di mood fi listen, sah.' Trivia released Luana, who had gone quiet. 'It's no use talkin'.'

While there were some objections, the promise of freedom through armed conflict was seductive and soon there were verbal clashes between the enslaved Africans, most of whom were drawn to the rallying cry and had discarded their masks. Inflated, Pollux tried to persuade the men that he shared their plight but he provoked a backlash from enslaved women like Luana, Nyla, Kyra and Nefili. His brother, Castor, had publicly derided a revered midwife, who had de-infibulated them years ago and saved scores of lives during childbirth. The women greeted Monifa as 'Mama' and their children called her 'Granny.'

'Hey, bwoy, yer puppah mek Ocean shit inna mi mout'.' Hearing the mutter amongst the men, Kumasi, whose voice carried weight in the strong gang, stepped forward. 'Yer puppah force me fi eat mi bes' frien' shit.' Big and restrained, it was not until he had joined the *Kumina* set that Monifa had cured his halitosis with herbal remedies. The fearless Ashanti, hailed as a voice for the voiceless, explained to the strong gang that any allegiance to the Darnleys would mean death. 'Di slave trade abolish, so it stan' to reason dat freedom soon com'. Gweh, bwoy.'

'Puddung oonu cutlass!' Monifa recalled how a dying Minah had sent for her son, Pollux, but all her children had rejected her on her deathbed. 'We will wait fi freedom!'

'Oonu is property to massa.' Pollux, desperate to break into the tight-knit strong gang that he had disparaged in boyhood, urged them to forget their grievances against his father and close rank. 'We will kill all di whites. Den we'll set fire to di canefields, sugar mill an' di trash 'ouse. Sistas, we spring fram di same common root: *Maddah Africa!*'

'Och! I should have put a neck-iron ring on you boys years ago.' Duncan rallied, seeing that his people were on his side. 'Ungrateful half-breeds!' He was mystified why an African woman, whom he tolerated because of Jane's fecundity, should seize the initiative and challenge the most pugnacious of Ezekiel Darnley's menacing sons, uniting all the tribes on Canongate. The strong gang was rallying under Kumasi's leadership, too, laying down their weapons which they had secretly strapped to their inside legs or concealed beneath their women's costumes. 'You've cut the rope from under you and your worthless brothers, boy.' Duncan's voice was hard, pronouncing sentence: 'Shoot those bull elks, Christopher.'

'Everybaddy, meet massa's grandson: Brice Foulkes!' Pollux and his brothers, who had held the upper hand, saw that the tables had turned to favour Duncan. He knew that this disclosure would have a significant impact on the worn-down Africans, all of whom were jeering. 'How much 'im worth to yuh, sah?' He prepared to bargain with Duncan. 'Speak now or I wohn be responsible fi wat I do. How much, massa?'

'Yuh smell like a musky civet cat, nasty ooman.' Castor thrust out his bottom lip when Gayle Brown tried to stop Pollux from man-handling her son further. 'Be t'ankful mi sistas talk me an' mi breddas into tekkin' you an' yer bastard son in.' Using the impoverished white woman as leverage against the Foulkeses, humiliating her to prove that white women were no better than their mixed-race sisters, he yanked her greasy hair and stared at Duncan, taunting him. 'In a way, I feel sorry fi di bitch an' her dutty son, sleepin' an' eatin' wid di pigs in di sty at Flamborough afta 'er faddah, dat beggarman Brown, drink 'imself to deat'. Ten guineas fi any buck who wahn mount dis slut in front of Massa Duncan.'

Christopher's jaw unclenched, glancing from his father to the barefoot boy, whose life hung in the balance. 'It is death to strike a white person! Let him go and I'll spare your life, boy. You there, let Miss Brown and her son go and you can all walk free.'

At a time of heightened tension, when there was no compromise, Duncan spoke in a whisper, 'In God's name, he is my grandson.' There was a loud gasp when Pollux held the boy in a tight neck grip. Such was the nervousness of the crowd that no one was surprised when the Devil's horse (part of the Jonkunnu) galloped off with Nimbus's black cape billowing like sails, inciting further chaos. Jane fainted when Pollux slashed the terrified barefoot boy's throat. His miserable life had been cut short and his body lay on the ground in a pool of blood while a smirking Pollux brandished the Bowie knife.

'Come away, children.' Fiona looked down. Marion had wet herself.

'It is finished.' It was a devastating blow for Duncan whose nose twitched like a dormouse. 'It is finished.' He had avoided temptation on the *Ballantrae* by spurning the proxy bride's advances yet, by a cruel trick of fate, she had given him his first grandchild. 'He is your legitimate son, Christopher,' he whispered. 'He is the grandson I have longed for – what a waste of a life.'

'Lawd!' Retaliation was instant. Pandemonium broke out when three bullets pierced the air, cutting down the Darnleys and sending the crowd into a panic. 'Whai!' Monifa observed with relief that Nana was being passed over the crowd's heads down to her. 'Weh Baba?' The boy was hiding behind her. 'Whai! Me seh me cahn believe it.'

'Guthrie, dump those dogs in Hutchinson's Hole!' Christopher, hearing the hounds howling, shut his ears to the cries of the brown women, who were already requesting a proper burial for their men. 'Mother, give Pinky a hand. Seraphima, see to the children.' Marian was retching violently. 'Kumasi, round up the strong gang.'

'Yes, sah.' For Kumasi, the moment of Duncan's downfall was a bitter sweet celebration. 'Yes, sah!' He nodded vigorously before commandeering the strong gang. Some of the women cried with relief while the young men pumped their fists in the air when they realised that Duncan was finished. 'Jonkunnu mash up, sah!'

'Nuh suh.' Although Trivia was no longer part of the strong gang, he felt an affinity with Kumasi, whom he hailed whenever their paths crossed. 'We haffe double di guard tonite, bredda.'

'Deat' com' callin' on massa.' Monifa perked up with enthusiasm, watching Pierre Fontane cover the barefoot white boy's bloodied corpse with his grandmother's tartan shawl. As she looked on, she thought, *Di dead bwoy birt' was no accident. Massa Duncan's nemesis.*

* * *

That was to be the last Jonkunnu celebration on Canongate. It was back to reality for women like Luana. She began to curse the Darnley women for keeping the conspiracy under wraps, blaming them for spoiling the malnourished children's free time while their mixed-race children had grown big and healthy in Flamborough where there were no whips or *cat o' nine tails*. The hardest workers had been looking forward to the masquerade, dancing and drumming until late. Some had donned their costumes, pretending that they were back in Africa.

What should have been a respite for the enslaved children to enjoy a break from work was cut short by the mini revolt, which caused the men in the strong gang to launch an attack on the other brown men, telling them to return to Flamborough – they would never swap a white driver for a whip-wielding Darnley. Throughout the heated exchange, led by Kumasi, he had said that he would rather 'stick to di devil me know' than throw his lot in with the Darnleys. Had the brothers ever worked in the canefields?

'Christopher, take your father into the house and put him to bed.' Fiona wiped tears from her face, not wanting to publicly fault him for bringing shame upon his family. 'That poor miserable boy.' The cruel irony was that Duncan had lived long enough to see the grandson he so desperately wanted, but the barefoot white boy had repulsed Fiona.

'A rebellion on Canongate? Unthinkable in the olden days when I first came out as a young bride. I always said Evan Brown or Ezekiel Darnley would be the death of your father.'

'They shall suffer the consequence of their treachery,' Christopher vowed. 'I shall burn Flamborough to the ground and make every man, woman and child homeless like a *walk-foot buckra*.' Whereas he had looked at the Maroons as a kind of dread in his youth, he had told his father often that Ezekiel Darnley was like a snake in the grass. 'Mother, go into the house ahead of me and prepare a cool bed for Father. Make haste. Josiah, Luke, please take charge of the boy's mother and book her on the next ship to Canada.' With a frosty demeanour, Christopher had no desire ever again to see Gayle Brown, the impoverished white woman who brought Canongate to the brink of rebellion and death. 'Madame Fontane, would you mind entertaining my guests?'

It was a private tragedy and a public humiliation for Christopher, who had not been certain that the barefoot white boy was his first child until Duncan had opened his eyes, repeating, *Grrr-son, Dougal, grrr-son*. A trickle of saliva had escaped from the corner of his mouth when he was carried into the house and up the stairs to the master bedroom, gradually turning into froth that reminded Christopher of a snail protecting itself from danger. Having settled his father into a cool bed, he and his mother now stood at the bottom rung of the stairs in the polished hallway. At last, he was officially the master of Canongate – his own fiefdom.

'Monsieur Fontane, I need your help.' Christopher recalled how Pollux's spittle-flecked invective had drawn backlash from most of the women, for Monifa meant the world to them. 'Please see to it that the slaves are returned to their huts while I take care of Father.'

'Yes, you go and see to your father, son.' Pierre now stood inside the hallway with René Dupont. The cuckoo clock disturbed his thoughts. It was 3pm. 'Your duty is to your father.'

'He devoted his life to Cannongate.' Christopher rued the day they gave Evan Brown a cool bed. Whatever his other failings, he felt that he did and would maintain a sense of dignity, which his family would need in the weeks ahead. 'This is the day, Mother; this is the day. Canongate is a one-man band now.'

'We'll continue as normal.' Fiona bowed her head, placing an arm around Jane's waist and helping her up the stairs. On the landing, she stopped and took one last look down into the hallway, shuddering. 'After all the years of building up Canongate, all your father wanted was to see his grandson. I'm glad Josiah and Luke are here for you.'

'My only son, a *walk-foot buckra*?' Welling up, Christopher followed behind the women and then returned to the master bedroom. 'I am here with you, Father.' Removing a plump pillow from the bed, he held it hesitantly, fighting the urge to fulfil a promise he had made not to leave his father in a vegetative state if the situation ever arose. 'Your hat fell off when I fired the first shot.' He heard his mother helping a distraught Jane into their bedroom, frightened that she would lose the expected child. 'You are resilient, Father. You'll soon pick yourself up and bounce back.' Duncan did not respond. 'Why did I agree to that blasted John Canoe?'

'Lachlan,' Seraphima called out tentatively, standing outside the open door and removing Jane's borrowed necklace on the landing. 'I sendin' di girls to Lafayette wid Madame Fontane tomorrow.' She had expected to feel elated, seeing the man who had caused her to abort two of his own grandchildren cut down, but the revenge she had dreamed of left a sour taste in her mouth now that the day had arrived. There was an anticlimax. 'Lachlan.' From the silence within, she knew that he wanted to be alone with his father. 'Dis is di day, Lachlan.'

'Go away!' Christopher yelled, gazing out the window, 'Mother!' Duncan's eyes had shot open, wide open, but his spirit had left his body, walking through the canefields. Ever since he had promised his father not to let him linger on when the time came, Christopher had gone over the scene in his head many times. Looking down on the lawn, he saw a heaving mass of Africans from the window, heard the drums beating and the old women ululating. 'I'm sending you back to Scotland, to Inverkin House. Given that Uncle Dougal has passed on, I shall write to Cousin Fergal. He'll receive you. Mother, hurry!'

'This is a day of self-denial and repentance, son.' Fiona brushed past Seraphima at the door. 'I hope you're happy, whore.' The next few hours would be hazy for the rest of her life. 'On our wedding day, a female slave pounded the ground between my bridal shoes and said, *Be a good wife*!' She remembered, too, the rhythmical sway of Duncan's kilt and how he had regretted giving Dougal his Targe. 'You know, your father was a good dancer. I can see him now, on our wedding day, dancing with upheld arms, performing the toe and heel steps to the tune of a lone piper.' The memory was almost too painful to bear, for their world had been ripped from beneath them by the Darnleys. With Duncan by her side, she was in her comfort zone. 'Och.' She could hear the breath leaving his body.

'I am so sorry, Mother,' Christopher said, watching her close his father's eyes in death. 'I've not always been a good son and husband.'

* * *

On the third day, Rev'd Robson Ellis awoke with a vision of thousands of black birds flying over Canongate. Duncan walked down the stairs dressed in black, wearing a top hat and carrying a gun. The minister had been invited to the Jonkunnu but was delayed in Falmouth, for he had been asked to conduct the funeral of an elderly Englishman whose only mourner was an attorney. Rev'd Ellis, who went wherever the Holy Spirit led him, was prowling the wharf at Falmouth when the horse-drawn hearse brought Duncan's coffin from Canongate to the harbour to be loaded aboard ship and taken to Edinburgh.

As the sun rose over Falmouth Harbour, Rev'd Ellis saw a mass of black crows circling overhead. Clutching his tattered King James Bible, he was not the only mourner waiting on the bustling waterfront, which was crowded with returnees, cargoes, sailors, enslaved Africans, freed persons and animals. The azure Caribbean Sea was choppy that day. Those who had gathered at the quayside and had enjoyed Duncan's hospitality at Canongate referred to him as a pillar of the community. Others praised his Puritan work ethic, patriotism and his devotion to family.

A short distance away, the horse-drawn hearse jolted when two black horses neighed nearby, and the crowd broke into applause. The news had spread of the hearse's journey from Canongate and people had turned out to pay their respects to The Much-Honoured Duncan Ellic Hutchinson VII (Foulkes). There was a pensive atmosphere as the white elite stood at the quayside, showing their appreciation of a Scotsman whom many had a personal connection with.

'Canongate was your father's great achievement,' Rev'd Ellis said gravely, watching British ships loading and unloading their cargoes. 'He once told me he could not have fathered a better son. It is too late to undo the wrong that has been done. You must restore confidence at Canongate, my son, or his life will have been for nothing.'

'He was a good man, exceptional.' Dressed in black and still in a daze, Christopher was struggling with the guilt of causing his father's death. Three days of introspection had led him to conclude that if he had not been so wilful, his father would have been far less troubled in his later years. 'On his ninetieth birthday, I told him to go to bed and he cracked a smile and scoffed, *I'm not in the ground yet. I'll sleep when I'm dead.* I had hoped to accompany him, Rev'd Ellis, but I can't leave my family. I am the master of Canongate now.'

'I share your grief, son.' By this time, Pierre had come to regard Christopher as the son whom he never had. His steely-grey eyes fell upon Rev'd Ellis. 'Where there is a will, there is a way.'

'*To sleep, perchance to dream.*' Rev'd Ellis bowed his head when he saw Duncan's dirk, powder horn, musket and a bouquet of tropical flowers strapped down on the casket, which was draped in black. He noticed the chaotic scene: people jostled to lift the leaded coffin to board the ship bound for Kingston and then on to Edinburgh, in Scotland, before being taken to the Highlands. He heard a banjo and saw a Black man by the quayside singing "Rock of Ages."

'If I have learnt anything in life,' Pierre said calmly, resting a hand on Christopher's right shoulder, 'it is that whatever happens to you, good or bad, use it. I picked myself up and sailed to this island with my family and my slaves after the revolution in St Domingue.'

'Me too.' René Dupont would be accompanying Duncan's coffin to Kingston, where he planned to purchase supplies from a Jewish merchant. 'For all we know, your father's spirit is already back in Scotland. I can see him sitting round a fire wrapped in a sheepskin blanket, or is it a tartan shawl?' He fell silent, watching the mourners arriving: a flotilla of planters sailing into Falmouth Harbour, or rolling up at the quayside and exiting from their fashionable carriages. Once again, the mourners spoke of Duncan as a kind and generous man and an upstanding member of the plantocracy. 'A cool bed at Canongate.' Then Dupont asked, 'Will you be going with the body, Rev'd Ellis?'

At these words, Christopher said haltingly, 'There's nothing to keep you here, Rev'd Ellis.' Throughout Duncan's sojourn in Jamaica, there had been an element of good luck, though the earlier years had seen some devastating hurricanes. Sleep-starved, Christopher had sat next to his father's coffin on its journey to the wharf in Falmouth. Since the Darnely uprising, there had been days when he hardly knew which way to turn. 'Will you take him home, Rev'd Ellis? I'll pay your passage, board and lodgings. You will know Inverkin House when you get there. It is at the end of a long gravelly drive with yew trees. Father spoke of it often. Cousin Fergal will receive you.'

'Today is a day of mourning.' Despite Rev'd Ellis's faith, there was a sudden lack of purpose and a great sense of fatigue; Jamaica had sapped his energy. '*I am my brother's keeper.*' He left a long pause before adding, 'The last time I saw your father, I mooted the idea of accompanying his casket on the voyage home. My trunk is already aboard ship. I have been here since yesterday, waiting for your carriage to arrive.' He began to hum, observing the black birds flying overhead like carrion crows on a red battlefield: '*As I came thro Sandgate, I heard a lassie sing. O weel may the keel row...*' The parting drew to an uneasy close and he made a Solomonic decision, as if he were a hermit emerging from his wilderness years: '*Here I am, Lord. Send me.*'

'You're a Godsend, Rev'd Ellis.' Shaking hands with the minister and members of the plantocracy, Christopher looked sombre as he gazed at his father's coffin draped in black. Fiona, who was devastated, had made up a bouquet of sweet-smelling flowers taken from the rose garden at Canongate. Christopher's body twitched when he heard the ship's horn. He was comforted by the condolences from his fellow whites and acknowledged the deep affection that the plantocracy had for his father. 'He wanted a memorial service at the Kirk of St Giles in Edinburgh.'

Ole age ketch massa on di road, thought Trivia (standing behind Christopher), having one last joke at Duncan's expense after Rev'd Ellis had promised to take Duncan's lead coffin to the Kirk of St Giles to lie in state for a day. Having been anally raped and mauled by dogs when he (Trivia) and many others in the strong gang had objected to toiling in the canefields, and after the initial shock of Duncan's sudden death, the mood on Canongate had changed to one of jubilation and a fierce desire for freedom. Trivia thought, smirking, *Yuh cahn buy yer way into 'eaven, Massa Duncan. A good*!

Acknowledgements

Many people have supported me during the researching, writing and publishing of the long-awaited novel, *Little River*. Above all, my husband Henry, who is my strength and my shield in times of trouble. A big shout out to my children, Gavin and Rebecca, for supplying me with ink cartridges and the endless cups of tea and biscuits. I am forever grateful to my late mother, Mrs Althea Jackson-Morris, who was as proud as a peacock when I published my first book, Hope Leaves Jamaica, in 1993.

I thank Professor Sir Geoff Palmer for kindly agreeing to write the foreword for the book. Many thanks to Dr Nicola Frith for writing the introduction. I should also thank the following people for endorsing the novel: Rev'd Delroy Sittol JP, Professor Tony Leiba, George Ruddock, Professor Constantine Sandis and Professor Linn Washington Jr.

I acknowledge Brother Cecil Gutzmore for the many discussions on the Maroons of Jamaica. I thank Sister Esther Stanford-Xosei for her work on reparatory justice. Over the years, I have been influenced by the thoughts and opinions of some outstanding female mentors of African descent, including Professor Carolyn Cooper and Professor Joan Anim-Addo.

Special thanks to my dear friends and relatives (I shan't name you all for fear of leaving anyone out), who provided practical help and encouraging words that kept me going in difficult times.

Finally, editorial assistance was provided by Dr Nicola Frith. Last but not least, I must also hail publisher Nana Ayebia Clarke and designer Paul Medcalf for their kind support.

VM